Night Fell, Morning Rose

Night Fell, Morning Rose

Danny Rittman

iUniverse, Inc.
New York   Bloomington

Night Fell, Morning Rose

This is a work of fiction. All of the characters, names, incidents, organizations, and dialogue in this novel are either the products of the author's imagination or are used fictitiously.

iUniverse books may be ordered through booksellers or by contacting:

iUniverse
1663 Liberty Drive
Bloomington, IN 47403
www.iuniverse.com
1-800-Authors (1-800-288-4677)

Because of the dynamic nature of the Internet, any Web addresses or links contained in this book may have changed since publication and may no longer be valid. The views expressed in this work are solely those of the author and do not necessarily reflect the views of the publisher, and the publisher hereby disclaims any responsibility for them.

ISBN: 978-1-4401-3676-4 (pbk)
ISBN: 978-1-4401-3674-0 (dj)
ISBN: 978-1-4401-3675-7 (ebk)

Library of Congress Control Number: 2009925937

Printed in the United States of America

iUniverse rev. date: 4/6/2009

Imagination was never explored in terms of reality.
Danny Rittman

Night Fell, Morning Rose

Ven was getting ready to start her special day – the Day of the Sun. As she reached her twelfth year, like any other girl in her tribe she was about to experience the most magnificent ceremony of her life. She would be carefully prepared by her family and taken to the big flat rock on top of Bear Mountain – a very steep, rocky mountain in the shape of a sleeping bear. Its beautiful forests nicely hid a unique flat rock beyond which was a sharp fall. No one was allowed to climb the mountain unless escorted by family and then only for the Day of the Sun ceremony. The mountain had been considered sacred for many generations.

The ceremony itself was not easy. The girl had to be escorted by female family members until they reached a moon-shaped tree at the foot of the mountain. The tree, revered by her tribe for many generations, was very tall and thick, with a large arch in its middle that looked like a very large moon. Its out of the ordinary shape was visible from far away and every wanderer that passed that way was amazed by it. Legend tells that many years ago a wise man was captured by a group of hostile men who tied him to the tree and left him there without food or water for many days. The wise man prayed to the moon every night until one day the moon sent its light beams and freed him. But it was too late for the wise man. He was too weak, and he died few days later. Before dying, he thanked and blessed the moon for being his only friend through many nights. Since then, the tree began to change its shape and grew in an amazing arc shape. Some people say that a few of the wise man's bones can be still found nearby.

The girl was escorted to the moon-shaped tree by her female kin. She would be provided with minimal clothing and little food. From this point on, she would have to survive alone. There is only one road leading to the top of Bear Mountain. It's very narrow and climbs steeply all the way to the top, ending with a flat area. There, she is to stay all day and through the night, until morning comes. Then she would experience the morning sunrise – the ceremony's vivid culmination. Owing to the mountain's contours, the sun rises with a certain pattern, flooding the flat top with a spectacular light throughout the morning. Ven had been waiting for this moment for months and now the time had arrived.

∞

As she, her sister, and mother neared the tree, Ven gazed upon its legendary moon shape. Without a word, her family members hugged her and then started down the mountain for their village. She watched as their images slowly faded away down the path. It was early morning and she was excited. She had a small bag with a few pieces of fruit and some water. Her mother also packed her feet wrappers – long pieces of cloth made from sheep's wool that would warm her feet at night. She stood for a few long minutes, looking at the tree. It was very tall. Huge, she thought as she observed the captivating arc shape.

Instinctively she searched for the wise man's bones, as told of in the legend, but could not find any. She looked at the narrow path that led up the mountain. I have all day, she thought, and started her journey. She was not in a hurry for she knew the trip to the top was not easy. The path became rough, which slowed her down. Sometimes she could hardly make any progress due to huge rocks that covered the entire path. It got much colder as she reached higher elevations so she wrapped her feet and continued the ordeal. This is why many girls simply gave up and went back, she thought as she felt her strength ebbing. Not me, this is my challenge and I am not giving up.

She steadfastly continued her climb until reaching the top. She stood there speechless at the magnificent spectacle the summit revealed to her. It was close to midnight and the bright moon shone over the valley underneath. In the clear night she could see the windings of the Black River as it created a path between the mountains. The high rocks stood up against the skies as though challenging them with their sheer size. The stars flickered above, creating light sparks over the dark rocks. The chilly night air hit her nostrils with the scent of fresh pines and flowers in bloom. This is magical, she thought and let her lungs fill with the fresh air, even though her body stiffened in the cold mountain night. It had all been worth it.

∞

Freezing, I am freezing, she thought as she shivered uncontrollably in the frigid night air. The top of the mountain was a giant flat rock with no vegetation. Not a tree or even a bush to ease the wind. Ven sat against the cold rock and tried to warm herself by rolling back and forth. That is why they call it a challenge, she thought, biting her lips as she tried to find some distraction in the clear skies. Her mother had told her to focus on the skies so as to forget the cold, but she had a hard time doing it. A falling star caught her attention and she watched it until it vanished among many other stars. I wish it was the sun! She was desperately hoping for the morning light but she lost all sense of time and could not estimate when the sun would come up. But her spirit was strong. I will not break. I will not leave this rock, she thought wildly. Even if no one can see me, I am staying here all night. She sat there, cold and hungry, waiting for the morning to save her from the cold dark night.

They were three, four or maybe even five men. She could not tell exactly since she was tied down with strong rope on the back of a moving horse, and her eyes were covered. It all happened early this morning just after she felt she had triumphed. After a horrific night that brought her to tears, she felt the glorious warmth of the first beams of the morning sun. A few minutes later she fell asleep, exhausted from the ordeal. Then she was abruptly grabbed, bound and blindfolded. She tried to scream but discovered her mouth was covered by a thick cloth and all she could do was breath through her nose. She was thrown on the back of a horse that then started to amble slowly. She could hear a few voices of men talking in an unknown language. The rope cut her skin and the pain was excruciating. Ven had an amazing resilience in adverse situations. She had supreme confidence and never doubted she could persevere. That spirit had helped her growing up and she knew it would help her now also. This morning has started bad, she thought with a touch of irony.

When she was brought down from the horse and her clothes were roughly torn off, she knew what to expect. She had witnessed the men in her tribe doing the same with enemy women they had captured. She just could not figure out where these men came from, as she was not familiar with their language or look. They were dark, short and had long facial hair. They seemed to be from far away. The real test is yet to come, she thought, surprised by her calm and self-control. The men continued to talk in their strange language while she lay naked on the ground.

I'll not give these men the pleasure of screaming, she thought. She did not make a sound, not even when they hit her all over her body, not even when they brutally violated her while screaming and hitting her. Her body started to feel numb from the constant kicking and biting. Then one of the men started to hit her with a large stick, which hurt her badly and left deep red welts. She almost screamed in great pain but then saw something. Despite her agony, she looked at the thick tree and saw someone among the branches. They kicked her sideways but she turned again towards the tree. She was astonished. A boy was looking straight at her. Her mind was clouded from the pain but somehow she wondered who he was and what he was doing there. Is he a savior sent to help me? The pain became severe. She looked at the boy again. He was hiding in the tree while the men were too preoccupied to see him. She rolled on the ground with pain, trying to escape from the blows that came upon her like hail. The world started to spin around her as she felt desperation slowly penetrating inside as her power slowly left her little body. Her vision became blurry as blood dripped into her eyes. As she rolled one more time she saw the boy again. Was it her imagination or did his face look sad and hopeless? Feeling that he was her only hope, she reached her little hand towards him. Amazingly she saw him reaching his hand towards her, and her spirit strengthened. I am not alone. She tried to smile but without much success – a desperate realization that made her strangely happy. It gave her hope. As she felt about to pass out, she gave a last look at the boy and reached her hand even farther towards him.

Then everything became dark.

They threw her battered and bloody body into a mud puddle, then made a campfire and started to roast something for their meal. After a while her consciousness slowly came back. Her whole body ached. She lay there awhile trying to regain some strength. Seeing that the men were busy with their meal, she crawled out of the puddle. Her body burned like fire and the pain was unbearable. She bit her lips and continued to crawl until she reached a small bush. She bled heavily and felt exhausted, but one thought kept her going – revenge.

She did not know why they did this to her. She did not know why they ended the most cherished day of her life this way. But she did not much care now. All she wanted was to get better and take revenge. While they were beating and raping her, she could only think of what she would do to them, if she survived. This thought gave her strength and even cheered her. Now this thought gave her the power to gather herself and think. It was dark and the men talked loudly, laughed and seemed to be enjoying their dinner. They had completely forgotten her. She heard the sound of flowing water near her. Following her keen senses of smell and hearing, she crawled and found a small creek. She sank her head in the water and slowly drank. It was fresh and cold and for her it had the taste of life. She washed her face and hair. She washed her body of the massive amount of blood caked to her. The bleeding had stopped but the wounds still hurt badly. A memory of the boy in the tree flashed through her mind, but she wasn't sure now that she hadn't imagined him. She slowly cleaned her shaking body and with great effort held back screaming from pain. She shivered in the cold night wind and knew that it would get colder. She had to get some clothes and get warm.

After that I'll find something to eat, gather my powers and see about these men, she thought as she moved slowly towards them. She looked at the four men around their campfire, eating, laughing loudly without feeling anything about what they had done to her. All of a sudden she did not feel the cold night air anymore. Slowly, naked in the dark, she walked towards the campfire.

∞

Anta was a thin young boy. He was twelve years old and all he wanted was to play games with friends. Every morning he immediately ran out of his tent to find his friends. His mother had a difficult time getting him even to eat breakfast. Anta belonged to a small tribe that lived near the big river since their main food came from it. The tribe lived mainly on fish and grains they grew along the banks. The river provided them plenty of water for drinking and irrigating their small fields.

On that day Anta played a hide and seek game with his two friends as he got lost in the woods. He did not panic since this was not the first time that he had gotten lost. It had happened many times and he always found his way back to the tribe. All he had to do was find the path of white flowers that leads to the big river. He was very familiar with the white flowers and sure that he'd find the path in a very short time. From there the way back would be easy. It was early in the morning and Anta continued to search for the white flowers, but this time it was different – he could not find them. Anta felt the fingers of fear along his spine. It's morning, the sun is shining, and I'll find the white flowers eventually, he thought to himself. It helped him stay calm.

Something caught his eye and he immediately stopped. He was familiar with forest animals and knew that extra precautions should be taken. A few days ago, during one of his games, he ran near a huge bear. He immediately checked the wind direction to make sure the bear would not be able to smell him, and changed his direction. Apparently he made a good decision for he evaded the bear. Now he saw something that caused him to shake. Right in front of him was a lion cub playing with coconut shells and unable to see a huge snake fixing on him. Anta could tell that the snake was evaluating a future meal. Where is the cub's mother? The cub looked so cute playing with the coconut and chasing after his tail. Anta looked at the snake and froze in fear. It was one giant snake – an anaconda – hanging from a very tall tree. Anta looked up, his mouth agape. The snake was coiled around the tree, all the way up. He could not even see the end of it. The head of the snake was so large that it looked like it could eat a grown lion in one bite. This cub would be only a nibble. The snake stared at the cub as though debating if the cub was worth the effort.

Anta thought quickly. He wanted to save the lion cub. The anaconda made his decision and slowly started to descend towards the cub, which was still playing, unaware of the great danger. If he sees me, he will definitely leave the cub, Anta thought. I am much larger than the cub, but the problem is, the snake can catch me in no time. Anta looked to the left. Within seconds he made his plan. He knew it was risky and his body tensed for action.

"Hoo ha! hoo ha!" yelled Anta, waving with his hands wildly to catch the snake's attention. The anaconda immediately turned his huge head towards Anta. He looked directly into the snake's huge yellow eyes and almost panicked. They looked cold, vicious and determined. I am going to die, thought Anta to himself, but he continued screaming at the snake while slowly pacing back and to the left. The snake, eager for a more appropriately-sized meal, started to move quickly towards Anta. He started to run towards a small pile of rocks, as the little cub recognized the danger and ran away, disappearing into the bushes. Anta was sprinting now, occasionally looking backwards at the amazingly fast snake. Anta knew what was going to happen for he once saw a huge constrictor catch his prey. The snake will wrap around him, strangling him to death and crushing every bone in his body with his immense power, then swallow him whole. Anta had other plans.

He reached the small pile of rocks and saw a few sticks nearby. He had played with such sticks for many years and knew they were rigid and made excellent hunting weapons for small animals and fish. He quickly grabbed one and turned around. The snake approached quickly and opened his mouth wide. Anta was terrified but knew that his life depended on executing his plan. To his relief, he did not see any poison fangs. This is going well so far. He will definitely try to grab me and strangle me first. To his surprise, the snake opened his mouth wider attempting to swallow Anta whole. All the better.

When the anaconda reached Anta, the boy looked inside its mouth in awe. It's like a huge cave! Then Anta craftily placed the stick inside the snake's mouth. The snake instinctively tried to snap his mouth closed but only impaled his jaws onto the stick.

Angered, the snake thrashed about and made a terrible noise. Now he was banging his head on the ground, violently trying to get rid of the stick between his jaws. But the stick was very strong and remained in place. Anta moved backwards in awe of the giant snake's thrashing efforts. He waited until the snake became tired then moved to the second part of his plan and started to throw rock after rock into the snake's mouth. After a while the weight of the rocks became too heavy and the snake could no longer move his head. Anta threw heavier rocks inside the snake's mouth until eventually it could not move its head anymore. Making squealing noises, the snake eventually lay on the ground with his mouth wide open, unable to move more than an inch or so.

Anta kept a safe distance since the snake's long tail was still dangerous. Victory, he thought. The nice thing is that the snake will survive also. He knew the stick would soften in the humid night air. He also knew the rocks inside the great snake were salt-based and would also get soft and eventually melt away. The snake will be able to close its mouth, probably tomorrow, and live out its life. After all, the snake is part of nature.

Anta continued to search for the white flowers that led back to his village. He hated to disturb nature. Some animals are predators but that is part of nature's way. His father taught him that when he was a little boy. Now he focused on finding his way back to the village.

∞

He could hear men ahead talking loud. I made it, he thought with relief, but he quickly thought different. The voices were coming right ahead of him. He inched forward until he saw the source. There were five men brutally assaulting a naked girl about his age. His heart skipped a few beats as he witnessed the cruelty. His mouth got dry and his brain worked extra fast to find a way to help her. He looked in all directions trying to find some way but it was in a clearing and he was alone. They will kill me in an instant if I try to do something. He was silently amazed that she did not make any sound during the assault.

Suddenly, she looked straight at him.

His eyes locked into hers and they shared a mysterious moment. It was as though nobody else was there, only those two. Everything around them seemed to stop. Her eyes expressed enormous pain and he felt immediate heartache. He could do nothing to help her.

Then one of the men hit her with a lengthy stick. Anta's lips became narrow and he almost shouted out in anger. The girl looked at him and he thought that she smiled at him, but maybe it was his imagination. Anta breathed heavily in frustration. She stretched her little hand towards him as if trying to tell him something or pleading for his help. He froze not knowing what to do. With tears in his eyes he motioned back to her. He wanted to encourage her somehow, to tell her that everything will be better. Then he felt anger taking over him. He wanted to kill these men for what they were doing to her. He could smash them like bugs, without any feelings. He turned his eyes from the scene. He felt helpless and like a failure. He could not make any rescue plans. He was too confused and sad. The girl stopped responding to their attacks and seemed to lose consciousness or die.

Anta cried silently. In those mysterious moments he felt that he and the girl had created a special bond, but now she was probably dead. He could not understand why these men treated her that way. She was just a child. He felt terrible for not being able to do anything to save her. They dropped her in a mud puddle and made a campfire nearby. His anger and rage took over again and he decided to avenge the little girl's murder. I'll show these men what cruelty is, he thought. I'll wait until dark and then I'll strike. He did not have a plan yet but he trusted himself to find one before nightfall.

∞

Ven stole some clothes from the men's horses and soon got warm as she carefully watched the men from a distance. She found fruit and bread in one of the saddlebags and was now eating slowly. After a while she smiled, and her white teeth glimmered in the dark. They will have a very surprising morning, she thought. She had already planned out her revenge.

There are many dangerous plants in the forest. One of the most dangerous is the curly, red grape bush. It looks very innocent, producing small red fruit during the winter. These grapes are edible during the winter only. Ven remembered her father allowing her and her sisters to eat these small red grapes during a certain time of the year. She and her sisters wanted to eat them all year long but had to patiently wait for their father's permission. Typically this was a few days after the first rain, when the grapes lost their toxic nature and became fun food for the kids in the tribe. They were allowed to eat the grapes until the first day of the summer. Then they all knew not to even get close to the plants. A few weeks into the summer they became extremely poisonous. Just to be on the safe side, parents forbade eating the grapes at the beginning of summer.

They would never forget what happened to one of the kids who did not listen to his parents and ate from the plant. His entire body was covered with red blisters shortly after eating the grapes. For many hours he suffered severe pains and eventually died, his entire body bleeding and covered with red pustules. It looked like his blood had boiled inside him. It was a horrifying death and they were all very scared. Ven could never forget his screams.

It was early in the morning and the five men were still sleeping, covered by woolen blankets. The embers of the campfire still produced occasional whiffs of smoke. The horses were silently feeding on the nearby grass, though they snorted from time to time. Ven sat near the men and quietly studied them. She was calm now. The clothes were ridiculously large on her but protected her from the chilly morning breeze and that's all that mattered to her. Her face was clean and she seemed at least somewhat recovered from yesterday's ordeals. Near her lay a coconut shell with a red mixture in it. A sudden sound of crackling leaves made her turn. She saw the boy. He was holding a long sharp spear and aiming it towards the sleeping men, his brows furrowed in anger. Then he noticed her. She quickly put her finger to her lips. "Shhh," she whispered to the boy. He was very surprised to see her alive. His anger changed to a shy smile. She signed for him to stay where he was and pointed to the half coconut shell. The boy looked at the shell, not understanding, but she signed for him to stay there and wait. Something told him to listen to her. He looked at the sleeping men and noticed their faces were smeared with red liquid. She must have put that on them while they were sleeping, he thought. Without yet grasping what was going on, he nonetheless felt that his revenge would no longer needed. He lowered his spear and silently waited. All of a sudden he felt a hidden joy.

The red grape plant has an amazing but devastating effect on the human body. A few drops of its juice can permeate the skin and rush into the bloodstream within seconds. But the actual effect does not start immediately. It takes a few minutes for the symptoms to show. The substance causes direct blood oxygenation within body tissue – a process similar to shaking a can of carbonated soda. The carbon dioxide explodes upon opening the can in a gush of bubbles. The powerful chemical reaction from the grapes causes the oxygen in the bloodstream to slowly bubble out. The results are catastrophic. It starts with excruciating pain in the shoulders, elbows, knees, and ankles. Then the oxygen in the blood bubbles its way out of the body through the organs and the skin. At first the skin itches then the reaction quickly leads to severe pain throughout the body. Red and marbled sores form and spread rapidly until the entire body is covered with large inflamed bleeding buboes. Brain parts start to fail serially, causing body dysfunction, systems paralysis, and eventually to slow painful death as the lungs fail.

Ven sat on a little rock near the sleeping men and ate an apple. Anta was standing near a tree about fifty feet away and watched carefully, ready to use his spear. Ven seemed calm and Anta had a feeling that she had already gained her revenge, knowing the men were doomed. He guessed that she had poisoned the men in their sleep. He had witnessed poison cases before. His tribe prepared their hunting arrows with a deadly poison, but when attacked they used it against the enemy. He was sure that she had done something but did not know exactly what or how it would unfold.

One of the men started to move in discomfort, then in a few minutes the others did the same. Ven knew that the poison was taking hold and there was no way to stop it. The closest man to her woke up in a panic and tried to stand up, but the pain overwhelmed him and he fell on the ground grunting wildly. Ven did not even look at him but stared at her apple instead. One after the other, the men woke up grunting and screaming in pain. They grabbed for their shoulders, elbows, knees, and ankles. Then their entire body started to itch until the pain rapidly became excruciating. All of them were now on the ground screaming and writhing in great pain. Ven still did not look at them, only at a spot in the thin air. Anta was shocked. He'd never seen such poisoning. He was transfixed by the scene of the agonized, dying men. Soon blood gushed from their mouths, noses and ears. Their bodies were covered with red blisters that grew rapidly until they exploded with blood. They thrashed on the ground, screaming loudly, trying somehow to counter the deadly process. Ven looked at them now. Her face showed no hint of remorse. She had no feeling. She remembered yesterday. After a long slow hour, the men's screams turned into mumbling as they convulsed on the ground more slowly now. The oxygenation of blood had reached crucial parts of their brains and lungs and turned them into vegetables. Their bleeding bodies became saggy then slowly stopped moving, as death saved them further agony. Another hour passed and they were merely bloody corpses strewn across the ground. The sun came out behind the hills and flashed into the valley. It will be much better day, thought Ven as she looked at Anta.

Anta was still shocked from the terrible scene and sat down on the ground in silence. After few minutes he stood and looked at Ven. She looked directly at him. He understood why she did what she did. As he was looking into her eyes he could again feel a special bond with her. They shared something horrible. Yet the event brought a bonding – something that he could not define or express. She looked at his blue eyes and felt that she and he belonged together from now on. After several silent moments, Anta nodded his head. Ven smiled back to him. Without saying a word, they knew that they had forged a bond and it would last a very long time, longer than they could possibly comprehend.

Ven jumped off her rock and started to walk towards him. Suddenly her eyes became large in horror. She wanted to scream and warn the boy but everything happened so fast. She just stepped back and watched in horror as a giant snake struck him from the top of a tree. Anta was looking at her when he felt something wrong. He thought that someone was attacking him from behind, but that was a fatal mistake. He gave a last look at Ven and quickly turned backwards with his spear aiming towards the attacker. But the snake attacked from above. It was too late for Anta. He looked up in horror as he saw a huge mouth coming directly at him. The snake wrapped Anta with his huge form, breaking every bone in his body. He curled around him so quickly that Ven could not see him anymore. All she saw was the long stout body of the snake. Within seconds she helplessly witnessed the snake swallow Anta whole. It was so fast she was breathless and open mouthed. The snake crawled into the deep forest to digest his meal. Knowing that it would take some time, the snake looked for a warm hiding place.

In shock, Ven stood near the little rock. In a short time she had developed powerful feelings towards the boy. He was her savior yesterday. Seeing him during the assault had given her strength. When he gently waved to her, he gave her hope. Seeing him again today and sharing her cruel revenge had been an extraordinary event. And now he was gone, forever. Her heart ached and her eyes filled with tears. She looked around and saw the bloody bodies of the men she had slain. She walked to the tree where the boy had been standing and where his spear lay. She picked it up and noticed markings on it. The boy had engraved something on it. She turned it around and saw an image of a little boy and girl standing close to each other. That's us, she thought as she began to cry. Did he foresee their meeting or did he draw this yesterday? She could also see images of the sun, moon and stars. What could this mean? Then she saw another engraving of two circles touching each other – ∞. She never saw anything like that. She let the tears roll down her cheeks as she looked out at the horizon. Deep inside she felt that a powerful bond had been made with this boy. Yet she did not even know his name. She had to continue her life without him, but a powerful voice inside her, one she had never heard before, told her they would meet again. Although he was dead, she was sure that part of him was still alive. Somewhere, sometime, they would meet again.

Not understanding her feelings, she started to walk back towards Bear Mountain. From there she knew the way back to the tribe. She arrived back at the tribe in the evening. Her family was happy to see her, especially her mother and sisters. She did not say a word about what she had experienced. That evening the tribe had a great feast for her successful completion of the Day of the

Sun. She did not feel happy at all. Later in life, Ven would marry and have children. She would have a full family life according to her tribe's tradition. In a very peculiar way she never forgot Anta, the boy she saw only for a few moments. Although constantly surrounded by family and friends throughout her life, somehow Ven always felt alone. Without being aware of this fact, their first and eternal connection had been made.

Night Fell.

Morning Rose.

Verna was upset. She was about to execute the only man she ever loved. Everything happened very fast. She woke up to a beautiful spring morning. Their village lay in a large valley among high mountains. The tops were still white with snow but their great valley was blooming in a variety of colors. It was springtime and there were flowers everywhere. The ground, still wet from the long cold winter, opened spring with an explosion of colors, smells and tastes. As with every spring, the village started to work the wheat fields. Early mornings, groups of men and women left for their duties in the fields. There was a lot to do. The land needed to be well prepared for a successful crop in the summer. The large fields of wheat were already fully grown and waited to get fully dry. They had to make a special mixture from eucalyptus trees and spread it throughout the fields to keep pests from eating their crop. Last year they suffered great damages from brown worms that ate the roots. This year they will be prepared. Verna herself taught all her people how to make the eucalyptus mixture. Special attention was needed to spread it in exact locations to ward off the worms and insects. She got the recipe from her mother.

Verna was the village wise woman, as were her adoptive mother and her mother's adoptive mother. They dealt with everything beyond the usual. They provided medicine for the sick, guidance for the young, and prayers for the needy. Nothing was done in their village without consulting her. She was involved with every subject from child-rearing to justice. She heard cases and meted out punishments, even executions. Verna had full control of her village and she liked it. She was in her late thirties and looked like her years has passed by without hard traces. She had long dark hair that she carefully arranged every morning after washing it in the cold river. In winter and summer alike, she meticulously cared for her long hair as part of her family's generation-long tradition. Her eyes were dark green and they slanted upwards slightly. Her mother claimed that this was due to ancient Asian blood in her family. Although in her late thirties, her body was as fit as when she was twenty-four. She had smooth golden skin and a slender figure. She moistened her entire body every night, as though in a ritual, with special herbs and scents – another recipe from her ancestors.

Although considered beautiful and appealing, Verna was forbidden to men. She was the village wise woman, and like all wise women they should never be with a man or have families of their own. She was a forbidden beauty. The wise woman would choose an orphaned girl as successor and train her in the arts. The life of a wise woman was dedicated to the good of her people. As told by her mother, she had passed through hard times. In her twenties, as many females in her village, she felt the urge to be with a man. She struggled to let go of her passion and self-control but most of all, she struggled against the desire to have a child of her own. With great sadness she watched the village's women marry and almost immediately bear children. Some had children before marriage. She conducted all the marriages in her village and it was very painful to witness the happiness of couples and know that she could never experience that joy. In time she learned to live with the pain. The long last dull ache always accompanied her wherever she went, but this morning something different happened. Something she never imagined would happen to her. She fell in love.

She was bathing in the early morning, as she did every day. She had a special spot in the stream that was for her alone. The entire village knew this spot and that it was forbidden to go there. Every morning Verna woke up early and devoted almost two hours to her bath. The ritual included rubbing herbs and scented oils all over her body. Then she relaxed in the early morning sun atop a flat rock behind a large olive tree. The rock was hidden by the tree and fully exposed to the sun. That was her time to herself. Many times she fell asleep there and woke up later in the day, especially during the summer when even the early sun was quite hot.

That morning, after bathing and anointing herself, she lay on the flat rock, her dark tresses spread all around her. She fell asleep and lost all sense of time. She woke from a soft noise, and there he was. A man stood very close by, just gazing at her. As she returned his gaze she suddenly felt panic take hold but then amazingly fall away, replaced by another feeling. She looked at the man's face. He was tall with long brown hair that fell all the way to his chest. His eyes were deep blue and mysterious. He had a proportional nose and full lips. He was handsome and she could not move her eyes from him, even though she knew she was naked before him. The man looked straight into her eyes, without any motion. They were locked into the moment. Then the man kneeled near her, took her hand in his, and kissed it. He said something in a language she did not understand. Then something extraordinary happened. All she could remember was that in a split second she was in his arms, afire.

The man kissed her passionately on her lips. His tongue boldly invaded her mouth and she almost passed out from the excitement. She could no longer control her body or soul. She looked at his face and then cupped it with her hands. His cheeks and chin felt rough from stubble, but she liked the feeling. He allowed her to explore his face. She felt like she had long known him, like they had already been together, although she knew that such a thing can never happen. A sudden thought occurred. She felt like her loved one came from far away and after many years. She kissed him gently on his lips, encouraging his animal passion. They passionately made love on the flat rock, touching, feeling, and exploring each other. They could not have enough of each other until nature's powers expended themselves and left them satisfied.

They lay there breathing heavily and relaxing sweetly. No words were spoken as he gently caressed her hair. She explored his body with all of her senses with his silent consent. Soon they were drifting again in a passionate harmony of love as though the world around them did not exist. Later as they lay together, it dawned on her. She violated the basic law of her existence. She was forbidden to be with a man. She was terrified but felt calm return as she looked over to her love. As long as I have him, everything is good, she thought and then smiled to him. He looked at her with love and thought, I do not even know her name.

They bathed together in the clear, cold river and made progress in communicating in sign language. She treasured seeing him rub his body with her herbs. He had many scars and she thought he must be a warrior of some kind. Then she anointed his body with her scented oil and was amused when he gently laughed at the ticklish sensations of her touch. An unexpected sound disturbed their moment. There was a girl from the village standing there, covering her mouth in order not to scream. All three froze for a moment before the girl ran back to the village. What is she doing here? Vernal thought in panic. Verna's heart raced wildly as she tried to think what to do. Obviously the girl had been sent to ask her something. Now the girl is on her way to the village with word of what she saw. Feeling her stress he looked at her, trying to calm her down. "Quick," she said urgently, "we have to get out of here," forgetting that he could not understand her spoken word. They dressed and descended from the flat rock and stopped at the sight of her entire village standing before them. She had violated the most sacred rule of her tribe for generations. Verna knew the penalty. They both would be put to death.

In desperation she searched for an answer.

∞

"Arrest him!" Verna commanded in an authoritative voice. She wrapped herself in her gown and pointed towards the man. He looked at her without any doubt. He completely trusted her, whatever she would do.

Silently the man was taken to the village.

She knew her village was fiercely loyal to her and would take her word. She will claim that he attacked her. She will become clean again, and he will be put on trial. That will buy some time. Without any hesitation, she gave the order to imprison the man.

According to tradition, trials were carried out the same day. She knew the punishment for the crime he was accused of. It was death and she would be the one to give the verdict and conduct the execution as well. The trial was set for midday. He was taken by her people and held in a dark cave near the river.

Slowly she went to her tent. The familiar scent welcomed her and for a second she felt relaxed. But then she thought of him and missed him terribly. Everything seemed hopeless. She will have to execute him shortly. She fell on her bed, feeling helpless. What have I done? she thought as she cried silently. Her world was collapsing.

The entire village assembled at the large round rock where they conducted trials and held assemblies for other important matters. Nature had created there an amazing, massive amphitheater. Circular structures of large rocks created an almost perfectly round shape. The unique topology meant no trees cluttered the site. Today the entire village stood there quietly and waited for the trial to start. They tied the man with thick ropes to a large rock before Verna arrived. Although the dire nature of the proceeding was known, the man looked calm. He ignored the crowd and stared at a certain spot in the sky. When a murmur in the crowd began, he turned to look. Verna arrived. She was attired in traditional clothing – a black gown with purple striping colored by vegetable dye.

She is beautiful, thought the man. Though he knew the likely outcome of the procedure, he could not stop gazing at her. He had traveled from far away to bring medicine to his sick mother. His village's medicine man told him there was only one way to save her – blue jasmine flower tea. The blue jasmine flower is very rare in their land and he journeyed far and wide to find some. All he needed was a few to dry and then crush to create tea leaves. The tea had to be given to his mother for seven days. His heart felt pain for his ill mother. I will not be able to save her, he thought sadly. Then he looked at Verna. Strange are nature's ways. Who would imagine that I'd meet this woman, desperately fall in love with her, but then die for it? At least I had the good fortune to fall in love.

He had never loved any woman before. Although many women were available in his village, he never found one he liked, let alone loved. Throughout the years, his mother constantly reminded him of her desire to have a grandchild, and he always smiled and told her, "When time comes." He wished his mother could see Verna but knew this was not to be. He was a warrior by nature and always looked for ways to escape danger, but he was under heavy guard and tightly bound. This time he knew that only a miracle could save him. The crowd became silent as Verna took her place in front of him. He looked at her but she held her face low. She began to speak in a language he could not understand. He closed his eyes.

On her way to the amphitheater Verna feared she would stumble, fall, and die. She was excited at the thought of seeing her love but felt pain all over her body and could not think clearly. The thought of trying and executing her loved one caused unimaginable agony. She wanted to die. While glumly walking down the path to where the trial would be conducted, she remembered the advice her father gave her just before he died. He had been attacked by a large bear and villagers found him few days later, severely wounded. He used to go on his hunting trips many times a year, sometimes for many days. Almost every time he came back with amazing stories. The entire village used to sit around the campfire at night and listen with open mouths to his stories. He always returned with something to show. Sometimes it was a bear hide, sometimes a deer head. As he got older his trips became shorter.

She had asked him many times to give up hunting, but he always had one answer. "This is part of me. If I give this up, I give up my soul." He said it often, smiling with a toothless grin. When she expressed concern that he was getting old and no longer a match for dangerous game, he said, "Then this is my way to go." He uttered these words when they found him. He lay under a huge tree, almost smiling. Verna rushed to him and could swear that he was indeed smiling.

"An extraordinary thing happened," he said quietly. "The bear did not kill me. I tracked him for days . . . chased him all the way here. Then he attacked me from behind." He showed Verna the huge wound on his back where the bear's claw had torn into him.

His clothes were soaked with blood and she knew he had lost too much blood. Tears came to her eyes. He noticed her sadness and slowly said,

"No need to be sad. It is my way to go."

She would never forget those words. He looked at her face and she could see the blood slowly draining from his flesh. "Never give up on yourself. If you want something, do whatever needed to get it. All that you have is within you." And then he closed his eyes, a faint smile still on his face. She sat there with him for many hours, looking upon his eternal smile and pondering its meaning. She felt happy for him. He died contented and in the way he always wanted.

As she slowly paced to the trial area, her eyes lit. She knew what to do. Yes, it will be a complete change in her life but she had to follow her instincts. Most of all, she had to follow her heart. Her spirit found new courage and she almost felt joy. I have to be careful, she thought as she took her place as judge. Things were not as they seemed and she was determined to keep it that way.

She stood in front of him, looking downward, as the entire village surrounded them in the natural amphitheater. She slowly raised her eyes and looked at him. She did not look sad anymore. He looked straight at her thinking about how much he would love to hold her again. Then he thought she gave him a slight smile. He had the feeling that their fortunes were about to change.

She uttered a few words, raised a hand above her head, and the trial was over. She sentenced him to death. She gave him a last look and then turned around and left. Only the guards remained to watch the condemned man. Tomorrow morning he would be executed.

∞

Executions took place at Giant Eagle Rock located on a high cliff viewing a large canyon, not too far from the village. The name came from an enormous eagle that lit upon the rock once a day, hoping to find prey. No one knew much about the huge bird.

No one ever saw it. Rumor held that it was very old and its wingspan was ten times that of a typical eagle. For generations the condemned were taken to the rock in the early morning hours, tightly bound and escorted by special guard. The immense eagle came around noon and the condemned would be eaten alive. The path to the rock was blocked by a stone gate that they had built. No one could open it from the cliff side. This left the condemned to face the eagle and the foreboding canyon below. Many prisoners chose to leap to their deaths rather than to be eaten alive. Guards returned the next morning to make sure that the execution had been done. In most of the cases they found remains. If not, they knew that the condemned had chosen to jump to death. Either way, it was a horrible way to die.

∞

Verna knew all about Giant Eagle Rock. She knew it so well that it figured highly in her plan. She would go to the rock to save her man, then they'd flee to a faraway place. Everything will be wonderful, she thought with a trace of a smile. We will be together, forever. Evening came and everything was ready. She dressed in dark clothing and prepared to leave her tent. She brought food and water and a sharp knife for the ropes. Slowly she prepared her gear and then looked at the sky. There was a full moon and she could see the mountain in the distance. She smiled in silence as she remembered the time they spent together and their passionate moments. She could not wait to be with him again. A sudden noise got her attention. She looked ahead and saw a few men from the village. They looked at her without saying a word. Many other men and women came out and surrounded her. She tried to pass through them but they formed a circle and would not let her pass. Angered, she tried to break through the circle, pushing, hitting and shoving aside, but without success. Her people silently closed around her. She fell back, looking at them, breathing heavily from the struggle. All she could think was one horrific thought. My man is going to die.

They returned her to her tent and stood outside. She lay in her tent, feeling hopeless. My loved one is going to die, she thought despairingly, and there is nothing I can do to help him. The only love I ever knew is going to be taken away from me. She lay in her tent quietly. She wanted to die.

∞

I must have been sleeping for a while, he thought as he woke up from a troubled sleep. He was bound to the back of a horse that plodded in the dark. His back hurt but he ignored the pain and tried to assess his situation. The horse was led by a guard. He could smell fresh pine trees and water as they crossed a creek. He could hear a few other horses and came to the conclusion that they were not alone. Where are they taking me, he wondered without feeling any fear. The night was cold but refreshing and he relaxed as much as he could on the way to an unknown place. After a while there were fewer trees and he could see the surroundings. With a full moon out, he could clearly see a path on a mountainside. Soon they were on a small path up a steep mountain.

The constant movement in the dark put him into drowsiness. A poke from a spear woke him up. He lay on the ground while the guards silently looked at him. The rock that he lay on was cold and jagged. The guards gave him a last look and left on their horses. He watched as they sealed a rock gate. Summoning all his powers he managed to roll on the ground. If I can move about, maybe I can find something to cut this rope, he thought as he increased his efforts. What kind of place is this? He was looking around but all he could see was flat rock. He rolled to the left and stopped at the last minute as he peered down a deep canyon. A little more and I'm at the bottom of this canyon, he thought in fear. The night wind was cold and he felt despair taking over. There was no way off the rock, and there was also the rock gate, which was carefully sealed. What is the purpose of this rock? Am I supposed to starve to death? Or maybe jump to my death into the canyon? After looking around for a while he lay on the rock and stared at the clear sky. Soon morning will come. I'll think of something then. Although it was cold, he soon fell asleep.

She did not sleep all night. She watched fearfully as the first sunbeams penetrated her tent. She knew that the giant eagle would soon visit the flat rock. She looked outside and saw her people still standing there. She felt she was falling from a high mountain.

He was awoken by loud flapping sounds. He looked up in disbelief at the sight of a giant bird circling above. The wings generated gusts of wind that almost caused him to lose his breath as the eagle searched for a spot to land. So this is the purpose I am here. This is the way they carry out death sentences, he thought. He felt the excitement of preparing for battle, but he felt no fear. He was accustomed to fighting for his life. "I am not giving up easily, big bird!" he shouted defiantly. It flew with a certain majesty, cutting the air with its huge wings. The huge black and white feathers gave the bird a stately quality. Its head was mostly white, with large black eyes and a bright red beak. He watched the bird circling the flat rock as it regarded its next meal, sure that its prey could not escape. The eagle had excellent instincts. It knew that its prey could not resist much. Even those who fell or leaped into the canyon would be very easy to be picked at. As the bird got older, it became harder to hunt large animals. Its vision was failing and it had lost its quickness. It was quite happy to see this type of prey. This one would be easy work. The eagle spied a good spot to land and moved toward it.

She tied the girl tightly with rope. Then she quickly donned the girl's attire, which covered most of her face. Young single girls cover their faces around men as a sign of availability. Married women went about without any face cover to declare they were taken. Lucky for her she was short and could neatly fit into the gown of the girl who had brought her food and water. She left the girl tied up in her tent and stealthily exited. No one stopped her. She could hardly keep from running as she walked towards the field where she kept her horse. Without losing any time she jumped on the horse's back and urged him to gallop towards the mountains. Disturbed from his calm breakfast, her steed responded somewhat slowly but soon developed a brisk pace. He sensed her urgency.

He had a brief moment of panic as he watched the giant eagle coming down towards him with its huge talons ready to strike. He had seen birds hunting before and knew the meaning. The big bird will stick its large claws into him, causing serious wounds and then death. His instincts came to full alert and adrenalin surged. He could see some matter hanging from the talons – probably the bird's recent prey. It's diving directly at me and I have only a few seconds to do something. His instincts provided a plan.

He had to somehow get the bird's sharp beak and claws to slash the ropes binding him. But how to prevent the bird from slashing into him? If the bird cut into him with its talons at full speed, his chances would be slim. The force would cause the claws to tear through his body like sharp knives. His only chance was to quickly roll to the side just before impact. Too early, the bird will adjust its attack. Too late, he was dead. He lay on his back and concentrated on timing his move. The sight of the huge bird plunging from the skies, screeching loudly with open claws, was frightening. He summoned all of his soldierly experience to stave off panic. The prey simply lay there, without any motion, and the eagle felt the nearness of victory. It positioned its talons downwards.

And then, a split second before the bird hit, the man deftly rolled to the left, causing the eagle to slow and try to readjust. But the giant bird was already at full speed and with age having dulled his responses, it could not stop. It crashed violently into the rock, screeching in pain as its talons clawed bare stone, and broke off. Knowing the peril was not yet over, the man crawled farther away. Its beak could still kill him instantly, but he could use its pained and clumsy efforts to cut the rope, allowing him to escape. He tried to think past that moment but knew the first move was to get free. The bird will pay a price for its method, he thought as his heart raced. When it strikes, it will strike itself. He just hoped to be fast enough to avoid what was coming.

The eagle was angry now. He was stumbling towards the man, searching for a soft spot to plunge into. The man rolled on his stomach, exposing his back. The bird struck wildly but the prey's reflexes were too good and he could only make serious but non-lethal wounds. The ropes became red with the man's blood yet his plan was working! With every wound came a slice into the ropes. In some places the ropes had been cut completely and the man thrashed about to further weaken them. The pain was excruciating but he focused on what had to be done. As the eagle angrily chased him, tearing into him at any chance, he felt close to freeing himself. He was covered with blood and started to feel the effects of so many wounds. Will I make it? Will I make it before passing out? Passing out meant being devoured by the great eagle. That thought drove him on.

He rolled again, harder this time, and suddenly felt the wonderful feeling of bursting free of his binds. He got rid of the rest of the rope by simply pushing it down through his legs. At last he was rid of the bonds and free! With his new freedom he looked at the eagle coming towards him once more, screeching noisily but now clearly conveying fatigue. Inspired, he roared back at it. The eagle was startled and moved backwards slightly, reappraising the situation. Stumbling badly, the bird sensed it had broken its talons, maybe also a limb, when it slammed into the rock.

What should I do now? The man thought briefly. But there was no time for that. The bird was still strong enough and able to kill him in an instant. The man looked around for a weapon of sorts, but the flat rock was completely empty except for the ropes. He knew he had to do something quickly or his blood loss would doom him. Then he had an idea.

He watched the eagle swooping down for another attack. He picked up some rope and carefully watched the eagle descend fearsomely. As the eagle approached more cautiously, he waited for the right moment then raced behind the great bird, which could not respond in time. The man threw the rope around the eagle's neck and created a loop, which he tightened with his remaining strength. The eagle felt it had become the prey, and panicked. That's exactly what the man was aiming for. To increase its panic, he shouted as loud as he could and pulled harder on the rope. The bird responded, as any bird would, by trying to fly away. The man held the rope firmly as the giant bird became airborne, screeching angrily and flapping its huge wings. The man grabbed hold as the bird flew over the canyon. His attacker would now fly him to freedom.

Neither his weight nor his motion affected the mammoth bird; it continued to fly smoothly. After a while his grip weakened, but to his relief the bird began to descend towards a thick forest, searching for a good spot to land – not an easy task for an immense bird. The eagle landed on a high branch of a majestic tree and looked into the skies quietly, hoping to recuperate. The man climbed onto a sturdy branch. A flock of birds alarmed the eagle and it flew off noisily, leaving the man in the tree. So long, friend, he thought. We shared quite an experience, and thanks to you I am off that rock! He almost liked the big bird, even though it had tried to kill him. After all, it bore no evil; it just acted according to instinct.

He looked around but could not see any way to get off the tree. The branch simply did not afford any way to descend. He started to see the world circling and felt the pain from his wounds become unbearable. He was so exhausted from his ordeal that he could hardly hold on any longer. I was so close, he thought as he breathed laboriously. His powers left him and he almost welcomed the cozy darkness as it took over. His last thought before falling was about his woman. He wished he could see her one more time.

∞

Fast, she thought wildly, I have to get their fast. She urged her horse on without mercy. The horse responded with a gallop, though its hooves were coming down on rock. She knew this was risky as the horse could stumble and bring them both crashing down, but there was no choice. She looked at the sun and determined it was just after midday. Pain filled her heart as she thought she may be too late and her loved one might no longer be alive. She felt despair descend upon her. No, she thought, he is strong. He is a survivor. He is alright. She shouted for her horse to increase its pace still more. She was struck by an inexplicable feeling – a certainty – that her loved one was alive.

Her horse's mouth frothed and panted, but she urged it on. As she approached the deep forest, she became encouraged knowing that the mountain path was close by but she had to slow down in the thick underbrush. As she was passing a particularly dense area, something crashed down just in front of her. A low thump sounded as the object fell atop of thick bushes. It looked like a human, she thought as she halted her horse. With difficulty, she looked through the brush as her horse welcomed a chance to catch its breath. Then she saw him. She stood in complete shock. She could not believe her eyes. It was her loved one – bloody and pale. She ran to him and hugged him but felt no sign of life. Her eyes filled with tears immediately and she uttered words incoherently. Her loved one was dead. She held him and kissed his face all over without any thought of time. She lay there, still hugging his lifeless form, until she could produce no more tears. She did not want to move. She felt her life too had ended.

∞

It was almost evening and the forest was growing dark. She thought she felt his head move – or was it her imagination? She paused her breath, held his head, and concentrated. There it was again. She immediately placed her ear to his nostrils. She could not believe it; he was breathing! Slowly, but he was breathing. His chest pumped slowly up and down, again and again. She exhaled all the despair she had experienced that day and all of her being became alive. He is alive! He is alive! she thought in a burst of happiness, hope and joy. She started to talk to him although she knew he did not understand her language. Still talking to him, she gently pulled him out of the bushes and laid him atop some soft vegetation. She brought fresh water from a nearby creek and washed the lacerations across his back, which she soon concluded had come from desperate struggle with the eagle. As the cold water stung his wounds, he began to stir. She covered him with a large cloth from her saddlebag. She knew that he was weak from the blood loss so she searched for white orchid flowers to prepare an elixir. She knew from the lore of generations all about healing concoctions from herbs and flowers. The white orchid elixir will revive him and give him the initial power to continue healing. She hid him under a thick bush and went to search for the flower. It was sunset but she could still see quite well.

Coming to consciousness slowly, he started to drink the potions. She knew his wounds were infected because of the green pus flowing from them. She repeatedly washed them with a medicine she made from the tree's stem and wild berries. The tricky part was that infections had to be cleaned constantly until they were completely dry. She held him all night, tending to his wounds, until finally she fell asleep.

He was looking at her when she woke up. She stopped breathing and looked into his deep blue eyes. Neither could believe their eyes. Then he smiled. "Oh . . . oh," she murmured and kissed his face all over, crying with happiness. "Oh . . . oh," he said in return, though his utterance was accompanied by a contorted face. "What's wrong?" she asked while carefully looking at him. Then she figured he was in considerable pain. "Sorry," she said with a smile and gently hugged him. He looked at her and could not believe his eyes. He had lost hope of ever seeing her again, but now they were reunited. He suddenly tired. It had been a long, exhausting journey. He allowed himself to fall asleep as she showered him with kisses once more. She watched him sleeping calmly and knew that they had made it. They would camp here for a few days and she would take care of him until he regained his health. The sun was shining, the birds sang beautiful morning songs, and all of a sudden the world looked like a beautiful place again.

∞

It was an enchanted evening. The full moon sparkled across the calm lake water, making it almost unreal. Splash! The calm water was disturbed by her leap from a rock. In the darkness he could only see the outlines of her beautiful, naked body as she entered the cool water. She swam briskly towards him then stopped near his feet to catch her breath. Her smile invited him to join her but he preferred to gaze at her for a while. When he did get in they swam harmoniously together across the calm surface – the water seeming to follow them like a white trail. Soon their passion took over and like two young people they reached shore, holding each other. The ground was still warm from the hot summer day and their passion ruled them as they rolled together in the rhythm of love. They became one body, one soul, as their love commanded their bodies. Their entire world exploded in brilliant colors as their love climaxed spectacularly. They rested, trembled, and held each other. Their perspiration mixed with the lake water, making them one with nature. They were together, and nothing else mattered.

She looked at him as he treasured her hair and the moonlight created silver glimmers in his eyes. He smiled and sank his face in her wet hair and breathed her in. He loved her scent. They lay on the ground enjoying the night skies. It had been almost three years since they met each other that day and endured so much to be together. They could speak the same language now. After their miraculous reunion they roamed for months until eventually finding their destiny in a small village within a beautiful valley near this huge lake. The villagers were very kind and hospitable, and they loved nature. They learned that these gentle people had been attacked many times by hostile tribes in the region. Despite their defenses, the village often suffered grievous casualties and loss of crops.

The man, a warrior by birth, trained the villagers in martial tactics and strategies. Verna, a medicine woman and teacher, assumed those roles in their new homeland. They soon became the village leaders, respected and honored by all. Verna found her man's name, Dror, simple yet strong. Verna and Dror found happiness in this little village between beautiful towering mountains and clear blue waters. They built a house on the shore, among tall trees and aquatic plants. They swam almost every night; it was almost a rite. The weather was warm and pleasant just about all year long. They were virtually inseparable. There happiness was complete – almost. They had no children even though they had tried for years. Every month she felt disappointment. Dror comforted her, assuring they'd succeed next month. Her natural potions were futile. Years passed and Verna started to lose hope. She was about to become thirty nine years of age.

Dror looked into her eyes. "You know how much I love you." She returned his gaze and felt tears bursting from her eyes, but could say nothing. "I know how much it grieves you," he said, pressing her hand to his chest. "But I know," he continued, "I know that the day will come when we will have a child." She raised her eyes and saw his gentle smile and it brought hope to her heart, as it did every month. What would she do without him, she wondered as she studied the detail of his face – the furrows of his forehead, the little wave in the corner of his lips that made him seem to be smiling, and the gray beginning to spread in his hair. She gently sank her face into his chest. They lay there in the night until the first beams of light woke them up. It was a new day with new hopes.

∞

Verna and Dror sat in Doru's large tent. Doru was the medicine man of a small and friendly village near theirs. Verna wanted to go to Doru regarding their fertility problem. After many requests Dror agreed, and there they sat, staring at him as he prepared all types of material. Doru did not speak much. During all the years they knew him, they had heard him utter only few words here or there. Usually he was quiet, speaking only when necessary and then only in a few words. Verna thought him very wise; Dror respected his knowledge and experience. They met Doru in times of crisis for both villages. Last summer they were attacked by a hostile tribe rampaging through their region. They held an emergency council with Doru and the other village leaders on how to protect their villages from the cruel tribe that looted, killed, and pillaged in the region. Joining their forces, they were able to defeat the invading tribe and drive it from the region. Dror's expertise in war had helped defend the villages many times in the past few years. Doru respected Dror for his wisdom, bravery, and knowledge.

Now they were ready for Doru to start a soothsaying session. It was evening and their shadows flickered in the campfire. Doru slowly moved a small lamp with an unusual flame. It was small and did not have the typical yellow color. Instead it was light blue. The lamp hung on a string that moved from side to side with Doru's hands. From time to time Doru added powder to the flame which made it briefly sparkle like small starbursts until calming down. Doru's eyes were closed and he chanted in an unrecognized language.

"A great war is coming," Doru stated all of a sudden, moving gently from side to side with the rhythm of the lamp. "It is coming very soon." They both focused on his face.

Dror looked calm but Verna felt uncomfortable. She did not like the thought of war. War, she knew, involved Dror and although he was experienced with every war came risks. Every war brought the shadow of death.

Then she interrupted the session. "Doru, we are here about children. What about our children?" she asked quietly yet impatiently. Dror looked at her and saw the sadness in her face. "This war will be bad," continued Doru, ignoring her interruption. "Many people will die in our villages." He stopped for few seconds and fed the lamp more powder. Then he drank from a small metal goblet. He looked up and almost stopped breathing. They were quiet. They felt something strong was coming. Doru looked at them.

"I have good news," he said, almost whispering. "What?" said Verna, excitedly. She felt that good news was coming but Dror felt different. He also had visionary powers, though he did not call upon them. He concentrated on daily activities, but this night he could not ignore the feeling he had. Something different is about to happened. It was hard to grasp the exact feeling though. He moved uncomfortably and looked at Doru, but his face revealed nothing.

"You will conceive a child," said Doru in his same tone. For Verna that was enough. She burst into tears and could not control herself. She hugged Dror, smiled with eyes full of tears and kissed him repeatedly. Surprised, Dror smiled weakly and felt happy. He was going to be a father soon. "I do not want to hear anything else. Let's go," said Verna in elation. "Let's celebrate," she whispered looking closely into Dror's eyes. "But wait, don't you want to hear what Doru has to say? He did not complete his session..." But Verna did not want to hear anything else. She came to hear what she wanted to hear, and was happy now.

Doru seems unaffected by the joy and continued moving with his lamp. His eyes were closed and he did not see that Verna and Dror had left, smiling and holding hands. "It will be a wry surprise for Doru," Verna whispered as they silently exited the tent. "He's our friend and will understand our happiness." Doru remained in a trance, his eyes closed. Suddenly his eyes opened wide and he desperately grasped for air. His heart raced and his breathing became fast. He could not see Verna and Dror anymore.

"Wait..." he implored. He wanted to tell them what he had seen. Something horrible was coming and he wanted to warn the couple. He grasped for more air then fell down. The lamp struck a pot and exploded into a thousand pieces. The flames spread to his clothes and blankets in his tent. He tried to stand and put out the fire but could not. The entire tent was one big flame. I wish to convey my vision to Verna and Dror, he thought. But he felt he would not survive this fire. As the pain began to numb him, he stopped fighting and accepted his fate. He could hardly breathe and saved any breath for few more moments. His last thought was, Whatever comes, it is all destiny.

∞

Verna had waited so long for this day. She and Dror were elated by Doru's prophecy. When word of his terrible death came, it was a great shock. They were the last people Doru saw and they performed several rituals in his memory. He had been their best friend and given them real hope. Dror still could not explain the eerie feeling that kept coming back to him on visiting Doru's tomb. Doru's remains were buried in a special place, high in the Mountain of the Great Leaders with all the previous village leaders. Dror visited the site not too long after his death, hoping to get some answers about his feeling, but without results. Verna focused on her upcoming pregnancy. She built a crib and knitted many items. All they had to do was wait for its arrival.

Months went by with no sign of a baby. Verna started to worry. One night they went for a long walk in the dark. Dror held her as they walked along the lakeshore. Dror felt her sadness but did not really know what to do. For the past few months he tried everything he could to make her happy, but with every month's passing she sank deeper into depression. "Verna..." he began, but could not continue. She just held him as they continued their walk. It was a quiet, moonless night, and the water was very dark.

Suddenly the earth shook, alarming Dror. The thundering from the ground was familiar to him. It was the sound of many galloping horses, most likely with mounted warriors. Dror knew what it meant. Verna woke up.

"What's that noise?" she asked sleepily.

"Horsemen," answered Dror, "going towards the village."

She was completely awake now and looked at Dror.

"I have to go there," he said and started to put his clothes on. Unexpectedly, Verna grabbed his hand.

"Be careful," she said and her voice sounded stressed. She typically did not say that. He stopped for a second and looked at her.

"Of course, my love."

"No, please be careful," she said insistently and holding his hand even tighter.

Dror hugged her gently. "I am always careful," he said as he smiled.

Although she could not see his smile in the darkness, she felt it and smiled back.

He left into the night and Verna remained alone in their bed still warm from his body.

Dror returned early in the morning. Verna looked at him and knew that battle had been waged well into the night. He was dusty with many bloodstains on his clothes, and his face was grimy. But more than that he had a look on his face – a look of great distance. She knew he had been born into a warrior family and trained long and hard for war, but his soul hated it. Only she knew how he felt after every war. Only she knew the look he returned with. For many days and nights after returning, he closed himself off and hardly talked. She experienced the long nights of holding him close to her breast, loving, crying and trying to bring him back to the present. He had to go to war – that's how he was trained by his family. He was quite accomplished in the arts of war, but his soul hated it. And only Verna knew it.

She took his hand and led him to the lake where they treasured a small rock structure that created a bath structure with a gentle current constantly running from one side to another. They had built it together as part of their home. They loved to cuddle there when they could, day or night. Verna undressed Dror, then undressed herself, and together they entered the bath. Dror remained quiet and distant. Verna gently massaged his back as the cold water flowed over him. They sat there for a while with only the gentle sound of the lake to be heard. It was early morning and the sun sent its warmth to their bodies.

"A bad war is coming."

Verna trembled. Typically Dror did not talk for few days. "What's happened?"

"Doru's prediction is coming true," he said as he looked at her. Gazing into her eyes, he went on. "A merciless warrior tribe arrived last night in the valley. I never encountered them before, but I remember my father's description of a particularly brutal band, and they fit it. They are vicious people who kill and destroy for no reason. They do not even use the conquered village's food and belongings. They simply kill and move on to the next village. That is their way of life." He looked at Verna and could feel her fear growing.

"What should we do?"

"We will have to be crafty with these people," answered Dror. "My father taught me well of this tribe, but I never expected to war with them. They are the worst nightmare that will ever come." He released a long sigh and looked at the clear blue lake.

"Now they are here," he continued. "We had an initial skirmish last night. They attacked late and we lost many men. They will be back tonight." He stopped again and rolled on his back allowing the cold water to wash his back. "We have to be prepared. I need to gather at least two villagers and make war plans."

Verna knew that when Dror spoke of war plans, it was serious. Typically he fought instinctively, without long-term strategy. This meant deep trouble.

"Are we going to be alright?" she asked, looking straight into his eyes.

"Yes," he said with a faint smile. He looked confident but then he always looked confident. His smile calmed her a little, but the knot in her stomach refused to let go.

"I'll have to go today, to train our people for the fight," he said with a faraway look. "My father warned of this war. He knew that one day this killer tribe would come." Dror looked at a point in the skies.

Verna felt something strange. She could not point to it. All of a sudden she felt nauseous. This news is too much for me, she thought and tried to breathe calmly to make the nausea go away.

Dror noticed something wrong with her.

"Are you alright?" he asked, his eyes becoming narrow lines.

"Yes, I just do not feel that well," replied Verna shyly. "I am sure it's nothing." As she completed her sentence she felt her stomach turning. Without control she vomited. "I'm so sorry," she said trying to control her sickness. "I am still not feeling well." They went into the house and Verna lay on the bed. After a while she fell asleep. Dror covered her with a blanket then remembered that his father gave him something many years ago. He was on his deathbed, saying goodbye to each family member. Dror was the last one to be called. His father was lying in his bed, very pale, making great efforts to talk.

"Be aware of this tribe, my son. It will be your greatest challenge," his father warned in a very low voice. Then he gave him his fortune stone. "A wise man gave me this when I was a child," he explained as his eyes sparkled, "and I wore it since then. I want you to have this stone." He handed him a white stone, some sort of crystal. There were five straight lines curved on the rock and Dror noticed that four of them were worn and almost faded away. The fifth line was also worn but less so than the others. "These lines are my life stages. As you see, I have completed my life stages and soon the fifth line will be gone also...and I will die. I give this to you for your life stages. One day you will challenge the killer tribe. Look at the stone then." Then his father slowly closed his eyes. He died the next day. Dror hung the stone around his neck.

At first he did not believe in the rock. He wore the rock simply out of respect. But the next morning all five lines were inexplicably visible. He tried to scratch out the lines but could not erase them. He tried to break it in many ways but could not. Somehow the stone resisted any damage. That's how he started his life cycle. He never told Verna about the stone. The last time he looked at it, it had three clear lines, now it had only a half of one, and it seemed to be dim. Dror rotated the stone in the light but the half line remained dim. What could this means? he wondered. Dror took a deep breath, attempting to presage what the future held for him. He looked at Verna sleeping calmly on the bed. So beautiful in her sleep, he thought, I do not know how to tell her.

When Verna woke up, Dror had prepared a meal she always enjoyed – oranges and apples mixed in lemon juice from their grove. Verna also ate a piece of fresh bread that they had baked, and a chunk of white cheese they had made from goat's milk. She was surprised when the meal was there before her as she arose.

"I hope you are hungry," said Dror with a shy smile as he leaned over to kiss her. "You slept for many hours and I did not want to wake you."

"I'm starving," answered Verna, smiling to him and giving him a hearty hug.

Dror smiled as he watched her eat ravenously. As Verna enjoyed her meal, a sense of dread came across her, so strong she stopped eating and stared at him. Her intuitive powers were acute and she looked with questions in her eyes.

"What is going on?" she whispered.

"Nothing," answered Dror. He did not know how to tell her. What if I am wrong? Then it will put her in a dark mood. He did not want that as he was going off to war. "I am just worrying about you – how do you feel?" Verna calmed somewhat and returned to her meal.

"I am well, my love. Maybe I was just hungry this morning..." her words faded and she looked at Dror seriously.

"What?" asked Dror concernedly. Did she feel something?

"I know!" she almost screamed. "Wait...one, two, three..." she continued counting in a whisper. She leaped atop Dror and screamed, "We did it, we did it!" Surprised by her exuberance, Dror almost fell from his seat and tried to maintain his balance but could not. They both fell to the floor with a thump.

"We did what?" he asked, laughing but still puzzled.

"Don't you get it, my love?" she said happily as she kissed him repeatedly. "We are going to be parents..."

The words stuck with him as he comprehended them.

"What? Are you saying that your illness this morning...it was a... baby..." He could not continue as a burst of happiness flashed through him. I am going to be a father, he thought with a great joy.

Dror was dressed in battle attire. She looked at him carefully. They had the tradition that before he went to battle, she made sure that all his gear was prepared. Another tradition was to ask Verna if she had a bad feeling. They did not know what they would do in case she had such a feeling, but it was a tradition for years and it was not going to change that day.

The day was somewhat different. Verna was joyed by her pregnancy, but now Dror was going off to war. She carefully reviewed his gear. Everything seemed in order but Dror looked strangely different today. She saw the little things on his face. A new wrinkle when he talked, the bead of sweat on his forehead, the tremor on his lip and his overall look. Something was different. She searched inside her soul, as she always did, to check her feelings. She felt the joy of pregnancy and attributed all the rest to side effects of that excitement.

"Any bad feeling?" he asked looking into her eyes with a serious look. He never asked her this way.

She stopped for a moment, getting in touch with her feelings, but nothing came to her.

"No bad feeling, my love. How do you feel?"

"Something is different but I cannot comprehend it," he said somewhat nervously. "But if you do not feel anything, it must be nothing."

"No!" she cried out. "Something is wrong...I can sense it. You are feeling something. Tell me!" she demanded, holding onto his hand.

"It's nothing, my love," he calmly told her. I cannot tell her my fears, he thought quietly biting his lips. It could make her lose the baby. "It is probably the news that we are going to be parents soon." He looked to the ground. "I want to see my child."

"Then do not leave," she said, almost begging.

"You know we can't do this, love. The village's trust is in our hands. Many people's lives, children..."

Verna looked to the ground without saying anything.

"Nothing is going to happen. I am sure that it is absolutely nothing," he said with a smile as he kissed her passionately. Verna replied with a passionate kiss and soon they found themselves captive in their eternal love, breathing, rolling and sailing in the sea of love. He would stay a few more hours and leave at nightfall.

They spent the afternoon together, holding hands, not saying a word. As the sunset brought golden flickers to the lake, Verna looked into his blue eyes and felt lost in their love. He looked at her green almond eyes and her golden hair and thought that her the most beautiful being he'd ever seen. He looked at her, tasted her lips and body, and wanted to keep her with him forever.

At nightfall he left to prepare for the night battle. She gave him a lock of her hair for good luck. He bore her lock in a small pouch on a necklace she had made for him. As he rode to the village, he touched the pouch, and it made him smile. She will always be close to my heart. Then he urged his steed on. There's lots of work to be done, tonight and maybe many nights to come. We must repel the invading tribe.

Verna remained alone in the house. She lay in their bed, slowly rubbing her belly, trying to feel her baby. She enjoyed the thought that soon she would get rounder and larger, as she had always dreamed. She concentrated on Dror and could not sense any bad feeling about him. He will be alright, she thought. She lay there for a while and soon fell asleep.

Dror completed the battle plan. It was almost midnight and they knew the enemy's position from spies they'd sent out. Dror knew they tended to attack late at night and prepared a surprise attack from the east. His father taught that the best way to defend is to attack unexpectedly. Jolting an enemy onto the defensive has psychological effects that better the attacker's odds. The enemy loses confidence and is more prone to panic. Dror had executed this stratagem numerous times in previous wars. He was ever victorious and hoped to remain so. His father also counseled that this menacing tribe was prone to overconfidence from their numbers and skills, and that attacking at night and using psychological tactics such as fire and fierce cries would increase the fear.

Dror prepared to lead his forces in a wide path behind the enemy to attack from behind. The dense forest would help with the surprise. They planned to attack around midnight, using flaming arrows and fireballs. The first attack would entail a rain of flaming arrows which would seem to come from nowhere. After the initial panic, a rain of fireballs will come. The tribe had built unique bows to shoot them. The fireballs were made from thin shells of large fruit, similar to cocoa nuts, filled with flammable fluid from animal oil. On impact, the fireballs spread flames in a large radius. At that point, the entire army would attack in waves, using swords and knives in hand-to-hand fighting. In all the consternation and confusion, defeating the invaders should be fairly easy and our casualties will be mercifully light, thought Dror as he reviewed the plans for the last time. He touched the little pouch around his neck and treasured the warm feelings it brought. It is as though she is here with me. Then he looked at the stone with the five life lines. Nothing had changed. Only half of the fifth line was clearly discernible. The other half was fading.

Maybe it means nothing, thought Dror. Maybe it will be like this until I die from old age. I will be back home shortly and become a father soon. The thought of his coming child warmed his heart and he became determined. Let's deal with this threat to our peace tonight, he thought. Then he saddled his steed. Shortly, all men were in place and they moved out into the night. It was warm, as it typically was this time of the year. Only a slight feeling of humidity was in the air.

∞

Verna woke up in a sweat. She tried to move but could not. She tried to get out of bed but she had been tied up. In the dim light of an oil lamp, she could see a few men looking at her and talking in a strange language. She did not panic. Instead, she regarded them carefully. Their clothes and look clearly showed they were not from her region. Her brain was working fast, trying to grasp her situation and what to do about it. She gestured to them with her untied hands that they were welcome in her home and could stay the night. She offered them food and comfortable beds, and signed that she was the village medicine woman. But they did not understand her. She knew the meaning of capturing a woman alone, but they did not know who they were dealing with. They did not look intelligent, a thought that made her form a hidden smile. After eating, they lay down and soon were snoring loudly. Verna determined to show these men what it meant to break into her home. Besides she had someone to protect now.

∞

The battle was about to start at the appointed hour. Dror and his captains were about to give the order to attack just as a mighty clap of thunder broke the silence. Dror looked up and smelled the air. There was no doubt – rain was in the air. At this time of the year? thought Dror angrily. Rain meant no fire and no element of surprise. His mind searched for an alternative but found nothing. We do not have much choice. We cannot call things off now – all of our forces are in place.

"How long until the rain starts?" Dror asked one of his captains.

"Probably not too soon," he answered. "But there's no way to know for sure."

"We have enough time to use the fire," answered Del, determinedly.

He took a deep breath and gave the order to let go with the first salvo.

∞

Verna was surprised by the men's behavior – pleasantly surprised. In the morning they gave her food and treated her respectfully. She communicated better with them through a dialect. They had come from far away, looking for wanted men. They did not want to risk being killed as intruders so they took the precaution of tying her. She explained that she and her husband were village leaders and that he is now at war.

The atmosphere became friendly. The leader seemed a decent person, and she was happy that things turned out this way. They asked her if a group of young men had passed by, but she had not seen any people of that description. It was almost noon, as the man were preparing to leave, when an arrow came out of nowhere and hit one of them in the chest. He held the arrow, which had gone well into his chest, in great disbelief and then fell backwards. A group of about ten men stood near them, weapons at the ready. They must hide in the bushes, thought Verna as she quickly turned and ran into the house. But the men did not move. They figured the woman was not a problem. The remaining two drew their swords. It was obvious that they were in poor condition. These must be the men they are after, thought Verna as her heart raced and she quickly prepared her weapon. Dror had trained her well in handling swords and knives. She went outside to help the two men.

The fighting was well underway. The two men fought bravely back-to-back while the bad men surrounded them and looked for their opportunity. Verna looked briefly at the leader. His look said for her to run away, that they'd cover her and fight to their deaths. Run away now. She saw a few of the men aiming for her but she determined not to desert her allies. She'd fight.

She used the metal stars – sharp pieces of metal that Dror had given her for defense. When used correctly, they can kill in an instant. Verna knew well how to use them and threw a pair at the two men coming at her. Both were caught by surprise and fell to the ground in astonishment. The bandit leader turned briefly, saw that he just lost two of his band, and laughed with a toothless grin. He'd take care of the woman later, he thought. Eight remained, and Verna planned her next move. Three men turned toward her and she used her second fighting skill – metal boomerangs, moon-shaped with a short handle on one side. A trained person could strike an object from a considerable distance. Verna judged the distance and the first boomerang was on its way. It hit the man, cut his entire arm from its base, lost only some speed and angle, and returned close to Verna. The man screamed in unexpected pain as his arm fell to the ground.

He's no threat anymore, she thought. Her second boomerang found its way to the second man, striking him on his neck and almost decapitating him. Without a word, he crumpled down, the boomerang stuck to his neck. Verna quickly grabbed the first boomerang and threw it at the third man, now running towards her. It hit his leg, causing him to immediately fall as his tendons were slit.

The toothless leader now focused on Verna, since he realized that she was devastating his band. Verna pulled her sword and prepared for face-to-face fighting. A big surprise lay ahead for this man.

∞

The attack was not beginning well. The fire attack was promising but shortly after the first salvo a downpour extinguished much of the fire his men had created. The enemy initially panicked, but found courage and mounted a tenacious defense. Dror had to deploy his forces sooner than expected and in larger numbers. The battlefield was littered with many casualties from both sides. Dror saw no choice in the matter. The enemy had to be stopped at any cost, and he had only one chance to do so. The bloody battle continued into the night.

∞

The toothless man fought Verna mercilessly. Using all of his strength, he struck her many times. Verna momentarily thought of her long training and thanked Dror for his efforts. She held her own and even fought back, as she had the advantage of being trimmer and more agile than her heavyset attacker. Her two allies were still fighting four bandits, one of whom soon fell, leaving only three to deal with. The heat and exhaustion started to take their toll on all of them. Verna drove back one of the weakening men. He sweated heavily and his face became redder. Verna used all her sword skills to press her attack. Dror would be proud of me, thought Verna when a sharp pain unexpectedly ripped into her back. A piercing scream came from her and she immediately felt a warm liquid on her back. She turned and saw one of the men stabbing her with his sword. She could not believe the sight of a sword now stuck deep in her back. She looked down and saw an even more horrible sight of the sword point protruding from her stomach. "No!" she screamed with great disbelief. She felt her powers leaving her rapidly. The leader of the allies saw his mortally wounded friend and he too screamed in empathy. She did not feel any pain yet. She looked into her attacker's eyes and he moved backwards, realizing what he had done. She sat on the ground and reached for the sword planted in her back. In a burst of rage, her allies finished off their opponents and ran to Verna. She stood there, breathing heavily. With panicked eyes, her assailant regarded her allies, but no one moved.

"I am so sorry," whispered the leader of her allies. She could see the pain in his eyes.

"That is well," whispered Verna with fading powers. Her ally looked at her wound, trying to assess if there was something he could do, but Verna stopped him with a weak smile.

"You did the best you could," she murmured, trying to overcome the pain that was now coming in waves. She felt astonished that this was actually happening to her. "I did not expect to die today," she said to them all. Even the bandits felt terrible. "I just found out yesterday that I am going to have a baby." She started to breath heavily.

"No, it can't be." mumbled the leader, looking downward. Thirsting for vengeance, he stood raised his sword at the responsible bandit.

"No, please," called out Verna, raising her hand in the air. "No more blood. Bring them to justice. Everyone deserves a fair trial." She did not hate the men for what they did. She felt sad that she would never have children. She will never experience the joy of raising her own child. A great void opened inside her. She did not care much about dying, more about missing being a mother. Then she thought of Dror and his life after her.

"Is there anything we can do?"

Verna did not answer right away. "Yes," she said slowly. "Could you please take me to my bed, inside the house?"

They carefully carried out her request. She covered herself with a blanket that she and Dror had made a few years ago. The touch of the soft, familiar silk gave her some strength and she smiled to the men.

"You fought well, my woman ally," said the toothless man trying to break the heavy atmosphere.

"Hours of training with my husband," she replied in a low voice.

"I would like to ask one favor please?" she asked the leader.

"Anything..."

She could tell he was upset. In the short time that she knew him and his men, she learned that they were men of honor.

"My husband...Dror," she coughed. The blood reached her lungs.

"Dror is in a battle against an invading tribe that threatens the region. I do not know when he will be back. It could be today and I want someone to be with him when he learns of my fate." She looked at the man with tears in her eyes.

"See, he and I are as one...and I do not know how he will take my death. We could not foresee this. Of course, no one predicts these things... I sense that you are a good man. I want you to tell him what happened." Then she took the man's hand. "I want you to hold him when he learns. Tell him that I asked you to do so."

The man looked at her with great sadness. "I will."

"I do not even know your names..." said Verna shyly. "I am going to die in your presence and would like at least to know your names..." She became weaker by the minute and increasingly pale as well.

"The name is Ren, and I am from the villages across the White Mountains."

"I am Jake..." said another.

"I am Henry..." said the third.

All looked downward in sorrow.

"Ren... I like your name," said Verna with a shadow of a smile.

She touched the blanket and noticed that it was soaked with blood.

"I guess it is closer than I think..." she said to the air. No one spoke.

She wished that Dror was there, right at that moment. She missed him, his touch, his smile. If he was here things would be much easier, she thought, but then again it is not fair to Dror. It probably would be harder for him. She thought of all their time together and for a brief moment she thought she could see them in a past life. She wondered if they had met sometime before. She had a strong feeling they had.

His scent lingered on the blanket – something from him. She reached for the bracelet that Dror had made. He made weapons from metal but also jewelry. The bracelet was a gift, two years ago, and she wore it ever since. On it he had engraved two doves, love birds.

"Our love is eternal," he always said to her. "Whenever and wherever we are, we are always together." She knew this was true. "I would like to be by myself now please," she said. "I would like to spend my last moments alone...with my love." Ren and the others nodded quietly. He held her hand gently. She smiled to him as they left the room.

She lay on their bed and wondered how it would be. She was not afraid to die; she just did not want to die without Dror. The numbness on her left side was spreading to her entire body now. She felt cold and knew this was the first sign of the end. She remembered the beautiful moments she and Dror had had over the years. Their first meeting and the passion of their love. The moment of reuniting and of knowing about the baby, which will never be born. All of a sudden she needed him and started to panic. She was not ready to leave life without him.

"Dror... she called out, her voice becoming scratchy. She moved from side to side, trying to find him and then felt a warm hand holding her hand. "All is well, Verna. I am here with you," a soft voice near her said. It was wonderful. "Dror, you made it," she said happily. Ren held her hand. He could not let her die alone. "Dror..." she whispered.

Ren did not answer. His eyes were full of tears and he had to hold back his sobbing. He held her hand, soothing her in these hard moments when life needs to leave. With her last strength she turned towards him. But she could not see anything anymore.

∞

Ren tied the two men outside the house. "Dror will decide what to do with you," he said emotionlessly. "It is beyond my judgment now." He and his men sat down and awaited Dror's return. Ren intended to keep his promise to Verna.

∞

The bloody battle ended early in the morning. The warriors of the villages had suffered heavy casualties but emerged victorious. The enemy was conquered and fled the region. Dror stood on the battlefield for a few hours, his heart empty. He was tired yet satisfied. They had saved the villages. He went down to the nearby stream. As he was washing himself in the cold water and feeling relief, he suddenly called out, "Verna!!"

∞

Dror reached their house, exhausted from his desperate gallop. His steed's mouth foamed and it breathed and snorted noisily. Dror entered the house, sword in hand. "Are you the one called Dror?" a voice asked. He turned quickly and saw Ren standing with his sword on the ground. "I mean no harm," he said quietly. How does he know my name? thought Dror. He does not look like a bad man. Dror held fast to his sword.

"My name is Ren," said the man looking straight into Dror's eyes.

"Where is my Verna?" demanded Dror anxiously. His senses told him something bad had happened to her.

"Inside, but wait..." answered Ren. But Dror had already run into the house where he found Verna in her bed, a peaceful smile still on her face. Dror instantly knew that she was dead. He sat near her. The blanket was wet to his touch and he realized that it was soaked in blood. What had happened? His brain urgently searched for an answer but could not find one. He sat there and looked at her ashen face. Even in death, she was lovely. She had kept him going. She signaled him in death that all was well and she died happily. In her hand he found the necklace he made for her. Ahhh, he thought. She died happily holding onto our memories. He lay near her and hugged her, touching her cold face and looking out at the view they loved so much. He was so full of sadness. It was beyond the help of tears.

Why, why had it to happened to them? Suddenly he knew this was not the first time they had lived as one. A supernatural feeling told him they'd been together before. Lying there, he felt a message, a message that all was well, that she was with him even then, and that she will always love him. There is no call to end your life because of this, my love. We will meet again. He wondered why he was not crying.

He stayed there with her and felt that everything would indeed be well. He kissed her on the forehead and covered her face. He stepped outside. It was evening already and he could see the sun setting over the lake. Verna was not there. She was not here to watch the sunset with him, or for their nightly walk, or to cuddle with. She would not be there tomorrow morning. She will not be here anymore. The realization caused him a sudden weakness and he almost fell. Someone was there to hold him up. Dror looked into his eyes, which were red from tears and sorrow. He held Ren's shoulders while Ren held his.

"I know it is hard," said Ren. "She asked me to hold you in this moment. That is why I am still here. I promised her to hold you, for her."

"Did you get the chance to know her? She was a fine woman," asked Dror with great anguish on his face.

"Only for a few hours," replied Ren sadly. "We were trailing bandits. There were too many." He looked to the ground and Dror could feel the man's guilt and shame at not protecting Verna.

"It was not your fault," said Dror, holding Ren. "They would've come here anyway. You did your best." Dror figured Ren's men fought the bandits in order to help Verna.

"She fought like a lioness," said Ren with a hidden smile. "You trained her very well. You should be very proud of her. She actually saved us."

Dror understood what happened.

"I am proud of her," he said quietly. "That is her. She always put others before her."

"She was very brave," said Ren. "I am very sorry for your loss." He added as tears flowed.

"I know," said Dror. "We learned only yesterday that she was expecting our child..." He continued looking at a hidden spot in the mountains.

Ren could not control his tears anymore and let them flow down his face.

"No one expects these things to happen," said Dror after a while.

"Those were her words also," said Ren quietly. "You are bonded together beyond life."

"Yes, we are," replied Del. "I really believe we are."

Dror and Ren looked at the night skies.

"What do you want to do with the two bandits?" asked Ren. "Verna prevented me from killing them. She wanted justice."

"Do you have a justice system in your homeland?" asked Dror, breathing deeply. He had no feelings of anger or revenge. Maybe Verna sent him a message of compassion for all.

"Yes, we put criminals on trial and a group of elders judge them and determine the sentences," answered Ren.

"Then that is your duty. Take them back and try them. You know best what they did and what happened here. You will do the right thing." He looked at Ren with a determined expression.

"I will," answered Ren quietly. He patted Dror on his back and went to prepare the horses.

Dror remained alone under the night sky. He was not used to be alone. He looked at the beautiful skies full of sparkling stars. He looked for answers, for destiny but most of all he looked for Verna.

"What should I do now, love?" he repeatedly asked without voice.

He felt Ren's hand on his back.

"We are leaving, Dror. Are you going to be alright?" He looked at Dror, concerned.

Dror turned around and looked at Ren, who was like a close friend. In the evening light he could still discern that Ren truly cared. He gathered his courage, smiled, and embraced him.

"You are a friend to me, Ren," he said. "You helped Verna, my everything in this world, in her last moments. I'll always be there for you if you'll need me."

"Thank you, Dror. You too may rely on me," said Ren, smiling somewhat. "Where can I find you?"

"Here or there. I have to search for a purpose in my life now."

Ren nodded and released a long sigh. "So long, my friend. I wish you only good."

Ren and his group left and Dror remain by himself. Soon the dawn will come. He has to prepare to put his loved one to rest.

He washed Verna's body and dressed her in her most beautiful clothes. He anointed her with herbs and perfumes, and applied powders to her lovely visage. As he finished his loving chore, the sun began to send its warm light upon the earth, to remind everyone that a new day was about to start.

Dror looked at Verna's face.

"It's time to bring you to rest, my love... Until we find each other again..."

∞

They ran into the woods to escape the killers. Their small village was being attacked by merciless horsemen. The men were dressed in black garb and rode into the tranquil village, killing and destroying. They shouted lustily while ripping open tents, putting people to their swords, and running over everyone they could with their immense black mounts. Men and women ran everywhere in panic. The riders did not hesitate to kill women with children in their hands and helpless old people. Screams sounded throughout the village. A father and mother held their baby and hid in a tent at the far side of the village. They peeked through the tent and saw riders approaching. The woman looked at the man and without saying a word, they knew what they had to do. They opened the tent and bolted toward the woods, their baby cushioned inside a basket carried by the mother. When they could no longer hear the screams, they felt safe enough to rest. They did not know what to do or where they were going. All they knew was that they had to get far away from their village.

In a few hours the massacre was complete. After destroying the village and killing hundreds of people, the mounted tribe left, leaving behind only a few living.

∞

Dror placed Verna's body on his horse and started to ride north. The realization of being alone hit him. He looked behind at the house that they had built together. I will never return here. There is no reason. He looked for the last time at the beautiful shoreline Verna and he used to walk along. He looked at the special spots where they would make spontaneous love, and felt aches all over his body. He suddenly knew where he wanted to go. Without looking back, he urged his horse on. The horse walked slowly in an unfamiliar direction. Dror reckoned that tomorrow morning he would near his destiny.

∞

They walked slowly in the deep forest. They did not know where they were going. All they knew was that they needed to be far away from their village. They hoped to find another friendly village to join. They came to the end of the thick forest and saw majestic mountains in the distance. They decided to rest and forage for food. The nearest tree had some type of red berries and they seemed to be edible. They sat for a while and rested as the midday sun hit with full force. Exhausted, the couple fell asleep. The woman woke to a growling sound. She looked around to find the source of the strange noise. She woke up her husband and they both began to look about.

What they saw froze them. They were surrounded by several huge, black panthers. They looked around to escape but the pack surrounded them and inched forward to attack. The man and woman looked at each other, realizing that they were going to die. The woman pointed desperately towards the baby. They had to find a hiding place for her. At that instant the panthers struck. With loud roars the first wave jumped on the man and woman. The man did not even have time to scream as two large panthers landed on him, breaking his spine and causing quick and painless death. The mother was less fortunate. Three of the beasts jumped on top of her, claws opened.

The basket and the baby fell onto the ground and rolled away. The baby woke up and started to cry, which attracted one of the largest panthers. It started to walk towards the basket while the others fought over various parts of their prey. For some reason, the great panther did not attack. Maybe the panther was a female and had maternal instincts, or maybe it was just not interested in such a small prize. The panther sniffed the baby a few times and went on its way. Soon the panthers finished their feast and departed, still dragging grisly portions of the two human bodies, perhaps for a later meal. The baby remained alone in the opening. Without any food or water, it would die in few hours. The strong sun would see to that.

The baby was giggling, unaware of his peril, when a huge shadow blocked the sun. He looked upwards, fearlessly. A loud screech sounded that scared the baby, causing him to cry and attracting the attention of a large eagle. The infant would normally be fine quarry, but the eagle did not go for it. Instead the predatory bird looked at it for a while, moving his large head from side to side and screeching loudly. He then grabbed the basket containing the baby and took off. The baby stopped crying and looked up at the huge eagle. The basket shielded the baby from seeing the height and feeling the wind, and soon she found her reasons to giggle at the eagle and the adventure she was on. There is nothing like a ride to tire a baby, and after a while she fell asleep. The giant bird continued on its journey to a very familiar place.

∞

Dror arrived at the flat rock mountain earlier than he expected. Although he rode at a leisurely pace, he found himself at the spot in the early evening. Since darkness came late in the day, the sun was still bright and it almost felt like the middle of the day. He felt his loneliness come over him once more, reminding him of his Verna. He looked down from the high cliff and pondered an escape from the loneliness that plagued him. As he looked into the abyss he was struck by the canyon's astonishing beauty. The massive rocky cliffs touched the ground in a scratchy path. There was a small creek at the center that nourished green trees and bushes along its way. Many birds nested between the rocks and he marveled at all the large birds flying in and out of the crevices.

The flat rock was at the summit and it afforded a spectacular view stretching out many miles. The canyon's zigzag shape gave it the appearance of a huge maze. Dror gazed at it and thought how romantic it would be if Verna were here. He thought of the irony: Verna sentenced him to be executed here and now he has come back, with her. He looked at her as he laid her on the ground. Her long hair spread with the mild wind and she looked so calm. He wanted to believe that she was just sleeping and would wake up soon. But reality intruded and he closed his eyes and felt the heartache. With every memory, with every moment, he looked at her. He took her in his arms.

"Here, my love, take a look at the beautiful view," he told her quietly as he stood on the tip of the rock. The wind hit his face and brought the scent of flowers. He closed his eyes and let nature touch them. This is it. All of a sudden, he felt a peacefulness from knowing just what to do. He'd fall with her into the canyon. They'd be together in their new destiny. He did not want to continue without her. He was happy that he was going to join Verna. He smiled up to the sky then looked at her. "I am coming home, my love," he whispered. He kissed her on her forehead.

A loud screech made him look up. It sounded familiar. He was amazed to see the giant eagle flying in circles above the flat rock, looking for a spot to land. The large bird landed on the other side of the rock and inched towards him. Oh no, my friend, he thought, this time I am ready for you. He laid Verna's body near the rocks and drew his sword. This time we will have a more even fight, my friend. But something was wrong with the big bird. It came towards him, limping, stumbling, and looking tired. Its screeches even sounded weak and sickly.

What ails the eagle? He watched it slowly approaching him. Dror waved his sword towards the eagle as it got closer. He wanted to warn the eagle not to engage him. The eagle tossed a small parcel toward him and stared at him strangely. Dror looked carefully at the basket and then uncovered it. He stopped breathing for a second. He was amazed at what he saw – a sleeping baby. The baby started to wake up and Dror helped her brush aside the cloth that covered part of his face. Dror looked at the eagle, which was looking on in silence. "You brought me a baby," said Dror, all amazed. He looked again at the eagle. The giant bird looked back at him eerily, stumbled a few times, and fell on its side. It looked near death. It lay there, breathing heavily without moving. Dror was not sure the eagle could stand anymore. "It seems we have a special bond," uttered Dror. "After all, we are old friends."

The baby opened her eyes and looked at Dror. Something wonderful happened – the baby smiled at him. It is so beautiful, thought Dror as he smiled back. It was a beautiful baby girl and Dror held her close to his chest. Mysterious are nature's ways, he thought. Is this Verna's gift? Nature's gift? Or a message to prevent me from dying? All these thoughts crossed his mind as he played with the baby. Yes to all. The answer came from inside him. You cannot die now, you have responsibility. He gave the baby some of his bread moistened with water and it seemed to be good food for her.

"What is your name?" he asked her as she smiled at him with little brown eyes. After giggling for a while, she fell asleep again as he rocked her inside the basket. He looked over at the eagle. He approached the eagle and saw its eyes were closed. It is dying, thought Dror. As he got closer, it opened its eyes and looked at him but could not move its head.

"Thank you, great bird," said Dror, gently touching its wings. "You gave me a reason to continue. Sleep well." Maybe it was his imagination but he thought the eagle's head nodded as if to bid him farewell. The bird soon closed its eyes, never to open them again. Dror felt sad. He had come to respect the eagle. Maybe it was sick or simply old. I was once its prey but we ended as respected friends. The eagle saved me. It gave me reason to live. But from where did the child come? He had a feeling the parents were dead and the bird instinctively delivered the baby to him. Or maybe it planned to care for the baby. Who knows.

Evening came and the sun vanished beneath the large rocks, only its red glow remaining. The sunset illuminated Dror holding the baby and the giant eagle lying nearby. Dror looked at the sleeping baby girl and took a deep breath. He did not know what happened to her parents. He did not know where she came from. All he knew was that she depended on him for everything. He looked at Verna in her calm, eternal sleep. "Verna will be your name," he told the baby quietly. "You will grow to be as beautiful and kind a woman as she was."

Dror buried Verna near the flat rock and covered her grave with rocks from the stone gate. Not far from the spot lay the giant eagle, as though guarding her. "Farewell, my love. You go first on the journey. I have a mission to raise little Verna. We'll meet again in time. I love you forever." He closed his eyes for few moments then put little Verna on his horse and began the ride down the mountain. It was dark now but he had a full moon to illuminate his way. He would stop for the night at the closest stream. He needed fresh water and food for the baby. The skies shone with billions of stars, sparkling in turns. Dror looked at the beautiful moon and thought that goodbye must be the hardest word in the universe.

∞

Dror traveled far and wide until he found a friendly village. He joined it as a medicine man and came to be respected for his skills and kindness. Over the years little Verna grew to be a beautiful young woman who taught the village children. Occasionally Dror told little Verna about his loved one and their wondrous story. He asked to be buried next to her on the cliff. Little Verna vowed to bring him there, when the time came. Dror relished being a medicine man and no longer a warrior. With the inspiration of little Verna, he started to teach his healing craft. Their village was peaceful, adjoining friendly tribes, and war was uncommon. Life seemed to amble along a smooth path, and he became aged and frail. One evening, when they had just finished their meal, Dror quietly held little Verna's hand and looked into her eyes.

"It is time." His long white hair moved gently with the evening winds. Little Verna looked with tears at the man she knew as her father. He has become old very fast, she thought. She was only in her twentieth year but already had long white tresses. She looked at his eyes and saw the happiness in them. "What?" She was surprised, and almost angry. "Are you happy to go, father?"

"Please do not be mad at me," he answered softly. "I've missed my loved one for many years and now I am happy to join her at last – it is nature." He smiled a loving smile. "You will be alright," he continued, holding her hand. "You are a beautiful, strong young woman. It is your turn to have your own family." They both knew that she had never married in order that she could be with her father. It did not matter how many times he urged her to find a husband, she always had a reason not to do so. "I'll take you there in the morning," she said holding back tears. "I will miss you terribly," he replied and pressed her to his heart. They held each other silently in the night. Soon he felt her tears on his garments.

∞

They left at dawn and arrived at the flat rock at sunset. Verna's grave was there as it had been since Dror constructed it. Near it lay the remains of the giant eagle. Little Verna looked with sorrow upon the pile of stones Dror had built many years ago. She'd seen it many times during their frequent visits to the spot they so relished. "I am not leaving you here alone in your last moments," said little Verna. Dror looked lovingly at her. "Of course not," he agreed. "I do not want to be alone." His time was close and he wanted to be with the two women he loved.

They prepared a place to sleep at night by placing blankets on the rock. Little Verna was exhausted from the long ride and fell asleep almost immediately. Dror looked at her and thought how amazing destiny is. Here he met her, and here he leaves her. Wings brought her to him, and now her wings will open and fly her into the world. This is how nature works, he thought as he kissed her face for the last time. He felt his powers leaving him rapidly. He was tired but not sleepy. His vision became blurry and his muscles could hardly hold him up. He lay on his blanket and looked at the beautiful moon. It was full and it illuminated the skies, brighter than ever. The stars sparkled and shone in their billions. The moon seemed to look at him, telling him it is time. It is the same evening as I said goodbye to my love. The thought filled him with joy. He reached out and touched Verna's gravestone. "I am coming home, my love," he said quietly. He remembered their days as though they were yesterday. Their wide-ranging adventures, enchanting night walks, and charming passion. They had a unique bond and lived like there was no tomorrow. Both felt that they had known each other from a previous life. His life without her had passed quickly, bringing him to this moment. He felt tired, no longer able to move. This is it, he thought without the slightest sense of fear.

He gazed at the moon as darkness came and took him in its cozy arms.

Little Verna woke up suddenly. It was about midnight and she felt that something had happened. Her father lay on his back, eyes open and looking towards the moon. He looked calm and peaceful. And the moon...she had never seen such a brilliant full moon. The entire sky was illuminated, almost like daylight. She had never seen so many stars. Her eyes filled with tears, but then she remembered what he had told her. "I'll be happy when I go and I want you to be happy with my decision. It is sad to leave you, but death is part of life and we have to accept it. I'll join my eternal love...which makes it a happy event." She replied to his motionless form in the moonlight, "I guess you were right, father. It is a happy event."

She buried him near Verna and covered them both with scented leaves according to their tradition. By early morning everything was done. The sun sent its morning light declaring a new day and little Verna knew she had to move on. I was privileged to have Dror as my father, she thought. Little Verna gave a last look at the two graves.

"Goodbye, father...and goodbye, Verna. Although I never knew you, you were like a mother to me. I am happy you are together again." Her voice broke and she touched the rocks for the last time before starting her journey back to the village. She would visit the site once a year for the rest of her life, as she and Dror had.

A large and beautiful eagle landed on the flat rock. It roamed about it for a while and regarded the two burial spots. His head turned to the sides and his eyes carefully observed the rocks. The eagle remained at the flat rock until the evening. Later, it built its home on it. The flat rock became its aerie for generations to come.

Night Fell.

Morning Rose.

Darren woke up and lay in his bed, looking at the sunny skies through the window. He had built his dwelling with large openings so he could do just that. Living in a small village has its benefits, he thought, continuing to enjoy the morning sun. He had no burdens like working by schedule and obeying orders, as in a town or castle. Here he was his own master. As the village doctor, he did not even have to pay taxes. Life is wonderful, he thought lazily. What to do today? He covered himself with a blanket to protect from the morning breeze. It was still early morning and although it was summer, mornings in England were rather cold.

He had to examine humble tillers coming in from his and surrounding villages. Most of them had simple illnesses like rashes, upset stomachs, and the like. Due to poor hygiene these were common health issues in medieval times. The majority of them he cured by suggesting simple cleaning procedures like washing hands and foods. Then all of a sudden a thought came to his mind and he became completely awake. Today is a very special day. He is going to perform surgery on a boy from the other side of the village. The surgery was unusual and quite risky. The boy had a large growth in his chest and Darren suspected some sort of infection. He remembered the first time he went to see the lad. His entire chest was blue and purple and enormously swollen. A light touch caused severe pain. The chest seemed to be congested with dark fluid and continuously enlarging. He had never seen a similar case like this one. The boy's condition had become severe in recent few weeks. He could no longer move. He had to perform surgery, otherwise the boy would shortly die.

He discussed the matter with the boy's parents and decided the surgery would be today. The surgery was new and all knew the boy's life hung in the balance. Darren usually performed improvised surgery, usually on people who had little chance to live anyway – such was the profession back then. He knew he needed greater caution this time, but this case baffled him. He quickly dressed and studied the notebook he had created over the years. Every case he saw or heard from other doctors was entered into his notebook, mainly in the form of sketches. He firmly believed that if every doctor documented his experience, the information could be shared and the art of medicine would benefit. Unfortunately not many doctors agreed. He searched through his book but could not find a similar case. He put the book down and looked at the sun's position. He knew the time had come. He liked the youth, who was sweet and innocent – unlike many people he treated. He released a sigh and started to prepare his gear. It's going to be a very long day.

The boy was looking straight at him as Darren examined his chest. The swelling had reached an alarming size, causing dangerous pressure on his lungs and breathing difficulties. He was inhaling and exhaling like an old man gasping for air. Darren tried to touch his chest but any contact caused great pain. He cleaned his instruments by exposing them to flame. Everything is ready except the knowledge of what to do, he though cynically. He tried to form a plan while several people stood around him and looked on silently. The chest is filled with old blood and fluids, he thought to himself, trying to focus. I need to remove those vile fluids. No medicine will help here. He looked slowly at the lad's chest and all of a sudden had an idea. He carefully took measurements and wrote it all in his book, then took a deep breath. It was time to tell the plan to those present. He will need the help of at least four strong men. Then he looked straight in the boy's eyes. "No worry, my friend. I have a plan but you will have to be strong and help me. Are you ready for this?" he asked. The boy saw Darren's difficulties. He sensed that Darren would try with all of his skill and knowledge to do everything to save him. He knew that this was his only chance to live. "Yes Darren, I am ready," he said with a brave little smile. "I trust you. I know that you'll do your best." Darren looked at him for few more seconds. "Good boy," he said with a smile. "We'll need to get help from some men here. It will not be easy."

The boy drank two goblets of wine and began to giggle incoherently – a sign he was sedated. Four men held him firmly while Darren prepared. He would make a small incision in the center of the chest and then push hard from the sides to expel the blood and other fluids. This would be painful for the lad and Darren hoped the boy would pass out, making his work a little easier. The intoxication would help in the beginning, even though the men would be using all their considerable strength to restrain the boy. Everything was ready so Darren covered the boy's eyes with a dark cloth and tightened it around his head to prevent the boy from seeing the procedure and panicking.

The process went rougher than expected. Although the boy was drunk, he screamed loudly and the men held him down as Darren made the incision. Black, old blood along with foul smelling fluid flowed from the cut; the lad's mother slowly poured cold water on the incision, washing away the vile fluids. Darren completed the incision and let the boy calm down. He sweated heavily and found it hard to concentrate while the boy screamed. Darren was surprised the boy did not faint.

"I am sorry," mumbled the boy tearfully. "I am trying...but the pain is so strong..." He lost his words. "I know," said Darren understandingly. "It is alright. You are doing excellently." He took a deep breath for he knew the worst was still to come.

He nodded to the men to hold tight and then to the surprise of those around him, put all of his strength into pressing the sides of the incision to expel the fluids. The boy screamed uncontrollably now and thrashed from side to side, trying to get loose. As Darren continued to push, the boy found the power to free himself from one of the men. A massive amount of blood and foul liquid gushed out of the incision and splashed all over Darren. The man regained his hold as Darren ignored everything and focused on pushing even more forcefully. With Darren's last push the youth's eyes rolled listlessly and he passed out.

"At last!" exclaimed Darren as he wiped his face. "I wish it had happened earlier."

His pressure produced red blood now. A good sign, thought Daren. The vile fluids are out. He washed the incision thoroughly and closed it with a plant that had adhesive qualities. Then he put a clean cloth on the wound and instructed the parents to clean it often during the day. "The most important thing is to avoid contamination that can lead to his death," he told them. He knew that they needed luck. The boy was young and healthy and so Darren had good reason to hope. "I'll visit him tomorrow morning," he told them, then left exhausted. The grueling procedure had taken all of his powers. He went to his home and fell asleep almost immediately. He did not even have the strength to change his clothes or wash.

The boy had a high fever the next day. It lasted three days and then eased. A few days later the swelling started to go down and a week later it completely disappeared. Only a large scar remained, a memory of his brush with death. Darren was elated with the results and documented the entire event in his book. If he or another doctor encountered a similar case, he would know what to do.

∞

Darren was looking at his book when he heard a horse neighing. It was early morning and he just had an inspiration regarding a procedure he conducted on a pregnant woman. The woman's whole body swelled shortly before she was to give birth. Typically this meant death but he experimented with herbal tea to reduce the swelling – an idea from a friend who learned of it overseas. Initially it seemed to work well and the woman's condition got better. But she soon became very sick and he decided to stop giving her the herbal tea. She gave birth to a baby girl earlier than expected and her swelling went down naturally. Darren knew that not all cases ended this way. They usually ended with the mother's and baby's deaths. He wondered if he could perform simple surgery on the mother in order to save the baby.

As he was writing down his idea he heard a man's voice. "Darren Wells?" Puzzled by the voice, he replied, "Yes, I am he," and went outside to see who it was. "Ruben, my old friend! How goes it in Drake's castle?" Darren smiled and hugged the big man. It was Ruben, Drake's chancellor at Hartford's castle. Darren hated everything about castles. Everything was enclosed within walls and everything went by rules. Hartford started as a large castle system and developed into a city ruled by his friend Drake Holmes. "I'll make this castle the center of a prosperous city one day, a city with an economy of its own, a culture and a promising future," Drake had told him several years ago. Drake dreamed to build an autonomous city, independent of the various feudal lords. Darren liked Ruben. He had good heart and was a kind person. And few enough men had such traits in those times.

"Life there is as always," laughed Ruben jovially. Ruben looked somewhat primitive to Darren. He was a large and chubby man with a beard covering almost everything on his face, but it nonetheless gave him a sweet look. People liked Ruben from first sight. "Why am I honored by your visit today?" laughed Darren as he invited Ruben into his home.

"Drake wants to see you," answered Ruben – with a serious face now. "He seeks your opinion regarding a witch that was brought to us last week."

Darren made a strong herbal concoction and they sipped it slowly.

"A witch?" asked Darren, raising an eyebrow. The last time he dealt with witches was a few months ago. He typically did not like witch matters since he was not convinced that there were such things. He thought it more legend than reality.

"Yes," continued Ruben. "Last week a witch was brought to the castle by the villages to the north." He sipped from his hot tea carefully. "There is something about this witch that is out of the ordinary," he said somberly.

Darren felt tense. Ruben's behavior alone convinced him there was something extraordinary in the matter. "What is it about her?" Darren asked as he prepared bread and cheese. "Is she really evil? Did she do any special sorcery?"

"We do not know really," answered Ruben pointing towards the cheese and bread. "All we know is that a group of peasants brought her, claiming that she is evil."

Darren motioned with his hand and that was enough for Ruben to start his meal. Without any further sign, he grabbed a large piece of bread and a generous chunk of cheese, and ate ravenously. "Careful, my friend," said Darren with a smile, "eat slowly – I have enough." He knew that Ruben loved to eat. For him it was almost a hobby.

"I think that they simply are afraid of her," said Ruben with a full mouth. "She is very pretty..." His voice trailed off to a whisper.

"Oh, another case of an innocent woman too pretty for the crowd," replied Darren with anger displayed. "I've seen too many of such cases." He ate his bread and cheese while slowly drinking his beverage.

"Yes, but Drake wants you to come and see this woman and give counsel," noted Ruben, grabbing more bread.

I really do not want to do this, thought Darren, but I really do not have a choice. His relationship with Drake, although friendly on the surface, was quite formal. He was obliged to assist Drake with every request and in return he never had to pay taxes. He liked Drake but at the same time did not trust him. He always had the feeling that Drake's friendship was a facade. And if Drake did not like something, he would not hesitate to kill him.

"Tell Drake that I'll come Thursday morning. I have several patients to see," answered Darren quietly.

"Alright..." Ruben suddenly stopped chewing. His face turned red. "Do you have water?" he asked uneasily. He started to cough uncontrollably and Darren quickly brought him water and pounded on his back. After a series of loud coughs Ruben seems to be better and even smiled as his eyes teared. It was not the first time that this happened to Ruben and it would not the last either, thought Darren as Ruben was preparing his horse for departure. With his eating habits it's a miracle that he is still alive.

Darren left Thursday morning for Hartford castle and arrived before noon. That time of day, when the heat was on the rise, reminded him why he despised cities so much. The narrow streets reeked of garbage and sewage, especially in the workers' quarters. Darren passed these streets as fast as he could to reach the more prosperous parts of town, where the cobbled streets were washed out now and then and the stench was at least tolerable. Eventually he arrived at Drake's castle. Drake had designed the castle and was personally in charge of the construction, which took almost ten years to complete. It was a beautiful architectural creation with five main towers, with one tower twice the height of the others. It was built of black brick imported from a region of North Africa renown for masonry. The underground portions were as complex as those aboveground. Drake wanted secured hiding places and many secret escape ways. There was a maze of tunnels and chambers that only Drake knew of. He also kept prisoners in certain chambers the location of which he alone knew.

"Darren, my friend," welcomed Drake with a jovial smile and a bear-like hug, "thank you for coming." Drake looked at Darren still perspiring from the journey on a hot day.

"I am happy to see that you haven't changed much, Drake," jested Darren, pointing to the array of food spread across an expansive table. It was well known that Drake loved to eat and drink and that he partook of only the finest foods and wine. He himself ate only sparingly but always had the best brought in from around the world. On his last visit Darren had enjoyed a delicacy made from Nigerian geese liver, and he remembered a previous dinner featuring a distinctive trout brought alive from Spain in casks of cool water. Somehow the casks punctured and the fishes spoiled, causing twenty people to get severely sick. Luckily he and Drake did not eat much and were fine. Drake executed the merchant he deemed responsible.

"Care for a meal?" asked Drake, pointing to an empty chair. "I already dined but shall be ever happy to join you for paté and wine." Darren washed his face from a small pail. "I am pleased it is not an exotic fish from I do not know where," he replied with humor and a raised eyebrow. Drake roared with laughter. "Not this time, my friend. There will be no more surprises like that.

After all, you know what happened to the merchant." He took a small sip from his wine glass. "Yes, I do know," said Darren, feigning amusement.

They dined leisurely while Drake spoke of everything in the world beside the reason for Darren's visit. Later they sat on a balcony and enjoyed a cool wind descending from the mountains. "You have a beautiful breeze here," noted Darren, fascinated by the beautiful view. Drake lived in the tallest tower. It had four balconies facing each point of the compass to ensure a breeze and view at almost all times of the day. Darren could see the rolling hills in the distance and could almost smell their pine trees. The day was cool and refreshing, the wine the same, and Darren relaxed and enjoyed the moment.

"I love this balcony the most," said Drake looking at the evening skies. "At night it is even lovelier, with all the stars above." There was silence for a while and then Darren broke it.

"So why did you request my visit, Drake?" He looked straight into Drake's eyes and Drake looked back at him with his deep blue eyes. In the evening light they looked cold as ice. Drake looked at him for a few long moments then diverted his look to a hidden point in the skies.

"I have encountered a serious problem, Darren," he said quietly. He looked distant.

Darren did not say a word and let Drake go on. "A few weeks ago several peasants brought me a woman from a faraway village. They claimed she was a witch and extremely evil." He paused for few seconds. "When I asked them what she did they could not point to anything specific – only vague things." He turned to Darren. "I thought that this was another case of ignorant peasants scared of a woman." He looked carefully at his glass. Darren still said nothing. "Well," Drake continued, "this was not the case. This woman is...well, different."

Drake was strange. He knew Drake loved pretty women but always wanted to get them through his charm. He was a handsome man and never had difficulty. Adding his position and status made him irresistible to almost every woman he ever wanted. This time

Darren sensed things were different. "So what happened?" asked Darren cautiously.

"This woman has powers even I cannot overcome," Drake said without looking at Darren.

"What are you saying?" laughed Darren, trying to make the conversation lighter. "Are you saying that at last a woman said no to you?" He sipped long from his wine and looked at Drake, but he completely ignored Darren's comment and continued as though nothing had been said. "I tried to have her. I invited her to a feast; I bought her expensive gifts, perfumes, clothes. I even wrote her a poem. Nothing worked." He looked at the first star that showed in the skies. "Then I tried to threaten her, telling her that I'd give her back to the peasants and they'd kill her. But nothing helped. She simply looked at me, smiling like she was in control and I could not do anything. She has powers. I cannot touch her...as much as I want to," he added quietly as though to himself. "Somehow, she has hold of my thoughts." He stood up and started to pace on the balcony. "She definitely has powers. I want you to meet her and tell me what you think." He turned towards Darren. All of a sudden anger flashed across his face. Darren froze, knowing its potential. "If she has evil powers... if she can control people...I'll have her killed." He said quietly, almost spitting his words.

"Calm yourself, Drake," Darren interrupted. "There is no reason to get angry. I'll take a look at her, but I never saw a woman with real powers. Some of them simply want to make people think they have powers, to gain some sort of control." He looked at Drake. "And even this is fairly easy to detect," he added. "On the contrary, the majority of the so-called witches are poor women – that are pretty – and then falsely accused of witchcraft." Darren stood and stretched. "Drake, I do not believe in witches. People are people. We are all human beings. I perform all type of things that can be called sorcery, but these are mainly to fix some problems of the mind, not of the body. I do not have magical powers, Drake – no one has. Trust me, I know the human body." He studied Drake's face for several moments. Drake returned his look and seemed to calm down from the words of a doctor of great repute. People sought his advice on many subjects. He was considered a very wise man. He would know.

"Still, I want you to see her. Try to talk to her." Darren thought him obsessed. "Try to see if you can get anything that I could not..." His voice broke and Darren again saw strangeness in Drake. "You can stay tonight in my guest chamber. I'll take you to her..." Before Darren had a chance to say anything, Drake added "right now."

∞

Darren walked behind Drake as he entered the castle's maze work. After going down many stairs, passing many halls and rooms, going up many additional stairs, Darren lost all sense of direction and was completely confused about their location. "As long as you do not leave me here, I'll be alright," he tried to joke. "I'll never find my way out," he added, trying to keep up with Drake's pace. Drake did not answer. He continued determinedly through passages only he knew. All of a sudden, he stopped before a huge brown door. Drake turned to Darren. "I want you to talk to her alone. Do not be afraid – she is not violent. There is a white rope at each corner of the room. In case you need me, just pull the rope and I'll be here instantly." Darren was confused – by the maze and by Drake's words.

"Drake, why can't you come inside the room with me? Maybe it will help you to see that she is just a human being."

"NO," Drake almost yelled. "I want you to experience your first meeting with her alone." And then he looked town to the floor and added, "As I did..." He stormed away before Darren had a chance to say anything. "The door will be opened shortly," he called out as he vanished in one of the hallways.

Darren stood alone in the large hall in which small torches illuminated the huge door before him. What kind of place is this? He knew about Drake's love for hidden places, but this was the first time he actually walked through the castle's underground. It was eerie. He stood there a few minutes in the dim light, in total silence. Then a boom sounded and the huge door started to open slowly. Darren saw a large room lit by the soft light from an oil lamp. Slowly he stepped inside. He heard a sound and turned back to see the heavy door closing after him. Some light came from above. Darren looked up and could not believe his eyes.

The full moon shone brightly on the entire room, illuminating it with a soft white light through glass windows. There were lamps fixed inside the walls, covered by thick-carved glass. Darren had thought he was deep underground. He stood there in stunned silence, fascinated by the clear skies above. In the center of the room there was a large table covered with a red tablecloth and magnificent urn. Darren noticed that to his right there was a bed with someone in it. He slowly approached.

Then he saw her.

The mixture of the soft moonlight and the shimmering glow from the lamps created an exotic and alluring look to her face. Her dark hair gently spread out and looked soft as a silk. Darren's heart missed a beat. He looked at her face and could not move his eyes. Then he felt fear crawling up his back. She looked oddly familiar. He was sure that he had never seen her before, yet he felt intimately familiar with every detail of her face. He shook his head and told himself that she is simply beautiful and that's all, but something inside him kept telling him that he knew her well – or had known her well.

He continued to study her every detail. She had high cheekbones, her lips were small and red. She wore a long gown the color of which eluded him in the dim light. She was sleeping calmly. Darren searched his mind for a clue to how he might know her but could not find one. After a while he decided that sometime in the past he had seen someone who resembled her. His soul told him differently but he logically rejected it. She moved gently and opened her eyes. As her eyes met his an immediate connection was made. An invisible trail of fire flew from her eyes to his and into his soul. An explosion of unknown feelings burst inside him. As she continued looking inside his eyes he stopped resisting, simply because to do so gave him great intimate pleasure. Her almond-brown eyes smiled to him as he got lost in them. Even if it was some type of black magic, Darren did not care anymore. He allowed himself to sink into her soul, unconsciously learning new things about himself and her.

∞

She was surprised that she was not scared to find a stranger in her room as she woke up. She wanted to say something, but her breath was taken away as her soul bonded with his. Maybe it is just a dream and I will be waking up soon and everything will disappear, she thought. But she soon knew this was real. She did not say a word, not even when he moved closer. She felt paralyzed when he kissed her on her lips. She thought it wasn't right but was helpless to resist, even when his kisses – their kisses – exploded with passion. Her body and soul felt an explosion of their own, sending them into a whirlwind of emotions and feelings. As though in the thrall of an ancient ceremony, they felt the fire inside them and abandoned all reluctance to their love. Naked as at birth, they hungrily explored each other's bodies – feeling, touching, kissing and tasting what had been forbidden them for generations. They obeyed the flame of love that fused them into one. Shaking and sweating, they lay in each other arms, breathing heavily and trying to understand what had just happened. They knew their souls had felt the joy of reunion.

∞

Darren wondered what had happened. They lay together, holding each other, refusing to let go, touching each other's face, body and soul. Darren had to awkwardly ask her name. "Janis," she replied quietly. Her voice sounded beautiful to him and he impulsively kissed her. "Janis," he repeated, rolling the word about in his mouth. She looked at him and her eyes became small slits as she laughed. "Yes, that is my name – and you are funny." After a pause she added, "And what is yours?"

"Darren," he said looking at her in a teasing manner.

"Darren, Darren...you are sweet," she added as her cheeks formed two perfect dimples.

He shook his head in disbelief. "What is happening to us? What is the explanation for all this?"

She became serious. "I do not know, Darren."

He loved hearing her say his name but then remembered the circumstances. If Drake discovered what had happened here, his reaction would be unpredictable but severe.

"Are you really a witch?"

She made a serious face for a moment but then could not stop from laughing. "No more than you are, but I have some knowledge of medicine. It is something that my father taught me. Beyond that, I have no esoteric knowledge at all. Since he died I've been pursued many times by ignorant people who accused me of being a witch. When my father was alive, life was easy. Since he passed away last summer though, I had to move from village to village." She looked at the air. "Everywhere, sooner or later, people came to believe I knew witchcraft." She buried her face in her hands. Darren pressed her to his chest. "Eventually they brought me here."

Darren hesitated to ask what had just begun to torment him. He looked at her meaningfully and she read his mind. "No, he did not touch me." Darren felt great relief. "He tried and he will try again... I am remaining strong as I learned from my father, but eventually I will be at his mercy."

Darren's brain worked fast. "We will do something. I'll find a solution. Do not worry my love." He held her beautiful face between his hands and kissed her, not knowing where he found his confidence. Inside, he did not have a clue as to what to do, but he had to give Janis the strength to survive.

It was difficult to leave her there. He tried to smile and be strong but his heart was full of fear. He promised her that he would come back soon and that he would then have a plan. She looked into his eyes, felt his agony and fear, then told him, "I believe you." Even if he did not come back, he had imparted strength to her. Come what may, they would be together forever. He pulled the white rope and shortly Drake arrived. Without a word he took Darren to the chamber he had had prepared for him.

Darren could not sleep. He feared Drake knew what had taken place, so he expected the worst. He knew Drake. Such a man would not wait for morning. Then he felt panic when he thought of Janis's danger. He had to breathe in and out for a while and try to calm down. The first priority was to find a way to get her out of the castle. He tried to form a plan but was too tired. Early in the morning his body gave up and he fell asleep just as Drake's servant arrived to take him to breakfast.

"Please excuse me. I had a few drinks last night and do not feel well," said Drake as he slowly sipped a goblet of water. Thank God for great wine, thought Darren as he gently coughed. "Well, I also am not in the best shape. I could not sleep well last night due to the heat." Darren relaxed and thought he had leeway to plan the rescue. Suddenly, he felt great joy.

"I cannot resist such an excellent morning meal," he declared happily. He then started to eat from the full table, replete with cheeses, breads, fruits and of course fine wine – even at breakfast. "Please help yourself. I am going to forego eating until later," said Drake, pointing to the rich table. "Let's eat at noon. I'll go for a ride – it always makes me feel better after a night of revelry." Darren replied, "Of course," feigning empathy. "I hope you feel better...and next time, control your drinking!" Now for the plan.

He still looks awful, thought Darren as they ate together a few hours later. "It looks to me like you had quite an evening," started Darren, easing the atmosphere. "I feel better," replied Drake, but his appearance did not support his words. He had dark shadows under his eyes and he looked exhausted.

Drake got straight to the point. "So what did you conclude about her?"

Darren poured himself some red wine from a decanter. "Before I give you my opinion I have to ask you straightforwardly," Darren stated assertively. "Did you have relations with her?"

Drake looked at him long and hard, then he turned his eyes to the outside. "I truly wanted to...but she rebuffed me."

Darren felt relief but was very careful not to show anything. "This is good, Drake," he casually said then started on a slab of roast beef. "I am glad that things went this way. It may sound hard for you, especially since I see you've developed feelings towards her." Then he stopped eating.

He knew what he was about to do was the only way to get her out of the castle. He decided to take a big chance.

"She is no good, Drake." He said in one breath. "I have determined that she really has dark powers," said Darren calmly. Drake was fascinated.

"I knew it," he said, and his face went down. "I felt that she has something out of the ordinary, but could not quite point to it."

"Indeed," continued Darren. "This is the first time that I've seen something like that. She can alter the mind..." He sounded serious.

"How did you find out?" asked Drake looking at him thoroughly.

Darren expected this question. Drake needed to know everything. His curiosity and caution had saved his life many times. "Well," started Darren, "I talked with her for a while, asking her about her life, where she lived, her family and these sorts of things. Although she gave me information, it was never clear. She never disclosed full details, only parts and pieces. She did not name anyone and never mentioned places. At first I assumed that she did it out of fear." Darren looked in deep thoughts, which made Drake more curious. "Then I tried the old doctor's trick of getting closer to her. I claimed that I was asked to check her health since there is an illness in the city, but even then she did not open to me and remained a mystery. I began my medical checks."

Drake became alert. Darren knew the topic was risky but it had to be raised. Mention of his closeness to her brought him to a fine line. If Drake even suspected his closeness to Janis was not for medical reasons, his life was in grave danger. "Then I felt her powers," said Darren quietly as his face darkened. "It was as though my thoughts had been taken from me. I could not think clearly...and I felt dizzy. She looked at me without saying a word...but I felt her dark control. I felt that she could read my every thought. I was an open book. I tried to logically explain to myself everything that was going on but nothing came to mind. After a while, without the power to express my desires, I instinctively moved backwards and far away from her." Darren was quiet and the only sound was the two men breathing. "After some time I gained control and could think again. When I looked at her, she smiled...as if she knew that she had won. Then she never even looked at me again."

"That's exactly what she did to me," exclaimed Drake. "She never spoke or even looked at me. Did she say anything later?"

"Actually yes," answered Darren "She asked me if I was alright and for a second I thought that she was sincere." He paused for few seconds. "That is, until I looked at her and could tell that she was enjoying my confusion. To my surprise she did not try to use her feminine powers on me. She has enough power already." Darren continued in a dry, medical tone. "She is very pretty – no doubt – but her powers are coming from a...different source." Darren took a long deep breath and slowly got back to his meal.

"As your friend and as a doctor I have to admit that such things I've never witnessed before. And although I usually recommend mercy," he looked straight at Drake, "this time I recommend... another course. True evil has to be eliminated. Otherwise it can grow and become dark control. I am sure that many men were captured within her evil beauty and forfeited their lives...or their souls." The last sentence he said like announcing a fatal disease. "I am afraid I have no choice. This woman must be executed."

Drake was astonished. He had known Darren for many years and knew such recommendations from him were rare. Darren knew he was still on that fine line and needed to prod Drake even more. The news is very hard on him, Darren thought. He is already in love with this woman and the thought of executing her is unbearable. Probably he already planned to have her in one way or another. Drake looked up at Darren's face and his eyes narrowed. Darren expected this. Drake was suspecting something was amiss. Without waiting for Drake's reaction he stood up and made an announcement. "I am sorry, Drake, but in my office as doctor of this county, I hereby declare this woman a witch. She is forbidden any communication until the day of her execution. She is a danger to all and must be executed posthaste. I'll personally supervise her execution and cremation, to ensure complete elimination of evil."

Darren made his pronouncement in a single breath, making a great impression on Drake. He had never before invoked his office and so it was quite striking to Drake. He touched Drake's shoulder in feigned sympathy. "Drake, my friend, I see how hard it is for you, but I am doing this for your own good," he said with equally feigned compassion. Drake did not look at him anymore and seemed to appreciate the situation. "I'll stay here another day. Please announce the time of execution for tomorrow morning. No one is to be in direct contact with the woman. I will deliver her food and water – I am trained to handle situations like this." He turned and whispered into Drake's ear. "And you, my friend...find some other woman – one that is good for you." Drake looked at him, fully convinced now. "Thank you, kind Darren. I am now aware that I was enthralled by her beauty. Such incredible beauty...it is hard to resist."

"Exactly," responded Darren with a slight smile, "but it is my duty, as your friend and doctor, to settle this matter." His smile disappeared and he became serious. "I do not want you to end in a bad place." He paused before stating his next words. "I will need a guard to escort me back and forth to the woman's chamber. This guard must wear a helmet to protect him from the witch's powers. Only the guard and I can be permitted to enter the chamber. I will try to communicate with her today in order to gain more knowledge about her sorcery. The guard will always be in the room with me, at a safe distance. All these precautions are necessary to ensure the proper study of this woman and to perform her execution." He knew that he had to play on Drake's ignorance. Darren was a doctor who gave orders regarding local medical matters. He did not even look at Drake as he gave his commands. "I'll provide you all that you need," said Drake as he sipped wine, "but I will not attend the execution."

Darren put his left hand on Drake's shoulder. "I understand, my friend," he said, "I understand."

Shortly thereafter, Darren was on his way to the dungeon, with escort. Darren instructed the guard to maintain some distance from him and the woman. When they arrived, she sat near the table, laying her head on the table. She stood in alarm and looked at Darren. He could see that she had been crying. Her hair was in disarray and she looked distraught. But when she saw him, her appearance changed. A slight smile came across her face and she immediately looked better. It is amazing how mood can improve one's look, thought Darren. Then he instructed the guard to wait just outside the door. "Enter only if I summon you!" he told him. "I need to examine the woman without interference." Darren knew that speaking with such commanding voice had great effect on most people. The guard meekly complied.

Darren moved towards Janis. He wanted to wildly grab her and hold her tight – forever. But he knew the guard was not too far away. He put his hands to his mouth. "Shhh..." he whispered. She looked at him and understood instantly. She sat there calmly as he placed a chair near her. They looked at each other without saying a word. No words were needed to express their love.

Darren left after several hours. He could hardly hide his stress and walked quickly towards his chamber. Janis trusted him with her very life and her trust came easily. Although he planned to the finest detail, he knew that there was always the chance of something going wrong. That could cost them their lives. He knew Drake would not hesitate to kill them both if he discovered their relationship. He rushed to his room and refreshed himself with a warm bath. Afterwards he took all of his coins and left the castle. He still remembered his father's advice, "Always carry money. You never know when you may need it!" He thanked his father a thousand times that night. Without his advice, Janis's life would be doomed.

∞

The executioner's head was covered with the traditional black mask, leaving only two small holes for his eyes. The slant of the eyelets made for a sinister look. Many people gathered in the court hours before executions, simply for socializing before the event. They were mainly peasants and workers looking for crude entertainment. The executions of witches were popular, as everyone wanted the chance to see an evil woman get what she deserved. The tradition was to tie the witch between two wooden poles for some time, to let the crowd view her. Sometimes the crowd got unruly, so the city built a high wooden platform. An iron piece formed the crossbar of the gallows. The condemned was lead to the center of the platform, where a rope would be placed around his or her neck.

It was early evening and the people cheered when they saw the executioner take his position. All moved closer to the platform. A woman was brought out and everyone became silent for a moment; everyone wanted to see the witch. The woman's hands were tied behind her back and she looked out at the crowd fearlessly. There was a surprising silence as the people studied her. She was surprisingly beautiful, not the grotesque crone they expected. The sunlight touched her face and she closed her eyes for a moment, breathing in the light breeze that brought the scent of flower blossoms from the cool hills.

"Kill her!" someone shouted. This was almost a signal and everyone seemed to stir and start to scream, "Kill the witch" and other derisive jeers. The woman looked into the sky above the sneering crowd. She seemed unbothered. The executioner took her straight to the gallows and the crowd was disappointed. They wanted her to be tied for a while. Without delay, the executioner took her to the center of the platform and prepared the rope. The mob jeered the executioner now. They wanted a longer show, but he seemed in a rush.

Behind the execution site stood Darren. He wore a long gown with a hood. He sweated heavily and his heart raced as he carefully watched the executioner. He had planned this laboriously and wanted to make sure that nothing went awry. Only a few feet away from him, his loved one seemed about to be put to death.

An executioner has a lonely job. No one is supposed to know him or worse, want to know him. Executioners are outcasts, without friends or family. The city hired them for their special skill and their only contacts with the outside world were the city aldermen. They provided executioners with details about the condemned. But even executioners can become ill. Darren met the executioner once when he became quite ill. Darren didn't think he would make it since he diagnosed him with severe congestion. As a last resort he treated him with an ancient remedy made from a eucalyptus tree. He had heard about this remedy long ago from a friend who lived in the city of York. The executioner had high fever for almost a week and then miraculously recovered. Darren had the chance to get to know the man and was amazed by his nature. Apparently Drake had selected him to be executioner at a young age. Drake thought him suited for the job.

But the man hated his work. Although he was told that the people he executed were criminals and did evil to society, he did not like to put them to death. Many nights Darren sat with him listening to sad stories about people he had to execute, even though he was convinced of their innocence. He described in painful detail the look on their faces just before death. They looked upon him as the last human being they would see. He could do nothing as to their last requests. He was just doing his job, as instructed by the city. He always tried to give them warm words. Through his eerie mask and clothes he tried to tell them, just before they died, that they are going to a better world – a final gesture of humanity. Darren was fascinated by this good soul and became his friend. Darren visited him often when in the city. Last night he came to him with a special request. The disaffected executioner agreed to help without a blink of an eye. Darren offered him money but was not surprised at all when the man refused.

The executioner neared Janis with the noose. The crowd yelled and screamed, loudly protesting the rushed procedure that deprived them of their demented sport. The executioner ignored them and continued with his work. He handled the rope in an expert way and made all necessary positioning. At last he was standing behind Janis – and ready. The crowd fell silent. Everyone awaited the alderman, who always arrived shortly before the execution to read the sentence. If the prisoner requested a priest, then the city provided one. But witches never received priests. The alderman arrived dressed in official attire and holding a scroll. Darren peered from his spot and almost stopped breathing. The alderman arrived with Drake! The two walked pointedly then took their places on the scaffold. What is he doing here? Darren's brain worked crazily trying to figure out if this would undo his plan. Drake was calm and showed no sign of suspecting anything. Darren decided to make his presence known. He quickly stepped out from his spot and walked towards the scaffold, ordering the crowd to make room. Many recognized the county doctor and allowed him to reach the platform.

"Drake, my friend," said Darren with a broad smile. Drake looked somewhat surprised then gave him a hug. "Why is your presence called for?" asked Darren, changing his tone to a more stern one. He looked serious now, like a teacher about to scold a student.

"I told you not to come to this execution. You are simply too involved with the witch."

"I know," admitted Drake, looking somewhat embarrassed. "I could not help it though." He looked straight into Darren's eyes. "But I have to see her for the last time."

Darren tried to control his racing heart. He needed to discern if Drake knew anything. He looked into his eyes but could not be sure. Does he know anything? thought Darren with more than a little fear. Does he wait for the right moment to thwart my plan? His heart continued to race and he felt cold sweat on his back. He summoned all his will to show calm yet strength. "Alright then, but be strong, my friend. Remember that she is evil and I am here to personally ensure that everything proceeds as it should." He studied Drake's face, trying to see if he had impressed him. "You know, I am going to check the body after the execution and escort it with two guards to a faraway place whence her powers cannot reach here anymore." Drake agreed with a short nod. He looks sad, thought Darren.

He knew the procedure had to continue. He looked at Janis. She stood there, certain his entire being wanted her. He felt her trust and knew that he could not fail her. More than that, he could not fail himself.

The alderman started to read a detailed description of the witch's crimes. People from a faraway village caught her using her evil powers on people. The crowd watched silently. Janis looked at the people, observing their faces. All she saw was ignorance. She had no fear in her heart. She trusted Darren completely. Even if I die, at least I have experienced the essence of love. She could not prevent a small smile from crossing her face. She wondered if anyone had seen her smile, but everyone was focused on the ceremony. They wanted her blood. She still did not feel fear when the alderman concluded his presentation with her death sentence, nor when the executioner started to put the noose around her delicate, white neck.

She could smell the scent of the man's body. She tried to see his face through his mask but could only see darkness. The executioner stopped for a moment and looked straight at her. She focused on his eyes but they told her nothing. What! Was it her imagination or had the executioner's eyes told her she would be fine? He delayed only a split second then continued placing the noose. The alderman stepped to the side and the crowd roared. From the corner of her eye she saw the executioner approaching with the lever. She felt a brief moment of panic. Where is Darren? Is it supposed to go this far? Did the executioner try to tell her something or was it her imagination? Everything happened too quickly and she actually was happy that it was like that. She did not have too much time to think. She closed her eyes and let herself sink into acceptance. She heard the executioner's footsteps and felt the rope tightening around her neck. The crowd roared more loudly. In the next second she felt the ground give way. The rope grabbed her neck violently and she felt her body suspended in the air. Then there was a drop. The sounds around her faded away as the entire universe became dark.

Drake watched as her body disappeared beneath the scaffold. He looked to the side and closed his eyes for a moment. Darren watched him for a few long moments. He put his hand on Drake's shoulder. "Go rest, my friend. Do something cheerful," advised Darren in the tone of an old friend. "We've done the right thing," he added solemnly. "Did we?" said Drake quietly. Then Drake left the place of execution, escorted by his guards. Darren felt an enormous relief.

Janis! he thought wildly. He looked around for the executioner and was relieved to hear "Right here" from below the scaffold. The wooden platform had a chamber under it for the condemned to fall into and the executioner pointed towards Janis lying on its floor. Darren ran to her and held her in his arms. "She is not breathing," he almost screamed to the executioner. "Shhh," the executioner silenced him. "She will wake up soon. She's blacked out due to lack of air. See, I used a flat rope, one that cut off her air but did not break her neck." The trick would work as long as the hanging was short. Janis would be thought dead and no one in his village would be the wiser about Darren's new wife. "I brought my wife from far away," he will claim when introducing Janis to the world, a few weeks from today. He held Janis close to his heart, waiting for her to wake up and look into eyes once more.

Janis heard sounds, as though from a great distance. Slowly the sounds got clearer and she could tell they were voices. Then she felt warm kisses on her face. Janis moved her head slightly, coughed a few times and opened her eyes. "Darren..." she whispered as a loving smile spread across her face. "It's me, my love," answered Darren. "We are here...forever." They kissed long and passionately. The rest of the world did not exist for them.

The executioner looked at them. I just helped to save these lovers, he thought to himself. I never had a loved one. He felt a hidden ache inside. And probably I never will. Such things, he knew, were not for him. Nonetheless he enjoyed seeing couples in love. They lived in their own world as though the outside one was none of their business and had no claims on them. The way they looked at each other, their touches, their way of getting lost in their love, always caused the executioner happiness and sadness at the same time. He was happy to see loving couples but there was an attendant loneliness. Now he was looking at Darren and Janis in their joy and happiness, and it filled his heart. He had helped his friend – a man who respected him and treated him with care. No one else had done that. Not the hangman.

Sensing someone watching, Darren and Janis turned towards the executioner. Janis smiled to him. "Thank you," she said simply. "Thank you for saving us and giving us ourselves." She looked at Darren lovingly. Darren kissed her gently then looked at the executioner and understood the source of his sadness. "No worry, my friend," he said quietly. "You too will find your loved one someday." The executioner nodded but Darren knew the executioner did not believe him. Before Darren could reassure him, the executioner said, "We have to get you out of here soon...before someone gets wind of something. The entire city thinks you are dead. We have to keep it that way." The couple hugged and thanked the executioner. In a moment of inspiration, he knew how to reward his friend for saving their lives.

Later that night Darren and Janis left from the executioner's stable on a speedy horse. They were the happiest couple in the world. They rode to freedom and eternal love. The next morning Darren introduced Janis to his village, as his soulmate whom he had met and romanced on a sojourn. No one asked questions. It was a small village and all were busy with their own lives.

A few weeks later Darren knocked on the door of the executioner, who was pleased to see him. "How are you my friend?"

"Very well, thank you." Darren smiled, as though hiding something. The executioner looked at him without knowing the visit's purpose.

"I would like to introduce someone to you," Darren said with a mysterious smile. The executioner just looked at him without understanding. Darren went outside and returned with a woman. The executioner looked at Darren, then at the woman, and then at Darren again. The woman wore a long gown with a hood that covered most of her face. Darren took a deep breath. He knew it was a gamble but felt that he had to try. He wanted to give his friend the greatest gift of all, the gift of love. The woman came from his village. She was very pretty, though blind since birth. Darren knew her entire family to be simple, goodhearted people. She had no suitors because of her blindness. All of her sisters had already married and she remained with her parents. Darren talked with her and asked her permission to introduce his friend. "He is a good soul...but I will not tell you his trade," he told her. "This he will have to tell you himself, someday."

She trusted Darren but asked one question that day. "Is his soul good?" she looked at Darren without seeing him.

"Yes, it is. I would trust him with my life – actually, I already have."

"Then I want to meet him," she concluded.

She removed her hood and the executioner looked at Darren, who simply said, "I would like to introduce you to this kind woman."

The woman turned her head towards Darren and the executioner. Darren led her to his friend and placed her hand in the executioner's.

"She can't see," Darren said simply.

The executioner looked, without saying a word, upon the woman's face and felt his heart warm. She was the most beautiful woman in the world. He stood there in great disbelief. She held his hand gently. Her hand was warm and soft. Then she touched his arms, his forehead, his hair and finally his face. Her gentle fingers gently touched his lips, nose and eyes. The executioner stood there with a racing heart.

"I do not know your trade, but I sense good in you," she said.

"Thank you, Darren. You can leave us now." She smiled to Darren who stood by in awe.

Darren looked at the executioner's face and quietly nodded. He had done enough and so he left the couple there. As he turned back for a moment, he saw his friend touching her face, just as she touched his. I have a good feeling about this, thought Darren. Then he left for his village. I'll return in few days and see how these two have come along. He never saw them again. When he returned, both were gone. His friend's house was empty. He asked neighbors but no one had word. An old man in a tavern told him he saw the executioner leaving town late at night with a large wagon – alone. And the city was in search of a new executioner. Darren thanked the old man and left the tavern.

He was walking towards the main gates with his horse, eager to return home. He almost never left his wife alone, not even for a few hours. A man in a black cloak stopped him. "Are you Darren...the doctor," he asked in a gravel voice. Darren could smell alcohol on his breath.

"Yes, I am – and who are you?" he asked.

"I have something for you," said the man, who then laughed. "Your friend asked me to give this to you." He waved a small package in his hand.

"I do not have any friend here," Darren retorted then he turned to go. Drunken old man, thought Darren as he continued towards the gate.

"Oh yes, you do," insisted the man. "He told me so. Your friend left the city with his wife a few nights ago. He knew that you would come to visit him and left this for you."

Darren stopped. Something told him to turn backwards. He approached the drunken man. "What do you have for me?" he asked cautiously.

"I need money to buy some ale..." replied the man with a laugh, exposing the rotten teeth in his mouth. Now that he had Darren's attention, he was in charge.

Darren regarded him suspiciously. The man looked like a typical drunk, with long beard, red eyes, and filthy clothes. Perhaps the executioner would choose such a man to leave me a message, thought Darren. After all, no one would suspect him. Crafty. He pulled out few coins from his pocket. "Here are three shillings... but first you have to tell me a few things."

The drunkard saw the coins and knew that he could sate his thirst for alcohol. He wanted to cooperate now. "I'll tell you anything you want." He could not take his eyes off of the three shillings in Darren's hand.

"Who is my friend? Where did he go...and was he alone?" asked Darren sternly.

"I do not know him – I swear. All I know is that he stopped me and told me that a friend of his will come to search for him and that I should give him this package. He was alone and left with a horse and wagon. He also told me that you are a doctor..." He added in fading voice, "Are you?"

"Give me the package," demanded Darren, sure now that the story was true. He tossed a few coins to the drunkard and watched him head off joyfully for a tavern. Darren opened the package and found a flat piece of wood from an olive tree. "Thank you, my dear friend – from both of us" was engraved on it. Darren smiled and looked at the full moon. You've found it, old friend. Farewell, wherever you both go. He felt great joy. I had a good feeling about the match. Janis will be happy to hear this. It was late and he wanted to go home. He missed his wife.

∞

Darren and Janis became beloved by all in the village. Everyone was fond of the beautiful woman Darren brought from far away. Janis had practiced homeopathy in the past and became Darren's assistant. They built a larger house outside the village, near the dark forest, and everyone who needed help came to them there. Janis cultivated a garden in which they grew fruits and vegetables. They loved to spend hours in their garden tending to their crops. They did not have to pay taxes because of their profession and received food and money from people who came for help. They were inseparable. Even when Darren had to leave to help people in other villages, Janis accompanied him. Darren avoided trips to Drake's city as often as possible and when he had to go, he made the visits short. After a few cold winters Janis told Darren that she was ready to have children.

∞

"Her name is Janis," said the fearful man.

Drake looked at him thoroughly. "And when did he bring her to his village?" he demanded.

"The people could not tell for sure, but one claimed about three years ago," answered the man.

"Three years ago..." mumbled Drake as he paced the room. "It matches the time. What is she doing? Do they have children?"

"They do not have children, sir," replied the man. "She is helping him with medicine. Some people claim she is a very good healer, too."

Drake questioned the man for several hours. It had all begun when his friend Ruben came back one day after visiting Darren's village. During dinner, Ruben told Drake about Darren's beautiful wife, which surprised Drake who did not know that Darren had married. He expected to have been invited to such an event. He asked about the couple and Ruben's answers described something familiar but not precisely recognizable. He felt an old yet inexplicable ache.

A few months earlier, Drake was witnessing yet another witch execution when it dawned on him. Ruben's description of Darren's wife matched the woman executed two or three years ago – at Darren's recommendation. Initially Drake rejected the idea that the wife was she. Then his thoughts took a different direction. Darren's visits were few and far between. Was Darren avoiding the castle...and him? Drake needed to know more. He sent an agent to Darren's village to inquire about the couple. Today he returned with information about the doctor, his wife, and the fond villagers. Drake paid the man for his services and sent him away. He had dinner in the high tower and had just finished his fourth sampling of wine but he was not yet drunk. He poured another round and went out onto the balcony. The skies were golden blue and he felt the cool breeze from the hills. He took a deep breath and thought about events of years past. Darren would never deceive me, he thought. He fears my darker side, and he is also my friend. True, he has not visited much lately, but perhaps he is simply burdened by work. It is definitely not to avoid me. He finished his fifth glass of wine and started to feel the warmness of the alcohol slowly spreading through his body and mind. Ah, he thought, I am becoming too suspicious. Darren is a good friend and would never do something like this, ever. I better drink more of this wonderful wine and invite some women to spend the evening here. I am not going to worry myself with this.

That night Drake finished a good deal more wine. He woke up the next morning nauseous. After vomiting violently, he lay in his bed exhausted. He looked outside at a beautiful sunny day. The skies were blue, the air cool and fresh. Drake stood and slowly walked onto the balcony. The mountain tops were already white from the first snows of late autumn. Below, he could hear city sounds – the crowd, the horses and carriages, and the busy market. Everyone was engaged in routine. Something is not right. Darren is hiding something from me. His senses never failed him. They had protected him and in some cases even saved his life in battle and in court intrigue. I have to check this personally. I'll go to the village by myself. The decision made him feel better. He immediately ordered his horse and gear to be readied for tonight.

∞

"Thank you very much, doctor," said the old man.

"You're welcome," said Janis with a smile. The old man visited her this morning for a severe rash. She examined him and concluded it was probably due to a plant that he had touched. "Be very careful not to touch any strange plants," instructed Janis. "And wash at least three times a day and apply this powder generously afterwards." The powder came from a white rock ground into powder. It had several minerals that countered infections and chaffing.

"Many thanks for your care," said the old man. He then offered goat cheese to Janis. "I do not have much. I have a few goats that give milk and I make cheese from their milk. It's wonderful! Please try it."

"Thank you. I'll have a few pieces. I like goat cheese." She really didn't. But she accepted his gift anyway since it would have disappointed him if she hadn't. The old man left happy and Janis walked with him for a while. It was a beautiful sunny day and she enjoyed the fresh air of the forest. Alas, Darren was in the village visiting the sick.

She marveled at her garden in which she had recently planted a new type of tomato, smaller than commonly found. A friend from the village had given them the seeds. The seeds were now bursting from the earth. Janis had a passion for new plants and always had a desire to learn of new vegetables and fruits. Janis allowed her thoughts to set upon a baby and warm almost ticklish sensations rushed across her heart. The thought had grown stronger in recent months and without telling Darren she was trying to get pregnant. She hoped to know soon.

"Hello Miss," she heard someone call. She looked and saw a man standing near the house. "The villagers sent me here to seek your advice. You see I have stomach pains," the man said pointing towards his stomach. Janis was in a pleasant mood and did not sense danger. "Sure, we'll see what your problem is. Please come in," she said with a smile. Janis offered the man some water. He looks dirty, she thought. He may have come from far away. He had a long gray beard and judging by his clothes, he was quite poor.

"Where are you coming from?" asked Janis as she poured some water.

"Thank you, miss," replied the man before quenching his thirst. It wasn't enough. "May I have some more, please? I come from far away."

She somehow got the feeling that she had seen him before but she could not remember where.

"I am coming from across the forest," he said after downing his second drink of water. "Friends say you can heal any illness and I am having these stomach pains for months now, mainly at night." The man slowly stopped talking and stared at her.

Janis searched her memory for his identity.

"Did we meet before?" she asked while preparing some herbs.

"I am not sure," answered the man. "I was never in this part of the county. Maybe we met at the May fair. I go there every year to purchase clothes."

"We'll take a look at your stomach and see what the matter is." She decided to ignore her feeling. She smiled and prepared lengthy, aromatic leaves to be placed on the stomach. "Please lie down." Janis probed his stomach but could not feel anything out of the ordinary. She applied the leaves onto his stomach. "Do you feel anything?"

"Not at all," said the man, though he continued looking at her strangely.

"Did you eat anything new recently?"

The man looked at her very thoroughly and she started to feel uncomfortable.

"Did you eat anything out of the ordinary recently?" she repeated.

"Oh yes, I am sorry," said the man. "No, I eat the same things every day. I am a farmer and my food is mainly what I grow..." His words faded.

"Ahh. Then did you get hit in your stomach area recently? Maybe while doing some farm work?"

The man was fascinated by her and hesitated answering her questions. Eventually Janis told him that she could not find anything wrong with him and that he needed to maintain better cleanliness. This advice always helped with stomach problems. The man mumbled a few more words, thanked her, and left.

What an odd man, she thought. He was not focused on his ailment and made little effort to help diagnose the problem. He simply stared at her. She could not get rid of a troubling feeling about this man. Maybe she had met him someplace before, but maybe not. She went back to work the field. She wanted to sample the new tomatoes soon. Darren returned and they embraced. That night they watched the stars and the moon, and she completely forgot about the man. In the morning she woke up with terrible nausea. Darren was still sleeping as she joyfully whispered in his ear, "Good morning, my handsome prince...and future father."

∞

Drake was almost in tears. He stood there in the shadows of trees and watched Janis. She was working a small field, weeding it and taking care of the plants. She can't be a witch, he thought as his heart began to ache. And those savages... The villagers wanted to execute her...and I almost did. He never admitted then, but now, after a few years, he knew he had been deeply in love with her. The power he felt from her came from beauty, not evil. And now she was married to Darren. He pursed his lips in anger. Darren stole her from me! He deceived him into thinking she was dead while he had her all to himself. She only loves him because he saved her life, thought Drake bitterly. She could easily fall in love with me then. After all, I offer much more than Darren, with all of his medical prestige. First, I'll need to see her close. She noticed him and motioned for him to approach her. I wonder if she'll recognize me. If so, I will tell her the truth – I wish only to meet her.

Her beauty only grew as he neared her. He could barely concentrate on the story of stomach pains. When she got close to him for the examination he had to struggle not to reach for her and kiss her. He was again hopelessly in love with her. She told him about methods to help his stomach pain, then he left.

But he remained hiding in the trees for long time, watching her. Then Darren arrived. He wanted to strike him with his sword, but then Janis ran to him and they kissed passionately. Drake watched expressionlessly. Anger coursed through him. His hand tightened around the hilt of his sword. His eyes narrowed to a malevolent squint. She once belonged to me. He stood there in the dark, watching their little house and listening to their voices. They sounded happy. But it did not matter to Drake – jealousy controlled him.

They were in the middle of breakfast when a knock on their door sounded. Darren was looking through his notes and Janis was preparing tea. "Who can it be so early in the morning?" asked Darren without taking his eyes from his notes. "Well, let us see," replied Janis, walking to the door. Darren looked to the door and exclaimed, "Ruben my friend, long time since our last encounter. And perfect timing, my good man – breakfast is on!" Typically Ruben would march in happily, grab a chair and begin his meal. Not this time. Darren sensed Ruben's dismay. He did not smile or even mention food.

"What's amiss, my friend?" said Darren, worriedly.

"I do not know, but Drake asked me to call on you urgently. He looked very worried," answered Ruben. "I'd love to stay for breakfast but we have to go. You have to see to Drake."

Darren looked at Janis. She was breathing heavily. "Any bad feeling, my love?" He knew she had a bad feeling about this. This was the first time that she felt that way. Darren looked to the ground. They all knew that one cannot refuse Drake's request. It was truly a command.

"Did Drake say why he wants to see me?" asked Darren quietly.

"Not really. Maybe he does not feel well and wishes your services."

Darren felt relieved, but he was nonetheless troubled by the unusual gravity in his friend this day. It may be a simple visit, he thought. After all I am his doctor. But even if Drake has some skullduggery in mind, he would not make Ruben a party to it.

What to do? Darren thought urgently. Was he worried about nothing or should he and Janis flee for their lives? But Drake's influence reached far and wide. And perhaps Drake is becoming dangerously paranoid. Ahhh! I'll just go and have done with the matter. "I'll go, my love, and come back shortly," said Darren. But she appeared disturbed and Darren felt her stress. He stopped for a while and tried to think of options but nothing came to mind. If he refuses Drake, he may get upset and come to the village. He looked at Ruben but could not get answers from him. He simply did not know anything. Janis looked at him and felt like her whole world was collapsing.

∞

He and Janis spent the entire night holding each other. She did not want him to leave and cried constantly. Darren saw no choice; otherwise, Drake would come. Even Ruben could not understand why this time it is so different. In the morning, he tried to allay her fears. "Janis, he'll be back in a day or two. I'll make sure he does. I can't believe you two lovebirds cannot be without each other a few days." And then he thought to himself, I wish I had love like this...

It was raining lightly when they left. Darren wanted to leave early to make it to the city by evening time. In this way, he hoped to be on his way back the next morning. Darren chatted with Ruben during their ride, which improved Darren's mood. After a few hours of passing through villages, they headed towards the dark forest. The woods were a thick and bushy, with tall and dense foliage that slowed their progress. Travelers tried to pick an existing path and stick to it, but even these paths were quickly overgrown and they had to use knives to slash through. Darren and Ruben picked a path and entered the dark forest. After about two hours, they reached an opening. "Goodness," said Darren with surprise, "I've never seen a bald spot in the middle of this forest." The surprise was a pleasant one as it meant less foliage to cut through.

"I'm familiar with this spot," replied Ruben, breathing heavily from the cutting efforts. "Maybe we could rest here awhile. I am tired and I'd be happy to eat the muffins Janis gave you."

"Ruben, you'll never change," scolded Darren with a laugh. "Here, how about if we rest and eat there, near that big rock."

"An excellent suggestion," said Ruben as he licked his lips to show his hunger.

"So you really do not know why Drake is calling for me?" asked Darren as he bit into a muffin.

"Not at all. But Drake never tells me his reasons," answered Ruben while eating with great enthusiasm. "I am just a messenger." His large teeth showed as he smiled.

Darren did not reply. He saw several men approaching from the distance. Ruben saw Darren's concern and looked in that direction also.

"What is that?" he mumbled. "I am not sharing my food with anyone," he added immediately.

Darren smiled "Do not worry my friend, we have enough food."

The men reached Darren and Ruben. One of them was Drake. Darren saw immediately that Drake's intentions were not friendly.

"Thank you, Ruben, you can go now," said Drake without any expression on his face.

"Ruben, you swine!" Darren turned. "You eat at my table then betray me."

"Hey, what's going on?" said Ruben with a loud laugh. "This is supposed to be a surprise for you, Darren? Right, Drake? Tell him." Ruben turned towards Drake, who remained astride his horse, not laughing at all. "Tell Darren of the surprise you have for him." He looked amused and turned back to Darren.

"Darren, my friend, Drake wanted me to bring you here to surprise you...agghh..."

Ruben's words halted as Drake's sword thrust from his back out through his stomach, ripping arteries, muscles and bones on its way. Ruben looked surprised at the sword sticking out from his stomach. Then he looked back at Drake.

"I never liked your friendship with Darren. You never told me about Janis." Drake said matter-of-factly, as though in an afternoon conversation.

Ruben looked incredulously at the torrent of blood flowing from his torso. He wanted to understand but could not. Darren immediately attempted to help his friend but realized within seconds that the wound was fatal and there was nothing he could do. Ruben slowly collapsed with a surprised look still on his face and muttered, "Why..why...?"

"There was no need to kill him," Darren said in a cold voice.

"He was your close friend...and a cover for you," replied Drake quietly.

"He knew nothing," replied Darren angrily. "He was a good man, and you murdered him in a cold blood."

As Drake looked at Ruben's slumping body, Darren could see a trace of shock or horror when Drake realized what he had done.

"What's wrong with you, Drake?" asked Darren quietly. "Why did you kill Ruben?" Darren felt that his darkest nightmare was about to happen.

"Why did you lie to me?" countered Drake, trembling in rage. "I loved her and you betrayed me and took her away." Drake regained his control.

"We fell in love, Drake. I did not plan it. I met her and at that moment our souls remembered each other, as though from past lives." Darren looked into the sky. This was the first time that he had actually expressed what he felt then. "Our souls had already been together. I know not when or where, but I know that we met." Then he turned towards Drake. "We knew that we have to be together, again. No one, especially you, would have understood, so we fled."

Drake looked at him with hatred. "But she was mine. I loved her and I would have had her but for you." He pressed his lips together.

"No, you wouldn't," answered Darren quietly. "She would never love you – she told me that."

Drake looked upwards with visible sadness. Somewhere inside him he knew that Darren was right, but his pride and anger took over.

"You took her away from me and for this I will never forgive you." Darren saw pure anger, jealousy and wounded pride. All three qualities were Drake's weaknesses. He was used to getting everything he wanted. When he realized what happened he could not control his anger. Darren looked at Drake's face and had a feeling that he will never see Janis's face again.

Drake nodded and the men tied Darren's hands. The band of men headed out. He knew Drake's look. He was set on a fixed course.

∞

The executioner was on his way to the city for provisions. He and his wife, saved by love, had been living joyfully in their small village for the past few years. He had purchased a plot of land on which they grew fruits and vegetables. They always talked of Darren and of his kindness, which had brought them together. They were eternally grateful to him. These thoughts and others were running though his mind as he passed through the dark forest. I should pay a visit to Darren and his wife, he thought. He would be glad to see Darren.

∞

"Drake, you don't have to do this," said Darren as they neared the end of the dark forest. Drake did not answer; he just continued to look out in the distance. His two helpers were ever quiet too.

"I should have told you what really happened," said Darren quietly. "I simply thought you could not handle it."

"And you were right," replied Drake calmly. "I would have hanged you with her on the same day."

"Are you angry because you loved her or because she is not one of your...companions?" asked Darren straightforwardly. "You have many girlfriends. Why did you want her?"

Drake turned his look away from Darren.

"She was something different, something that I really never had. A mystery, a beauty, an unobtainable woman. To have her would be a supreme achievement. For the first time in my life I wanted a woman for love. But she always told me we were not a match." He paused for a few seconds. "Believe it or not, she said she is waiting for the right one – the one that when she sees him, she'll melt into his arms and they will finally be together. She did not know what she was talking about." He added bitterly.

"But Drake, she did know what she was talking about. When we saw each other we knew that we were destined for each other. We belonged to each other, from generations in the past. She simply did not want you as her husband. It was her free choice."

Darren simply had to say it. He hoped that Drake would understand the love between Janis and himself. Drake looked calm and Darren thought he had assuaged his anger, but within seconds Drake turned to him with a scarlet face.

"She did not know what she was talking about! I could offer her much more than you and eventually she would realize it and love me. You blinded her with your doctor nonsense and she fell for you because of that."

"But Drake, look at us now..." objected Darren, but Drake turned his head away.

"You should be punished for what you have done to me – and with all severity."

Darren knew the way Drake thought. In Drake's eyes there is only one punishment for such a crime – death.

∞

He saw a group of riders at a distance. The executioner squinted his eyes but could not discern who they were. Oh well, he thought, I am going that way anyway. I'll meet them when I get closer. He continued to ride towards them.

∞

"I am not going to kill you personally," Drake stated. "You will die by nature."

Darren looked at him without comprehending what he was saying.

"Drake, I am asking you to think again. As your friend..."

"You are not my friend anymore," interjected Drake. "You took the most beautiful thing from me...I could have had her...She would have loved me after a while."

"Drake, can't you see what you are saying?" Darren almost screamed at him. "You want her to get used to you? To accept you because you are forcing yourself on her? She does not love you. She never did and never could. You have to accept that." Darren was shaking from the emotions that ran through him. "Don't you see she has the right to love whom she wants? You will find your true love one day. She found love and so did I."

Drake was unaffected.

"You will be left in the lion's valley, down below," he said, nodding towards a steep path. "No one can survive there. It is the home of many wild lions. No one dares go there. You will be bound and placed at their gathering place. Soon enough, they'll smell and find you. You will have plenty of time to think about what you have done."

"But she never loved you."

"It does not matter, she would have eventually fallen in love with me, even if it had been forced. We eventually recognize the people who are good to us and then we love them. That's how it is with our parents, siblings and husbands. Eventually we develop love."

"Drake, she is pregnant..." Darren tried once more to reach Drake's soul.

Drake looked at him briefly, then nodded.

"Prepare him," he said to one of his men. It was early afternoon and the sun already started its way down towards the horizon.

Darren did not say a word. He looked at Drake with great disbelief. Then he looked at the sun that was going down and realized that this was probably the last sunset he would see.

∞

They took Darren down the path into the rocky valley. There were only a few trees and bushes here and there, but magnificent large rocks lay randomly as though heaved about by an immense force. The path soon became flat and narrow. They took Darren to a large spot where there were no rocks and pushed him to the ground. "We have to get in and out quickly," explained Drake to Darren. "Otherwise the lions will come for us too." He paused for a few seconds and looked around. "There are many lions in this place, perhaps scores of them. I use the place only for special cases."

"I hope that you'll be happy with your decision," Darren said, trying a different approach that would play upon Drake's conscience. He looked straight into Drake's eyes. "You really think I deserve this? Look into your heart, Drake, and tell me that I deserve to die like this...and I'll accept it like a man."

Drake seemed affected for a moment but then Darren could see his anger taking over again. His eyes became narrow, his lips curled down and his face grimaced. Darren lost hope. Drake may regret this tomorrow, but it will be too late for him. He closed his eyes and released a long sigh. I have to accept this, he thought and turned his face away. He and Drake did not speak anymore. The group of men left back up the path. It would be dark soon and the lions would hunt for dinner.

∞

The executioner stopped and waited at a distance as he watched a man being tied up. I am alone and no match for all of them. And maybe this man has done wrong. The group took the man and walked him towards an unknown place. The executioner debated what to do. His instincts told him to be careful so he decided to follow the men for a while. They soon vanished on a path towards the canyon. The executioner was familiar with this canyon but had never entered it. He knew that there is only one way in and out. They will have to come out shortly, he thought. I'll just wait here.

The sun was halfway towards the horizon as the men rode out of the canyon.

The executioner noticed that one was missing. Is it the man who was tied? Did they kill him and leave him in the canyon? Did they take him to somewhere? He did not know what to think. He decided to approach the men. Suddenly they urged their horses on to a gallop. He did the same.

∞

Darren lay on the ground. The ropes were tight and hurt badly. The sun had already turned orange as it slowly made its way down towards the rocky horizon. Soon the day would be over and the night would start. He never thought his life would end like this...but then again, who does? When it comes, it's all too often unexpected. The thought of never seeing his child brought tears to his eyes. He yearned to see Janis. He would give anything to be in her arms for just one moment. He shouted her name and the canyon walls echoed her name until fading away. Darren wondered how long until the lions came. He thought again of Janis. She will have to live alone for a long time, probably the rest of her life. He had a feeling that she would never remarry. But it was all imponderable. He closed his eyes and pressed an ear to the ground. He could not hear anything.

Janis was right – he should have never left home.

∞

The young lion woke from his nap. The entire pack had been sleeping almost all day. They had caught a large deer in the early morning and after the feast they lay in the warm sun until all fell asleep. The young lion sniffed the air. He smelled something different. It wasn't another deer; it was some new form of prey. If he found it first, his instincts told him, he'd have the best portion. Sniffing the air more, he went on his way to find it.

∞

Darren lost hope. He tried to cut the ropes by rubbing them against rocks, but the ropes were too strong. He only exhausted himself. Worse, he cut himself and was now bleeding. He lay on his back to reduce the scent of his blood that was doubtlessly wafting through the valley. Maybe someone will happen by. I could call out...but that would likely only attract predators. I am going to die. His medical mind wondered how death will feel. He never imagined being killed by an animal. He had treated people injured by wild beasts. The wounds were hideous. Most victims soon died; some managed to live, though severely maimed. He felt something that, amazingly, he had not felt until then – fear.

He heard a soft sound behind him. He made an effort to roll backwards, but as he did so, he froze. He found himself looking straight into the eyes of a large lion only a few feet away. Darren could tell he was young. His main nobly surrounded his large head and his orange-brown eyes looked directly into his. He radiated youth and stamina. Oddly, the lion struck him as quite beautiful. The lion was surprised by Darren's roll and stared back inquisitively. Darren's fear somehow vanished. So, are you the lion that is going to kill me? You're such a handsome animal. A small lizard darted before Darren, breaking the moment. The lion opened his gaping maw and roared, though mildly. Darren instinctively moved backwards. He is a lion, and I am his prey.

∞

The young lion approached. Was it already dead? Sometimes lions found dead humans in the valley – easy prey. He walked slowly without making a sound. As he got closer, he crouched down and continued slowly, ready to attack. Suddenly the man rolled back and looked straight at him. The lion immediately halted. The human looked at him without any trace of the fear found in prey. The lion felt something from the human. His instincts did not allow reflection but he suddenly lost his urge to hunt. The lion sat and looked at him. Lions, like many mammals, have the uncanny ability to sense feelings and emotions in humans and other animals. A few long minutes passed and he comprehended what he sensed from the human. The lion sensed deep sadness.

∞

Darren was profoundly sad. Not because he was about to die or for any other reason. He was sad because he would never see Janis again. While he looked at the lion he realized this would be the site and time of his death. In a way, it is noble, he thought. But nothing could assuage his deep sadness. He turned his look from the lion, hoping that he'd simply pounce on him and end it. He said his goodbyes to Janis and his unborn child in his heart and prepared for imminent death. For the first time since he was brought to this place, he was ready to die. He lay there for a while with his eyes closed, waiting for the pain. But it refused to arrive.

∞

He felt a wet tongue across his face. He turned and felt it again. Darren blinked his eyes in surprise. The huge lion was gently licking him. Darren instinctively talked softly to him, which the lion seemed to enjoy. "Do you feel my pain?" he quietly asked the lion. "Or maybe you simply are not hungry." He tried to explain the experience in the logical manner with which he approached medicine. The lion simply sat there and looked at him. Sometimes he licked his paws and fur. Maybe this lion can be trained, Darren thought. "I wish I could touch you," said Darren, "but my hands are bound. All I can do is lie here and talk to you." The lion seemed to be engaged. "You see, I miss my wife..."

I got someone to listen to me. I'll tell it what happened in my life. "I was lonely for many years until a few years ago when I was called to Drake's city..." Darren narrated to the lion the tragic chain of events and in doing so, tears came to his eyes. As his eyes filled with tears, the lion licked his face as though he felt and maybe even empathized with Darren's sadness. He closed his eyes momentarily. He started to like the lion's licks.

∞

Affected by the man's emotions, the lion wanted to comfort him. So he followed his instincts and licked the man with a sentiment innate in his species and others – love. He remembered moments when his mother, the senior lioness in his pack, licked him when he felt fear or hunger. Her attention comforted him and made him feel better. From an unknowable reason, this man was sad and he wanted to do what every good friend does – give love and comfort. The man seemed to communicate with him in return, and he liked the soothing resonance in his voice.

∞

Darren continued with his story. "I wish Janis was here now. Well, maybe not when I am about to be eaten. But you understand..." Darren found himself laughing. "Look at me. I am talking to you – a lion that is about to eat me." The lion looked at him and started to lick his paws. "What's going to happen now, my friend? Are you going to eat me eventually?" A thought came to his mind. "Maybe he is just playing with his prey..." Darren quickly overruled this idea. He sensed kindness in the lion. He was sure it was there. Darren was exhausted. His fear, emotions and exertions had worn him down. He closed his eyes. The lion licked his face from time to time. Comforted and safe, he fell asleep.

∞

The lion felt as though he were protecting his cub. The lion sniffed the air and sensed the approach of his pack. The lionesses were nearing their prey. The lion sensed danger. The pack will not behave like him. They are hungry. They are looking for food. The man had to get away. He started to nudge the sleeping man. You have to leave. There are hungry lions coming.

∞

"What?" asked Darren. "Do you want me to flee? I can't, my friend. I am tied up. See my hands and legs?" Darren moved his arms and legs as much as he could to show the lion, but the lion did not seem to understand. "If you could just talk and understand me." The lion continued to push Darren and even managed to roll him over. The lion's efforts elicited an emotional response in Darren. "Why do you do this, my friend? Are you trying to release me? I do not think you can." The lion sniffed the air and then Darren understood. Others are coming. Darren felt affection, perhaps even love for the great lion. "I understand, the others are coming and you are telling me to go. I am sorry, big friend, but I simply can't." Darren saw concern and dismay in the lion's face.

Darren talked calmly to the lion. "It's alright, my friend. You did your best." Then he looked at the lion and with his open hand he caressed his tail. The lion calmed and they shred an empathic moment.

∞

You must flee! the lion tried to tell the man. Soon the rest of the pack will be here. He would not be able to save him from the others; they are too many. He urgently pushed him back and forth but without much success. The man seemed unable to rise up and just continued to lie on the ground. The man talked to him and caressed his tail. This calmed the big lion and he sat down near him, sniffing the air. Whatever happened, he would sit here near his friend. He would protect him.

∞

Darren thought he had earned a special death. Not every day a lion becomes your best friend and tries to protect you. He lay there a while, looking at his new friend. "Thank you for being with me during my last hours." The lion looked anxious as he sniffed the air continuously. "I guess the rest of the pack is coming." He took a deep breath to prepare for the idea. The lion stopped sniffing and now was looking at him. Darren found a solution.

"You will have to kill me, my friend." His eyes filled with tears. "I will miss you also, my friend, but this is the best solution. If all the other lions come, they will devour me alive. You have to kill me quickly...it will save me a lot of pain. Do you understand me?" The lion looked straight at him. "All you have to do is use your powerful jaws to break my neck. I'll die instantly." He was weary from all of it. What is it with me that I expect the lion to understand me, he thought in his exhaustion. It does not matter anymore...I am too tired...I'll wait here and the lions will kill me soon.

He rolled backwards and lay his head on the lion's tail. The lion gently pawed his head then left his paw on Darren's head. Darren looked into the lion's eyes. Was it his imagination or had the lion understood him?

∞

Man and lion communicated again. It seemed the human had become very tired. The pack was on its way and would be upon them shortly. He would not be able to protect the man. The lion felt a face warming his tail and moved his paw to touch him. The man had tired of fighting for his life. He had given up. Sadness. Slowly the lion comprehended what had to be done.

∞

Darren could hear the occasional roars getting nearer. "Your pack is arriving now, my friend. There isn't much time," he said gently to the lion. "I'll always remember you, my big friend. You were with me during my last moments. You have to help me now." Darren looked straight into the lion's eyes and rolled on his back. "Do it quickly...please." The lion seemed to understand. The lion stood up and started to pace nervously around Darren. "Goodbye, Janis. I am happy that I found you...and sad to leave you," Darren mumbled. "I know we'll meet again my love... I am so tired...so tired." He closed his eyes.

∞

I'll wait until he is near sleep and then I'll strike. I'll go for the neck – a fast kill. The human will not feel much pain. The lion was sad but knew that this was the best course for his new friend. He heard the pack gathering around them.

∞

Darren heard a mighty roar and instinctively opened his eyes. The lion was racing towards him. "Thank you, my friend," he said with his last breath. I love you Janis... The lion's roar and his own fear were too much for him. His heart stopped beating as the lion closed his jaws around his neck with great precision. Darren opened his eyes in surprise, but could not see anything anymore.

∞

Janis was about to prepare a small dinner for herself. She hated to eat alone and hoped that Darren would return by tomorrow. Every once in a while she stopped for a few seconds and touched her belly. She did it even more often today when she knew that Darren would not be back for the night. It was good to know that she had little Darren inside her to comfort her.

Shortly after dinner she felt great anxiety. She had to hold on to the table in order not to fall. Her entire being felt something horrible had happened. She tried to explain to herself that it's probably due to the pregnancy but her body and soul would not accept her mind's explanation. She was out of breath and gasped for air. Her hands shook and her heart raced. She was covered with cold sweat. She ran outside and looked at the trees, at the surrounding mountains, and at the skies, trying to calm down. Eventually she could not hold herself anymore and burst into tears, screaming into the night air, "Darren!"

∞

The executioner followed the band of men until they reached the city. There, they stopped at the inn, and he followed them inside. As he identified the party, he felt fear grip him. It was Drake. A disturbing thought overcame him. He now was almost sure that he recognized the man that they had bound.

∞

Drake entered his chamber and sat on his bed, exhausted from the day's events. He had a dark feeling all the way back home and hoped to forget it in the inn, but without success. What have I done? How could I do something like this? Darren and Ruben were my close friends... An answer came from his anger. They betrayed you. They lied to you. They took your true love. You did the right thing.

Drake tried to relax. He took a long bath, ate a large dinner and even drank an entire decanter of wine. Nothing helped. Eventually he gave up and sat on his balcony, looking at the clear skies. He was almost in a depression.

∞

A powerful hand grabbed Drake from behind and covered his mouth. He gasped for air but could get only a small amount. Drake was a strong man and tried to free himself, but could not do so. He struggled then felt a blow to his head and everything turned dark.

Drake slowly woke up. He could hear noises and then started to see indistinct images. He tried to move and discovered that his hands were tied behind his back. "Who was the man you took to the canyon?" demanded a voice from behind. When the man came in front of Drake, he tried to identify him in the dim light.

"You do not recognize me?" he asked.

"Not, but I know your voice. We met before..."

"Do you recognize me now?" the man got closer.

Drake looked at him, trying to concentrate. Then he remembered and his blood ran cold.

"You are the executioner. You vanished several years ago."

"Indeed," replied the executioner "Now again, who was the man you took into the canyon?"

"Why do you want to know?" asked Drake, though he knew the answer. "You performed an execution on a witch about three years ago, did you not?" The executioner did not answer. "You saved her life...according to Darren's request. Then they left secretly, as did you shortly thereafter. You thought that I'd never discover." Drake looked straight into the place where he estimated the executioner's eyes were. It was too dark to see details. Drake's anger took over. "But I found them. One of my men reported to me on Darren and his wife. For a while I did not want to believe so I sent a spy. He confirmed everything." Drake paused for a few seconds. "Then I went to see for myself. I pretended to be a sick old man and she tried to help me. I found them." Drake seemed to be happy in his success to break the case.

"Did she try to help you?" asked the executioner quietly.

"Yes," answered Drake, "but she..."

"Did Darren always help you?" interrupted the executioner.

Drake was confused, "Yes, but I..."

"Was he always at your service and willing to give you anything he had?" continued the executioner sternly.

Drake was silent now.

"Was he your friend...someone who cared for you?"

Drake looked at the floor.

"He found his love, the love that he never had. You have everything you want; he was living a life of a doctor who helped people. He did only good."

"He stole her from me...he lied to me!" exclaimed Drake.

"Only because he knew how you would react if he told you. He knew that you would not be able to control your jealousy."

He paused for a moment and looked at Drake. He looked broken. The executioner untied him.

"I believe that you understood enough of what you have done," said the executioner. "See," he continued, "Darren knew me for many years and saw how lonely I was. He also knew that a person like me is condemned to live without love, but he always pondered how to help me. One day he introduced me to a beautiful woman."

Drake was transfixed.

"And we looked at each other and knew from the first look that we were meant for each other." He paused and looked at Drake. "Can you understand that? We just knew it from first look. It does not happen to many people. Did it ever happen to you?"

Drake turned his look to the clear night skies. "Never..."

"Did it happen to you when you saw the witch?"

Drake did not answer. The executioner thought he saw Drake's eyes getting wet.

"It happened to Darren and Janis. The first moment they saw each other they felt they were reuniting from past lives – the ultimate form of love. It overpowered everything."

The executioner became quiet, then released a long sigh.

"Once more – who was the man you took to the canyon?" He did not even look at Drake. He already knew the answer.

∞

They rode through the night, finding their way by the moon and stars. Drake wanted to get to the canyon posthaste. "Maybe we can still save him," he said with tears in his eyes, now obsessed with saving Darren. They arrived at first light and slowly descended the path to the bald spot where they had left Darren. He wasn't there.

"Are you sure this is the place?" asked the executioner.

"Yes, I'm quite sure. Maybe he managed to escape." The executioner heard hope in his voice.

"I don't think so," said the executioner solemnly.

"What? Did you see something?" Drake walked quickly to where the executioner stood. There were lengths of thick rope, obviously chewed upon by a large animal, and soaked with blood. Drake fell to his knees. He held the rope and trembled.

"It can't be... Maybe he managed to run away. We do not know for sure..." His voice cracked. He held the bloody rope to his chest and cried like a child.

The executioner did not say a word as he mounted his horse. "You know, when I came to your chamber last night, I thought that I'd perform one last execution – this time for the right reason. With all the executions that I've done in my life, I never knew if the convicted was truly guilty. I was just the executioner. My job was not to know about the crime, only to execute. With you I thought that it would be my last execution...and a justified one. You destroyed a perfect love, two good-hearted people who were kind to their fellow villagers...and to you personally. And why? Because you could not control your jealousy and anger." Drake could find no words.

"I will not execute you, Drake." He looked at him without any emotion. "When I married my wife I swore not to kill anymore. My hands had enough blood on them and I determined to do only good, hoping to earn mercy for my soul when my turn comes. I was set to break my vow but I am glad that we came here. You are on your own now. You have to live with what you have done." He released another long sigh.

"I have to bring the ill tidings to Darren's wife now."

He looked one more time at Drake and turned his horse around. Drake is already punished. There is nothing else for him to do here. The executioner had a difficult mission now. He took a deep breath and urged his horse on. It was still early morning. If he rode fast, he'd reach Darren's dwelling by evening.

∞

Drake sat helplessly on the ground, staring upward. I killed Darren, he thought. As he began to fully comprehend Darren's friendship, he felt terribly alone. Darren supported him in hard times and illnesses. He could rely on Darren, and Darren never asked for anything in return. Tears streamed down his face. I just killed the only family I had.

∞

The lioness was on her morning hunt when she smelled prey. She signaled to the other lionesses and they all quickly followed her.

∞

Drake's horse neighed nervously, but he did not care why. After more warnings, the horse raced into the canyon without knowing he was heading towards death. Drake heard roars nearby but remained heedless, oblivious to the world. He did not move when the pride of lions attacked and tore open his horse's neck. He did not move when a lioness appeared in front of him and slowly approached him. He did not even move when the lioness sprang on him, ripping open his shoulders. Shortly thereafter the other lionesses joined the feast. They dragged the prey back to their cubs. It was morning and there were many hungry cubs in the canyon.

∞

Janis knew something was wrong. Since last night she felt something had happened to Darren, but she hoped that it stemmed from the emotional changes of pregnancy. She hardly slept. Early in the morning she went to tend to her garden, which always relaxed her. This morning she was working a row of beautiful red roses, which were in bloom and offering their scent to the world. But even their delightful scent could not rid her of dread and physical pain. She walked between the tall flowers and bowed to better enjoy the blossoms. Her entire being felt looming disaster and she started to cry. She raised her head towards the skies. She could not control herself anymore and screamed towards the skies with al of her powers, "Darren..." Tears streamed from her eyes as she fell on her knees and trembled.

A powerful arm picked her up. For a second she stood in disbelief. "Darren?" she mumbled. The executioner looked at her wordlessly. She could read the message as though written on his face. She saw his red eyes, the dark circles under them, and his world-weary face. She held his hand and they slowly walked towards the bench under a large sycamore tree. They sat there for a while. "Are you hungry...thirsty?" Janis asked after a while, trying to smile somewhat.

He just shook his head.

"I arrived too late..." he broke into tears.

She hugged him as he cried like a child.

Now she was prepared. "What's happened?"

The executioner finally found words. "Drake ambushed him and Ruben. I found Ruben's body in the field. They just killed him and left him there." He moved his head in disbelief. "He was a good man."

"Yes..." said Janis quietly.

"He was not involved in the plan. Drake probably told him to bring Darren, like so many times before. He had no clue."

"They took Darren to a canyon. Drake took me there later. We thought that we might be able to save him, but... All we found was the rope he was tied with...covered in blood."

"Drake?" Janis asked without understanding.

"I thought I'd make him my last execution but I decided not to." He paused and looked at Janis's face. Janis listened quietly.

"He realized he had acted in jealousy and anger," continued the executioner. "I left him in the canyon. As I rode off I could hear lions coming for him."

His head hung low and she gently caressed it. They sat there for a while quietly mourning their loss.

"Come in. I'll make you something to eat and drink. You've had a long ride," Janis invited.

"What are you going to do?" he asked. "We do not have much but we will happily share all we have."

Janis managed to smile.

"Thank you, good friend. I'll rest here for a while and then see. I am moved by your kind offer." She made him dinner and provided him with food and drink for the road.

"Please consider staying with us," he reminded. He could not talk much.

Janis looked at him with strangely cheerful eyes. "Thanks for letting me know." She watched him for a while until he disappeared near the forest. Then she slowly went back to the house and lay on the bed. She touched the blanket. She could smell Darren. She closed her eyes and let her imagination take her away. They were walking together as the sun rose, passionately making love in nature and holding hands, forever. She did not want these dreams to end. Tears rolled down her cheeks uncontrollably. Her life seemed gone. Only a void was left – one that would never be filled. She looked at the night skies through the small window and thought she was ready to die.

A sharp pain brought her back to the present. She felt a warm sticky liquid on her legs. She felt under her dress and found blood. She stood up and felt a sharp pain shoot through her back. She screamed in agony. She had just lost Darren's baby.

∞

The executioner and his wife prepared their horses. They were on their way to visit Janis. The wife thought she should not be alone. If she does not want to come to stay with them, they will stay with her for a while, at least for some time.

∞

Janis could not sleep. Her eyes stayed open, staring at the ceiling. As a young girl she ran carefree in the fields of her family's lands. She smiled from time to time but also got angry when a bad memory came to her. She loved her childhood, for she was blessed with a happy family that worked the land as farmers. She and her sister used to roam about their fields and sometimes even beyond it. She frowned as she remembered how strangers showed up one day and cruelly killed her parents as she and her sister hid. Hard times followed as they were homeless and had to find their way. They wandered from village to village, working any job, until one day reaching the small farm of an old farmer.

Starving and on the verge of despair, they asked to work his farm in exchange for room and board. He took them in and in time treated them as his daughters. They learned his wife and children had perished from a fever a few years ago, and he carried on alone. Soon they became a family and life was good. Her sister found her love in the next village, got married and left the farm. Janis met a woman in the village who taught her magic and sorcery. The old farmer asked her many times not to visit this woman. "She is no good," he used to say. But she was attracted to her arts. She secretly visited her and learned from her. She had a good and evil side. She placed a curse on a man who once hurt her. Her face became dark and her eyes turned narrow while her lips closed in determination. Janis felt fear but never asked what happened to the man. One day the old farmer who had become their father died, and she remained alone. The next day she visited her mentor but she was not there. Villagers informed her that she had been accused of witchcraft and put to death.

Some of the villagers accused Janis of witchcraft as well and took her to the city, where Drake saw her. He was immediately smitten by her. She thought him a shallow man whose life was based solely on power. He was willing to give anything to have her, but she rebuffed him. While imprisoned, she thought of relenting and having a life of comfort. She could easily manipulate Drake, but she did not want him. She waited for the one, and had to find him. She knew she was getting older but her heart refused to give up. She would meet him, the one she already knows, the one she knew long ago in a past life. She learned about past lives from the sorceress and came to believe she had had a past love. "You, my dear, are one part of two star-crossed lovers," the sorceress told her as she listened in fascination. "Your man and you are meant to be. It is a rare love – the strongest. But this type of love is accompanied by tragedy and heartbreak that pass across generations."

She never understood until Darren entered her chamber and she felt her soul recognize him. "He is the one," her spirit told her. They found themselves in each other's arms. She smiled and closed her eyes. The world ceased to exist. There was only Darren and her. Then her face crumbled as she remembered how things ended. She hated the world. She hated Drake, his castle, and the people who helped him. She remembered the horrible crowd as she dropped from the gallows. Her eyes got dark. "I will avenge my love." She looked outside. The first beams of light were appearing. "It will be a beautiful day...but not for the world."

∞

The moonlight made Janis appear menacing, even evil. She sat on the ground near a small campfire and stared into it with total concentration. That day started with preparation for the night ceremony – the same ceremony her mentor had performed on the man of uncertain fate. She looked at the full moon and whispered spells into the night air. She threw powder into the fire, eliciting bright green flames to shoot high into the air. Her eyes were closed and large beads of sweat appeared on her forehead. She knew that she was doing wrong, but her soul was in such pain that nothing mattered anymore.

A bright blue flash appeared in the center of the campfire. She looked on with great surprise as she did not think she could recreate the ceremony. She did not know exactly what would happen or to whom, nor did she care. The fire suddenly diminished. Within seconds it was gone and even the coals were no longer red. A ponderous cloud moved across the bright moon and darkness covered everything. The fire ran away from something. What could frighten fire? She felt great fear.

"What have I done?"

∞

A drunkard meandered through the city's streets, bumping into walls from time to time. It was after midnight and he had just left a boisterous tavern. He had had a few drinks, maybe one too many, and could not remember where he lived. He tried to ask people along the street, but they just laughed at him, called him a drunk and told him to go home. That's exactly what he was looking to do – go home. Where can it be? Eventually he decided to rest awhile and sat near the entrance to another tavern. He felt an itch on the back of his neck. He sent his hand there and was surprised to find small lumps. He had suffered for the past few days from terrible headaches and nausea, and had sought relief in a tavern and the brewed remedies therein. The small lumps were hard and quite painful. As puzzling as the lumps were, he soon fell asleep.

"Go home!" he heard as someone shook him. "It's morning... go home," said the tavern owner, helping the old sot to his feet. "Thank you...I will," he mumbled and walked away to his small room on the other side of the city. How did I arrive here? he thought as he slowly dragged himself home. He had a terrible headache and started to feel the familiar nausea. When he arrived home, he took a bath, hoping it would help the pain. As he entered the bath, he noticed a pain under his armpits. He touched the areas and felt large lumps. He almost screamed in pain. They were huge, almost the size of small apples. What is happening to me?

The doctor had not seen such lumps before. He thought them some sort of abscess and gave him herbs to make tea with. The next morning he woke up with severe pain in his groin. He decided to stay home, rest and drink the herbal tea. The following morning his neighbor heard loud screams. He rushed to the man's home and found him thrashing on the floor. He had huge black lumps on his neck, some of which had burst open, oozing pus and blood. When the doctor arrived, he found huge lumps on the man's inner thighs, under his armpits and on his neck. The doctor sent for other doctors to examine the man and his mysterious malady. The man had blood in his urine and stool, and blood was accumulating under his skin, causing black spots.

The stench of the pus and blood was horrible. Nothing they put on his lumps reduced them. The next day they had opened and black blood was coming out. In the afternoon the man developed a high fever and suffered frequent convulsions. The doctors gave up all efforts to save the man and simply watched his condition. It was clear that he was going to die soon. The next day the man lost conscious. Towards evening he stopped breathing.

The first doctor looked at the man's face. "He has found peace, at last. I hope his malady does not spread." His colleagues looked at him with visible fear. He looked at them, nodded his head and added: "If it does, it will be the greatest disaster that we ever experienced..."

The doctor did not know how close to the truth he was.

∞

Janis heard of an outbreak of an unknown, deadly disease in Hartford, and went there. Dressed in a dark gown and with her head covered, she rode into the city late in the day. People were pulling carts filled with bodies all around her. There was a horrible stench in the air and she had to cover her mouth and nose with the hood. People looked scared and hardly spoke with each other. Everyone rushed home and soon the streets were almost empty. A hand grabbed her. "Water...please...I haven't drunk water for days now..." A vagrant grabbed her hand as he fell to the ground. His face was covered with dark spots that looked like internal pustules. He was filthy and covered with some sort of dust. His eyes showed great pain. "Please...I am very thirsty," he cried.

Janis gave him one of her water flasks and he drank from it noisily.

"What happened?" asked Janis. She could hardly hide her revulsion.

"I have the plague...but I do not really care..." replied the man, smiling somewhat and revealing rows of rotten teeth. "I have no reason to live," he continued. "I have no family or friends, but I feel sorry for the rest of the people. Everyone seems to get this black death," he said quietly. "Everyone in the city is dying."

"What is it? How did it start?" asked Janis as she regarded him carefully. "Where did it come from?"

"No one really knows," answered the man, pulling his shoulders. "I heard they think it came from across the sea, but no one knows for sure. Since it started a few weeks ago, everyone that gets it, dies." He rolled his eyes. "Myself, I got used to the pain. Here... look." He turned his neck to her. She could see two black lumps that were beginning to ooze pus. It was disgusting. The stench became stronger. "See? I am going to die in the next few days. But I do not care. What's the reason to live for me anyway?" The man looked at her without any hope.

Janis looked at him and felt sudden pain. Is it my curse that brought this disease? She tried to look closer at the stranger's face in order to discern more details about the disease but without success. "Here is some food," she said as she gave him some of the bread from her saddlebag. His eyes brightened and he quickly grabbed the piece of bread and bit in.

"Thank you, my lady," he said with a happy look on his ravaged face.

"You're welcome," she answered – and it made her feel better. This bread is his entire world. She felt like a boulder was lying on her stomach. In a moment of anger, she had brought this plague on everyone.

"Farewell," she said to the man and then prepared to leave as he started to cough violently.

"No need to worry..." he told her between his bark-like coughs. "This happened to me many times for the past few days, I am used..." His words were ended by a fit of uncontrollable hacking. The man spat up blood this time. Janis gave him her scarf.

"I am alright, dear lady, really..." Janis tried to give him some water but nothing helped. The man gasped for air. "I can't... breathe." He choked and fell, holding his neck.

Janis turned him to the side, trying to help him breathe. His eyes bulged and his whole body shook as he gasped for air. After a few desperate minutes he managed to breathe though still with considerable difficulty. She touched his face as he slowly calmed.

"I get this often," he said quietly. "Just never that strong."

"You are alright now," Janis said with a faint smile.

"Yes..." he found the power to smile, too.

"You are burning though. You have a high fever. Please take these herbs, boil them and make yourself this medicine. You have to drink it every few hours until your fever breaks."

He sneezed loudly.

"Apologies, my lady."

"Get better." She kissed his forehead.

The man did not say a word. He just looked at her, amazed that someone cared about him. "Thank you." He continued to mumble as she mounted her horse and continued into the city. Wherever she went, she could see people coughing, crying and screaming in pain. She felt fear slowly crawling up her back. She passed near Drake's castle. Most of it was dark and there were no sounds. It looked like no one lived there anymore.

She directed her horse towards the poor people's quarters. The visions were horrific. Among the waste in the streets lay many sick people. They vomited, screamed in pain and called for help. Few doctors would come here and those that did had no medicine that helped. The dim light from street lamps created eerie shadows of people dragging themselves along the narrow streets. A nightmare, thought Janis as she rushed to exit the city. She wanted to go home. Darren, where are you? cried her soul.

She searched for the sick man she had just left and soon noticed a crumpled form near the wall. It was him. She dismounted and found a small candle burning near him. As she got closer she almost screamed. He lay there in a grotesque position of death. His face was twisted into a horrible look, either from coughing fits or laughing at the absurdity all around him.

In his hand she saw the bread that she had earlier given him. The lumps on his body had putrefied so badly that she had to cover her nose. She turned him on his back and noticed his entire skin was covered with black spots, many of which were open and bleeding. His clothes were covered with vomit. She screamed and backed off when a large rat crawled from underneath the man and quickly vanished down the street. Her entire being felt awful. She could not get rid of the thought that her ritual had brought this on the city. It can't be... This is too serious for a human to have wrought. No sorcery could unleash this into the world. The Black Death had hit Hartford with all of its power.

∞

Janis planted more flowers. She and Darren loved to have fresh flowers in their home. It always gave them a sense of celebration of their love. Almost every night, they dined as though it were their first night together, or as though they knew their time together was limited and would someday end. Her tears watered the fresh morning soil. The sun was warm but all of a sudden she felt chills and then a strange itch under her armpits. She found small lumps. Then she sat on the ground, looked at the beautiful horizon and breathed in the scents of a thousand blossoms. She took a deep breath and relaxed with nature. She wanted to enjoy every moment of nature. Although she heard that a few people survived this disease, she knew that soon everything would change. She was about to face the Black Death.

She remembered the old man in the city with the hideous lumps. Hers were smaller, at least for now. She must have gotten the plague from him or maybe it was carried in the air. How ironic. I probably brought this disease into the world and now I am going to die from it. Is this my punishment? She took another deep breath and sat there quietly. The realization brought a small smile to her face. I am going to join Darren soon.

Within a day she had a high fever and the lumps under her armpits had grown markedly. She prepared herbal tea to reduce the fever and ease the pain. The lumps hurt like no other pain she had experienced before. Maybe a few days left? The Black Death has come to take me, she thought as she was arranged the house for the last time. Wanting to preserve their memory, she placed her and Darren's belongings side by side. The next morning she worked the field, though knowing it would soon grow wild. She watered the plants of the garden and meticulously removed pests. During the day she started to vomit and suffered terrible headaches. She discovered a few more lumps on her neck. That night, her entire body hurt severely and she could not stop coughing. She drank a strong concoction to help with the cough and it seemed to help, but the high fever remained.

The next morning she did not have the strength to get out of her bed. The overnight struggle weakened her and she could not eat anything. Her powers were leaving her rapidly. Her entire body was covered with black spots. Some of them opened and pus flowed from them. She was unable to wash herself anymore and she smelled bad. Towards the evening she tried to reach her teapot but could not. She clutched a dozen or so flowers and fell on the floor. She knew that she would not last the night.

She lay on the floor helplessly. The fever caused her to sweat and her throat was very dry. Water, she thought and tried to crawl toward a pitcher. But it was high on the table, which was at the end of the world for her now. One of the big lumps on her neck burst and she felt it bleed. She closed her eyes and cried, for the last time. She cried for dying without dignity. She cried for not having Darren near her, to hold her then. She cried for letting Darren go to Drake.

Then she smiled at the ceiling as she remembered the past few years. These were the most pleasant years of my life. She thought of their talks, arguments, and childish behavior. She started to laugh but it hurt, so she simply smiled. Strange images from their past life passed in front of her eyes. She saw another couple in different times, yet it wasn't another couple. The couple was separated at some point due to death. She wondered if these were hallucinations from high fever or a glimpse at some other time and place no less real than hers. She closed her eyes and tried to sleep. Maybe I'll die during sleep and will never know about it.

Then she saw Darren.

"My love, please do not go..." she could hear herself saying to him. He came and pressed her to his heart.

"No worry, my love. I am not going anywhere." He then kissed her at length.

"But I am dying. What am I doing here?"

"I wanted to show you something, my love," said Darren with a mysterious smile. She saw images – beautiful images – flowing into billowing white and blue clouds.

"Look there... See? We were together before – long ago"

"How can..." started Janis, but she was too enthralled by the visions. Beneath them was a beautiful high cliff over a wild canyon, above which an eagle soared. Janis could see an old man lying near a grave. He laid his hand on the grave marker, looked at the skies and then closed his eyes.

"Who is this man?" she asked quietly.

"These are our souls, my love," said Darren with an illuminated smile. "We met many years ago..."

"How...how can it be?"

Darren kissed her and gently caressed her hair. She became lost in the feeling and closed her eyes. When she opened them she saw a little boy looking lovingly at a young woman. They watched each other from a distance. Janis could feel the love between the two.

"Who are they? Us again?"

Darren nodded.

"See, my love...we were lovers in the past and we will be so in the future."

Janis looked at him. He looked so good, she thought – exactly as she remembered him from their first meeting. Bright hazel eyes, straight brown hair, strong facial features, but most of all endless kindness and goodness shone from his face.

He softly looked at her, moving her hair to the sides of her face.

"We will be together again, my love, in a different time and different place." He smiled to her. "All you have to do is to remember. Remember you and I, together. That's all. You'll recognize us in our next meeting, even if it is many years in the future."

She could not talk. Tears ran from her eyes without control.

"But I do not want to say goodbye, Darren."

"You do not have to say goodbye. All you have to say is that you'll love me forever..."

Janis cried in anguish. "What am I going to do without you?"

"You will never be without me," he replied as he held her hand gently, then started to fade away. "You will never be without me..."

"No, no," she cried loudly, "do not leave me. Please no..."

"I never will, I am always with you..." It was all beyond her will, and Darren faded away. "You will never be without me..."

She woke up sweating and shaking, still lying on the floor. She knew she had cried in her sleep. Did I dream that or did Darren really visit me? She came to believe that Darren had indeed visited her. He wanted to tell her of their eternal love.

Although her body was extremely weak, her soul had found courage. "You did come to visit me, my love," she mumbled to herself. She tried again to move but could not. She lay on the floor and waited for the end. Her fever rose slowly and she sweated profusely. She arranged her dress and hair. I am going to look well when I go, she thought – and it almost made her laugh. Even in her last moments she wanted to be groomed.

Then she noticed a light. It is morning already. The thought flooded her with joy. I'd love to see the morning one more time. The light was bright and slowly started to fill the room. Yes, come on, beautiful sunshine. As the light grew brighter, she realized something. This is it, what a painless death...and beautiful! The light became brighter and covered her. "Darren, my love, I'll see you soon..." She closed her eyes. The light grew stronger until it encompassed all. Her hand lost its grip and released the dozen flowers she had picked a day earlier. They spread all over the floor, making a floral deathbed for her.

∞

The executioner and his wife found no one at home. He opened the door and was struck by a horrible stench. On the floor was Janis. She looked beautiful, in death as in life. The many flowers spread around her gave a dignified setting. "They could not live without each other..." said his wife quietly. The executioner did not say a word. He looked to the side to hide his tears. "What are we going to do?" he asked his wife. But in a moment he knew the right thing for Janis and Darren.

∞

They washed Janis and took her to the canyon. The executioner lay her gently on the rock where he had found the bonds that had held Darren. He and Janis would rest at the same place. The wife arranged Janis's hair and placed flowers around her. Then they left the canyon and wordlessly headed back to their home.

∞

The young lion picked up a scent. He yawned protractedly and started to walk lazily towards the canyon. The sun was already touching the horizon, sending its last light for the day. It was dinnertime and he'd be there first. The scent was familiar. It was the smell of his human friend. He carefully approached the rock. He noticed another human there. He smelled the human and determined it had no life. The body smelled foul; something was wrong with it. He wondered if this human was akin to his friend, and something told him they were. *I could not save my old friend, but I may be able to bring them together.*

He dragged the body to where his friend's remains were. The two belonged together. The young lion remained there for a while, as though honoring the two humans, then he slowly shook his big head and left the canyon just as he had entered it. According to the lion's comprehension, they would be there together, forever.

A strong evening wind blew through the canyon. Fresh blossoms and green leaves were cast about, covering the bodies and providing them a natural blanket. After a while they were completely covered. The sun had completely disappeared from the horizon and the night air immediately became cold. Janis and Darren were together in eternal peace.

Night Fell.

Morning Rose.

Andy Cooper was frightened. He had volunteered for the army a few weeks ago and was now receiving orders to go into battle. With him were a few hundred other soldiers who sat in the large amphitheater and listened carefully to the commanding general. The general did not have any intention to make things pretty. He described in gory detail the consequences of failure or being captured.

"We will attack the Indians at first light. At all cost, and I repeat, at all cost, do not get captured." He then recounted horrible stories of men captured and tortured to death. Andy could not even hear the tribe's name as he fought the intense fear inside. He had completed his cursory training a few weeks ago and was posted to this camp in the Nebraska Territory. Andy missed his home. A sheltered youth from Portland, Maine, Andy came from a family that owned a large tract of land surrounded by beautiful, expansive orchards. He and his brother were educated by private tutors as his family believed strongly in education. He could still remember his father say, "Education is everything. Disaster can take away all your land and money, but education will ever be yours, wherever you go." His father would make a serious face and raise his eyebrows. Of course, he never really listened to his father's lectures, but now, out on the frontier, he yearned to hear them once more, as they held the warmth and security of home. It was midmorning and the air was still chilly so he pulled up his hood. They were about to attack this Indian village and he did not even know the name of the tribe.

∞

Orenda was to have turned sixteen and attained independence. She had to earn it through a grueling ordeal of seven days isolation in the woods. She hunted her food, found her water and created shelter for the night. She roamed the woods for seven days to prove she was capable of surviving on her own.

The ceremony for Orenda was beautiful. The women dressed her in a lengthy skirt made from long leaves and they scented her with the puberty perfumes. She danced through the night to signal her availability, and drank a sweet concoction that made her dizzy. With this ceremony she became independent and permitted to choose a husband to create her own family with. Although Orenda was beautiful, she never had any boys approach her. Her aggressive, controlling and somewhat intimidating character caused her to become respected and admired but without romantic interest. A girl completing her independence ceremony usually had a boyfriend ready to join her but Orenda did not have anyone. Nor did she care, for she was used to be alone. All she wanted was her own tipi and own life. She was now the happiest girl in the tribe. She built her tipi, decorated it and prepared it for dwelling in. She lit a few candles and prepared for a quiet night. After dinner she lay on a blanket and looked at the stars above. She wondered if she would ever have a family of her own. She did not want a family unless it was with the right boy and not one chosen for her. She gave up to her exhaustion and fell asleep as the candles burned out. She never imagined that everything would change that night.

∞

Andy felt adrenaline coursing through him as his unit rushed into the village. They came with torches to throw in the tipis to cause panic. Pushed forward by an officer, he heard the villagers screaming all around him. The intent of the raid was to drive the Indians from the territory. Deep inside, Andy thought ill of the plan. He did not think the Indians would leave. It had been their land for generations and he knew they would fight forever to keep it. Some fellow soldiers agreed with him. Others said it was not their business to decide the matter and left it to the generals. Andy went into battle with a heavy heart.

The tipis were made of animal hides and sent thick smoke into the air when set afire. Women, children and animals ran in panic, desperately looking for safety. The soldiers rode through them mercilessly, their horses trampling over the less adroit and less fortunate. The Indians fought back with arrows and tomahawks and with a few firearms they had obtained. Andy remembered the commander's warning: Do not get captured by them. If you are, you are considered dead. Andy drove his horse on, but was careful not to trample children who were running around, screaming at the top of their lungs. After a while he could hear the bugle sound recall, signaling the close of battle. The mayhem is over. Let's get out of here.

A child ran into his path. Instinctively, Andy pulled his horse away from the child. The speedy horse lost his balance and fell on his side, crashing into a small tipi. Andy was abruptly thrown to the ground. The horse screamed in panic as an Indian brave mounted him and rode him into the soldiers, shouting loudly and waving his tomahawk. Andy tried to stand up, still confused from the hard fall. His head hurt and he could not feel his left arm. He assumed he had broken it in the fall. I have to rejoin my troop, he thought as he saw the soldiers leaving the village. He tried to run but his right leg betrayed him and he fell to the ground. He touched his right leg and found it all bloody. He tried to get as far away as he could. He noticed something to his left. He wheeled his pistol towards the movement but was too late. A brave struck him on his head. Andy blacked out immediately and fell onto a tipi, breaking the poles and sending it to the ground.

∞

Orenda had been violently awakened earlier by loud screams and gunshots. As she peeked from her tent she saw the chaos. Many of the tipis were on fire and her fellow villagers were fleeing in panic. She would not give in without a fight and immediately looked for a weapon. She remembered seeing friends taken away after other attacks and knew the brutality of men towards women. She determined not to be captured. She took hold of a thick wooden stick that she kept, crawled out of her tipi, and waited. A sudden motion caught her eye as she saw a soldier fall from his horse. He seemed hurt as he tried to run but could not. She saw a pistol in his hand and as he neared her, struck him with all her might. Without any sound, the man fell. I hope I did not kill him, she immediately thought. It was quite dark inside her tipi so she lit a candle. She froze. It wasn't from the blood streaming down his face. It was a strange attraction. She instantly fell in love with the man – this man who was her enemy only a moment ago, this man she felt she already knew. He had delicate facial features. His almost arrogant nose mixed together with a small chin and a smooth face made him very handsome, she thought. Her heart erupted with passion.

She became confused and backed off. Why? she asked herself as an emotional storm flooded her. I've never seen this man. He belongs to a different people. It just can't be. Her entire body ached, telling her, "You know this man. You were together. You belong to each other." She touched his face. She closed her eyes and saw visions that she had never seen before. She saw lions and horses and eagles and many people yelling. She saw mountains and clear skies near a beautiful creek. She saw a man and a woman passionately kissing on a flat rock amid a magnificent forest. She saw so many things that she could not understand. She pulled her hand back.

The man lay there. His eyes were closed but she could feel his soul. She took his hand in hers. It was gentle and warm. In the dim candlelight, she felt she knew the hand. She knew it like she knew her own. She could not hold back her emotions anymore. She gently kissed his hand. She could not let this man die. In a mysterious way, she was in love with him. It was as though her husband had come back home.

She peeked out of her tent, saw the attack was over and immediately prepared some herbal packs, which she gently applied to his head and leg wounds. His head looked better than his leg. The horse had fallen hard on the leg and it was now dark and swollen. She made a splint with her stick, wrapping it with a cloth packed with herbal mud – a remedy she learned from the medicine woman. After a while she was done and she sat near him, waiting for him to wake up. My parents will kill me if they discover I have him here with me, she thought. But as she continued looking at his face another thought took over, He is worth the danger.

Andy felt terrible pain in his leg. He could barely feel the rest of his injuries. He could smell a burning pine tree and heard crackling sounds. A campfire, he thought as waves of pain crashed upon him. Then he remembered the chain of events and his entire body became rigid, instinctively preparing for a fight. As he tried to stand up, the pain threw him back to the ground. He noticed he was inside a tent and saw a small fire in the center. Where am I? Then he saw her. Her large green, almond shaped eyes hypnotized him. Her long, dark hair curled around her face and fell naturally on her shoulders and then to her midsection. She had beautiful full lips and a smallish nose. He could not take his eyes from her. She did not say a word.

She gave her open hand to him, almost like a handshake. Surprised, he looked at her delicate hand. Although she did rough work, her hands were as delicate as fresh blossoms. He did not feel fear anymore. Her hand felt invitingly warm. But there was something else, something he could not explain. He felt something he had never felt before. The flood of feelings was so intense he instinctively closed his eyes. What are you doing? demanded his mind. She is the enemy and you are closing your eyes with great pleasure. She can kill you in an instant. But his soul reacted differently, joining with this girl through her hand, and he did not know why. His logic was pushed to the side and quickly disappeared as he drifted in an emotional storm. He was no longer aware of any pain. He was almost in a trance, and he wondered if she had plied him with a potion.

Her eyes did not talk war but something different. He tried to understand their meaning but could not. All he could feel was something that he refused to believe was happening. He could swear that he felt love. She gently nodded and smiled. He closed his eyes and smiled back to her. They continued to hold hands for a long while as their souls joined together in the joy of reunion.

Early in the morning he fell asleep and slept for a long time.

∞

She had to hide him. The little village woke up to the dismal aftermath of the army's cruel raid. Everyone was busy fixing tents and collecting belongings. Some were preparing to bury their dead. Orenda covered him gently and moved him to the side behind a buffalo hide that she had tanned last summer. She had to get food, so she went out to hunt rabbit. Her man needed to get strong. She gathered her weapons and headed for the fields. I will take care of my man. He will get better and we will be together. My destiny has arrived at last. They had somehow been separated during their past life and found each other now. The fact that they were somehow enemies was an absurd accident, as was the language difference.

∞

Andy woke up surprised that most of his pain was gone. The scented mud must be good. He was lying in the recesses of the tent, under thick furs. He allowed himself to relax. The light coming through a seam told him it was daytime. Going out would mean instant death. He remembered the beautiful girl. She captured me...and my heart as well, he mused. She was magical. Her coal-black hair was long and gave her face a wild look. Her full yet small lips were almost a contradiction to her eyes. She was petite and her body moved as though hovering. Her energy fascinated him most of all. She radiated a strong yet soft energy – a unique combination of sweetness and toughness, an independent soul yet needing love. He felt they already knew each other and he could not understand why. It was all too confusing for him. He was still in thought as she quietly stepped into the tent. It was only when she moved the flap that he turned to look. She was quiet as a puma and she was holding a few dead rabbits.

She put her finger to her lips, as though saying, "Silence." She put her prizes on the ground, got closer to him and took his hand. They again became lost in each other's eyes. She took his hand with her two hands and moved it slowly to her face. He could feel her soft skin and lips. This is not right, his brain told him but he could not stop. She led his hands to her shoulders and then to the rest of her body. Within seconds, like a fire spreading in dry summer, they found themselves in a naked embrace and passionately exploring the beauty of love. Many years of separation had created a thirst for unity. Their bodied combined in the ultimate force of lovers' passion. They kissed each other, touched and hugged for many hours, making love again and again, using their bodies as a conduit of love and joy until eventually falling asleep when their bodies could not continue.

It was almost evening when he woke to the aroma of meat being cooked. He rubbed his eyes, sat up and noticed a small fire with a pot over it. Noticing that he was awake, she presented him a slice of rabbit meat. He nodded thanks and began to eat. When she joined him, he noted that she took large bites. She eats like a man! And she must have used spices that I've never come across before.

"This is wonderful," said Andy. She froze as she heard an unknown language. "This is good...the meat," said Andy, this time pointing towards the meat, smiling and making hand gestures to convey praise. This time she understood and the tension was gone. She returned a nod and smiled. She has a beautiful smile, he thought and smiled back. They continued to eat for a while, communicating in an improvised sign language. By the end of the evening Andy would have gone to the ends of the world for her.

∞

Time passed swiftly. The rest of the world stopped as they enjoyed their time together. In time, they communicated very well. Andy hid in the tent during the day as she found them food. His leg healed nicely. At night they could venture out for walks in the beautiful, thick forest. They learned about each other intuitively. They explored each other's desires, wishes and dreams. They cooked their meals together, sharing the culinary knowledge each had. Andy taught Orenda what he knew from home as she taught him what he learned in nature. They quickly created their own traditions. They became inseparable. Every night they cuddled together inside the warm fur and explored each other's body and soul. Some nights they lay on the ground and gazed at the stars for hours, holding hands in the dark. Their respective languages ceased to be a problem. Orenda talked with Andy many times in her language and he started to understand full sentences. Andy helped with her English and it got better day by day. Improvised sign language was still used. Their main problem was their hidden life. Life was wonderful yet both knew that soon they would have to change. Meanwhile they let their reunited souls rejoice.

∞

It happened one morning, as it was bound to. Orenda went to hunt and Andy remained in the tipi. The night before, they took a long walk in the forest and spent almost all night at Blue Moon Lake – a magnificent body of water beneath snowcapped mountains usually shrouded by dense clouds. Legend held that one of the bravest of the villagers tried to climb to the top of the mountain but encountered a blinding snowstorm. He struggled against the elements for almost a week, persisting in his journey to the peak. Alas, he froze to death just before reaching the top. Friends that searched for him claimed that it was so cold near the peak that every living thing froze rapidly. They could not find him, only a blue powder scattered about. They believed that he froze to death and powerful gusts shattered his body into dust. Since then, when the moon is seen near the peak it takes on a blue hue. Andy and Orenda loved Blue Moon Mountain. Orenda thought the moon indeed looked a little blue on some nights. Andy saw no such hue, only white – as it should be. They teased each other about this until eventually they began passionate lovemaking.

Last night, Andy saw blue. It was clear, not too cold, and near the top of the mountain there were many clouds. Orenda, laughed loudly and told him, with the little English that he taught her, that she saw it a long time ago. Andy was in deep thought. The night before he told her that they cannot go on living as they were and that things needed to change. Orenda agreed but saw no option. It made her very sad. She did not want to lose Andy. They did not talk much that night and returned to the camp early in the morning. Andy was tired this morning.

Andy woke up in midmorning, alone. The sun had heated the tipi for several hours. He peeked through the tent and breathed the fresh air with thousands of nature's scents from the trees, the flowers, the rivers and the sun. He loved the morning. Although there was a brisk breeze, the sun was strong as it hit Andy's face. He did not mind. He walked out, naked, and exposed his face and neck to the sun and enjoyed it, his eyes closed.

A piercing scream made him jump. He turned and froze. In the tent's entrance was a young Indian woman about Orenda's age, standing there in shock. Quickly he covered himself with a blanket. Thousands of thoughts passed through Andy's mind. What to do? She will go and call the entire tribe. He and his love will be brutally put to death. Sweat drops appeared on his forehead. For a second he considered killing the young woman but he quickly rejected it; he could not murder a human being in cold blood. Maybe hold her until Orenda came back. She will know what to do. Nothing reasonable came to mind. All of a sudden the woman turned to go out.

"No..." yelled Andy as he reached for her. This was the first time she heard his voice and that made her stop and look backwards. He stood up and the blanket fell. She looked at him. "Please do not go to tell the others," he said quietly. She looked carefully at him. Her instincts told her that he did not want her to tell the other villagers. But she knew him to be one of the soldiers that attacked the village. What is he doing here? And where is Orenda?

Her name was Mei and she was Orenda's close friend. Since she had not seen Orenda for a long time, she decided to visit her this morning and see if she wanted to join her in gathering nuts, as they had often done. She looked at his nakedness. A handsome man, she thought. Warm surges coursed through her. She was almost nineteen years old and never had a boyfriend. Mei was a pretty girl and many boys were looking for her company, but her parents kept her far away from boys. They wanted her to grow to be a medicine woman. Does he belong to Orenda? Now he was talking to her, asking her not to tell the tribe. She pointed towards the outside and said, "I can call my people..."

Andy comprehended. "No, please," he asked again. She did not understand English but she grasped his meaning. She looked at his deep blue eyes and for a moment felt a mild tremor. *It can't be. Am I attracted to this man?*

She entered the tent. Andy sat and covered himself with his uniform. *He is one of our enemies...yet so beautiful and manly...* Strangely, she found herself daydreaming about the man in front of her. Her emotions astir, she smiled. He was shocked and he released a short sigh. He had been sure that he and Orenda were doomed, but it seemed this girl liked him somehow and would not inform. He felt relief. *Maybe she is a friend of Orenda and has figured things out. Maybe we are safe after all.*

"Are you a friend of Orenda?" he asked, speaking slowly, hoping she would understand. She just looked at him. He tried to communicate to her their condition. "We love each other...Orenda and I," he said, as he pointed towards himself. He smiled back to her. "I am a friend," he added, hoping that she'd understand he meant no harm. *I'll try to keep her busy until Orenda returns.*

Mei felt an excitement she never felt before as her young body responded to a young man. She could not think straight. She forgot Orenda and the nut-gathering plans. She was flooded with new feelings reverberating through her entire being as she looked at his chest, his long hair, his beard, his hands, nose and lips. She slowly gained control of her breathing. Nature took over her young body and mind; she knew what she wanted. She wanted to mate with this man before her.

Andy felt the tension but did not grasp its nature. He tried to communicate with her, but without response. She only stared at him. He thought she was frightened of an enemy near her. He told her stories in the few Indian words he had learned form Orenda.

"Mei," she interrupted. She pointed towards herself. "Mei..."

Andy stopped his speech and slowly indicated comprehension. "Beautiful name, Mei," he said. "I am Andy. How old you, Mei?" he asked accompanied with some signs but it did not look like she understood him. Mei approached Andy. Surprised by her approach, he instinctively stepped backwards, but she stepped forward, almost touching him. Andy looked at her carefully. She looked at his eyes without saying anything. He could smell her body, which radiated a scent of flowers. He noticed her breath becoming faster as she reached for his hand.

Mei could not control herself. She was only inches from this man and her entire body ached. She felt goose bumps all over and her stomach became tight. She took his hand and put it on her breast. Andy was frozen for a second and only then understood. He slowly pulled his hand back.

"Mei...I cannot," he tried to explain in a soft voice. "Orenda and I...in love...meant to be." She understood – all too well. Her eyes flared in anger. She ran to the tent's opening and pointed outside, threatening in her tongue to tell all to her people. Andy tried to explain that he understood her feelings but his heart belonged to Orenda. Mei did not understand or did not want to understand. She kept pointing towards the outside, repeating her threats. Andy searched for a way to defuse the situation. Why hasn't Orenda come home? She shouted louder and louder and someone was bound to hear her.

"Shhhh..." said Andy as he signed for Mei to approach him. Mei got quiet and slowly complied. He smiled and pointed towards the blankets and fur that lay on the ground. He slowly sat down, offering his hand to her and inviting her to be near him. Suspicious, she hesitated then sat close to him. She took off her leather shirt. He signed for her to lie near him then grabbed her hands and pulled them backwards. She screamed out of frustration more than pain as she realized that he was about to bind her. She started to thrash about and though he tried to restrain her, she got loose. She reached into a pouch on her waist and threw a powder in Andy's face, which made him sneeze and water. Mei stood up as Andy flailed about blindly. He searched for water to wash his eyes but was stricken by a sudden sense of weakness. He could not stand. His head filled with heavy clouds and he could move only slowly. The entire tent was slowly changing colors from blue to pink and eventually to purple, yet strangely he felt calm and happy. There is no need to worry. Everything will be fine, wherever I am.

Mei sat quietly as a smile formed on her face. She had done the right thing. The man wanted to attack her for some unknown reason and she defended herself with hunting dust, which stunned small animals. Her family made it from poppies and knew well its effect. The animal became disoriented and drowsy, which made it easy prey. She used a handful on Andy and it took effect almost immediately. Andy was now laughing uncontrollably, and her smile only got wider. She slowly lay near him, shed her clothes and wrapped her body around him. He saw only a cascade of colors. *I will teach him a lesson. He will learn to respect my desires – welcome or not.*

∞

Orenda finished hunting around midday. It took her longer than usual as she wanted a turkey. Andy loved her roasted turkey and she spent an entire three hours searching for the elusive bird. Eventually she found a whole family of them and managed to kill two young birds. She was tired and rushed home. *Andy will be very happy to taste the news.*

She entered the hot humid tipi. She smelled something different in the air. It took her eyes a moment to adjust to the low light and at first she did not see Andy. The smell of sweat reached her nose. This was a lovemaking smell. From the corner of her eye she saw movement. To the left she saw a girl's head raise up. The two turkeys fell from her hand. "Mei," she cried out. Mei silently looked at Orenda. Her hair was strewn about her face and Orenda could see perspiration on her forehead. Then Andy's head appeared. They lay in the tent's corner, wrapped in her blankets and hides. It was obvious what had gone on.

Orenda closed her eyes. Thousands of feelings flooded her, the most dominant being anger. She wanted to club Mei until every bone in her body was broken. She wanted to kill them both and burn their remains in a bonfire. She shook from anger and despondency. The love of her life, the love that she had waited for many years had been taken away. *How could this happen?* she thought in disbelief as she tried to grasp the meaning. *What have I done wrong? We were the perfect love, an impossible love that even different cultures could not break. Is Mei more beautiful than I? More loving?*

Orenda fell on her knees and cried until she had no more tears. She pounded the ground until her hands became bruised. It must be my destiny, she thought. Her mother told her a long time a go that everyone has a destiny, regardless of one's hopes. Destiny makes the decision for us and determines our path. No use to kill Mei or Andy. It is not in their hands. She has to accept her destiny. But her mother also taught her that she does not have to be where she does not want to be, that she does not have to do things she does not want to do. She decided never to return to her tipi. She would leave it and everything in it. Andy and Mei will not exist anymore.

Orenda slowly stood and looked around. She would build a new tipi. She would make new tools and build a new home. This chapter in her life is over. She gave a last look at Mei and Andy then closed her eyes for a moment. She took a deep breath and left the tipi. She breathed the air and looked around. The village's tipis were scattered over a wide area and ended near the bottom of a high, snowy mountain. No one built a tent near the foothills. It was bad luck to challenge the mountain. She determined to build her tent there, where no one else would live.

∞

Andy awoke in the night with a terrible headache and had difficulties opening his eyes. It was dark in the tent and the small fire in the center projected flames onto the tent walls. As he recalled events, he felt about to pass out. Hot and cold flashes ran through his body, leaving him in a cold sweat. He looked all around in panic. Orenda was not there, but Mei sat near the fire, staring at him. Anger threatened to take over but he forced himself to calm down. He already lost once to Mei. He did not want to lose to her again. If I can explain to Orenda what happened, she will forgive me. Mei explained in words and sign that no one could find her and that he belonged to her now. In keeping with tribal custom, she had won him. He countered that this was not how it worked in his world. People have feelings for each other. He is not just property. But Mei could not comprehend him. He wanted to search the village for her but knew it was too risky. Mei went out for food and returned after a while. She roasted meat and it tasted quite good. He eventually concluded that it was useless trying to explain love to her. She could not understand the concept. She was motivated by nature's insistence and that's all. Andy was very upset that night. Mei kept offering herself but he just turned his back. He could not stop thinking how he had lost the love of his life. He could not sleep all night. By morning he had a plan.

Andy waited three long days and nights, but Orenda did not come back. Every night he searched the places they had gone to, hoping to find her. Every morning he woke up hoping to hear her little feet walking into the tent. Every day he snuck to the forest, hoping to find her hunting or searching for food, but she was never there. He tried to talk with Mei, to explain to her his pain, but she only misunderstood. She offered comfort and love but he did not want them. He asked her to find Orenda, but refused. In her eyes he belonged now to her, forever. After a while Andy abandoned hope that Mei would help him. Another excruciating three days passed. He hardly slept or ate. He knew what he must do.

"Mei, I know it is not your fault. You do not even understand what is going on," he said on the third night. Mei seemed happy and smiled, holding his hand. She was always happy when he talked to her. Even if she did not understand him, she liked the attention. "I have to go back to my world, Mei, and I'll do it when you are asleep. If by any chance Orenda returns, please tell her I am leaving for Virginia, probably to join the navy. I always wanted to sail the high seas." He held her chin and looked into her eyes. "You will never understand me, will you?"

Mei was happy. She loved him and he was hers – that was all that mattered. She could felt his sadness, but he would get over it and she would be here to comfort him and give herself to him. She wanted him badly, but did not want to make him more upset. She'd wait patiently. There is no rush – he is in her hands anyway.

∞

It was about midnight when Andy donned his uniform. It was wrinkled and smelled of mildew, as it had been a long time since he wore it. He packed fruit and checked his pistol. He gave a last look at his former love nest. Amazing how things can change so fast, he thought as he looked at Mei sleeping calmly. He would never have imagined such an end. Well, destiny seemed to end their love story. He closed his eyes and remembered Orenda's touch, her smile, the sunshine in her eyes and kissing her lips. He released a long sigh. He'd probably never find someone like her again. With her there was a spiritual connection that he never had before. Destiny had Mei enter. And now Orenda was gone and he had to make his life without her. His eyes moistened and he blinked a few times to dry them. There is no hope here. I have to go back. He gave a last look at the tent and Mei then left into the night.

It was a full moon, which helped Andy find his way. He did not know in which exact direction his camp was. He roughly remembered that they passed near a green valley and a ridge line. At night, he could not clearly identify the landscape but he hoped to find a familiar path. He pressed on, leaving behind everything he ever loved.

He walked all night, and morning light showed him his camp in the distance.

∞

"I'm glad to see you. We thought..." said John Thorn his best friend as he patted Andy hard on his back. John was a huge guy and so everyone called him Big John. Despite his menacing look and great strength, Big John had a gentle heart and everyone loved him. "Hey John, mercy...please. You almost broke my back," complained Andy. But with a loud laugh he hugged John. "You big bear, I missed you." After some joviality, John became serious. "Now tell me, what's wrong? I know you. You should be happy to be back from capture."

"John, just between you and me?"

"Cross my heart," replied John as they started to walk through the camp.

"It's a long story, John..." started Andy with a sigh.

"I have all night."

143

Andy related his entire adventure. His being captured by Orenda, how he fell in love with her at first sight, and how they lived together for some time.

"Glory be!" said John. "That's quite a story. You told a different story to the captain, though."

"Of course," replied Andy grumpily, "what would you expect me to do, tell them that I fell in love with an Indian girl that captured me?"

"I understand," said John with an amused smile. "Go on."

Andy then continued, with Mei and how Orenda left and never returned. John looked deeply moved.

"I understand, my friend," he said sadly. "It must be painful."

"I never knew what love was, until I met her. She was special. Something that I'll never be able to find again."

John looked at Andy and many thoughts passed through his mind. He wanted to tell him many things. He wanted to tell him that he understands, but better that all things come to an end. After all, he and Orenda belonged to different worlds. He wanted to tell him that he felt sorry for losing the love of his life. He also wanted to tell him that love eventually wins, although he could not see any chance of winning in this case. Instead he did not say a word. He hugged Andy. There is nothing like losing your loved one, he thought. And no words can give comfort.

∞

Orenda ran through the woods. She had already run for hours and could not remember when she had started. After she left her tipi she built a new one on the other side of the village, near the mountains. She did not want to see anyone, not even her family. For a few days she stayed in her tipi, staring in the distance. Her sleep was fitful. What more did I have to do to make him love me? I gave him everything. For days she could not comprehend how he chose Mei over her. After a few days she went hunting. She walked aimlessly in the woods and then started to run. Without knowing where or why, she ran. She ran as fast as she could.

Bushes and small thorns poked her legs, leaving trails of blood. She ignored the pain and continued. Frightened rabbits crossed her path but she ignored them. She ran with her eyes constantly tearing up. After a few hours, she fell. Her lungs heaved in great efforts to get oxygen as she lay on the ground. Youth was on her side as her body recovered from the enormous stress and her breathing became regular again. She lay on her back and looked up at the blue skies. She closed her eyes. One thought crept into her mind, Alone again, naturally.

∞

Mei was devastated. She woke up the next morning and her man was not there. She searched for him all day, covering the entire village, the creek that flows nearby and the caves. But she could not find him or pick up a trail. She returned to the tipi and sat down despondently. What went wrong? I am young and pretty and can bare children. I gave him everything. Yes, he was sad because he lost Orenda, but so what? The winner takes all and I had won. He seemed to understand that concept. What went wrong then? As much as she tried to find an explanation, she could not find one.

∞

"I am going to request a transfer to the navy," said Andy in a low voice. John nodded silently. Andy was not the same man he knew before the raid. He never regained his joy of life. There had always been a glimmer of sunshine in his eyes and he was full of joy, even in hard moments. He needed to be near Andy to get through tough moments. As much as John tried to return him to his joyful self, he could not. He rarely laughed and seemed to have lost his passion for the world. John knew that Andy always had a special love for the sea. When Andy mentioned his desire to join the navy, he sadly approved. Yes, he will lose his best friend but maybe Andy will find his happiness again.

"I'll miss you, my friend," said John with a faint smile.

Andy looked at his eyes and could see them moisten. He loved John like a brother.

"Old friend, you can visit me in Norfolk. We can walk about the town or have a drink in a bar." He tried to comfort himself more then John.

"Of course..." said John as he looked at the ground.

They both knew that this would never happen. Norfolk was far away from Nebraska.

John looked at Andy's eyes and they hugged each other.

"I hope you find your happiness, my friend." John tapped on Andy's head as little kids do. "You need to find it."

Andy looked at John and nodded silently. He needed all of his strength not to burst into tears. But he had to do something to help him forget Orenda.

According to his request, Andy was reassigned to the navy in Virginia. After brief training, he was assigned to a wooden frigate. On October 29, 1861 Andy's squadron would set sail from Hampton Roads to Port Royal Sound in South Carolina. The Union planned to take that strategic position. Three days later they would pass Cape Hatteras, North Carolina, which protrudes to the southeast along the northeast-to-southwest line of the Atlantic coast, making it a key point for navigation along the eastern seaboard. Many ships had been lost there due to frequent hurricanes that move up the East Coast. That is why the waters off Cape Hatteras are called the "Graveyard of the Atlantic."

∞

Orenda's sixth sense woke her. It was about midnight on a moonless night. She listened carefully, for at night she trusted only her hearing. Everything sounded normal but she stayed alert anyway. Her tipi was behind a large rock so she knew that she was hidden from anyone coming from the mountain. She peeked through her tent. Something was not the same. She waited then heard horse hooves in the distance, soon followed by the trampling of feet. Braves from another tribe were approaching and would attack her village within minutes. She sneaked around the big rock and ran as fast as she could to the village. As she neared the village she started to call out the tribe's warning signal. Within moments, the men assembled with their weapons just as the attackers neared, shouting their war cries. Orenda saw a flash of a knife blade to her left and instinctively moved away. She fought back with her ax and knife against a large man. Suddenly a club came down her on her head and the world became darker than the night.

∞

The horizon became orange as the sun slowly sent its first light. Andy was on deck for almost every sunrise. The magnificent view of the sun rising out of the dark and illuminating the sea reminded him of the mornings he and Orenda used to share. Their nocturnal walks often ended at dawn and the sunrise always fascinated them. They used to stop when the first sunbeams showed themselves. Then they picked a high spot and sat to watch the beginning of a new day. The sun seemed to be coming up slowly, as though hesitating, or too shy to show itself. The sun's slow appearance was like a battle of light against darkness. First there was the dark, then a few hopeful beams showed. But darkness did not give up easily and it always seemed to them that the sun had to make tremendous efforts to break the night. The sun illuminated the formerly dark clouds, establishing light over darkness. In just a few minutes, the sun overwhelmed the night and her light was everywhere in the world, comforting and reassuring. There is light.

Many nights, Andy and Orenda had walked somberly, searching for a solution to their plight. Their love would not let them consider separation but they also knew they could not continue as they were. Days were long periods of hiding but nights meant openness. Sunrise gave hope. The light winning out against darkness gave them hope for the next day. Something will come for us, Orenda thought after every sunrise. A solution will come and in a natural way.

At sunrise, wherever he was, Andy felt Orenda, wherever she was. He closed his eyes and let himself drift into memories. There, he and Orenda were together again as husband and wife. Andy was on a high cliff, holding hands with Orenda. They looked at the stormy sea below as huge waves broke violently onto the rocks, splashing briny seawater everywhere. Andy turned towards Orenda and saw her beautiful smile. He smiled back and they kissed. Andy opened his eyes and she was gone. He watched the sun climbing in the sky. You already finished your battle of the day, he thought. You won, but what about me? How do I continue from here?

∞

Orenda saw white shadows. They faded away and she blinked a few times. The left side of her head hurt. She saw the treetops clearly and realized she was on the ground. She slowly turned to her right. She could tell by the chilly, fresh air that it was dawn. She could see the village tents and many of her tribe searching for relatives. Her head hurt badly. She passed out and her attacker probably thought her dead. I wonder if we had many casualties. She rested for a while and then went down to the creek to wash. She let herself lie in the ice-cold water, which helped her pain and after a while she felt better. She cleaned her body thoroughly, dressed and went to the village. The village suffered great devastation. Many tents were burned and she saw dozens of bodies around them. Orenda felt anger building inside her when she saw the corpses of several of her relatives, some tragically young. She walked towards the end of the village and saw her old tent. What if he was still there? What if something happened to him during the attack? The thought filled her with dread. As she approached the tent, she saw it crumpled, as though someone had smashed it. She hoped to find her old tent empty.

She looked inside but did not see Andy. Relief flooded her. Then she heard a murmur and saw a hand move from a fur blanket. It was too young and delicate to be Andy's. It was a young girl's hand – Mei's. She was lying on her back, her hair moist and sticky. Her eyes were closed as though sleeping. An occasional moan indicated she was in pain.

Mei, she thought, was the reason for her separation from Andy. She had sneaked into her tent while she was not there and seduced Andy. She hated Mei. Then Mei's head turned to the side and Orenda saw her hair was caked in dry blood. Orenda removed the blanket covering her body. There was a huge wound in her stomach, perhaps from a horse hoof. Orenda could see bones jutting out from the wound. Something had also hit Mei on the head, inflicting a catastrophic wound. Mei was dying. Her anger disappeared as fast as it had arrived, and she put her hand on her best friend's head. Mei gently coughed and opened her eyes. They were bloody and Mei looked straight towards Orenda, without seeing anything.

"Mei?" said Orenda quietly.

Mei's head turned towards her voice.

"I cannot see you. What's happened?" Mei was not completely coherent.

"You were hit during the attack last night," answered Orenda in a low voice.

"Orenda? But you left..." Mei stopped as she remembered everything. Her head turned away from Orenda's voice. She could not say anything.

Orenda sat near her, tears rolling from her eyes. She held Mei's hand. It was warm and sticky with blood.

"I am so sorry, Orenda..." she started. "I do not know what happened. I just wanted him to myself and I could not control myself anymore."

Orenda felt the anger grow again but she forced herself to stay calm. Mei continued. "He did not want me. I threatened to tell everyone about him and you..."

You did what?" she almost yelled.

"I threatened to tell about him to our people." Mei turned towards Orenda's voice and Orenda got the false feeling that Mei could see her. "I did a very bad thing, Orenda..." Mei's voice broke as she cried quietly. "I realized it only later."

"Yes, you did," Orenda responded. She took a deep breath and looked outside. It was not Andy's fault. That's what he tried to tell her but she never gave him the chance. She forced herself on him. Mei was having difficulties breathing.

"I am very sorry, Orenda," repeated Mei in a quavering voice. "He waited for you here for days, hoping you'd come back."

"I didn't," said Orenda in a rough, scratchy voice.

Mei did not answer but tried to keep her breathing regular. Her lungs were filling with blood and it was only a matter of time until she suffocated.

"You have to find him. You belong to each other. I did not understand it then." Mei looked at Orenda with great pain. "All he wanted was you..." Mei closed her eyes.

Orenda took a deep breath and allowed herself to relax. Mei seemed to gain control of her breathing, shallow though it was. But soon her body started to shake. Orenda covered her with the blanket, which helped for a short while. Then Mei turned to Orenda. "Do you forgive me?"

Orenda held Mei's hand. "Yes, I do."

A shadow of a smile spread across Mei's face and she looked calm. She was ready.

"I am very tired, Orenda. Can I go to sleep now?"

A warm memory came to Orenda. She and Mei went to sleep many times together as children, and Mei would always ask if she could go to sleep. Orenda would caress Mei's long hair and sing to her until sleep took hold. This would be the last time she helped her friend find sleep. For a moment she thought that Mei could see her.

"Yes, little Mei, you can go to sleep now," replied Orenda, tears streaming down her face. She held Mei's hand and caressed her hair. For a while they forgot everything. For a while they were again two little girls, best friends. For a while Orenda was again helping her best friend to sleep.

Mei smiled and slowly closed her eyes as Orenda's gentle voice sang to her. Mei's breathing slowed but Orenda did not stop. Not even when Mei's body twitched as her lungs collapsed. Not even when Mei gently exhaled for the last time. Not even when Mei's hand lost warmth. She sang to her past midnight and then began to cry. She cried for losing Mei, and for losing Andy. Exhausted, she fell asleep near Mei. She cuddled with her lost friend, as she did as a little girl.

∞

Mei's family had been killed in the raid, so it fell to Orenda to bury her friend. She washed her and dressed her in pleasing clothes. Orenda brushed Mei's hair and adorned her with the scented flowers. When she laid her on her colorful blanket just before interment, Mei appeared to be sleeping calmly. Orenda gazed upon her for the last time. A large tear rolled down Orenda's cheek and landed on Mei's cheek. It looked like Mei was crying also.

"Goodbye Mei. May your spirit fly high with the noble spirits of nature that you always loved..." She thought she saw a smile come faintly across her face. She buried her in her blanket to provide her spirit a familiar setting, in accordance with the tribe's tradition. Then Orenda packed food and clothes and left towards the great valley. She was determined to find Andy.

∞

Big John had a taste for blueberries. Although it was after midnight he had to have some and he knew of wild blueberry bushes just outside camp. Every once in a while he would go and get a small sack of them. He looked at the skies. A gibbous moon lit the sky. Just in case I'll take a lantern. He quickly made the calculation for a short trip and within a few minutes he was on his way to the northern perimeter, hefting a new breechloading rifle – again, just in case. As he passed the guard post he promised the sentry a treat.

There were no clouds that night as John wended his way down the path into the forest. The bushes were just behind a small clump of trees. The last time he was there – about two weeks ago – there were many ripe berries. The thought of big ripe blueberries made him happy and he picked up his pace. Hey, sweet berries. Papa is coming...

∞

Orenda was tired – too tired to detect movement behind her. She had walked all day, trying to guess where Andy's camp was. She knew that she could not enter the camp. She thought to hide nearby and contact him somehow. When night fell, it was harder to continue but she refused to stop. Orenda did not hear the muted sound of a bobcat stalking her. It was large and hungry from an unsuccessful hunt. But now he was waiting for a chance to pounce on this girl. Orenda started to think about stopping for the night. Her legs were aching and she was tired and hungry. She saw berry bushes and was elated that she could eat and rest the night. She collected a generous amount and settled under a tall tree to enjoy them. Orenda sat on her blanket and enjoyed the scenery. Exhaustion seized her and she fell asleep.

Her instinct woke her up. She listened carefully to the night but could not hear anything unusual. Still, her gut told her differently and she respected that feeling. Then she heard it, bushes crackling under a running animal. Orenda's mind worked fast. The animal is very close and no longer needs to be stealthy. She quickly stood up and surveyed her surroundings. She could not see anything, even though the moon shone bright.

I have to get clear, she thought as her heart beat wildly and she grasped her knife. She knew that if it was a large bobcat or lioness, it will be a tough struggle and she prepared herself. From the corner of her eye she noticed sudden movement. Just a few dozen feet behind her, a large bobcat jumped over the berry bushes and raced after her. She was afraid to look behind her. Never run from a pursuing animal. Your chances are worse than if you face it. She had to turn around and face the bobcat. otherwise she was dead.

∞

Big John stopped. Right in front of him was someone being chased by a bobcat. It was hard to see in the dark but he could not mistake the sight of the big cat. "Thunderation," said John reflexively as he raised his rifle. "What do we have here?" As the person neared he shouted, "Halt!" and he saw the face of a terrified Indian girl. The bobcat was closing fast and John had to react quickly. He fired a shot in the air to frighten the beast. The bobcat veered but continued his pursuit. The girl changed direction and was running directly towards him now, hoping for help. "Why the hell do these things always happen to me..." complained John as he finished reloading. A running target is very difficult but John was a crack shot. The bobcat closed on the girl and leaped. John closed one eye, drew a bead and fired. He hit the big cat in midair and it fell like a heavy sack. John remained at the ready in case the bobcat still had fight in him. After a minute of stillness, John released a long sigh and lowered his rifle.

"That was close..." His breechloader fell as the young girl ran into him, almost knocking him down. Her arms hugged him tightly and her little face sank into his coat. "Easy, everything is alright now..." He stood there awhile, holding her shaking body until she calmed down. Then she raised her head from his chest and looked up to him. In the dim light of his lantern he could see a beautiful young girl's face. She was definitely Indian and absolutely beautiful, thought John.

"Are you alright?" he asked gently. She seemed to be better.

She started to talk in her language. John recognized an Indian language but could not understand her stream of words.

"Hey, slow down. I cannot understand anything..."

She talked fast and many sentences at a time, constantly pointing to his army uniform.

"What is it? Is there something with my uniform?" asked John, trying to understand her signs.

She struggled to communicate, pointed at his blue coat and said, "Andy."

John froze.

"Andy? You know Andy?" She nodded and smiled. She recognized his language as Andy's native tongue. This is the girl Andy met at the Indian village. This is his loved one. She is the reason his heart is broken. I can see why. She came here to find him. "Are you looking for Andy?" he asked her slowly.

"Andy" she repeated after him and nodded. "Andy..." He wondered if she was asking or telling him.

"Orenda?" asked John.

Her eyes became round in surprise and she realized that he knew Andy. She became happy and talked incessantly, mentioning Andy's name from time to time.

"Orenda?" repeated John. She nodded, answering his question. "I am so sorry, sweetheart, Andy is not here anymore. He headed to Virginia. He joined the navy." She did not understand him and continued to be happy and talkative. "Andy is not here anymore," repeated John. He improvised sign language, showing her hand symbols that Andy moved away to sail on ships. Orenda eventually understood and her smile faded away. She had come all the way to find out Andy was not here anymore. She signed him if he knew where Andy was and John explained to her as much as he could that he was on a wooden ship.

"He is in Virginia now," John said gently. On the ground he sketched the sea and sailing ships – one with a man on it. "This is Andy." Orenda pointed at the figure and repeated, "Andy?"

"Yes, this is Andy."

She sat there quietly with her face down. John could feel her sorrow. She lifted her face and John could see her big sad eyes. What a true love, thought John. I never saw a love as miraculous as this one. It is sad that it has to be in two different worlds. They sat there in silence. Something flashed in John's mind. I cannot let this story end like this. I must find a way to reunite them. They'll find a way to bring together their different worlds. John's face illuminated as he had an idea.

"I can tell you where you can find Andy." He knew a thing or two about the base in Virginia. Once he wanted to join the navy.

∞

Orenda walked as fast as she could. Many times along the way she thanked the heavens that she had found John. Without him, she'd know nothing about the navy base. It was a long way – John estimated about ten to twelve days – but she was determined to walk day and night, taking only short breaks to eat and rest, and navigating by the stars as her parents taught her. Amazingly she made it in seven days.

She arrived on the Virginia shoreline just in time to witness a flotilla sailing against the strong winds in Hampton Roads. The channel contains several natural harbors where the mouths of the Elizabeth and James Rivers along with several smaller streams empty into the Chesapeake Bay, near the Atlantic Ocean. It was an astonishing view, as Orenda had never seen such ships. The flotilla sailed through the Roads towards the Atlantic. She could see many cannon on the decks and protruding from openings below, and she wondered where they were heading. The sea air hit her face, leaving a salty taste. After her arduous trek, she allowed herself to stand before the sea and observe the majestic ships rocking from side to side as they passed the cape and took wide turns to the south. She could not know that the ships were sailing to capture Port Royal.

She descended the cliff towards the water where, hidden among trees, she watched the ships pick up a strong northerly wind. The ships were quite close and she could see sailors on deck. They struggled with the rough weather, constantly trimming or setting sails. The ships rising and lowering in the seas frightened her. Orenda had feared water since childhood when she and her father fished what settlers called the Platte River, which rises in the Rockies and flows into the Missouri. The Indians mastered the art of fishing in kayaks, using bow and arrow in the clear water in which fish could be easily seen. Although they were skilled, even the best found it fraught with danger. The strong current sometimes took small kayaks into the rapids and over falls.

On one trip they chased several large fish down the river but without luck. It was a hot summer day and the sun hit hard. Her father was focused on a large fish and frustrated by his lack of success, failed to take heed of the falls. Little Orenda heard them getting nearer. She warned her father once but he ignored her. She knew they should be heading back upstream. Her father fired into the river and shouted in elation as he finally got a fish. Then the rushing noise took over and he stood up, realizing their peril. He immediately started to paddle upstream with all his might, but the kayak was pulled into the center of the river, spun in circles and shot towards the falls. She did not remember much of what followed. Her father grabbed her just before they hit the falls. She clearly remembered the view as she looked down and saw the drop and the swirling, hissing waters. She could not look anymore so she pressed herself into her father's chest.

They hit the water at such great speed that her father broke his spine and died instantly. She was driven deep into the cold water. The pressure on her ears was painful and she instinctively tried to push her way up. The air had been forced from her lungs on impact and she started her way back up with almost no air. She pushed the water to the sides in a desperate effort to reach the surface. Her lungs burned and her face reddened. She looked up and saw glimmers of light far away as her strength faded and her vision got blurry. She wiggled about in a last effort to reach air, but her mouth opened and she took in cold water. Panic struck as the water reached her lungs and she lost the ability to breath. Efforts to inhale air only took in more water. Efforts to scream brought no sound. She noticed movement near her as her body went into convulsions. All of a sudden she was not scared anymore. Nothing mattered as she welcomed the soft, painless darkness.

She woke up three days later in her mother's arms. Her mother saw their fall from her kayak and went to save her. She reached her at the last minute and managed to drag her out. She was unconscious for about three days. The feeling of not being able to breath stayed with her. She never again ventured out on a kayak. Even when walking near the river, she kept a safe distance. She wanted never to go near water again.

As the ships passed just in front of her, one after another, she focused her eyes on a man. Just in front of her, on the main deck of a proud frigate, she saw Andy. She could clearly discern his slender, tall figure. She could not belive her eyes. It was beginning to rain and the seas were picking up. The crew was constantly working the sails to keep the ship stable and on course. Andy simply stood there and looked out to sea. Orenda began to shout his name and wave her arms. But the strong wind carried her shouts away and she knew her efforts were futile. She cried in frustration and sadness. She was so close to him but he could not see her. She continued to watch his ship until it slowly rounded the cape.

The fleet was sailing close to shore as it made its wide turn. This is it, she thought. I've not come all this way to miss him by moments. She saw a few boats docked beneath the cliff. She descended and found a small craft that she thought she could handle. She would reach his ship and find a way to get to him. She had to. She would have to contend with her fear of water.

∞

Andy stood on deck, fixed on the stormy waters. It was their second day of their expedition to Port Royal. The captain announced they were nearing Cape Hatteras. The rain, seas, and winds had all picked up. Andy looked at the gray skies and knew that a tempest was coming. He could smell it. As a boy he learned how certain skies and scents meant storm. He loved storms – the hard rain hitting him, the winds buffeting him from side to side, and even the bright lightning and loud thunder. Whenever he sensed a storm, he welcomed it with a smile. That day was no different. Hello, old friend, he thought as he closed his eyes and within a few minutes he was drenched. Then came the wind, whistling across the sails, masts and ropes. As the storm grew, Andy became worried.

The storm was developing into a gale. This one reminded him of a terrifying storm from his youth in which he almost died. He and his family went to visit his uncle in Florida. Andy loved to spend the entire day at the nearby beach. One afternoon the skies swiftly became stormy. It was the beginning of a hurricane, though Andy did not know and so he stayed and welcomed the storm. Initially it was quite pleasant as his body was nudged about by the wind. Then the winds became stronger and within minutes some gusts reached a hundred miles per hour. He started to run but he was picked up by the wind and smashed against a tree. He broke his arm and leg, and the pain was unbearable. He lay down, unable to walk far. He noticed a pile of boulders and spied a crevice he could crawl into. After four hours, the winds slowed enough that he could emerge. He looked out at the sea and felt respect and awe. Slowly, though in great pain, he reached home. From that day on Andy had a sense for bad weather. Now he was sniffing the air and observing the dark gray skies. He was sure they were in store for a hurricane.

∞

Orenda rowed as fast as she could but was unable to close on the ships – in fact they were getting farther away. She was exhausted. The oars fell from her hands and she burst into tears. She had missed her chance to reunite with him and she let the little boat rock in the sea. She lay down and fell asleep to the gentle motion.

She woke up violently as she was tossed about and pelted with heavy rain. The skies were leaden with an eerie greenish tint. She watched the waves and felt panic taking over as her old fear of water paid her an unexpected visit. The waves rose to immense heights and she could only look on as her little boat slowly climbed then crashed down wave after wave. The storm was terrifying yet at the same time fascinating as she imagined herself and her little boat facing off against all the powers in nature. The imagined contest eased her fear, putting it aside amid the ongoing ordeal. She soon observed that her boat could handle the harrowing rises and falls of the waves, which indeed might have been more dangerous for larger ships. Out on the dark horizon she could see Andy's fleet. She wasn't sure at first but after a while she was certain of it. The storm was pushing her closer to the ships – and closer to Andy.

She could even make out the ship she had seen Andy on. The storm and her fears abated. She was about to see Andy. The formerly deadly waves and powerful winds now were her friends. Amid the watery hell, Orenda was quite happy.

∞

Andy stood and watched in fascination of nature's power. He stood on the stern watching the rest of ships struggle. He already told the captain that the weather would worsen. It was a strong hurricane, no doubt about it. Andy noticed a small boat climbing the high waves and quickly disappearing between them. Who is so unwise to be in a small boat in a sea like that? He discerned someone in the boat. The waves brought the boat closer. As Andy stood and watched the tiny boat buffeted in the wild sea he stopped breathing for a moment. He looked down one particularly mammoth wave and he could not believe his eyes. He thought he saw Orenda! It was so fleeting that he refused to believe it. Am I missing her so much that I am imagining things? Another wave brought the boat to its crest and...it was Orenda! She was in the small boat, smiling widely, oblivious to the danger. Orenda looked elated. Had she gone completely mad?

∞

Andy forgot where he was and shouted her name and signaled with his hands. At first the wind carried his voice away but as her boat got closer to his ship, she noticed him. Their eyes fused. They called out to each other at the same time. Orenda maneuvered the little boat as best she could and Andy grabbed a lifeline. The crew was busy battling the storm and no one noticed the plight of two people. Andy encouraged Orenda to row faster to avoid a serious collision with the larger vessel. Andy tied the rope to a large barrel and threw it with all his might. She grabbed it with both hands and prepared herself. "Jump!" he shouted to her.

It was just a matter of time until the little boat was smashed to pieces. Orenda hoped for a momentary stillness before jumping, knowing that if she missed the ship the waves would carry her off into the frigid darkness. Andy's eyes were focused on Orenda as she calmly waited for her moment. At last it arrived. Orenda pursed her lips, held the rope tight with both hands and jumped. Her legs slammed into the ship's hull but she maintained balance by pushing forward and literally standing perpendicular to the ship. As the ship heaved and waves crashed just below her, Orenda skillfully ascended towards Andy. Orenda felt Andy's powerful hands holding her and pulling her up into his arms.

They stood there, holding each other, unmindful of the rough weather raging around them. Time and place did not matter.

"I feared I'd never see you again," whimpered Andy. "I can't believe that you tracked me all the way here." He looked around them in disbelief. "Are you crazy? Rowing in such a tiny boat in weather like this?" Although she did not understand his words, she got the idea and shook her head, moving her shoulders with a mischievous smile.

"I found you," she told him in her language, which he understood. "Yes, you did," he answered quietly. He held her precious chin and gave her a loving kiss. Their bodies entwined ravenously and they forgot the world around them. Only their love existed. Their lips pressed together and their breathing became faster from the excitement of their touch. They wanted to join in the beauty of intimacy. Finding a covered boat on the rear deck, they curled in the little space it offered. Although drenched, they felt no cold at all. Kissing and touching each other, they took off their worldly rags. Orenda's eyes closed in wonder. She had embarked upon her journey with this very dream.

They were together, making passionate love in a small boat – and this was the most beautiful thing that ever happened to them. Their bodies craved each other and they explored each other. Andy kissed her all over, making sure he was not dreaming. Their passion took over and they wandered together down the wild path of love until completely satisfied. They lay in each other's arms, sweating and trembling. They did not want the moment to end.

"I am not letting you leave again," Andy whispered.

She understood and answered with a soft kiss.

"I leaving not," she said in her English.

Andy opened his mouth in surprise on hearing English from her. "You remembered some words!" They needed to be near each other. They were incomplete apart.

∞

They were woken by the cries of the crew. Andy lifted the canvas and peeked outside. It was night and there was still a strong wind and steady rain. The air was cold or maybe it was just cold comparing to their nest. The entire crew was scurrying about. He could hear commands to set sail. "Oh, my heavens!" Andy heard the captain exclaim. Andy sensed danger. They dressed hurriedly and stepped from their hiding place, darting between momentary places of hiding. Eventually they could see the crew on the foredeck, staring at something dead ahead. It was hard to see too far as there was a driving rain, but they studied the sea ahead of them. Then they froze.

∞

Mid-ocean waves of seven meters are not unusual. In some conditions they can reach fifteen meters. However, maritime folklore has long told of vastly more massive waves — veritable monsters up to forty meters in height, which appear without warning and against the prevailing currents. Such waves are described by survivors an almost vertical wall of water preceded by a trough so deep that it was referred to as a "hole in the sea." A ship encountering such a wave would be unlikely to survive the tremendous force of the breaking water, and would almost certainly be sunk in a matter of seconds. The crew of the wooden vessel stopped all their activities and watched the deadly yet strangely magnificent sight. The first glimpse was a dark shadow that suddenly dimmed the daylight from the north. The day was gray in general, but this shadow was different. "Look there!" shouted one hand. Everyone looked ahead then fell silent.

Maybe it was unrelated to the rough weather. Maybe it was due to seismic activity. It was still fairly far away but it looked fearsome. Everyone stood in stunned silence. Most impressive was its height. The wall of water rose to such height that it looked like a moving mountain. The silent movement of the giant wave was almost a contradiction to the danger it posed – to the death it promised. It appeared to swallow up another ship in their flotilla, but no one could say for sure. Calmly and slowly the enormous wave rolled forward towards the seemingly small ship. Many on the deck knew it was the end. There was no way to escape. Even if it did not break on the vessel, there was no way the ship could float to the top then over without capsizing. They stared at the inevitable.

∞

Orenda felt panic pervade her. Andy's face turned pale and he held Orenda tight. He shook his head in disbelief. Orenda's fear of water reached new levels. She started to breathe fast and felt the lack of oxygen. "Look at me, sweet one..." he told her. "Look into my eyes, my love." Andy turned her face towards his and forced himself to stay calm in order to calm her.

She held him and buried her face into his chest. Andy held her tightly and thought, After all this, we are going to die. We just found each other and it's going to end right now. Fate can be cruel. He had a jarring feeling of deja vu. He had the feeling he had been separated from Orenda before, in a different time and place. He shook his head. No, the first time I saw her was when we attacked her village...but maybe not. He found no explanation. He held her and looked into her eyes. She was calm now and looked back at him. The feeling of another time and place stayed with him.

They kissed gently then calmly turned to face the wave. They saw it now as a breathtaking part of nature. The huge mass rolled forward, moving like an old giant that knows its stature and the respect he commands. The image was so large it almost looked unreal, yet everyone was frozen in helpless fascination.

Andy turned to Orenda. "I love you," he told her simply. The cold wind blew droplets across her face and for a moment panic took hold again. She hugged him as their fate neared. "No need to be afraid, my love. We are here together. We are going to a new adventure together. That is how it is with us." Orenda's panic faded. They are going to visit the great spirits together. She could not imagine a life without Andy. She crossed rivers and seas for him and now they will face the greatest journey of all together. It is just a new path. She gave Andy her most loving smile and his eyes illuminated. It must have appeared strange to an outsider. Eternal lovers happy to be together, though death loomed.

There was movement on deck. Some of the crew jumped overboard and others ran for cover. Pointless though that was, it was the human instinct for self-preservation. Some stopped as they saw Andy and Orenda, wondering what these two were doing but soon returned to their efforts to survive.

In Orenda's tribe, husband and wife are buried together, in embrace, so they'll continue their journey to the spirits together. As she was looked into Andy's eyes, she was able to look deep into his soul, and what she saw puzzled her. His face changed and she saw someone else. The face was familiar but it was not Andy's. It was the face of a man about to die. Her soul reached out to the strange man but she could not do anything. Then she understood. This was not the first time that their spirits had met. They had been together in the past. They'd been separated but then reunited. They were about to be separated again, but she was sure they would meet again in another time and place, as a different man and woman. She trembled at the insight.

The huge wave curled quietly towards the ship, which looked ridiculously small in comparison. The deck was completely empty, except for the two lovers. When the wave reached the ship, Andy and Orenda could hear a great roar, like the sound of a wave nearing the shore but complemented by a great rush of air being pushed forward. They wrapped their arms around each other. Orenda buried her face into Andy's chest. Andy sank his head into Orenda's long hair and closed his eyes. They were ready.

The ship started to climb the slope of the wave but it was obvious it would never make it to the top. The wave nobly continued its progress and hammered down upon the frigate. Seawater crashed down, overwhelmed any other noise, and gushed into every opening, filling them with salty foam. The ship's hull emitted a dim groan as it broke into several pieces before completely disintegrating under the full brunt. It looked like a huge hammer had struck a nicely crafted toy. Pushed down by tons of water, the remnants of the ship began their slow journey to the bottom of the Atlantic.

Night Fell.

Morning Rose.

Daniel opened the letter with shaky hands. "Yes!" He hopped about like a jubilant child as he learned he got a mechanical engineering job at the Krakow machinery factory. He had graduated the previous summer from AGH University of Science and Technology in Krakow and had been searching for a job. "Independence day is coming…" he mumbled to himself as he got dressed. Daniel was twenty-one years old and lived with his parents. He hated living there. His father was a chemical engineer and worked in a local hospital, while his mother taught music at a conservatory. Daniel thought that they were wonderful parents but they wanted to know every little thing that happened to him.

Many times he talked with them about the fact that he is already twenty-one and can and should take care of himself. But it did not help. It reached a peak last month when his father wanted to go with him to one of his job interviews. It took him a long time to persuade his father, without hurting his feelings, that he could do the interviews by himself. Just last winter he reached a life achievement when his mother did not ask him anymore if he needed a sweater or coat when he leaves home. Now Daniel smiled while getting dressed. I love my parents dearly, he thought, but it is time for the bird to leave the nest. He'll always cherish his parents' support and love, but now he has to prepare for his new job. He'll go to the library to learn about the factory. He ate his breakfast quickly and left the house. On his way to the library he bumped into the newspaper kid that always stood on his corner, shouting the headline. "Seventeen thousand Polish Jews deported from Germany, now at Polish frontier," shouted out the little boy as he waved the paper. Daniel gave him a brief look and rushed on his way. It was already October and cold weather had arrived early this year.

∞

"And here is your office," the secretary said as she showed Daniel about the workplace. Daniel could hardly hide his excitement. He liked the director, the machinery they made and now his office. It was equipped with a large desk, stationery, large chair and calculation devices. Daniel's eyes sparkled as he remembered his father's words when he was twelve years old. "When you get your first job you'll understand the meaning of having your own respectable office. It's a great feeling." Daniel could not grasp his father's words then. Now he did. He sat in his comfortable chair and looked around his office. The pens, notebook and brand new desk looked at him, saying, "Good morning, boss." He closed his eyes and allowed himself to float into career worlds. Here he is after a few years, after many sleepless nights: he develops a machine that no one imagined before. Soon the entire academic world is visiting his plant to see the new device. He receives awards and praise from around the world. The plant makes him the chief engineer and gives him an entire team that works together on the next generation of mechanical-engineering breakthroughs...

"With status and comfort comes responsibility." The words of director Hans Miller brought him down to earth. Daniel immediately straightened his posture and focused. "Yes, of course. I am sorry...I was thinking about..."

"That's alright, Daniel," smiled Hans. "I felt the same when I got my first office as a young engineer, but of course that was many years ago..." He released a sigh and sat in front of Daniel. This broke the ice and the conversation became informal.

"So, do you like your new office?" asked Hans, slightly smiling.

"Oh yes, of course," answered Daniel with some embarrassment. "It has everything I always wanted."

"We are investing a great deal of time on creating high-quality products," continued Hans, "and this is a demanding task."

"I know. I like..."

"You have to be aware of management and employees," interrupted Hans. "Investing many hours to make things better and to meet our schedules is key for this factory. That is why we are leaders in our field all of Europe." He paused and looked at Daniel thoroughly. "I demand the best from my employees. Are you willing to give your best efforts?"

"I promise!" he answered, looking straight into Hans's eyes. "I'll do my absolute best!"

Hans smiled. "Good. I need people like you." He turned serious. "I just read that war is nearing. Hitler's troops deported Polish Jews. There are rumors that the Germans' next destination is Poland. I suspect that Krakow will be one of their targets." He became quiet.

"I briefly heard the news this morning," answered Daniel, "but I did not have the time to think about it. I was here, studying my material."

"I have four hundred employees in my plant. Many of them are Jews. If the Nazis seize Krakow, I will probably lose many of them. We've all heard how the Nazis are treating Jews."

"Yes, I heard," answered Daniel quietly. "They deport them to camps."

"Correct," answered Hans. "It can cause a major problem for me. They have all kind of regulations to turn factories into war plants, but still I am not sure how it will go. In any case, hard times are soon coming."

Then he looked straight at Daniel. "Are you Jewish?"

Daniel was not surprised by the question. Like many other Poles he had heard about the threat of war. He heard horrible stories about the camps in Germany. "They are all nonsense," even many Polish Jews said. "Just rumors and stories." But many other Jews believed the stories and left Poland. He was so busy with his college and job search that he never really gave the subject a thought.

"My mother is Jewish...that makes me Jewish."

"It is more than that, Daniel," continued Hans. "I have good friends in Germany. On their last visit here they told me stories." He turned and looked through the window. Outside it was a beautiful, sunny autumn day. "Some stories I prefer not to believe – stories that do not seem possible from humans. And that is why I prefer not to believe them." He walked towards the door. "But if any of these stories are true," he stopped near the door and looked to the side, "then we are all in deep trouble, Daniel." He turned and looked in Daniel's eyes. "And this is beyond our work."

Daniel looked at him with questioning eyes.

"This is about our lives," added Hans. He nodded and left the room, leaving Daniel with his thoughts.

∞

Daniel sat back on his seat and looked through the windows. What if Hans is right? Many of his close friends had already made plans to leave Poland. They believed that when the Nazis come, it will bring danger to all people, especially Jews. I just got a great job. Something like that comes once in a lifetime. I can't give it up that easy. Then he remembered his father's funny saying. "If more than two people tell you you are drunk, then go to sleep." He always thought it a joke. What if it isn't?

∞

He finished not too late and left the office, making sure he was departing after Hans so as to ensure that he worked at least the same hours as his boss. But it was more than that. Daniel really liked his job. The technical topics were the most advanced in his field and Hans spared no expense. He had all the most sophisticated equipment for mechanical engineering design. Daniel was elated to work for Hans.

Still thinking about his conversation with Hans, Daniel almost missed the tram as it pulled up. He thanked an old man who alerted him, climbed aboard and tossed in his fare. The tram makes a circuit around Krakow but he gets off at a station near the park and from there walks about fifteen minutes to his home. Though it was in a secluded and quiet neighborhood, it was not to his taste. He wanted to live downtown where all the attractions are within walking distance. "It is a matter of age and experience," his mother used to tell him. "When you reach our age, you also will want peace and quiet." She always smiled pleasantly after saying that, assuring him that she understood his desire to live downtown.

The tram was almost empty. There was an elderly couple sitting in the back, a girl who looked like a student and a few kids on their way to the playground. As he walked toward a seat, he got closer to the girl. The sun was about to go down affording him a view of her sunlit face. It was enough to make him stop. His heart raced as he gazed upon her lovely visage. Although embarrassed, he simply could not move his eyes from her. She soon noticed that he was looking at her and they were both caught in the moment. His soul looked into hers, recognizing it and responding to it unconsciously, as though at opposite ends of a tunnel and reaching a moment of reunion. Years if not generations of separation came to an end. "Here we are," exclaimed his soul to hers, and their human hosts merged in an eternal dance of love.

"May I sit near you, please?" Daniel eventually said in an awkward voice. He hoped that the dim light hid the embarrassment coloring his face. "Sure...of course," she replied after pausing to find her voice. He sat near her while his brain raced thousands of miles per hour to control his emotions. She was absolutely the most lovely girl he had ever seen. Her face, her voice, her entire being were enchanting. How do I start a conversation? He looked in all directions beside hers. Daniel, typically full of confidence, was speechless.

She was too. What is it with this man? she thought. I am dying to talk with him! She sneaked occasional glances his way but he quickly turned the other way and feigned interest in a passing shop. She could not control her feelings and wondered what had happened to her. She was not the type to get excited about someone so fast. She typically held her emotions in check upon meeting someone. This time she fell into her feelings.

The tram reached its station but he stayed put. What is going on with me? he screamed inside. I should have gotten off at my station. What am I doing here? Instead he continued sitting near her, occasionally glancing at her and then looking on city sights he already knew well.

What is happening? she thought wildly as the tram passed her station. She hoped for a conversation to start but it never happened. Very well, I can get off at the next station. It's only a short walk, she thought, trying to convince herself that she is about to do the logical thing. The next station arrived and she stayed put. The tram waited a few seconds then moved on. She was almost in pain but could not move. Not before talking to him.

This tram circled the town twice before stopping briefly and beginning a different route. After about an hour it reached its terminus. Everyone got off...except for two people. The elderly driver walked to their seats. "So, are you going to sit here forever?" he said, smiling at the obviously smitten pair. "You know, I've been working on these trams for many years but never had a lovely young couple complete two routes. You must really like each other!" Then he returned to his seat, leaving the two embarrassed passengers.

Daniel found his words eventually. "My name is Daniel...What's yours?"

"I thought this moment would never come," she said with a shy smile. "I am Julia."

"Was it that hard?" joked the old driver through his white beard. "Now, what are you going to do? You obviously missed your stations." But Daniel and Julia were in their own world just then.

Without knowing how he got the courage, Daniel placed his hand on hers. Her touch was delightful. He could not move his gaze from her face. With her other hand she touched his unshaven face, providing him a sublime pleasure. "You two have found the real thing," said the driver with a smile. "The tram is leaving in a few minutes. You can continue to your stations with me. Have some time to yourselves now. It looks like you haven't seen each other for a lifetime." He could never have imagined how true that was.

∞

Daniel and Julia had a hard time without each other during the day. She was in her last year of medical school and he was still learning his job. Both lived with their parents, which prevented the privacy they needed. They used to meet every evening at a small restaurant and have dinner. Then they took long walks through Krakow. They talked about every subject in the world. They held hands, hugged, kissed and were the happiest couple in the universe. They could not wait to reach the public park on the other side of town. Although the nights were cold they could hold each other tenderly on a secluded bench, inspired by the lovely sky. Like teenagers, they found private places but could not fulfill their love yet. Every night they had to go home with burning, unfulfilled love. One chilly night Daniel showed up at the cozy restaurant eager to tell his secret. "Why are you so... What happened?" asked Julia as she took off her coat and sat beside him.

"I have a surprise for you." Daniel was smiling ear to ear as his cheeks reddened in the warm restaurant. "I reserved a room for us in a country inn outside town." He looked at her with sparkling eyes. Without waiting for her answer he grabbed her and they hugged joyfully.

"Where is it?" she asked, all excited, "and the most important question, when?"

"This weekend, my love. In exactly three days..." he smiled like a naughty boy. "Not that I am counting..."

"You are my genius..." said Julia, and then she kissed him passionately.

They got lost within their kiss, forgetting they were in a public place. Their bodies naturally pressed against each other. They could hardly stop and were breathing heavily when they broke it off to sit back and look at the menu. They had a hard time concentrating and it took them a while to order.

Three days later they stood before the inn. It was absolutely beautiful. It was located in a small town almost surrounded by a pine forest whose scent was everywhere. Snowcapped mountains were visible from almost every room. They stood there, fascinated by nature, breathing the brisk, pine-scented air. "Are you going to stay outside all night?" an old bearded man asked cheerfully as he approached them. "It will get cold soon and there's a fireplace for you in the lobby...or in your room. Is this your baggage?" They could not see his lips through his thick beard.

"He looks like Santa Claus," whispered Daniel as he found his words. "Yes, those are ours. But please, we can take it ourselves."

"Not here, you don't," replied the old man as he lifted their suitcases. "Here we take pride in hospitality. What did you say your name is, sir?"

Daniel and Julia looked at each other with big eyes. They already loved their small vacation.

The old man insisted on escorting them to their room. "This is the best room in our entire inn," he said. "We usually reserve it for special occasions...like honeymooners," he looked at them with a meaningful smile. They felt embarrassed and looked at each other with innocent red faces. He opened the door to their room and they stood there, mouths agape, as they took in the view given by a large window. A fireplace warmed the room from the far end corner. The spacious bed was covered with a thick, fluffy blanket. The two long candles on an antique table emitted a gentle, stimulating scent.

As soon as the innkeeper left, Daniel pulled Julia to him. They could not control their hunger for each other and fell onto the bed, passionately kissing and touching each other. Quickly they shed their clothes and let their love roam free. Their physical love had been bounded for so long it exploded in a variety of forms and they could not have enough of it. They moved together in the rhythm of excitement until their entire beings burst into millions of bright lights. Exhausted, they lay together, covered with perspiration, holding each other. Soon their ardor was reawakened and they gently made love once more. They lost all sense of time and eventually fell asleep together, their bodies entwined.

A knock on the door awoke Daniel. "Breakfast time," the innkeeper cheerfully announced. "Do you want your breakfast in your room?"

"Yes, please," he answered softly, trying not to wake Julia. "Could you bring it in about half an hour?" he added.

"Of course." He heard the footsteps fade as he went to his way.

He looked at Julia asleep next to him. She is astonishing...and I love her so much. He looked out on the majestic mountain and realized that nothing really mattered now...nothing beside them.

Breakfast was amazing. The inn had been owned for many years by this elderly couple that served guests personally. They served fresh eggs, fruit salad, whole wheat toast and homemade jam. The eggs were quite an experience as was the berry jam that the old man's wife had made. Daniel and Julia spent the day touring the village and hiking the surrounding mountains, then returned in the evening to the inn. After a sumptuous dinner they lay on the bed watching the night overtake the mountain.

"This is going to be too short a vacation, Daniel..." said Julia almost in sadness. "In two days we have to go back to our city lives...and I do not want to. I'll be able to see you only late at night, without any place to ourselves."

Daniel felt his heart begin to ache.

"I know, my love" he replied, hugging her. "But no worry, we will work on this. I want to marry you," he told her softly the pausing. "Will you marry me, love of my life?"

Julia looked at him in disbelief as her eyes moistened.

"I will...with all my heart, Daniel." She held his face lovingly in her little hands. Her warm tears watered both of them as she whispered, "I'll always be yours...always..."

On Monday they informed their parents about their intention to marry. They did not set a date.

∞

The newspaper headlines were talking about Kristallnacht, or the Night of Broken Glass. It was a massive, coordinated attack on Jews throughout Germany, beginning on the night of November 9, 1938, and continuing into the next day. The German police stood by and crowds of spectators watched in support as members of the SS and Hitler Youth beat and murdered Jews, broke into and ransacked Jewish homes, and brutalized Jewish women and children. All over Germany, Austria and other Nazi-controlled areas, Jewish shops and department stores had their windows smashed and contents destroyed.

Synagogues were vandalized, their Torah scrolls desecrated. As hundreds of synagogues were systematically burned, fire departments stood by or only prevented fires from spreading. About 25,000 Jewish men were rounded up and sent to concentration camps, where they were brutalized by SS guards and in some cases randomly chosen to be beaten to death. The reaction outside Germany to Kristallnacht was shock and outrage, creating a storm of negative publicity in newspapers and among radio commentators that served to isolate Hitler's Germany from the civilized nations and weaken any pro-Nazi sentiment in those countries. Shortly after Kristallnacht, the United States recalled its ambassador, permanently.

∞

Daniel and Julia sat wordlessly at their regular restaurant. The stories about the Nazis were all that anyone talked about. A war atmosphere hung over Krakow. But the most disturbing of all was the talk about the Jews. The newspapers were describing, on a daily basis, the Nazi actions against Jews. Everyone talked about the day that the Nazis would invade Poland. The fate of Polish

Jews will be similar to that of their German brothers. Many were making plans to leave Europe. Others would not leave. These are only vicious rumors, they said. Cruel and inhumane actions like these will never happen. People and governments will never allow such behavior. War has bad sides but nothing like that.

Daniel and Julia did not know what to think. Daniel was upset since he just got a great job and did not want to leave it. Julia was in her last year of medical school and was supposed to graduate next summer. Both their parents urged them to leave Europe. "I can't believe that people are running away just because of rumors," said Daniel quietly as he ate dessert. Typically he loved cake, but today he had no appetite for it at all.

"My father wants me to quit the university and leave for America. We have family in New York and they already sent us a letter saying they will arrange a program so I can complete my medical degree there." She held Daniel's hand tight. "I do not want to leave you..."

"And we will not be separated," answered Daniel determinedly. He kissed her hand and smiled. "Whatever happens, we go together."

Julia wiped her tears and looked at him. He gave her strength. Whatever happens, we will be together, she thought. She held both his hands, curled into his chest and closed her eyes.

∞

A few weeks later Daniel's father approached him at breakfast. "Daniel, I would like to talk with you tomorrow. Could you come home before you two meet?"

"Why?" asked Daniel as he hurriedly ate his toast and drank his coffee.

"Daniel, please do not eat too fast. It is dangerous, you know," scolded his mom as she poured him more coffee.

Daniel ignored her and looked at his father's worried face. Daniel stopped eating. "What's happened?" he asked. His father's forehead had sweat. He looked pale and sickly.

"Are you not well, father?"

"I have been talking with friends – people in key positions in the government."

He then looked at his mother who simply stared at him.

"The Nazis are coming to Poland, Daniel. It is almost for sure. The only question is when. We think that they will seize Poland in mid 1939."

"How can you know?" Daniel was upset and returned to his meal a little angry. "I know what you are about to tell me. I just got a new job and Julia and I want to get married soon. How can we do that without a job?"

"Daniel, when the Nazis seize Krakow they will arrest all of us, including you and Julia. Then you will have no job...and even worse." His voice fell almost to a whisper. "They can send you to work camps. They kill the Jews in these camps. Everyone knows that." He looked straight into Daniel's eyes. "A few friends are organizing groups of young people to leave for friendly places – Holland, Scandinavia and any other country far away from here."

"And what are we supposed to do there?" answered Daniel cynically. Then he saw his father's eyes and released a long sigh. "Everyone is talking about what is going to happen when the Nazis come. But can you understand our side also?" he looked at his father and mother with a desperate look. "How are we supposed to start our lives together far away, without jobs... and Julia has not even finished her degree yet." He scratched his forehead and looked at his parents. He could feel their sincere concern.

"You both are young. You will be able to start over anywhere in the world," said his father, looking somewhat relieved. Daniel seemed to entertain the idea.

"We will not consider this before Julia completes her degree," he answered.

"That may be too late," replied his mother somberly.

Daniel turned his look towards his mother. She hardly ever got involved in family arguments and this was the first time he had heard her state an opinion.

"I am also talking with my friends on a daily basis." She looked seriously at Daniel. "The situation is not good. They are not here yet so we all have a false sense of security. It can change within days. They are already killing Jews in Germany and every other country they have seized. I do not think you have time to wait until summer."

Daniel looked very frustrated. "What about you two? You are sending us and staying here?"

His father took a deep breath. "We want to leave soon. I've already talked with my brother in Brussels. He will find us a small place until the war is over." He got closer to Daniel. "You both are more than welcome to come stay with us. It is only until the war is over."

"Ahh," Daniel answered with deep bitterness. "Who knows how many years it will go on..."

His parents did not say anything more; they simply concentrated on their breakfast.

"I'll talk with Julia," said Daniel after a long while. His father nodded silently.

Finishing his breakfast and leaving for the office, he could hear the newspaper boy, as every morning, screaming the headlines. He could not stop his urge to see the headlines. He went to the corner and bought a paper. "Jewish pupils expelled from German schools," shouted the headlines in bold letters. Daniel read it in disbelief. He did not even look at the rest. He knew his parents had good reason to leave Poland.

∞

"Are you crazy? You're asking me to leave before I get my medical degree?" Julia was furious. They sat in the restaurant as Daniel told her about his discussion with his parents. Julia stopped eating and looked at him in astonishment.

"Julia," tried Daniel, "have you read the newspapers? Did you hear the talk? Everyone is talking about what's going on. I did not have the time to look at the news when I was searching for a job, but the truth is that the situation is getting bad – terrible." Daniel took a long sip of coffee and looked at her with a serious look.

"The Nazis are coming to Poland. It's just a matter of time." He released a long sigh. "You know, I also worked hard to get my job and I can't even think about quitting now. The freedom to do whatever we want depends on our jobs, or in your case your degree." He paused a few seconds, took a deep breath and continued. "But the situation endangers our very lives."

He held her hand. "Look, I too was a skeptical. But I took time today and talked with people. We are among the few that still do not pay attention to what's going on."

"So why are people not leaving?" challenged Julia.

"It isn't easy. Many people simply do not believe that something like this will happen. Others do not believe the rumors. They think that even if the Nazis invade Poland, they will not be barbarians." Daniel stopped and looked outside. "Even for me these stories sound like old propaganda. Did you hear some of the stories or read the newspapers?"

Julia resumed eating. "No, and I do not want to hear about it. I have enough worries without the stupid war. Let them deal with it." She continued eating anxiously. Then she stopped and held her head, looking at the table.

"What we are supposed to do anyway? The Nazis are going to invade the whole world. One of the professors said it today during class. They will be everywhere." She looked at him sadly. "Can we just wait until the war is over? After all, it will have to end at some point. The thought of quitting now, just a few months before graduation, is killing me." She wiped a tear. "You know how much I put into school. I love this profession and I'm good at it. I want to be a pediatrician. A move will deprive me of this... Do you really think it is the right thing to do?"

Daniel could see the pain in her eyes. He knew how much she wanted to be a doctor. He knew how much she wants to help people, especially children. He saw her tears and could not say anything. Instead he held her. They held each other a long time, gently rocking, and looking at the streets that were slowly emptying. Snow started to fall, covering the city with a white, sparkly blanket.

∞

"We are going to leave in the summer, when Julia completes her degree," announced Daniel a week later during breakfast.

His father and mother stopped eating and looked at each other, without saying a word. Then they continued their breakfast.

No one said anything else that morning.

∞

Daniel and Julia hardly ate their dinner. It was a cold December night and they had their late dinner, as every weekend. The city was covered with snow and the flakes had fallen slowly for many days now. The snow reached up to five feet in certain places, and the city's plows worked around the clock to clear the streets.

"I read that they instated a law for compulsory Aryanization of all Jewish businesses," said Julia quietly, as she stared at the snow outside. "It is all over the papers." She looked straight at Daniel.

"Hans told me that yesterday," replied Daniel. He tried to concentrate on his cup of coffee. "I can't believe these things are happening."

"The situation is getting worse. My father and mother are telling me on a daily basis about the Jews in Germany."

"The Germans are coming here, Julia," said Daniel almost whispering. "They are coming soon. Everyone is talking about it. Many people have left the factory. They left for other countries, some even left Europe." He held her hand. "I think that we may need to move sooner." He paused. "There's real danger, my love."

"I know." Julia had tears in her eyes. "I see it coming too." She held his hand tightly. "It is just so hard for me to leave school. I worked for this for years. Leaving it at the end is breaking my heart." She could not stop her tears.

"We will have to make plans," said Daniel, looking through the window at the snowy streets, "...and very soon."

"Where do you want to go?" his eyes sparkled. "My father has connections in America, and we can start a new life there." She did not say a word. Feeling her sadness, Daniel continued. "I am sure that you can complete your medical degree in New York. We'll get all the help we need there. There is a group of guys that are planning to leave together. A friend from work told me this yesterday. They are planning to go on a ship around April or May. They will depart from Italy, heading to New York." Daniel looked excited. Julia, however, did not.

"Let's go meet them next week," she said after a while.

"Your parents will be very happy and so will mine," replied Daniel, holding her tight.

"They are leaving Poland next week," Julia said without any change of tone. She was upset.

Julia's parents left Poland for Scandinavia. Daniel and Julia had their own place now and some privacy. It made Julia happy, except for the impending departure. Cooking together a few times a week was a ritual; each time something new. On the weekends they went out for a special dinner. Julia anxiously continued her last semester, trying to achieve the highest scores in her final exams. She was determined to bring the best grades with her. She wanted to be accepted into a prestigious medical school, wherever they went.

∞

On Thursday they went to the group's initial meeting at the house of one of the founders. There were about thirty-five people, young couples and singles, all in their early to late twenties. They introduced themselves to other members and quickly found friends with similar backgrounds. Now they were all sitting and listening to the group's founder, Henry Cohen. "Thank you all for coming here tonight. As you know, the Nazi outrages continue, especially towards Jews." He paused and looked at everyone, trying to convey the enormity to them. "We have all seen what happened in Germany. The Jews there are humiliated, robbed, then expelled or murdered. There are those people that say it will never reach here, it will never happen to us. I say, it is almost here. Just a few months ago we saw how fifteen thousand Polish-German Jews were deported from Germany – without their belongings. They were left at the border for several months until Poland accepted them." He paused and wiped his forehead. "But worse, we hear things that we do not want to hear or do not want to believe. We hear that Jews are murdered in Germany. We hear that Jewish children are banned from schools. We hear things that are inhuman."

He looked at the people in the room thoroughly. "I think that it will get even worse. The Nazis do not care about human life. They blame the Jews for every problem to incite the crowds. They want to kill us all." He paused for water. "And they are coming to Poland. Some say they will invade in a few months, and some say in a few years. I say, it really doesn't matter. When they come, they will destroy us. Even if they do not kill us all, we will not be able to hold our jobs or send our children to school or own a business. Therefore I've organized this group quietly and secretly. I will recruit more. I am planning to get us all on a ship departing from Italy on July this year. We will go to America, the land of the free. As I see it today, even England and France are not safe. The Nazis may reach there also. We are young, healthy and holding a wide variety of professions. We will be able to find a new home in a new land. At least until Europe is in better hands." A murmur sounded among the people.

"I personally think that the Nazis will not rule for too long. The world will deal with them, eventually." And then he continued in a lower voice. "What I am afraid of is what will happen to the Jews until then..." There was a complete silence in the crowd. Cigarettes smoke silently made its way towards the ceiling.

Weeks later, Daniel was encouraged. He noticed that Julia was much happier than before. It all started last week, not that long after the group meeting. All of a sudden during breakfast she was in an extremely happy mood. Of course, he was happy also but wondered what had changed. She was no longer so concerned about her degree.

"Oh, I'll continue it somewhere else," she told him that day and then devoured her breakfast.

"Great," he responded in elation, but still wondering what had brought on her change.

Seeing that he did not grasp the change, she added, "It is the right thing to do anyway, and if I cannot fight it then I better join it. It will be just fine...wherever we go." She left for her class and he remained there, surprised.

∞

The next day he found out why.

It all happened when they met for lunch. He came to her university cafeteria and ordered their meals. He noticed that she did not eat. Within a few minutes she looked sick.

"Are you alright?" he asked worriedly.

"I'm not hungry," she replied quietly, trying to suppress her nausea. It was obvious she did not feel well. She left for the restroom and returned after a few minutes. "I feel much better now... But I'll eat only the green apple," she said as she held his hand. "And there is another thing that I need to tell you."

He felt that something big was coming and remained quiet. She looked at him for a while.

"We are going to be parents," she whispered with a mysterious smile.

"What..." replied Daniel instinctively and then understood everything. "My..." he did not know what to say. Then he felt joy spreading through his body. I am going to be a father. Julia was waiting patiently to see his response. He grabbed her and held her tight to his chest. "We are going to be parents..." he simply said.

They made plans for the event. The baby was due around July and she could use her student benefits at the local hospital. They decided to have the baby in Krakow and shortly after that, depart with the group. They hoped they would not miss the ship's departure. "Worst case, we leave Europe by train," suggested Daniel. "We'll travel to a safe country and settle there until the war is over." They saved as much as they could for those days to come.

∞

In February 1939, the Nazis forced German Jews to hand over all gold and silver. The Jews there were at the mercy of mobs. Anyone could beat them, rob them or even murder them. German schools presented anti-Semitic propaganda, creating hatred towards Jews, even among children. Many Jews were forced out of their homes and had all of their belongings stolen. The spirit of pogrom pervaded Germany.

"I worry that we will not be able to leave on time," said Daniel one night as they cuddled on the couch. "The newspapers are telling horrible stories. If the Nazis come here soon, we're in danger."

"You look tired, my love," Julia said, kissing him. "The war is not here and we do not have to worry about it. Let's focus on our plan. We have to do the best we can. Save money, have the baby and then leave. Maybe the war will be over by then. Who knows." She gave him a loving look. "Here, I'll bring you some of the cake that you like. There are only two more pieces..."

She's quite happy and not worried, thought Daniel. "Sure, I'll have a piece of this delightful cake, but only if you'll share it with me."

"You know I will..." She headed for the kitchen.

He watched her and reminded himself how beautiful she was. I wish I could avoid worrying. He looked again at the newspaper. He could feel trouble coming their way.

∞

Julia passed the difficult part of her pregnancy and started to eat normally again. She used her student benefits to get free checkups at the university hospital. The baby became her own world and that was all she talked about.

In March 1939, Nazi troops seized the Sudetenland of Czechoslovakia, which had a Jewish population of 350,000. In April, Czechoslovakia passed its own Nuremberg Laws. The Nuremberg Race Laws of 1935 deprived German Jews of their rights of citizenship, making them "subjects" in Hitler's Reich. The laws also forbade Jews to marry or have sexual relations with Aryans, or to employ young Aryan women as household help. After 1935, the Nazis issued a dozen supplemental decrees that deprived Jews of their rights as human beings. In April, Jews lost the rights as tenants and were relocated into Jewish dwellings.

∞

"We have to get out soon." Daniel was disturbed. "I have a bad feeling." He looked at Julia sitting on the chair in deep thought. "All my friends at the factory are urging me to leave. The Germans have already invaded Czechoslovakia. We're next." He walked back and forth in the small living room. "I say we pack the essentials and leave this weekend. We'll go far away... somewhere in Western Europe. We have savings and I can work any job."

"We do not have enough money to get by and then have the baby," replied Julia quietly. "We have to have the baby here... before we leave." She looked at him sadly. "Otherwise we have no chance, especially with a new baby. How soon until you can find a job in another country? Will they even give us work permits? Here, we are citizens. We can complete all the necessary matters and then leave. At least we will have the baby, and we can save more money."

"They will be here soon," said Daniel, breathless from emotion.

"They've said that for the past six months now," replied Julia. "And I still don't see the Nazis." She took a sip from her tea. "I do not want to listen to rumors. The fact is that we do not know just when they are coming. But that's not really a good thing." She looked at him. "When they come, it will be a surprise."

"Very true," said Daniel as he sat near her. "And also too late for us."

Julia buried her head in his chest. She knew he was right.

∞

"The St. Louis, a ship crowded with 930 Jewish refugees, was turned away by Cuba, the United States and other countries. It then returned to Europe." Hans tossed the newspaper on Daniel's desk. Daniel was immersed in technical documents but he grabbed the paper and read it quietly. Hans sat and looked out the window. "I would never imagine that such madness would take over." He looked over at Daniel. "What are you going to do about this?" Daniel just nodded nervously. "I would leave this place tomorrow if not for this factory," Hans continued. He pursed his lips and turned towards the window. "This plant has been in our family for generations. My father dedicated his life to it, and his father and his father." He turned back to Daniel. "So I have to stay here." Daniel still did not say a word.

"But you don't!" exclaimed Hans as he stood up and approached Daniel. "Don't you understand the danger? They are almost here! The moment they get here, your fate will be that of the Jews in Germany." He paced about the room. "It is a matter of life and death. I honestly believe it is." He turned again towards Daniel. "Look Daniel, I think that you are a bright engineer and of course I want you here with us. Since you've came on board, you've done excellent work and I'm really proud of you. When the situation gets better, I'll take you back." Daniel looked at him with admiration. "I just don't want you to make a bad decision based on work." He released a long sigh. "Life is much more than just work."

"Work is not the issue, Hans," said Daniel after a while. "Julia is pregnant." Hans stood and stared. "We simply do not have enough money to move to another country and start a new life there. It's too complicated. We want to marry and live abroad until the war is over. But it is not that easy. Circumstances have changed. Now we have to think about the baby."

Hans looked at him for a while and then started walking around the room again, deep in thought. "First, this is great news," he said with a warm smile. "In other circumstances, it would be a wonderful event. But just now we are in a difficult time." He continued his pacing. "But even for this there are solutions." A thought came to him. "Daniel, I like you and I want to help. I would like to help you two with some money to leave Poland for a while. At least until the war is over."

"No, thank you. I cannot..."

Hans interrupted. "Shhh... I am not rich but I do not have a wife and kids. This is the least I can do. Just think about it and let me know tomorrow how much you think you'll need." He was on his way out but he stopped at the door, remembering something. "But you have to decide fast. Really fast. I have the feeling that war is almost here." He left the room before Daniel had a chance to say anything.

∞

"Daniel... it's time," Julia said quietly as she touched Daniel's shoulder.

"What, honey...?" Daniel mumbled, barely out of sleep.

"It is time, Daniel! We need to go to the hospital!" this time Julia was emphatic.

He was awake now. He briefly looked at his watch. It was almost midnight. He turned to Julia, lying calmly next to him.

"Are you sure?" he asked her as he touched her stomach. "The baby is about to come out?" He smiled in excitement.

"I am all wet, Daniel. My water broke. It is time to go now."

That was enough for Daniel. Quickly they dressed, took the bag they had prepared and left for the hospital. It was a typical warm July night and there wasn't much traffic as their taxi rushed them to the hospital. After five hours of labor, Julia gave birth to a beautiful baby boy. They named the baby Isaac. Julia loved that name. Julia and Daniel were happy parents. They forgot the rest of the world. For them little Isaac was everything. Hans held a small party at the factory. The entire factory celebrated Isaac's circumcision.

Urged on by Hans, they prepared to leave Poland in August. Their plan was to cross Poland to the south and go to Italy. There, they would stay awhile. Daniel had close friends in a small port town, who offered them a room for a few months. Everyone believed that the war would be over by then.

"The situation is actually getting worse," said Daniel during dinner. "I hear that the Nazis are savage with Jews." Julia was feeding the baby and did not respond. "They are confining them to the ghettos, forcing them to work for nothing." Daniel was eating his dinner slowly, deep in thought. "Hans wants us to leave as soon as possible."

"Daniel," responded Julia at last, "we will. I am going to complete my last exam next week. Then we can leave." She finished feeding the baby and was now rocking him to sleep.

Daniel looked through the window at Krakow's streets. The streets are too empty. What's happening? War was in the air. "I just hope that it's not too late" he said quietly. Julia did not hear him. She fell asleep, along with Isaac.

A week later the German army invaded Poland.

∞

At dawn on September 1, 1939, the German army launched a ferocious assault across the Polish border. First, the Luftwaffe sent its bombers and fighters to attack airfields, railheads, troop concentrations and anything else vital to the command and control of the Polish armed forces. The first Blitzkrieg had begun. One hour later German troops attacked from the north and south, intent on encircling the Polish army. The Poles fell back only to find German troops in their rear. Two days later, honoring their obligations to Poland, France and Britain declared war on Germany. This was of no help to Poland. The final blow came on September 17 when Soviet forces, under terms of a secret agreement with Germany, marched in from the east. Warsaw surrendered on September 27. By October 6, it was all over. Poland ceased to exist as a country. World War II had begun.

Poland was immediately divided between the Soviet Union and Nazi Germany. The Soviets absorbed the eastern portion including Byelorussia and the West Ukraine. The Germans declared the western portion of Poland a part of Greater Germany. The portion in the middle including Warsaw was declared a German colony ruled from the city of Krakow.

∞

Two weeks later, Julia, Daniel and Isaac were at the train station with two large suitcases. Their train would take them to the southern border. From there they would take another train to Firenze, Italy.

"Isaac looks so cute," said Julia with a smile. They had bought him a new baby outfit for the trip. Daniel felt better now that they were on their way. Hans was very pleased that they were leaving. He gave them some money and promised to rehire Daniel when the war was over. "Just stay there until all this insanity is over," he said.

The loudspeaker announced the train's destination, and they went aboard. It was to be a long trip – almost seven hours – but Daniel did not care. As they get farther away from Krakow, he felt better. The train ride was relaxing. Little Isaac was already asleep and they all watched the passing countryside.

"I remember the first time we met..." whispered Julia, resting her head on Daniel's shoulder.

"Yes," said Daniel as he was looking outside. "I remember that day." He looked at Julia and kissed her.

"I could not stop looking at you," continued Julia. "My heart pounded so hard I thought that you could hear it." She smiled and kissed his neck.

"And I thought that I just saw the most beautiful girl in the world," said Daniel "and I wasn't leaving the trolley without her." He looked at her with love.

"It was so funny," Julia laughed wildly. "We circled town three times, refusing to leave each other, yet we were too shy to talk with each other."

"But it was worth it all!" declared Daniel as he hugged her.

"And now look what we have created – little Isaac." They both looked at the sleeping baby. His little cheeks were red and he was breathing calmly.

"I wish I could be a baby," said Daniel, looking at his son. "Such a worry-free life. He does not really care what is going on. As long as he gets his food and sleep, he is happy."

"Yes, but he depends completely on us, his parents," replied Julia. She touched Isaac's little hand and he moved slightly.

"But he does not know that..." Daniel smiled and touched Isaac's little head. "Go on sleeping, my baby, do not worry. Mommy and daddy are here to take care of you..."

"Newspaper! Newspaper!" came the call from the hallway. Their cabin door was opened and a paperboy asked, "Care for a newspaper? There is big news: The Nazis have invaded Poland." Daniel was instantly covered with cold sweat. His and Julia's eyes crossed as they looked at each other wordlessly. "No, thank you," said Daniel quietly. "That won't be necessary..." When they arrived at the next station, their cabin door opened and two German officers regarded them. Julia and Daniel looked at each other.

"Passports, please," said one of them. He looked at the sleeping baby and added, "What a cute baby..." Though smiling, the officer had a cold, steel look in his eyes, noted Daniel as he handed their passports.

"Daniel and Julia Stern?" he asked. They nodded.

"This is your last stop." He looked at them again – this time without any smile.

∞

The officers took them off the train, where they stood in a long line with many other people. When they asked the purpose of the check, the answer was "a routine passport check." The train left and they were told they could take the next one. They were allowed to go to the restrooms at the train station and also buy some food. After about two hours, their identification was verified. Out of nowhere, yellow Star of David patches were brought out and handed to everyone. They were told to attach the patches to their clothes in an easily visible place.

Daniel was upset. They were told that they are going to take a different train to a different location. "I'll ask the soldiers where they are taking us and why. We need to get to Italy tonight," he told Julia. But she just looked at him and said nothing. She looked scared. Daniel looked at her for few seconds and then hugged her. "Don't worry, honey," he said in an assuring voice. "Everything will be fine. I never really believed the rumors about the Nazis. After all, what would they do to a young couple with a baby?" He sounded almost cheerful. "We are all human beings after all, especially when dealing with babies..." He continued with a pleasant look. "Aren't we?" Julia held back her tears and nodded. I wish I could believe that, she thought. She had a sense of dread.

The soldiers arranged a few tables, notebooks and some papers. Little Isaac was hungry and Julia prepared to breast feed him. From the corner of her eye she saw the soldiers making a banner, which was then placed on one of the tables. She turned her head to read the banner.

It read, "Dachau."

∞

Everything unfolded as in an unreal, bad dream. A long line of boxcars was brought to the station by a large steam locomotive. It was clear that these boxcars were designed for animal transport. They were covered with mud and dried animal droppings. The people were then pushed in like animals. Many complained loudly but the soldiers ignored them or shouted angrily at them to get in. When they asked where they were going, the only answer was "relocation." They asked for details but received a stone face and no answer.

The boxcar was fully packed with men, women and a few children. All had to stand and lean against each other. The small openings did not allow in much air and everyone sweated. The change from humanity to brutality was so drastic that people had difficulty believing it was actually happening. Only hours ago they were free human beings, but now they were mere objects as soldiers pushed, yelled at and beat them. Shocked, scared and refusing to believe what was going on, they entered the boxcars and before they had a chance to comprehend what was happening, the train started to move towards Dachau.

∞

Julia and Daniel stood near each other. Julia held Isaac to Daniel who was holding the opening. "I can't believe they shoved us all in here like animals, even children and babies." It all seemed like a nightmare. Julia wordlessly concentrated on holding little Isaac, keeping him a sleep. No one spoke. From time to time someone groaned or complained about the heat. An older man cried out, "We are all thirsty in here! We are not animals!" The others calmed him. The train continued its journey.

"I have a very bad feeling abut this," said Julia quietly. Daniel looked at Julia and could see pain in her eyes. He had the same feeling but did not want to make her even more frightened. His brain constantly sought a way to get out of the situation, but without any success. It seems like we missed our chance, he thought with bitterness. From now on, our destiny is unknown. We should have listened to everyone who told us to leave earlier.

"I am not giving up Isaac," whispered Julia quietly, as though she had read his thoughts.

∞

After many hours, the train arrived at Dachau concentration camp. The boxcars doors were opened by SS soldiers who roughly herded the people out. Daniel and Julia were pushed along with other Jews to a field where they were ordered to assemble in rows. Julia was able to hide little Isaac under her coat. Luckily he was sleeping.

"You are prisoners of war," the loudspeakers screamed in a metallic sound. "You will stay in this camp and work for Nazi Germany. You will obey the camp rules. Those who do not obey will be executed." The loudspeaker system continued to bark more and more instructions. The people listened silently. Their expressions ranged from confusion to shock. Men, women, the elderly and children stood in rows without understanding what was happening.

Daniel could not believe it. We are prisoners just because we are Jews, he thought, trying to grasp the meaning. All that we heard about the German Jews was true then. He looked around the camp and saw the foreboding buildings, the fences and the SS guards. His spirit wanted to scream, "We are innocent! We did no harm to anyone!" But he remained silent. He knew there was worse to come. Help us, please, he prayed inside his heart, for little Isaac's sake. He turned and looked at Julia. Amazingly she was standing, holding little Isaac to her heart, covered by her coat. She looks strong. Her spirit to defend her child is strong, he thought in amazement. I wish I was that strong.

Their belongings were taken from them. They received two sets of prison clothes and one pair of shoes, then were divided into men and women. Each received sleeping quarters in separate buildings. Daniel was assigned to work on the road outside the camp while Julia worked at the large sawmill at the farther side of the camp.

It was just the beginning.

It was almost 1940 and Dachau concentration camp held a few thousand prisoners. Initially the internees consisted primarily of German Communists, Social Democrats, trade unionists, and other political opponents of the Nazi regime. Over time, other groups were also interned there: Gypsies, homosexuals, as well as "antisocial" types and repeat criminals. During its early years, relatively few Jews were interned in Dachau and then usually because they belonged to one of the above groups or had completed prison sentences after being convicted for violating the Nuremberg Laws. The number of Jewish prisoners at Dachau rose with the increased persecution of Jews, and on November 10-11, 1938, in the aftermath of the Night of Broken Glass, more than 10,000 Jews were interned there.

Daniel and Julia's group was just one of many.

∞

At the beginning, the conditions were fairly decent. Since Dachau was a model camp to the world, the Nazis kept it presentable, especially when visitors arrived. As the war progressed, however, the living conditions deteriorated and many prisoners died due to weakness or disease.

Daniel and Julia could see each other every night near the showers. Both were exhausted from the workday but could not wait for the moment. Daniel used to say that one day all this would be gone and they'd be free again. Julia kept little Isaac with her so his father could see him. He fell asleep after every breast feeding, which made it easier to hide him from the guards.

"I want to marry you...in a religious ceremony," told her Daniel one night.

Julia wept.

"Daniel, nothing would make me happier than to marry you according to our tradition." Although tired, she could not hide her happiness.

"I'll talk with the Rabbi in our quarters," replied Daniel as they embraced. We have to do that as soon as possible. Who knows what tomorrow brings.

They arranged the ceremony for a few weeks later. His entire building would be their witnesses and they could hardly wait for the moment. All they wanted was to get married in a life-bonding ceremony, even in these conditions.

∞

Two weeks later they were standing under an improvised chuppah that was quickly fashioned from sticks and cloth. As the Rabbi gave the blessing, Daniel and Julia looked at each other and forgot the dismal world that surrounded them. They forgot the chilly night breeze. They forgot they were going to wake up tomorrow morning into a miserable reality. They forgot that tomorrow they may die. They were lost in their moment. Many people quietly surrounded the chuppah as the ceremony went on.

"I do not understand these couple," said one man to another next to him. "These people are getting married as though they have a future. We may have no tomorrow..."

The man near him smiled.

"That is the best way to make a future," he answered, exposing rotten teeth. "This proves that we did not lose our spirit of life. No evil war will prevent us from being human beings. Life must go on. This is the only way we can win this war..." His last sentence faded. He was trying to catch his breath as a sudden cough took over. The man looked at him in disbelief. "Nonsense! Within the next few months the Nazis will kill us all. I know it!" He looked straight into the other man's face. "You know it, everyone knows it. I do not know why everyone continues to pretend we have a future. We simply don't..."

He left the gathering and walked into the barracks.

The other man looked after him. His smile had faded away. He looked at the couple under the chuppah and thought the man might be right.

"Mazal Tov," the Rabbi blessed the young couple. Daniel stepped on a glass and the witnesses cheered. It was strange to see a wedding party dressed in prison clothes, dirty and emaciated, but nonetheless with sparks of hope in their eyes. No matter what the Nazis did, their spirit could not be broken. The wedding was living proof of their passion for life. It did not matter what happened, as long as they were alive. Life must go on and traditions be kept.

Daniel looked at Julia's eyes and they kissed a long while as the guests sang and cheered. They gave them part of the quarters to be alone. Julia's friend watched little Isaac as they shared the most precious moment in their life – their wedding night.

∞

The next morning they witnessed the first summary execution.

The commandant ordered everyone to stand in rows in the courtyard. One of the prisoners had tried to escape the previous night. An electrified fence, a ditch, and a wall with seven guard towers surrounded the camp. It was not easy to escape. The prisoner trying to escape was caught on the electric barbwire. The commandant wanted to demonstrate the punishment for trying to escape. A prisoner was brought in front of the assembly as the commandant berated him and paced back and forth. In time, the commandant simply drew his pistol and shot the man in the head. The sound of the shot passed into the crowd. Everyone was stunned. They witnessed a helpless man, shot to death and bleeding profusely from the head.

Julia cried quietly as Daniel pursed his lips and watched the body fall to the ground. It's just started, thought Daniel. He looked to the gray skies, hoping to find some answers, but none came.

Executions became an almost daily event as the number of Jews in the camp increased. Once a week a new train arrived and the population grew. Every day the reason for execution was different. The SS officers liked this new game of murdering Jews without any reason. The dawn of mass murder had begun.

∞

"Daniel I am really worried about Isaac," said Julia one night at their meeting. It was becoming harder to hide him. Julia built him a small area in her barracks where he could stay during the day. Every time she had a short break, she was off to feed him. She was worried that if he made some noises while she was not there, the SS guards would find him.

The next morning at the morning routine, the commandant marched between the lines, reviewing the prisoners. He moved back and forth between the lines, looking at people's faces. This morning he looked disturbed. Daniel watched him in fear as he approached him. The commandant walked slowly near Daniel and stopped in front of him. Daniel held his breath. He knew the meaning – arbitrarily picking a prisoner to be executed. Sometimes the commandant just yelled at the prisoner and hit him, but it usually ended with shooting him to death.

Today Daniel was chosen.

The commandant looked thoroughly at Daniel. He felt fear taking over. This came as a total surprise. They tried to stand in the rear rows so they would not be picked but today the commandant started at the rear rows. I am going to die, thought Daniel. His breathing got faster. He started to sweat and shake. Today is my turn. But I am not ready for this. Daniel closed his eyes. The commandant looked at him and could see his fear.

"What's your name?" he asked him.

Daniel opened his eyes. "Daniel," he said automatically. His face was pale.

"How long are you here?"

"I do not know, sir. A few months now," responded Daniel robotically. Then he looked at the commandant. Incredible – he is my age! The man resembled one of his friends from the university. Daniel, to his surprise, had become calm. Maybe it was the young officer or maybe the composed expression on his face. Daniel well knew that the commandant had killed many people in recent weeks, but he no longer felt fear.

"Get out and stand in courtyard," barked the officer.

This was the beginning. Typically after shouting, beating and kicking, the prisoner was shot.

"No..." he could hear Julia cry in the row behind him. He looked back to see her briefly and put his finger to his mouth. He exited his row and walked to the center of the courtyard. She should be quiet, so as not to be caught.

He stopped at the center of the courtyard as everyone looked on. They had all seen it happen many times before. They knew the outcome.

"How do you feel today?" the young officer screamed at Daniel.

Here it starts, thought Daniel, still strangely calm. "I am well, sir."

His calm answer annoyed the commander and he walked faster towards him and hit him hard on the back with his walking stick.

"You are well?" he screamed, his face reddening in rage.

Daniel grimaced in pain but continued to stand. He looked the commandant in the eye.

"Yes, I am well, thank you."

What is making him so angry at us? Daniel thought as the pain stabbed through him.

The young Nazi looked at him with great anger, breathing heavily. Then, as with cases before, he drew his P-38 and aimed it at Daniel's head. The crowd murmured in fear.

The commandant stood there several minutes with his pistol at Daniel's head. Daniel gently looked at his eyes. The commandant's breathing slowed.

"Why do you do this?" Daniel could not believe he said that. Where did he find his courage? "Why do you want to kill me?" he asked the young commandant.

The young officer was astonished. No one had talked to him at this moment before. No one communicated opinion or desire.

In anger he pistol whipped Daniel's face.

"Do not ask me why. You are a Jew and this is enough reason to kill you and your entire family." He again filled with rage. He pressed the P-38 firmly into Daniel's neck and pulled the hammer back, but he did not pull the trigger.

Daniel stood there with his head pushed to the side by the pistol. He waited for the inevitable, without fear. The officer was surprised that Daniel did not show fear; all the others had. Daniel stared into the officer's eyes. Then something unexpected happened. The commandant carefully let the hammer down and pulled his pistol away from Daniel.

Daniel stood straight again and slowly rubbed his neck. He looked at the confused look on the commandant's face. "You are a good man," said Daniel quietly. "We are all human beings. We did not do anything wrong to anyone." Daniel looked straight into his eyes and for few seconds the commandant appeared to understand his actions. Then a conditioned response came. "You are a filthy Jew. You are trying to do your tricks on me as your people have done on us..." His voice broke as he pointed his pistol again at Daniel. His hand shook from anger and Daniel thought this was his end. But the young officer again calmed. Daniel simply gave a kind look at the commandant.

No one that day knew what passed inside the commandant's mind. Maybe some of Daniel's words sunk in or maybe he realized for a brief moment what he was doing. He looked for a long while at Daniel and then at the assembled prisoners. Daniel thought he saw a mild shock in the man's eyes, or maybe it was only his imagination. "Go back to your position," the commandant eventually said in a moderate voice. He wiped his sweaty forehead and added, "You are dismissed to return to your work."

The commandant looked quietly as all the prisoners quickly ran to their groups. From there they would go to their work. Some would go to work on the roads and some in construction crews. After that morning there were no more summary executions for many days. A few months later, the young commandant was found dead in his room. He had shot himself in the head. His P-38 lay on the floor. In the letter he left behind he wrote only few words, "Please have mercy on my soul."

∞

A few months later, SS doctors arrived at Dachau to begin the regular Auswahl – the German word for "selection." The purpose of Auswahl was to remove prisoners judged too ill or weak to work. Those were transferred to Hartheim, in Austria, which was a death camp where medical staff gassed prisoners as part of an operation code-named "Special Treatment 14f13."

Later that month the Germans reordered the camp. Dachau was divided into two sections, the camp area and the crematoria area. The camp area consisted of thirty-two barracks, including one for clergy imprisoned for opposing the Nazi regime and another reserved for medical experiments. The camp area also had a group of support buildings containing the kitchen, laundry, showers, workshops, as well as a prison block. The camp administration was located in the gatehouse at the main entrance.

∞

"I heard that they are going to move us soon," she quietly told Daniel. He held Julia and slowly caressed her hair. "I also heard from the other girls that the new camp has fairly good conditions. In other camps, the prisoners do not have showers or even regular food. The new camp, they say, at least has some facilities."

"I heard worse..." said Daniel in a tired voice. "In other camps there is systematic mass killing of Jews."

They looked at each other without saying a word. They were more than a year now at Dachau. The Nazis were torturing and killing prisoners on a daily basis. Others slowly starved to death.

"Whatever happens, we have to save Isaac..." she sobbed.

"I know, honey," answered Daniel with tears in his eyes. He looked up at the dark night skies. "I know..."

The next morning they were told that they would be transferred to another work camp. "This one is larger, with better facilities. You will be able to write letters to your relatives, have clean clothes and live in nicer barracks. This relocation will offer new workplaces until the end of the war." This news was announced on the loudspeaker system as classical music played. The atmosphere was that of a celebration. The prisoners became happy. They smiled and laughed. They wanted to be transferred to the new camp as soon as possible. The commandant told them that the transfer would start tomorrow morning. Every day two trains would go to the new camp.

Julia was happy at their nightly meeting, but Daniel did not share her enthusiasm. He had a sense of dread about the new camp. Still, he maintained a happy face. It will not help anyone to get us more depressed, he thought. That night Julia brought little Isaac, and father and son played merrily, though quietly. Little Isaac was about eighteen months old now, a toddler rather than an infant. Whenever Daniel played with Isaac, he forgot the world around them. Although they could not do as much as they wanted, these few hours were the most precious to them. They enjoyed the family time that Dachau's conditions allowed.

The next morning the new commandant started to read the names of the first group to go to the new camp. Neither Julia's nor Daniel's name was on the list. They were to be shipped in a few days, an officer told them. "No worry. All Jews will be eventually transferred to the new camp." The new camp was located near Krakow and this news cheered them. It was almost like going home. "Maybe even the war will be over shortly," the Nazi officer told them with a smile. The Nazis were surprisingly nice to them during the preparations for relocation. The officer told them that the new camp was located in Oswiecim, outside of Krakow. In German, it is called Auschwitz.

∞

Julia was playing with little Isaac, as she did every morning before she left for work, when an SS guard unexpectedly entered the women's quarters and saw them. He looked at them quietly. Little Isaac was waddling through the building, then stopped and looked with curiosity at the guard. The nickel-chrome buttons on his tunic caught his attention and he approached him to get a closer look. I want them! he thought as he reached up toward the black tunic. Julia tried to stop him but was too late. Isaac reached out his little arms and jumped up with all of his might.

Julia froze as the SS guard bent down and lifted Isaac. "What a cute baby," he said beaming. "Here he is." He handed her Isaac. "You are going to move to the new camp soon. They will help you with your baby." He smiled again and left the barracks. Julia stood there, holding Isaac, shaking from the near calamity. She was sure that he would take Isaac away. He did not, she thought. He also gave him back to me – and smiled. But his eyes were cold as ice. Something is not right.

Two days later they were loaded onto the train for Auschwitz.

∞

They awoke to shouting soldiers, "Everyone up! Raus! You are moving!" Quickly the group got dressed and a half hour later stood in rows in the courtyard. Daniel was in one of the back rows and Julia was behind him, hiding little Isaac. Close to her breast, Isaac was asleep. As the main gates opened, the SS guards arrived in their black uniforms and with their leashed, snarling German Shepherd dogs. The prisoners were ordered to march.

Daniel took a last glance at Dachau – their home for more than a year. I believed that if Julia and I could endure just a little while longer, the war would come to its end, thought Daniel bitterly. But the Nazis were on the march throughout Europe.

The group now marched down a winding road, roughly parallel to the railroad tracks that had just been built. The tracks, once so busy, looked deserted now. The prisoners raised clouds of dust that swirled in the air and surrounded them, but they did not care. They were being transferred to a different camp, a camp with much better conditions. Many of them were smiling and laughing. "Schnell! Schnell!" The SS guards ordered them to hurry. After about an hour of walking in the dust they arrived at a road alongside of which there were three parallel tracks. They could see about fifty cattle cars on one of the tracks, and about a dozen SS soldiers waiting for them. The group was tired from the long walk but glad to see the train.

The floor of the cars was more than a meter off the ground and difficult to climb up to, especially for women. The guards again yelled, "Raus!" and people were beaten and pushed with butts of their Mauser rifles. Though the cars were nearly full, they kept shoving more in. Only when the wagons were packed were the doors rolled shut. To avoid beatings, some inmates ran like the animals these cars were built to carry. Daniel remained close to Julia and pushed her forward into one of the cars as an SS guard struck him on the back while shouting, "Schnell!" Some inmates reached out to help Daniel and Julia pull themselves up into the car. More and more inmates were forced in. The wagon door slammed closed behind them, clanging hard and chillingly.

The insides of the aging cattle cars were three meters high. On the side, about two-and–a–half meters up from the splintered floorboard, were four 20-x-28-centimeter openings. Each had two iron bars across it, wrapped with barbwire. Only the very tall inmates standing on their toes could reach them. The SS men are talking and joking, which means that we aren't leaving yet, thought Daniel. He slowly bit his lips to remain calm as he listened to the guards' banter. They said the inmates were doomed, then laughed. Julia was rocking little Isaac and closed her eyes. She now also lost hope about the new camp, and expected the worst. She thought only about saving Isaac. Soon the stifling heat became unbearable and tempers flared.

"We'll all die here. These are our coffins," someone shouted in panic.

"Give me a little room. I can't get any air," another cried.

Daniel stood in front of Julia and Isaac to protect them as people pushed and begged for a little space that was not there.

As the sun set, they had still not departed. Finally, after dark, they heard an engine whistle. Around ten o'clock, the train moved out. Each time the locomotive slowed or banked in a curve, they were jostled about. Julia tried to sit on the floor, but without success. They were told that it would take two days to reach their new location but no one knew what to believe anymore. It was dark, but occasionally moonlight passed through the small air slots in the wagon. Daniel slowly pushed Julia between the people until they were near the slots. Daniel suggested that Julia sit and rest. Since they were in a corner there was room and Julia sat on the rough wooden floor and fed little Isaac. Amazingly, the baby was cooperative. He was quiet and happy near the warm body that gave him nourishment, security and comfort.

A new morning arrived and they continued their travel. The train had just come to a screeching halt, and Daniel looked outside and saw a handful of SS guards smoking near the train before walking away. It was midday and the heat started to come up. Physical needs arose. Things once done in private had to be done in public. Soup bowls became chamber pots. They tried to dispose of the excrement through the wired windows but without much success. People that were not well or very weak simply gave up and did not dispose of their bodily waste anymore. Soon the entire car began to smell like an ill-kept public restroom. In the heat of midday, it got much worse.

Daniel had a small piece of bread from Dachau.

"Would you like to eat?" he asked Julia quietly.

He did not want anyone to hear him. Julia just shook her head.

"No dear, keep it for later...for yourself."

They were both terribly thirsty, as was everyone in the car. Their cries for water did not let up.

"Water! Water!" someone dared to say to a passing guard.

"Shut your mouth," he barked back. It was past noon. The cars moved a few meters forward but then lurched back. Each time the locomotive whistled, they thought they were about to leave. Most had stripped to the waist. The cars got underway again, and each tilt of the wagon toppled people on top of each other. Finally, when the train stopped, a few people looked through the openings. One inmate at another window could see the cars at the end of the train.

"They must have added more cars at the last stop," he observed. "We're now at least a hundred cars. The train stretches all the way around the bend."

Suddenly the car's door rolled open noisily and an SS soldier placed a bucket of water in the car. Each person was allowed to take about two handfuls then pass the bucket to the next person. Each drop was precious. It did a lot to reduce the pressing thirst. The SS guard left the door open, somewhat easing the foul smell pervading the car.

The train began to move again. Daniel thought they had passed Nowe Miastonad Warta, a town southeast of Poznan. "If we continue on this track," Daniel told Julia, "we will pass through Katowice." Daniel visited the renown coal-mining community once with his parents and remembered the little town's look. Nighttime was a bit cooler and brought some relief. The rocking of the train put most to sleep and the ghost train slowly made its way through the night. The train arrived at Pleszew with the cars jolting back and forth until fully stopping. Daniel and Julia peered through the cracks. The train was on a sidetrack about two hundred meters from the train station. Since they were the least important cargo, they would have to wait.

"Can you believe this?" Daniel mumbled. He imagined that after all this time he would accept the way the Nazis treated them, but there was always a new outrage. "They just left us here on the side tracks, like animals or something..." He felt depression sinking in. We'll never get out of this. Julia put her hand on his back and the touch of her gentle hand brought him back. He closed his eyes and imagined Julia and him at their small hotel room among the beautiful trees. He took a deep breath. He had to continue. As long as he was alive, he had to continue – to protect Julia and little Isaac.

The train remained motionless outside Pleszew until morning. During the night a half dozen trains passed carrying German soldiers and civilians. Some watched as the comfortable, brightly lit passenger cars rushed by. Occasionally a passenger inadvertently glanced in the prisoners' direction and they looked back at them through barbed-wired vents. By midmorning a few civilians had gathered around the train. One of the men inside begged for water.

"They heard me!" he shouted. "Someone is bringing us water."

The train was about to close the doors when a loud voice outside ordered, "Halt!" Daniel could hear the same voice yelling, "Turn back!" An SS guard had seen the civilian carrying a pail of water.

An inmate sighed, "The guard made the man pour it out on the ground." There was no water for them at that station. Julia cried quietly as she held little Isaac. This was the second day and it should have been the end of their trip. The little food they had brought from Dachau was gone, and hunger and thirst were intense. One man asked the guard where they were being taken. "I don't know," a man with a Croatian accent answered in rough German.

The train began moving again. With each whistle they believed the train would stop and they would be at the new camp. In the early evening, they arrived at Katowice. The streets were lit and the factories spewed dark smoke. The war hadn't brought much damage here. Even the railroad station was brightly illuminated. They passed through the city and kept moving.

The people became desperate. They hoped this traveling hell would soon end. The locomotive labored hard and loud, pulling the long train up a mountain. At night it slowed further, and they again stopped. After the usual tugging and screeching, they stopped on a dead track. The guard slid the door open wide so they could empty their buckets. It rained during the night – a blessing, for the rain cooled the car and the people inside, and helped with the human waste. At four in the morning they still sat there. As the sun rose they could see the mountains. Suddenly there was excitement.

"Boruch Hashem!" (Thank God), someone yelled, as vats and baskets were moved to the train. Julia tried to get up, but her body was stiff from sitting so long. Daniel helped her up and she stood close to him, looking through the slots. It took about an hour before the SS guards opened the wagon. Understandably, chaos broke out. Although they got a nearly double portion of bread and a cup of coffee each, they gulped it all down at once. Why keep some for later? It would only cause a struggle.

Many in the car were happy. "They want to keep us alive," they said. The heat was not excessive that day. The door had been ajar for a while, and their thirst and hunger sated somewhat. This was the best day of the journey. Then all too soon, the guards slid the wagon doors shut and slammed the latches. They were ready to take them farther on.

Julia scratched her head. They all suffered from lice for the past year in Dachau. She had been able to wash her hair at night at the camp, but now, without any way to wash and with the close contact, her hair was full of lice. They were about to begin their fourth day on the train. They slept on and off, as much as the standing position could allow. They continued towards their destination – a destination that many still believed would be a better camp.

∞

Daniel woke up numb. It was night, but he did not know the exact time. The train slowed and the whistle shrieked. Smoke drifted into the car through the cracks and windows. Probably the locomotive's smoke. The train crept on, a centimeter at a time. Strange, we're not near any town. Daniel scratched his head. Why did the trains move so slowly? People near the window said they could see only barren fields. He did not know what to think. What are they doing to us now?

Traumatized, starved, and covered with human waste, they looked to be the inhuman, useless creatures the Nazis had characterized them as. It was dark when the train stopped, though dawn came a few minutes later and light began breaking through the vents. We are not at a station. Why did they stop? A few minutes later the wheels began to roll again slowly. They crept forward awhile until coming once more to rest. It was light enough to see distant barbwire fences.

"We've probably arrived at the new camp," said Daniel to Julia. He could not hide his relief. He thought their journey had reached its end.

Then they all smelled smoke.

"What is that smell?" asked Julia covering her nose. "It's awful!"

"Must be from the locomotives or something," answered Daniel. He was trying to look outside to see more details about their location and almost did not even notice the smell.

As the locomotive moved forward, they saw strange men dressed in striped uniforms with matching caps, walking like zombies and staring at their train as though they had been expecting visitors. They yelled, asking them what this place was, but no answers came. One of them slid his finger across his throat in a slitting gesture. Others looked at the arriving train with a desperate expression. Daniel and Julia felt the fingers of fear taking over.

"What is this place?" cried Julia quietly.

Daniel held her but did not answer. He wondered why his body was shaking. They stared, frightened, in disbelief. They all knew this place meant death. In the quiet that followed, a boy of perhaps sixteen asked what the strange gesture meant. No one answered. No one wanted to share his grimmest thoughts. It is hard to describe their macabre feelings. Some now understood the strange smell. It was from the burning of the dead. A few started to pray.

The train rolled on. They passed more uniformed people. They looked on while SS men held flashlights and while other prisoners made more strange gestures. Some raised their arms and flexed their biceps, mimicking a circus strongman. A constant stream of smoke billowed into the air. The train slowed then stopped. The doors rolled open and startled them with loud bangs. "Raus! Everybody out! Leave everything behind!" the SS soldiers shouted. The cement platform was crowded with SS men, yelling and waving impatiently for them to get out of the cars. "Raus!" they yelled as their dogs growled, showing menacing teeth. As they jumped out, Daniel look around and saw the small sign at the train station –

Auschwitz

∞

As Daniel, Julia and the other prisoners were getting out of the train, that name hung over them like an ill omen. Many had heard of this camp when they were in Dachau. They had heard rumors about the camp but did not want to believe such a place existed. They heard about the Auswahl (Selection) and death. In Auschwitz, Jews were turned into ashes. There was no way out of Auschwitz. People began to pray. "Shma Israel Adonoi Eloheino Adonoi Aichad" (God is one. God is mighty).

Brandishing their weapons, the SS soldiers yelled at and herded the prisoners. After being locked in the wagons for days, their limbs had molded to the people nearby and would not easily straighten again. "Leave everything on the platform!" the guards yelled. Daniel and Julia left the few belongings they brought from Dachau in the car. Julia was wearing a long coat with Isaac hidden inside. Panic erupted as SS men ran into them, whipping them for no reason. A whip lashed across Daniel's body. "Raus!" the SS man shouted as he whipped Daniel. Daniel rushed into a group of men upon seeing Julia had joined a group of women that arrived in other cars. They were separated again.

More prisoners in zebra-striped uniforms gathered, watching them from behind the fence. They look at us as though seeing the dead, thought Daniel. He knew that their chances to get out were negligible. He felt his spirit giving up. He lost all of his will to live. He felt already dead.

They were ordered to undress and leave their clothes on the platform. Carpenters, lawyers, shoemakers, businessmen, students, and professors – they were all just Jews to the Nazis. They ordered them into the customary rows of fives. The skies were gray and there was a cool morning breeze blowing across the platform. The prisoners gathered close to each other for warmth. The SS soldiers saw this and ran into them to spread them out. Then they all heard the SS officers shouting a dreaded order at them. "Auswahl," they yelled loudly. "Auswahl. Everyone moves forward." Daniel shuddered. He knew what this meant. He heard about the procedure but never believed he would face it. They thought they knew all about Auschwitz but soon discovered how little they actually did know. Each of them quietly evaluated his chance of survival. There is no way to escape form here. Daniel looked for a way to get out of this. He saw Julia with the women, who were taken to their quarters. Somehow the women did not go through the Auswahl process, at least not yet.

∞

I am fairly healthy, so most likely I will be taken to work. This judgment calmed him. First let me settle in, then I'll think of what to do. He stood straight. He will look healthy.

The line moved only grudgingly. Some people cried, others gathered courage to appear healthy. Daniel was several rows away from the SS men who, flashlights in hand, were inspecting the naked men. A few more minutes and it will all be over. Daniel was trying to control his fear. Eventually his turn arrived and he stood in front of the inspectors. A high-ranking SS officer wore a crisp black uniform with a doctor's badge – a serpent wound around a sword. He was tall and slim, with a dark complexion. His thick black hair was cut short. He left no uncertainty that he was in charge. The procedure seemed well practiced. As his assistants paraded a row of prisoners before him, he made mysterious gestures. Only the guards understood, and they quickly executed his secret orders. A blink of his eyes, a wave of his hand, or a twitch of his finger – each was a sign. Some people were ordered right and others left. It soon became apparent that one line contained healthier men than did the other. The right line was for workers and the left for those destined to die.

Two of the five men ahead of Daniel were ordered to the left line. One of them boldly attempted to persuade his judge to let him go with the others. "Look! I am strong," he said. "I can work. I laid rails for more than two years and did not miss one day." But an SS man shoved him back in the left line. The supply of people, demand for labor and space in the barracks were important factors in determining who lived and who died.

Before Daniel's turn came, a fellow captive behind him whispered, "Lift your head. Look strong and healthy."

The judges asked the first question of Daniel.

"What is your age?"

"Twenty-three," Daniel said shaking slightly.

"Occupation?"

"Mechanical engineer."

They ordered Daniel to the right. Daniel released a long sigh as he stepped aside and looked at the left line. These men...are doomed. He stood in his line silently. I wonder how Julia and Isaac are. He hoped that they were still alive but could not put off the tremors taking hold.

Suddenly a commotion erupted as one man tried to flee the platform. He was quickly shot down. His body fell on the train track. His body remained on the track until the next train ripped it apart. The brutal killing shocked everyone and they turned away from the grotesque sight. The prisoners realized that their lives had no meaning here.

A group of about hundred people were taken away. Huge clouds of smoke billowed from the chimneys as they passed them. Daniel looked at the skies and wondered how many bodies were turning to ash. He turned away. I must keep my sanity, he thought and kept looking forward. He had more immediate things to worry about. I need to contact Julia tonight.

After walking a hundred meters or so, they were loaded onto trucks and driven along a double fence, passing rows of three-story brick buildings. They saw groups of people marching. Their clothes were dirty and they wore miners' lamps on their heads. They were on their way to work. It is life's irony, thought Daniel with a sardonic smile. The coal these people mine is used to move the death trains that carried us here. Some looked lifeless, barely dragging their feet. In front of each group walked someone in the same striped clothes wearing a black armband. Daniel later learned that this was the Kapo – an inmate working with the SS in exchange for preferential treatment. The other prisoners hated the Kapos.

The camp did not look like Dachau. The old camp was fairly friendly, Daniel sadly thought. The perimeter fence at Auschwitz was made of heavy wire with barbwire on top. Along the inside ran an electric line. Perched above, in towers, were black-uniformed SS soldiers. Their machine guns pointed into the camp. As they were driven farther, they heard classical music playing from a loudspeaker. They passed a group of doctors and prisoners. It looked like another Auswahl – one done with classical music in the background.

A sign at the gate read "Stop – High Voltage!" Above the gate another sign read "Auschwitz," and below it the motto, "Arbeit Macht Frei" (Work Makes You Free). He knew it wasn't meant to be a promise, nor even a pledge. The truth was that they were here to work until they died. Daniel continued walking with the group. I hope someone escapes to tell the world what is going on in here.

In front of a small shack a conductor directed about thirty musicians. The scene was surreal. The musicians followed his baton as if playing in a symphony orchestra. Their truck turned left and stopped in front of one of the three-story brick buildings. A neatly dressed SS sergeant took charge of them. "Down," he yelled, as the rest of the SS soldiers began to enforce his order. Daniel was shivering, his face slightly blue. We are going to perform some hard labor for them. Daniel convinced himself to stay focused and not let fear take over. He noticed someone signaling to him. An inmate was waving from the opposite side of a fence, pointing at his boots. "You'll have to leave them anyhow. Throw them to me," he yelled. "I'll help you with some extra food when you get to the camp. I'm a Kapo." Daniel froze. What to do? Everyone is out for himself now. It was live or die, and he did not trust anyone.

As Daniel thought about the Kapo's offer, the SS officer ordered them to leave everything behind. Daniel threw his boots over the fence. He soon realized that he did not know how to find the guy. As it turned out, it really didn't matter. They were not allowed to mix with inmates in the main camp anyway. The officer ordered them into the cellblock. As they entered through a long corridor, they passed other SS men who searched them once more. This time they made them spread their legs and bend over. Farther down the corridor, they walked through brackish fluid that smelled of kerosene, more of which was showered on them moments later. "Schnell, schnell," the SS soldiers pressed them to pass through the disinfection process. They all ran as fast as they could to avoid the German Shepherds. Then they were led to the yard once again.

The sun had cleared the fog and it now shone upon them. Naked and wet, they were freezing despite the sun. Scratches and scrapes on their bodies reddened from the caustic fluid, and were painful. They were ordered into another building with a sign, "Showers." This, they feared the most. It can't be, thought Daniel wildly. They are already killing us? We were selected for labor. Everyone dreaded the word "showers." The rumor at Dachau now stood starkly in front of them. We are really in a gas chamber, everyone thought. "Quickly...inside," the guards barked. No one had time to react; they were pushed through the door. The large metal door locked behind them with a clanging sound. There in the large room, Daniel noticed narrow pipes along the walls leading to shower heads hanging from the ceiling. The mechanical engineer in him quickly assessed that the pipes carried water. Yet, fear stayed with him. *There can still be gas pipes someplace else.* He looked for them.

There were only a few yellow light bulbs illuminating the room. In the mustard-yellow light, fear and panic could be seen on many faces. Some began to pray. They heard another clang and everyone became quiet. *This may be the end,* thought Daniel. His heart raced. He thought about Julia and Isaac and said his goodbyes to them. He closed his eyes and stopped breathing, fearing that deadly gas would descend at any minute. A passive silence persisted.

Daniel felt a trickle of water and looked up. The shower heads started to emit water. Soon the water flowed steadily – and it did not smell or taste odd. They all gasped in relief and gulped the water. Water had never tasted so good! Daniel came to enjoy the shower, cold though it was. They all felt that new life had been given them. It would be their only happy moment in Auschwitz.

The doors opened and they were ordered into the next room – a large hall that was now a temporary barbershop. It was full of inmates sitting on benches. The barbers were also inmates. "Sit. Stand. Turn around." Each of the eight barbers ordered inmates about. Daniel's turn came and the barber began to shear him bald. "Auschwitz is full. You were lucky to escape the chimney," he told Daniel as he shaved his head. Daniel learned that "the chimney" was slang for being gassed and cremated. "Only if there is demand for workers does Dr. Mengele let Jews into camp." He added, "At times they are short of gas."

Daniel listened without any response, stunned by these words. Then he told the barber that most of them had been in other camps, as much as two years, in places like Dachau where they worked building railroad tracks.

"This is why we are still alive," murmured Daniel.

"I doubt it," the barber said. "You are in the main camp of Auschwitz." He mentioned the many satellite camps around Auschwitz. "Buna, Trzebinia, Jawizowiec, Janinagrube, and Günthergrube, just to mention a few," he said. "Their organization will amaze you." He stopped talking, but Daniel wanted to know more.

"What is that number you have on your arm?"

"Everyone is known by a number here. You will get one too, and then...you'll be known only by a number. You'll have to remember it and respond to it when called."

"We are identified like animals, like serial-numbered products..."

"You'll be tattooed as soon as you leave here." The barber continued without responding to Daniel's reaction.

"How long can one survive here?" Daniel wondered aloud. That question puzzled him.

"Auschwitz is a much different place now than it was when I came here," he said quietly. "When we first arrived here, one sign read, 'You can expect to survive three months here, at most six. And if you don't like it, go to the fence and end it now.'" That confirmed Daniel's suspicion that deadly electricity did indeed flow through the inner fence. He continued explaining that obedience was the inmate's unalterable duty. "Remember, never walk in Auschwitz. Run." He then urged them to learn the names of the SS rankings and use them correctly. "When you pass SS men, take your cap off and walk in military steps. Play by those rules, regardless how ridiculous or demeaning they may seem to you." Throughout it all he kept repeating how lucky they were. "At times you have to have luck here," he said. "Another reason that many of you passed the Auswahl was because there were no women, children, or elderly among you." He had survived eighteen months in Auschwitz and that left Daniel with some hope.

"What's happening with the women and children?" Daniel asked fearfully. "My wife is here also..."

"Women are also selected for labor or death. If your wife is healthy, she'll go to work – same conditions. No children though. Unless they are taken for medical experiments, they are exterminated."

Daniel remained in his thoughts. The barber's final observation to him was, "No matter how sick you are, never go to the infirmary. Working is the only way out of dying."

Naked and shaved from head to toe, they followed one another into the next barracks. Pairs of clogs, jackets, and pants were thrown at them, regardless of the size or fit. "If these don't fit you, swap with others," the inmates behind the counters told them. The clothing reeked of the caustic fluid they had been sprayed with. They each received gray-striped underwear and a striped cap. The jackets were either too large or too small, and most of the pants pulled up to the chin. Their names became numbers. In time they knew why. Numbers had no faces and were much easier to deal with. The dehumanization process had just begun.

∞

The numbering procedure began. A prisoner with a tool similar to a fountain pen began to inject black dye into Daniel's lower left arm. At first it didn't hurt, but as the procedure went on, it became quite painful. After a few minutes Daniel pulled his arm away. The numbering was done. Afterward they received patches with their numbers and were told to sew them onto their jackets and pants.

They learned to fear the Kapos. Some were in charge of cellblocks, others work gangs. Nearly all were non-Jews, and most were German. They came from a wide variety of backgrounds. They had been thieves, desperadoes, murderers, and petty criminals. Among them were also former soldiers from the International Legion. Though some of them had once been opposed to Hitler, they changed their allegiance when given the opportunity to leave jail and become trustees in concentration camps. All showed contempt for newcomers and acted as if all Jews were their enemies. Although they faced the same life that the Jews did, Jews seemed to them arrogant and indifferent.

It was amazing how the Nazis had singled them out from the rest of the inmates. If there had ever been any harmony between Jews and non-Jews in the camps, there was none seen in Auschwitz. In spite of their common plight, the other prisoners didn't associate with Jews.

Most non-Jews did not have to fear Auswahl. The gas chambers were only for Jews and gypsies.

∞

Julia's experience was similar, although the order of events was different – a fact that enabled her to save little Isaac's life. First the group of women was taken into their barracks, where Julia found a hiding place for Isaac. If they had been taken to Auswahl first, he would have been taken from her, permanently. As she learned at Dachau, she arranged a small hiding place under her bed. Little Isaac had known such a place before and so accepted his new playpen with excitement. After all, it was a new place to play and he had gotten a bit tired of being under his mother's coat all the time. She gave him a sign to stay quiet and ran outside just as her group was ordered to Auswahl. Like Daniel's group, Julia had to go through that inhuman process. As she watched the older women fated to die, an SS soldier reached towards one of them and grabbed a small bundle. "No, not my baby..." screamed the mother running after the SS soldier. The women held their breath as they saw the naked mother begging for mercy for her baby. As she approached him he turned back, drew his pistol and shot her in the head. She fell to the ground, blood gushing from her head. The women screamed in horror.

"Quiet! Quiet in line!" ordered the SS soldiers. They pushed and hit the women with their rifle butts. Stunned, the women were assembled in front of SS doctors for Auswahl. Julia could hardly breathe and her heart raced wildly after what she had just seen. As she stood in line all she could think was that it could have been her and little Isaac instead. I have to be in control, she thought. Isaac's life depends on me. Focusing on this, she calmed herself and when she appeared in front of the doctor she breathed normally. After a perfunctory examination, she was selected for work. They then went through the same procedure as the men, including having their heads shaved. They received a piece of cloth to cover their bald heads and were sent to their building until assigned workplaces.

Julia was elated to be back with Isaac. He was waiting for her patiently in the little playpen she created for him. She held him close to her heart and wanted to forget the world. "You know this cannot continue forever..." said her bunkmate, Sara. She was a much older woman and looked fondly upon Julia and little Isaac. "You know they will find him and take him. It's just a matter of time..." she looked at Julia with sympathetic eyes. "No! No! No!" answered Julia as she is hugged her baby. "They'll never find him...and besides, something will happen. The world will eventually find out what is going on in here and rescue us. It cannot continue this way, it is madness..."

Sara sighed and looked at little Isaac playing with his mother's hand. "I wish you were right. I am almost two years in the camps and the only reason I am still alive is because I am able to work and look younger than my age. I am thirty-seven but luckily look younger – otherwise I would not be here," added Sara quietly. "I know that all this is madness and in the beginning I did not believe these things were happening. Today, I do believe. And I do believe that one day there will be an end to all this and the murderers will be punished by the world." She looked straight at Julia's eyes. "The only question is, will we survive to see that day..." Her voice broke and she turned away from Julia. She could hear her crying quietly.

Julia touched Sara's back. "We are all together here now. We will help each other. We will help each other until our day of freedom comes. And if we do not survive to see this day...at least we lived in hope." Isaac smiled to Sara. "Besides, we have to try to save future lives. This little child can be a whole world. We have to save him!" Sara wiped her tears and looked at little Isaac. Without understanding what they were talking about, he giggled and looked at Sara. Then he giggled again and grabbed her hand. Sara was completely captivated by his charms, and smiled in return. She nodded while playing with him. "We will protect you to the end, little fellow. So that, hopefully, you will survive this."

Then they could hear the SS women calling them out to stand in lines. It was time to start their slave work in the camp of Auschwitz.

∞

Daniel's group was taken to meet their Kapo. "Where were you all this time?" the Kapo yelled as though berating them for not coming to Auschwitz sooner. A clerk next to him took roll. The clerk was tall, about two meters, and bowlegged. He wore a red triangle with a P, signifying a political prisoner from Poland. He looked massive. Of the three assistants to the Kapo on that block, he turned out to be the least cruel and most decent.

In a rough voice, he encouraged them to be hopeful. "You will probably be sent to one of Auschwitz's sub-camps, of which there are thirty-nine in a forty-kilometer radius. After two weeks, barring any problems, you can expect to be sent out to work." When he began to talk, he demonstrated how humans became more aggressive than animals in Auschwitz. Significantly, he was well-nourished. He laid down the rules. "Anyone who leaves this block will receive ten lashes. If anyone brings food into the barracks, ten lashes. If you leave your bunk unmade, ten lashes. Missing roll call, ten lashes. Stealing, twenty lashes." These people were probably abused by the Nazis, thought Daniel. Otherwise, why would they behave like this to us? They are prisoners also. After the introductory lecture, they were allowed to go to their quarters.

"In Dachau we always got our meals regularly," said Daniel to the man in front of him as they stood in line for their first meal in Auschwitz. "My name is Joseph Brodsky," answered the man in front of him as he turned to shake hands. They did so quietly and continued to inch forward. "My wife and I arrived from Dachau," said Daniel as he neared the food. "I arrived from Treblinka a few days ago," said Joseph, "and I hope not to be here so long..." He laughed and Daniel looked at him in great surprise at his good mood. "Do not worry...I am not crazy," explained Joseph. "See, I'm a comedian and I used to give shows in theaters." But he became serious, "I cannot be sad. If I have to die, at least I'll die with a laugh... Oh, here is our French cuisine. Would you like a glass of wine with your food, sir?" Daniel could not stop from laughing. "Crazy fellow, sure I'll have a glass of Chardonnay, please..." He actually found it encouraging to play along.

They received soup morning and night. It always came with a scrap of moldy bread. When the block orderly arrived with vats of soup, they each received two big pots of boiled water with bits of potatoes and an overcooked turnip in it. They had no spoons and had to drink from the bowl.

More people kept arriving. Almost ten thousand people had been brought since Daniel and his family had come. According to the norm, only twenty-five percent actually passed into the camp. That meant that in the two weeks since they arrived, more than forty thousand people had been transported to Auschwitz. That also meant that thirty thousand had been killed in the same amount of time.

Daniel was not able to see Julia because she was in the women's camp. Nor did he have much contact with the outside world. They heard of allied forces landing somewhere in Europe, but had no details. They could never know what was real and what was rumor. One day, late in the afternoon, twelve inmates were marched past their barracks. Usually inmates were escorted by Kapos, but these men were led by SS guards. Their faces exuded fear. "They are being taken to the penalty bunker," said Joseph quietly. There was no humor in his voice.

"What's that?" asked Daniel as he watched the men pass by.

"The penalty bunker has no light or toilet. It is barely big enough for one person to stand up in. They would have been better off to have gone to the electric fence," he said without any expression on his face.

"What sick mind can invent such horror?" Again he could not comprehend the meaning of the thing.

The two watched the terrified prisoners disappear down the road.

"I do not mind dying, but I want the world to know what happened here," said Daniel as he bit his lips. "The world must know what is going on here and how human beings do inhuman things. The world should punish them for this..." his voice broke off and tears flooded his eyes.

Joseph gently hugged him.

"I miss my wife and son..." cried Daniel. Joseph did not answer but continued holding him gently. He was not sure that Daniel's wife and child were still alive.

∞

One day they were told that they weren't to go out because there was no work. This was the worst news they could have been told. No work meant they were simply consuming food and water, and hence were dispensable. The next day they passed Dr. Mengele's Auswahl. He selected only a few men. Everyone knew their fate: medical experiments. The rumors about Dr. Mengele's "patients" were horrific.

They knew that to remain alive they had to keep working. Being idle beyond a certain point meant death. Joseph remained in a good mood and Daniel started to suspect that something was wrong with him. Joseph always claimed he wasn't crazy; he simply refused to get depressed despite the circumstances. Daniel had suspicions. After years of living so close to death, he probably cannot think straight anymore.

One day the Kapo kept them outside in the cold rain for more than an hour. When they finally got back into the barracks, they were dripping wet. They hung their clothes around the room to dry. When the Kapo saw that, he demanded to know whose idea it was. Since they all did it, no one claimed the idea. Then he ordered them to go outside naked and circle the barracks. He stood by the door and whipped them as they exited. Joseph was whipped badly, but even though some lashes drew blood, he didn't cry out. Daniel thought that his young heart had turned to stone. Later several prisoners came down with fever and were taken to the infirmary. No one ever saw or heard from them again.

They had been in isolation for more than two weeks. The small food rations barely kept them alive. Everyone lost a great deal of weight. Soon all of them looked like walking skeletons. The weak did not survive. Every day there were people that simply could not get out of bed. They were taken away and never seen again. The life expectancy was about three months.

In cloudy weather, the camp was shrouded in black smoke. Courage had long sustained them, but now that was in decline. Reality had become twisted beyond anything recognizable. At times they stared blankly for hours. Some wandered alone around the barracks. Although they had passed Dr. Mengele's Auswahl, they knew they would fail someday. Suicide, though, was rare. Only a few Jewish inmates gave in this way. Perhaps their generation's experiences had endowed them with a great ability to endure. Some determined to survive in order to tell the world someday what had happened at Auschwitz. This became their life's purpose. Undaunted believers still prayed every day. Daniel was amazed that despite the jarring discontinuity in their lives, they remembered word-for-word the prayers of Shaharith, Minhah, and Maarib – the morning, afternoon, and evening payers.

One day a number of civilians came to the quarters, accompanied by senior SS officers. The civilians were from a large German chemical and pharmaceutical company, IG Farben, that already employed prisoners in a nearby sub-camp called Monowitz where they made synthetic rubber. There, they were told, the inmate death rate was very high, and they had continuous need for replacements. They believed that it had to be better than their present situation. They just wanted to work. Work meant life.

Some of them moved to the sub-camp outside Auschwitz and the rest remained. They had to wait a few days in their camp until the SS made their decision. After four days, about five hundred prisoners were selected to work at Monowitz. The selected prisoners were happy. They felt they had been given another chance for life. Daniel remained at Auschwitz and was put on another work detail in a different part of the camp. The next morning he discovered he was near the women's quarters. He became obsessed with contacting Julia. Every night he asked women on the other side of the fence if they knew a woman named Julia. Joseph helped Daniel's effort. Both knew they risked punishment at the hands of the Kapo if they were caught communicating with women. A few weeks passed and Daniel did not find Julia or even get word of her.

"She must be in another women's section," said Daniel one night to Joseph.

"We will not lose hope. We'll continue searching for her. No worry, my friend. I am sure we will find her eventually." Joseph was ever confident and cheerful. The next day they were assigned to construct more buildings for future prisoners. They were put on a tight schedule to complete a series of new barracks. From what they heard, these buildings were planned for a large shipment of gypsies. "Like cattle," murmured Daniel as he hauled blocks. "They treat us like cattle. They feed us like cattle. House us like cattle. And exterminate us like cattle when we are useless to them."

"Don't take it too hard," Joseph said, as always with a smile. He worked near him carrying the large heavy blocks, one by one. "You are a couple of years in the system; you should not be surprised anymore by their actions." Daniel had not realized he was thinking out loud. "Still, I cannot believe these things are done," continued Daniel. "Just as I cannot believe you are able to laugh and find happiness amid all this." Joseph's face was red from the exertion. "Well, my friend...this is what keeps me going." He breathed heavily as he passed by Daniel to put his load near the wall.

Daniel looked after him, amazed. He'd never understand this man.

∞

The Kapo came upon them suddenly. "Did you talk with him?" He was talking to Joseph, pointing at Daniel.

Daniel froze. The Kapo looked in an especially sadistic mood.

"Yes, I did," Joseph said quietly, looking straight into the Kapo's eyes.

"Twenty-five lashes," the Kapo shouted. "You know it is forbidden to talk while working."

Everyone around them was quietly shocked. Twenty-five lashes was a severe punishment. Ten was usual.

"Your lashes do not scare me," said Joseph quietly.

Daniel wanted to scream, "Joseph, stop..." but everything happened too fast.

"Fifty lashes," screamed the Kapo into Joseph's face. "Right now." He took out his whip and two SS soldiers undressed Joseph and turned him upside down.

Daniel looked on helplessly as the Kapo flogged Joseph. After the twentieth blow Joseph's back was bleeding profusely. After the thirtieth, Joseph passed out. But the Kapo continued all the way to the fiftieth lash, breathing heavily afterward from the effort. Joseph lay on the ground, motionless.

"That will teach you not to talk while working." The Kapo spat to the side and looked down at Joseph's still body.

Daniel was about to erupt. He had to recruit all of his will to resist storming at the Kapo and strangling him. For the first time in his life he felt he could kill someone. All of his logic and sense told him that if he gave in to his rage he would be killed in an instant. The SS soldiers would shoot him as they would a dog. He waited until the Kapo left before he helped Joseph sit up.

"How are you, Joseph?" he asked, realizing immediately how foolish his question was. Joseph was bleeding heavily and could hardly talk.

"I...do not...know," replied Joseph in a low voice, suddenly adding, "I need a vacation..." He looked at Daniel's surprise and it gave him the power to smile weakly.

"You stubborn mule," said Daniel, helping him to stand. "Look what you've done. Now I have to drag you with me back to the building. Why did you have to talk to him at all?"

"An inspiration...from the moment," answered Joseph, in between breaths.

The end of their workday arrived and Daniel helped Joseph all the way to their building. Then he and another inmate gently washed his wounds. At night Joseph came down with a high fever. An inmate who was a doctor examined him.

"He will not make it without hospital treatment," he told Daniel quietly. "He has an infection and in our conditions he will die in a few days."

They all knew what this meant. Tomorrow morning Joseph will not be able to go to work and he will be taken to his death.

Daniel released a long sigh and fought back tears. Everyone left and he remained with Joseph. He looked at him and realized how much he loved him. During the past months Joseph was his living spirit. In desperate times, when he missed Julia and Isaac, Joseph was there to comfort and encourage him. He could always make him laugh, even in the hopeless surroundings. He gave him the passion to continue. He gave him hope. Now he was going to be put to death and Daniel couldn't do anything to stop the process. As though feeling Daniel's emotions, Joseph slowly turned and faced Daniel.

"I can't feel my back..."

Daniel was unable to speak. His eyes full of tears, he looked down.

"Oh, do not cry for me," Joseph said with familiar wit. "I'm the lucky one...I'm leaving. You are the one staying. You have to be strong. You have to find Julia and your son," said Joseph.

"I know..." Joseph gathered all of his powers and reached for Daniel's hand, which fever had made alarmingly warm.

"You are a good friend...like a brother," said Joseph faintly. Even now his eyes had the spark of wit.

"You too, Joseph," said Daniel, smiling softly as tears flowed. "You are my best friend... I have a last request..." His eyes became quite earnest.

"Of course, Joseph...anything."

"I have a terrible itch on my back, could you please..." Joseph laughed loudly and Daniel joined in. Joseph allowed himself a luxury and laughed riotously, for the last time.

Laughter could not last too long. He had lost too much blood.

"I do not think that I'll last until morning, Daniel."

"I know..."

"I personally think it is better than dying by their hands... Can you please grant me a favor? Seriously now."

"Of course..."

"I was in love once..." Joseph's face was moist and red. It was increasingly difficult for him to speak.

Daniel held his hand and nodded. "Yes..."

"It was twelve years ago," he continued. "I lived in a little town called Zawiercie and had a close relationship with a woman named Paula. We were together for almost seven years." He looked above for a while, deep in memories. "I should have married her, but I was afraid of commitment. It got so bad that I left her and moved to a different town. I broke her heart. I know it...and I was always sorry for that."

Daniel handed him a cup of water and he gulped it down.

"I met her again a few years later when I passed through Zawiercie on business. She had a child...Misha was his name. He was about four years old."

Daniel was intrigued. "And..."

Joseph took a deep breath. "Misha is my son. She offered for me to stay with them, and I did for a while. Just when I thought to propose to her and become a family man, I had to leave on a long trip. My job pushed me back on the road. She did not want me to go for so long. She said that as the father I should get a job nearby and stay with my family. We got into an argument...and I left." Joseph eyes were remorseful. "When I came back, they had left. I never found them again. Then the Nazis came and I was taken away. I never saw them again..." Joseph's eyes filled with tears. "I came back to tell her that she was right and I was going to stay forever with them...with my family. I never got the chance to tell her I am sorry..." tears rolled down his cheeks.

Daniel held his hand tight.

"I want to ask you this favor. When all this madness is over...go find her and tell her that I love her...and that I am very sorry I left."

"I will," said Daniel. He looked down, oddly ashamed of his tears. "I promise...I'll find her and tell her."

"I just hope that she and Misha made it...escaped the Nazis... escaped...this," Joseph added. He was too weak to say anything more.

Daniel placed a cool, wet cloth on his forehead. "Rest now, my friend. I'll be here in case you need anything."

Joseph smiled then pressed Daniel's hand. His eyes got larger, as though making efforts to stay awake. Then he released a long sigh and closed his eyes. Daniel remained near him, holding his hands until his body lost its warmth. Then he covered his friend with his blanket.

"Goodbye...you are in a better place now," he murmured.

Daniel could not sleep that night. He thought of Joseph, the hope he imparted, and his pledge to him. Daniel was alone with those thoughts. Alone there in the night, surrounded by Auschwitz.

∞

Julia's group had not worked for the past week and the women started to worry. Every morning they received their food and were ordered to stay in the barracks. In the evening they received another meal. Some of the women always gave small amounts of their food to Isaac. The same routine repeated itself the next day. Julia was happy because she could spend more time with Isaac, but Sara was worried. "No work is not good," She said repeatedly. "It means we're not needed. Our existence depends on work. If we are not needed for work, the Nazis will not keep us alive much longer." As Julia played with Isaac, she replied, "Every passing day brings us closer to the war's end..."

No one could know what the Nazis had planned for them.

∞

Daniel had a hard time focusing on his job. When Joseph died, he took with him hope for life. He was optimistic and jovial even about horrible things. It looked absurd at the time, but his spirit gave hope to theirs. The power of laughter was enormous, especially in their condition. The unceasing slow rain left them all wet, cold and hopeless. And now everything looked darker than before.

It was another gloomy winter day as Daniel worked a construction site. The SS soldiers were smoking under the roof of the new building while the inmates had to work outside in the rain and wind. Many suffered from malnutrition and the rain and cold made many come down with fever. They could not let on about their illness so they worked until they collapsed.

"No! I did not do anything..." Daniel heard a high-pitch cry. He looked around and saw an SS soldier beating someone. Everyone turned away and continued working. One thing they had all learned was if it does not relate to you, it is not your business. Many people were killed simply from the caprice of SS soldiers and Kapos. A prisoner's fate could hinge on mood or temper. They could pick anyone and start hitting him without any reason. The victim was lucky if they simply left him after a while. Typically it ended in death – if not immediately then the next day. Poor conditions meant infections, slow recovery and often death.

"Leave me alone...I did not do anything..." again came the high-pitch cry. Daniel realized the voice was not from a man. A boy was being beaten. He never knew what caused him to run to the scene but he did. There, he saw an SS soldier cruelly beating a child, probably twelve or thirteen years old.

"Leave him...please. He did not do anything..." he heard himself shouting at the SS soldier. Maybe he had lost all hope or maybe he was angry because of Joseph's death. Maybe he had lost his mind. He knew that this action would result in one outcome – death.

"What?" the Nazi soldier was dumbfounded that a prisoner had interrupted him. The prisoners were always quiet and submissive. Unaccustomed to this, he halted his beating.

"What did you do?" Daniel asked the boy.

The boy couldn't stop crying and was surprised that someone had come to his aid. "Nothing...I was just working and he came and started hitting me..." He wiped his eyes and looked at Daniel.

"Everyone to the front of the building in rows," barked the other SS soldiers. It was time for a count. The workday was over and they were taken back to their barracks.

The SS soldier recovered from his surprise. "You," he shouted at Daniel. "Stay here."

Pointing to the boy, he added, "You can leave." The boy ran to the others to be counted.

Daniel thought that these were his last moments. He is going to shoot me. The soldier loaded his Mauser, aimed it at Daniel and squeezed the trigger. But the rifle did not fire. He reloaded the rifle and tried to shoot again. Again it would not fire. Again and again he tried but his rifle was malfunctioning. In a rage, the SS soldier started to bludgeon Daniel with his rifle. Daniel protected his head with his arms as the soldier beat him and screamed at him. "All to the front of the building for counting..." came the order. "Go join the rest. I'll deal with you later," the soldier stated. As Daniel ran to join the others he had an ill feeling this event was not over.

∞

Daniel lay on his bunk and stared at the ceiling, thinking about Julia and little Isaac. He had not seen them for almost six months now and missed them more every day. He wondered if he'd see them again. After all, Auschwitz was an extermination camp. He felt his passion for life within him slowly fading. He closed his eyes and thought that death did not look that bad.

"Hello."

He opened his eyes and saw the boy from the construction site standing with one of the men. "He was looking for you, I believe," said the man, who then left.

"Hello...do you feel better?" asked Daniel, sitting up.

"Yes, thanks. I wanted to come and thank you – you saved my life." There was something familiar about this boy. He tried to remember if he had seen him before somewhere. Dachau? Krakow? They all seemed so remote now.

"How long are you here?" asked Daniel.

"Many months," he answered, scratching his head. "I do not even remember when my mother and I were taken here. It was long ago."

Daniel did not respond. The boy felt Daniel's thoughts. "I haven't seen my mother since we arrived. We were separated at an Auswahl." He became silent.

"I was separated from my wife and son when we arrived." Daniel sighed longingly and looked outside through the small window. "I do not know if they are alive or dead."

There was a moment of silence as both shared common worries and dreads.

"My name is Misha...and yours?" the boy said quietly.

Daniel was caught in the middle of his thoughts but then turned and looked closely at the boy. "Misha is your name?"

Misha did not understand Daniel's puzzled yet warm look. "Yes, it is. Why?"

"Where did you live before you were taken here?" asked Daniel, looking carefully at Misha's face for a familiar eyebrow or lip.

"We lived in a village named Wolbrom," answered Misha, still not understanding.

"Hmmm..." Daniel did not remember that name and stood up. "I'm sorry. I thought I knew your family, but I was probably mistaken."

He looked at Misha and smiled. "You are a good boy, Misha."

"They are moving our group to a sub-camp outside Auschwitz tomorrow," said Misha with a smile. "This is good news. Everyone knows that you have a better chance working outside Auschwitz. That is why I came here tonight...to thank you for saving my life." He looked gratefully into Daniel's eyes.

"I did not do anything extraordinary, Misha. I was just there at the right time..." Daniel's heart felt warmth he had not often felt recently. Darkness went away and light flowed in.

"Are you hungry, Misha? I have some bread. I always keep a little food."

"Yes, thank you. I am always hungry here..." Misha looked down shyly.

"No need to be bashful, my friend. I am also always hungry. The Nazis do not serve French cuisine here," Daniel joked. "I loved the bakery that was near my home," he continued with a wistful look. "My father used to buy us baguettes and cream-filled pastry every Friday night, for the Shabbat meal. Ah, I'll never forget those..."

Misha smiled.

"I can almost smell them." Daniel closed his eyes and smelled the moldy piece of bread he held. "Almost...almost." Then he opened his eyes and laughed.

"My mother also used to buy us special cookies for Shabbat," Misha said as he chewed his bread. "In Zawiercie, there was a bakery everyone loved. They made chocolate-coated cookies that I loved. My mother would buy me a whole bag of them every Friday. There were ten cookies in a bag and they are so big! When you buy them fresh, they are crunchy and the chocolate just melts in your mouth..." Misha delighted in thinking of life before all this.

"Well, I'll tell you. One day when the war is over, I'll go and buy you an entire bag of cookies. What do you say?" Daniel smiled at Misha.

"Wonderful!" exclaimed Misha, smiling back to him. "And my mom can join us also?"

"Of course."

"Don't worry, I think that my mom is still alive," responded Misha anticipating Daniel's thoughts. "I am sure that she is well." He looked at Daniel with the confidence of boyhood.

"Yes, of course..." said Daniel. I once had his confidence.

Daniel became serious. Something had gone by him almost unnoticed. "Wait... Did you say in Zawiercie?"

"Yes..." answered Misha, again confused.

"But you said you lived in Wolbrom..."

"Yes, but we used to live in Zawiercie before we moved to Wolbrom," continued Misha. "We lived there many years – since I was a baby. I grew up in Zawiercie."

Daniel was shaking from excitement. "What is your mother's name?"

"Paula..."

"I can't believe it!" Daniel grabbed Misha's head with both hands. "You were right here and he did not even know about it." He looked almost in pain. "Now I know why your eyes looked familiar. You have your father's eyes."

"What?" Misha was even more confused.

Daniel sat near Misha.

"Misha, what did you know about your father?"

"Not much. My mother told me he lived in a different city and that he came to see me once. Besides that, I never saw him." Misha looked curious. "She told me that he was a good man... and quite funny." He then looked at Daniel in expectation.

"Misha, your father was my bunkmate. He slept right here...on the lower bed."

Misha gushed in astonishment. "Right here? With you?"

"Yes...until a few weeks a go." Daniel felt tears coming. "He died in my arms here, Misha. He was a great man – probably the best friend I ever had." Daniel emitted a short, bitter laugh. "All my life I had friends for a longer time but only here did I realize the meaning of a best friend, of an unconditional friendship."

Misha looked confused, unsure what to say. Daniel pressed him to his heart. Although Misha had not had any connection with his father over the years, his curiosity came out and he asked many questions about him. Daniel told him everything he knew. He told him about his good nature, about his unfailing optimism, and about his sense of humor that never left him even in dispiriting moments. He told him about his good heart and kindness, about his always being there for him and others who needed help, support and a shoulder. He told him that when he passed away, he took with him the light – the light that helped him and others to go through the darkness of this camp. The light of hope.

It was late when Daniel finished. Misha sat there, enchanted by the stories of his father, who had always been a mystery. When Daniel told him of his father's final request, Misha hung his head and quietly cried. "Now you know your father..." Daniel said tearfully. "I hoped that you would be far away from here and the war would be over when I found you and related all this you... but unfortunately you are here, right in this horrendous place. If he had known that you were only one building away from him... Well, at least I am happy that you were saved from the soldier." Daniel smiled weakly.

Misha started to cry. He cried tears borne of knowing too much pain at a young age. He cried to release the horrors he had seen there. He cried because he had never cried there. He cried because he realized that he would never see his father, not even in a picture. He cried because all these years he had had hopes of seeing his father one day. These hopes would never be realized. Daniel cried with him for a while and then held him until he could cry no more. Early in the morning Misha fell asleep. Daniel put him in the bed where his father died and covered him with his father's blanket. He can sleep for an hour or so, he thought. I'll wake him up to go his building.

He sat there and looked at the sleeping boy – Misha, Joseph's son.

Misha woke up by himself and sat up.

"Good morning, Misha," said Daniel gently.

"Good morning..."

"Thank you for telling me about my father... At least I know what happened to him." He paused. "At least I know what kind of person he was..."

Daniel nodded and smiled. "It is important that you remember that your father always believed in the good, even in these horrible times that we are now in. You should always have hope. Hope to survive, hope for life."

Misha thought of what lay ahead. "I am leaving today for a sub-camp outside Auschwitz. Everyone says that this is good...and that people are not killed there. We are needed for work there, so I think that we will make it," said Misha with a world-weary face that children should not have. "This is good," he continued. "Maybe one day I will be able to tell my mother about my father."

"Yes, you will. I am sure." Daniel smiled. The night revived his spirit. Whatever happened from here on, he'd be alright. Joseph's son brought the light of hope again. "You take care of yourself. Stay alive – you have to deliver a message to your mother..."

They hugged one last time and then Misha left. Daniel never saw him again.

∞

In the morning they were ordered to a health inspection outside their building. They all knew what it meant. Every month the Nazis performed a health inspection after which the sick and weak were taken away. They all knew that these prisoners were sent to their deaths.

That morning the weather was extremely cold. The skies were gray and a light rain constantly descended on them. The doctors and the SS officers were dressed for the cold. The inmates were told to stand outside, naked, in two lines. They could tell that the SS and medical personnel wanted to finish the task quickly. The prisoners shivered and stood together to retain body heat.

For the inmates it was a horrible ordeal, but for the SS soldiers and doctors it was an ordinary procedure. Many of the prisoners were sick and coughing. They could hide some symptoms but not a high fever or a hacking cough. The SS doctors quickly picked out the sick from the healthy. The sick group got larger and the relatively healthy group smaller. Daniel stood in front of the SS doctor. It was his turn.

"How you are feeling?" the doctor asked as he probed his stomach.

"Good," Daniel replied.

"Any fever or cough?"

"No."

"Diarrhea or stomach pains?"

"No."

The doctor seemed satisfied and ordered the SS soldier to place him with the healthy group. But the SS soldier interrupted. "This one goes over there." He pointed towards the sick. The SS doctor looked at him with a surprised look. The SS soldier gave him a meaningful nod. "This one is sick..."

The doctor looked at the soldier's face and concluded it was a personal matter. They had enough for the work and they had received word that a new group was on its way. He was not about to argue over a prisoner. He motioned Daniel to the sick group and the SS soldier led him there.

Daniel walked mechanically with the soldier. He recognized him as the soldier at the construction site. An evil smile on his face, he looked at Daniel for few seconds and then left. Daniel stood among the weak and sick, only beginning to comprehend what had just happened.

In that way, Daniel's fate was determined.

∞

After a while the Auswahl was complete. The healthy returned to their barracks. The sick and weak were taken to another barracks. As Daniel walked, he was surprised he did not feel any fear. He was content that he had saved Joseph's son. It looks like he will have a real chance to live.

Then he thought how much he missed Julia.

∞

"Everyone outside! Stand in rows!" The SS soldier's shouts carried loudly over the gentle patter of rain. It was a dreary morning, about three weeks after their last work. "It looks like today we are getting work." Julia was dressing little Isaac as fast as she could. "I hope so. It's time. If we don't work, I fear for our lives," said Sara as she did her best to comb her hair. The lack of soap caused her hair to be sticky and smelly. Their hair was short, nonetheless many of the women had lice.

That morning Isaac seemed to want his mother more than usual and refused to stay in his hiding place. Although Julia tried her best to convince him with all type of pleas and offers, little Isaac insisted on cuddling with his mother. He had gotten used to being with her for the past three weeks and it was hard for him to let her go. "He is growing up. It will be harder to keep him in one spot..." Sara said as she saw Julia's efforts. "Out! Out!" the SS soldiers yelled. "Go out, Sara. I'll be there in a minute," said Julia as she hugged and kissed her little boy.

They stood in formation as the SS women counted them. "Today you are moving from your barracks." The loudspeaker announced in a grating, metallic tone. "Do not take anything with you. After rollcall, you will be taken to the new location where you will have new assignments. You will go through disinfection and after that you will be reassigned." Murmurs ran among the prisoners. Maybe it was good news.

The counting continued outside as Julia tried to calm little Isaac. She started to worry. Isaac did not want to stay alone. No matter what she tried to convince him to get into his hiding place, he insisted on staying with her. She was afraid that once she left he would make noises – or worse, go outside looking for her.

She could hear the counting going on and knew she had to go out soon. Little Isaac snuggled in her arms and rested there. She rocked him gently, hoping he'd fall asleep. But he stayed awake.

The situation did not look good.

∞

The rain was chilling and persistent. They had to walk for a couple of hours in the rain to a central area where they were ordered to form rows. Daniel could see a few buildings to their left. To their right, there was a long fence behind which he could see groups of women also ordered in rows. They were told to wait until being taken to another location. Many of the sick collapsed and were taken away. Others coughed blood due to pneumonia and other infections. Some were so emaciated they looked like skeletons. Daniel looked at them and wondered how they'd survived so long. He looked around and could see only death. Even if these people are alive, they are dead, he thought. Again he wondered how such things can happen. It is definitely not a dream. Even the most horrific dream cannot reach such levels. He then came to the only conclusion. This must be reality. Still it was hard to comprehend.

∞

Helga Kurt was a young SS soldier in her second year at Auschwitz and was about to search for prisoners hiding in the barracks. She was born in Berlin and lived there all her life. An average German woman in her late twenties, she had deep blue eyes and blond hair – the profile of the pure Aryan race. Her parents fervently believed in the Third Reich. That was why Helga volunteered to serve in the SS task force – to serve the Reich. When the SS called for young, dedicated men and women to join its elite units, she did not hesitate. Her parents were proud of her. She was sent to Auschwitz concentration camp for training. At the time, Auschwitz was a camp for Polish political prisoners, intellectuals and those who resisted the Nazi occupation. After a few months of training, she was assigned to supervise the first group of Jewish women that arrived in the camp in early 1942. Since then, Helga worked closely with the high-ranking women officers. Due to her dedication and performance, the SS thought she would rise through the ranks. Helga visited her home in Berlin every few months. Her parents were thrilled to see the medals and honors she brought with her on every visit. They were happy about her achievements and contributions as a dedicated and faithful Nazi. Helga was excelling in her field. Everyone was very happy – her parents, her SS supervisors and her fellow SS personnel.

∞

Helga knew what to search for. There were always women that thought they could hide. She knew to search under every bed and behind any object. She used her rifle's muzzle to move objects and probe blankets. She knew this group of women was going to be exterminated. They did not have enough work and new shipments arrived frequently. The orders were strict and clear. All excess women were to be eliminated.

She walked through the barracks officiously. The entire building stank badly as the conditions were very poor. Many beds were covered with vomit and other bodily fluids. Helga had to hold her nose. She showed no expression while she dutifully examined the barracks for hidden women.

She suddenly stopped.

A woman sat on a corner bed. She had obviously been crying as her eyes were red and puffed. But this was not the reason Helga stopped. On the woman's lap sat a small child looking at her with curiosity. The woman was rocking the child in her arms, probably to soothe the child. The boy was enjoying it. The image was so incongruous with the world of Auschwitz that Helga froze for a moment. The image was one encountered in a park back in Berlin, not in a concentration camp. In Auschwitz, everyone knew that babies and children were eliminated first.

How did this child manage to survive? Helga thought for a second. How had the mother managed to keep him here with her?

As she searched for words and raised her Mauser, the woman looked at her and started to speak. "I tried to calm him so he'd be quiet...but I don't know what got into him today. He would not let me leave his sight. Maybe the past three weeks when I was with him all the time caused him to be like that..." Then she looked at Helga. "And then maybe he is just done with this life..." She looked at little Isaac with love, her eyes full of tears. "I cannot blame him..."

Helga lowered her rifle. Something in this woman captivated her – haunted her. Maybe it was her knowledge that the woman and child were soon to die, or maybe it was something else, something in her nature long repressed. The fact was that Helga stood there and listened.

"See?" Julia continued, wiping her eyes and nose. "I hid him for almost two years in Dachau. There he learned to be quiet and remain under my bed during the day until I returned. When we were taken here, I managed to hide him and he was really good." She paused for a few seconds and hugged her child. "Well, until today... He was quiet during the day and played alone in the little area I created for him." Helga looked at the pieces of rotten wood that the woman had assembled around her bed as her son's refuge. He could not stand on his feet there, only sit or crawl. Helga noticed a small cloth that probably was a blanket. A large roach was crawling on it. Helga blinked in shock.

The mother continued to rock her child. Helga looked at her and saw her desperation. She saw her powerful but hopeless desire to protect her baby, to the end. She saw that she was beyond this now, accepting the fact that after so many years she had failed to protect him and he would be killed soon. She saw that the child, as with all the children this age she had seen, was not aware his fate was sealed. By giving his mother trouble this gray morning, he would be taken way and killed. Of course he was not aware of this. Or is he? she wondered. They say that young children sense what is going on around them. Why did this woman tell me her story? She is not a friend.

"My name is Julia and this is Isaac." Helga still could not find words. "I am sorry I bothered you with my story. I tried my best today, but I have failed." She smiled bitterly. "Without even knowing what he had caused, little Isaac will have to die now..."

239

She looked at him as tears streamed down her cheeks. Then she turned to Helga, looking at her intensely. "How can you do these things to people?" She had lost hope for herself and her son and was now searching for answers that had long troubled her. "I really would love to know how you live with yourself watching German soldiers killing children, old people, women and everyone else." She wiped her face with her filthy shirt. "How can you not see that we are humans, living people, who yesterday were your neighbors, your colleagues, your friends..."

Helga could not say a word.

"But even beyond this," she continued, "I see horrible things done here to people, especially Jews. You kill them; you are murdering them in cold blood. Old people, young, children and babies... Are babies your enemy also? Do you really believe that these babies and children are doing evil to you and your people? These children do not even know where they are or what is happening..." Her voice broke and she looked at Helga without saying anything else.

Helga sat on one of the bunks, her face still expressionless. She looked at Julia's face and could not think straight. Visions of what she had experienced flashed before her eyes. The systematic murders, the tortures, the evil propaganda about the Jews corrupting Germany, and the desensitization she had gone through. She had remained silent and accepting of everything. She was a quiet follower, never saying a word, even when she witnessed horrifying scenes as part of her SS training, such as simply shooting Jews one by one. She continued her life, went home and told her parents about her achievements, contributions and the great service she was providing her country. When she told them what she once saw, her father said, "War has costs. We all have to make sacrifices..." She looked at him without comprehending how he could say this. She knew they were human beings, but according to his thinking they were not. Deep inside her, in places she rarely ventured to go, she could never understand how the Nazis could do this to other humans. But her place in life left no choice. The mind has an amazing capacity to hide things inside, pushing them into the furthest and darkest corner of the mind. It was a useful self-defense mechanism and so Helga kept shoving all this to that back corner.

Now all of these memories were coming to the fore and she realized the enormity of the crimes they were committing. They were exterminating humans like animals – worse, like insects. They were killing babies and children, but for what reason? What justification can there be for murdering children? Every time she witnessed a murder, she blinked nervously. It was an unconscious tick. She took it all in without the capability to take it out. Her entire soul resisted these actions, despised them and never wanted any part of them, but she was duty-bound to stand by and watch and sometimes even help in the actions.

In jolting flashbacks she remembered the evening when she went back to her apartment outside the camp and could not sleep well the entire night due to the nightmares that kept waking her. She saw men, women and children walking by her, in and endless stream, looking at her silently and wondering why – looking to her for an answer. When she tried to speak, she woke up as though suffocating. She functioned silently during the day in the camp as her soul cried out to her every night. Her silence broke now as she realized at once what was going on and her role in it. All of her body started to tremble and her rifle fell to the floorboards. She held her head in both hands and opened her mouth to scream but no sound would come out. She tried to shriek in horror but could not. Her entire being convulsed with the ghastly realization of the truth: they were cold-blooded murderers and she was one of the cold-blooded murderers. She sat on the bed and moved her head from side to side, as though saying, "No, I did not do this... I was only... Nicht schuldig...(not guilty)

Julia looked at her and realized that she was different now. She was no longer simply an SS guard. She put little Isaac on the floor and he toddled over to Helga. He touched her knee, looked at her face and smiled. Helga slowly looked at the child. His face was dirty, his little fingernails were almost black from filth and his clothes stank badly. But the warmth and sincerity of his smile stood out, making the clothes and grime irrelevant details that faded in this image of the essence of hope and humanity. He reached for her face and gently touched it. She smiled at him, though she was not conscious of doing so. It was a magical moment. Julia froze, not believing her eyes. An SS soldier, capable of unspeakable cruelties, was serenely smiling at her son. The image was surreal, nothing she could have expected to see. Helga began to shake again. She covered her face with her hands.

"I am so sorry..." she cried as she shivered, "I am so sorry... for everything..." She spoke only with great difficulty. "I never wanted this... I never did..." She could not stop crying. I feel this woman's pain, thought Julia. She never realized she could do this. Julia sat near her and hugged her. Helga looked at Julia's emaciated face and frame but focused on her good and comforting eyes. She wanted to help her. Here I am in this hell and she wants to help me through my pain, Helga thought in disbelief. She hugged Julia and let her tears and pain out. Little Isaac held Helga's hand and slowly caressed it.

The barking of guards continued outside. The count continued as preliminary to the relocation of the women to the new camp.

"What have we done?" Helga asked no one. "All these children..." An idea came to her amid her turmoil. "I have to tell them all..." She looked outside.

"Wait," Julia said in soft voice. "You can't – you'll be killed."

Helga was like a tormented animal that wants to get out of her cage. "We have to do something," she continued with tears in her eyes. "We have to save them..."

"You can't save them all. The SS soldiers are too many...they'll kill you..." Julia thought more reasonably. She held Helga's hands. "But you can help us..." She did not know where she took the courage to say this.

Helga looked at her and began to think more reasonably, too. "I can't save you..." Julia could see the pain of that realization in her eyes. She truly wanted to help her. "But I can save your dear child..."

Julia took a deep breath. The thought of separation from her Isaac was not something she was ready for. But the thought of Isaac, her son with Daniel, the most precious thing in life for her, surviving all this, quickly took on a transcendent meaning above anything else. She could hardly talk but she forced herself to stay calm. She needed to, for Isaac's life.

"By saving little Isaac, you are saving his father and me," continued Julia. Summoning all of her powers, she smiled faintly.

Helga empathized with the motherly pain that Julia was feeling, the pain of leaving one's child forever, the pain that none other can approach.

"I'll save little Isaac. I'll take him out of Auschwitz. I'll make sure he gets far away from here. I promise you." She looked straight at Julia's eyes.

Julia saw Helga's soul through her words. She knew that she would do everything humanly possible to see that her son escaped. She was completely calm. But she had to help Helga find the strength to save little Isaac. She wanted to thank her but what words are there? There are none, not in any language.

"Helga, it does not matter what you did in the past. You are a saint now." Julia held her again, then let go. "We are almost ready." She turned towards Isaac. "My little Isaac," she said, fighting her tears, "I'll always be with you. Remember this... you have to go with this nice woman now, alright?" Isaac dimly sensed the brink of some change before him. He looked at his mother without really comprehending. Everything looked normal to him but he started to observe other things, her hair, face and eyes. Then he looked to the other woman. He liked her. She radiated goodness. Julia knew his expression and smiled quietly. Then she pressed him to her heart, for the last time. Little Isaac knew well the soothing sound of his mother's heart but could not know that this was to be the last time he heard it. Julia looked at him for a few minutes wanting to impress his essence into her, and hers into him. She breathed him in for the last time.

"We are ready now..."

Helga had looked on as mother and son bade each other goodbye. She arranged her hair. She had to become the crisp SS Nazi soldier again. "I'll take little Isaac with me and lead you outside to the count." She knew what lay ahead for Julia even though she did not.

"Nothing more needs to be said," Julia softly stated.

Helga noticed a glimmer of life and hope in her eye. She is going to die happy.

Helga stood there a few more seconds, admiring Julia's will. Then she lifted up little Isaac and held him to her heart. She straightened her cap, firmly held Julia in her arm and together they stepped out into the chilly morning.

∞

After a couple of hours they were told they had been designated to move to another area. First they had to go through another disinfection process. Daniel did not pay attention to the loudspeaker. He was thinking of his wife and son. I wish I could see them one more time, just one more time. I would give anything. He then laughed bitterly. What an irony. I really do not have anything to give.

∞

Helga placed Julia in a row just as the counting was ending.

"I found this one in the barracks," she announced in a cold voice to the SS soldier in charge that morning. He nodded and continued to mark his paperwork. It was very important to keep the books accurate.

∞

They arranged them in two long rows for the disinfection shower. Daniel was in the second line, towards its end. There were many SS soldiers accompanying these lines. Almost every fifth person was an SS soldier. Why the extra watch? wondered Daniel. It's just disinfection. It must be more than that. Daniel had the feeling that this was the end. The majority of the people in line were sick or weak, and did not care anyway. Daniel looked to the left and saw a similar structure on the women's side. There was movement and he saw a line of women forming. One after another, the long line of women started to move towards the showers.

∞

Helga looked for the last time at Julia standing bravely in line. Julia gave her a small smile and winked to little Isaac. He wanted to jump out of Helga's hands and run to his mother, but Helga tightened her hold and anyway something told him to stay still. Helga took a deep breath, turned around and walked away from the barracks. Julia watched until Helga and Isaac disappeared behind one of Auschwitz's grim buildings. "Goodbye, my little Isaac," she whispered quietly. "I am always with you…"

Then she felt her world collapsing. She wanted to cry, she wanted to scream but forced herself to stay calm. She knew that he would be alright and this made her feel better. She looked to the sky and offered a prayer for him. A blue patch appeared and the rain stopped. Julia thought this a sign of hope.

∞

They took them to a central area and ordered them into two long lines for the disinfection showers. The lines were heavily guarded and Julia sensed what it meant. She knew it probably was her last look at the sky, but she was calm. She knew that little Isaac was safe. I wish I could see Daniel one more time, she thought, missing him terribly. Then she noticed a line of men to her right. She wiped her eyes and looked at the line slowly moving forward.

∞

Daniel was moving slowly forward as he looked at the line of women to his left, behind a high fence. Their line also moved towards similar-looking buildings. They do not look sick or weak, thought Daniel. Why are they going to their deaths? I will never see Julia or little Isaac again, he thought despairingly. Everything looked hopeless and for a second he considered running away. It's better to be shot by an SS soldier. Then he noticed someone behind the fence, someone familiar. He could not believe his eyes. It's Julia! Her hair was cut short and she was frail, but it was her.

He felt incredible anguish. She is also going to die. Why her? She is strong and capable of work. And where is Isaac?

He shouted out her name.

∞

Julia heard her name being called. The voice came from behind the fence, where the men were. It was not the cold voice of a guard; it was a familiar voice – one she had not heard since she first arrived. What is it? Am I dreaming? Has my last wish been granted from above? She asked herself these questions with a joy she had not felt in months. It was him! It was Daniel! As joyful as it was to see him, the somber reality quickly struck. She knew they were both about to die. But why him? He is strong and healthy...

She waved to him exuberantly. He sent wondrous kisses through the air, as though they caught glimpse of each other from across a busy street in Krakow. Her eyes filled with tears. The long lines curled at some point and neared each other at the fence. Daniel and Julia waited for this point. They would be able to touch each other through the fence, if only momentarily.

The line moved only grudgingly, but their moment came.

Daniel ran to the fence, as did Julia. Their hands touched and they passionately kissed through the fence, ignoring the cold metal. Their eyes were closed with happiness and their fingers intertwined and became substitute for the embrace they both yearned for. They wanted the moment to go on forever. At first, the SS guards did not notice, but one on Daniel's side spotted them and ran towards them, yelling to get back in line. He struck Daniel with the butt of his rifle.

"Back in line!"

Daniel fell backwards as Julia screamed helplessly.

Another SS guard arrived from Julia's side and roughly pulled her back in line.

Daniel looked longingly as she was put back in her position and he to his.

"Little Isaac is safe!" exclaimed Julia with joy as both lines inched ahead.

"Safe? But how?" Daniel asked in a low voice to avoid the SS guards' attention. Thankfully, she could hear him.

Julia smiled through her tears, "Don't worry, he is safe..."

Daniel looked at her with all his love, trusting in her confidence of their only child's deliverance from Auschwitz and the fate so many endured there. Thank you, Almighty, that I could see her this last time. Thank you for letting me know that little Isaac is safe.

They were together for this time, in these dire circumstances, as they walked slowly towards death. Daniel was ready to die. The dark feelings and desperation he had for the past few days, vanished. Light returned to his soul, as it did to Julia's. The euphoria they felt was like that of their first meeting.

"I love you forever, my love..." Daniel's whispered without sound.

"You are always with me..." Julia's lips answered.

They continued to move slowly forward. Their eyes did not move from each other's.

"Our vacation in the mountains..." Daniel reminded her.

"I'll be there..." Julia looked happy.

"I'll be there first..." Daniel managed to smile faintly.

They did not say anything more for a while. Their euphoria made words superfluous anyway. Daniel saw that his line was almost to the building. The SS guards yelled, "Leave everything behind. Move forward."

He knew this was the end of their reunion.

He concentrated on Julia's face, memorizing every small feature. Julia looked at him wordlessly as her line also had come to the building. Their souls, they knew, had already been reunited from the past, and strengthened by their special connection in this life. They would continue for generations to come. They closed their eyes almost at the same moment of physical separation. Daniel was pushed by an SS guard as he was trying to walk towards Julia. And she was pushed by another SS guard into her building.

"Farewell, my love...I am always with you..." Daniel lips whispered as he looked at Julia for the last time.

"I am forever yours..." whispered Julia.

Daniel was forced into an inner chamber.

Their moment had ended.

Julia too was forced inside.

We had our last moment together, Julia thought with happiness. It's given me the courage for what is to come. They were ordered to undress and leave everything behind. Julia was not scared. She was content. Little Isaac would be well and she had seen Daniel near the end. Of course, it is relative, she observed ironically. Yet she had gotten everything she wanted. She even received a final kiss from her husband.

They were pushed into a large chamber that looked like an immense shower room, though the shower heads hung from the ceiling. The lights turned off and everyone screamed in panic. Slowly, small yellow lights illuminated the chamber from above.

∞

Julia sat near the wall. The floor's brick was cold but she ignored it and closed her eyes. She was able to isolate herself from the screams and whimpers of the panicked women around her, and soon she was sailing far away in her imagination. She was at home, with little Isaac and Daniel. A broad smile spread across her thin face as the yellow lights turned off. She did not even hear the sudden eruption of screams, nor did she hear the murmurs of relief when the lights returned. But fear and desperation came back immediately when an odd smell spread through the air. Julia was still elsewhere. She was in the country, on their vacation in the mountains. They were walking hand in hand with little Isaac. She looked at little Isaac and he gave her one of his precious smiles. He is the most lovely baby in the world. She kissed Daniel and they both looked at little Isaac. He pointed towards the skies and they all looked up. The sunlight became brilliant and everything became white.

∞

Daniel entered a large chamber along with about two hundred other men. He searched for a corner and sat down on the floor. He lay his head back on the cold wall and closed his eyes. He wanted to be with Julia and little Isaac in his last moments. As the lights turned off and a strange smell spread throughout the chamber, he began to have fleeting but vivid glimpses of scenes. He could not remember them yet they seemed strangely familiar. He saw a woman about to be executed by hanging. He was looking on from behind the scaffold and could not see her face. The crowd cheered as the executioner prepared the woman for death. He needed to see the woman's face. He darted to the side just before the black hood was placed on her head and he caught a glimpse of her face. A sense of recognition – timeless recognition – flashed trough his mind. It was his Julia. She was in medieval attire and her hair was longer, but there was no doubt it was her.

All of his being wanted to save her but he could not. He was trapped in his time and place and could not move. He tried with all of his will to get free and run to her, but without success. He shouted out, but no one heard him. He was not truly there. The executioner pulled the lever and she dropped without making a sound. Then suddenly he saw two people engaged in a sword fight in a pastoral setting he did not recognize. As he got closer, he could see that one was a woman. She fought valiantly and with great skill against several men. Again, the woman was Julia. Again, her clothes and look were strange, but it was her. One of the men came upon her from behind and brutally stabbed her with a long sword. Everything happened so fast. "No!" he screamed at the top of his lungs, but no one heard him.

Then he was home with Julia and little Isaac. She was gently rocking back and forth in a chair as she held little Isaac, asleep in her arms. Julia looked up and smiled. "I love you..." she said, and he was the happiest man in the world.

He embraced his loving family as everything became illuminated in a powerful white light.

∞

"You are so smart," Helga complimented Isaac with a smile.

She had smuggled him into her apartment a few miles from the concentration camp. As an officer, she could afford and was entitled to live outside the military housing in which the enlisted SS personnel were billeted. She had bought food and was trying to get Isaac to take in a little nourishment. He badly needed it. But Isaac constantly looked for his mother. He would look about and then explore the apartment. Helga allowed him to do so freely. It was heartrending to hear him call for his mother.

She did not know what to do. How to tell a baby that he will never see his mother again?

In time, he realized that his mother was not there and sat on the floor. Tears formed as he tried to cry, but could not. He looked at Helga and cried without a sound. His little hands reached towards the sky as though asking, "Where is my mommy?" It was painful to see him cry and tremble. She welcomed feeling such things again. Helga held him firmly to her heart and cried along with him. She cried for the lost mother. She cried for so many lost mothers and prisoners that she had seen murdered. She cried for all the horrific scenes that she had witnessed in Auschwitz. Most of all she cried because she had seen it all and could not, or did not, do anything. Seeing all those helpless, innocent souls murdered in cold blood and not doing anything about it, ripped into her inner being. So many times she wanted to raise her rifle and scream, "Stop this madness..." So many times she wanted to start shooting her fellow SS officers, men and women, for what they were doing. So many times she wanted to comfort the men and women going to their deaths. But how...how to comfort doomed people? She could never have found the words. So she let them go, looking after them as they walked hopelessly to the gas chambers.

How can we do this? she asked herself every night. She tried to find explanations and justifications but could not. After a while she got used to murder. It was her profession, her duty. She became numb inside. But she could never accept the murder of children. She almost shot an SS officer who took a baby from his mother and hurled him into a mass grave. That evening she climbed down into the grave and searched about among the corpses, but the abyss was too large and too horrible. She wanted to strangle her friend, a woman officer, when she ordered a seven-year-old girl to walk forward with her hands in the air and then shot her in the back. She remembered glaring at her colleague angrily and having to stave off the thought of shooting her.

There were years of darkness – darkness that she had to go through without the ability to change it, darkness of the human kind and all the unfathomable evil it was capable of.

Little Isaac noticed her pain and reached with his little hands towards her face. He touched her wet cheek as Helga trembled and cried. He felt her pain and anguish. He wanted to help her. He touched her face and her crying eased. Helga could not believe it, but little Isaac was comforting her. And she realized that she needed him, just as he needed her.

"We're both alone, little one," she told him, taking his little hands in hers. They were soft and warm and elicited feelings in her she thought had been lost. Little Isaac understood her. His mother was not there and he was with Helga now. He sensed Helga's goodness. He sensed Helga needed his help. And he hugged her.

Little Isaac pointed towards the bread on the table. Some things predominate in children. "You are hungry?" Helga wiped her tears and laughed. She sat him on her couch and served him his first real meal in years, in a little plate. He was puzzled as he looked at the chicken, bread, and mashed potato. He had never seen anything like it. But instinct prevailed and he grabbed the bread and started to eat. The food tasted what he would know to be good, and he had lots of it. He gave Helga a contented smile and continued to eat with great enthusiasm. "Eat, little man. Eat as much as you want..." whispered Helga. "You are safe now...I'll think what to do next"

They cuddled on her couch in front of her apartment's window. They saw blinking stars in the dark night sky. It was a beautiful night and Isaac's eyes were wide open, taking it in. She looked deep into his eyes for a long while. A special bond was made that night between Helga and little Isaac, almost like that of mother and son. Almost. He fell asleep and she gently put him in her bed. Watching him sleeping calmly, she knew what she had to do. She would leave the SS and run far away with him, to a place where no one could find them. One day, when he's grown, she'd tell him who his real mother was. One day, she'd tell him what happened in Auschwitz.

"Rest in peace, Julia and Daniel," she said quietly. The names would become familiar and cherished, as though those of her own family. "Little Isaac is safe..."

Night Fell.

Morning Rose.

"I do not want to move to Washington!" Danny was talking on a cordless phone while working on his computer. "There is nothing there."

"It's just for a few months," countered his friend Michael.

Michael and Danny had worked together for the past few months, contracting for integrated circuit design companies. They met many years ago and were working together for the past few months in Sunnyvale, California. Their contract was about to end and Michael found them another in Washington State. Danny liked the Bay Area and did not want to move. It was the year 2000, the era of the Hi-Tech and professional engineers were in high demand,

"Yes, I know it's just a few months, but making the move and returning will be a big pain," complained Danny as he struggled with a program flaw.

"That's true, but this area is dry – no contracts. Are you willing to do nothing for six months or so?"

"I don't think it will take that long." Danny scanned the screen trying to find the bug.

"I already pulled all of my contacts; there are no jobs in the area now. You know the situation as well as I do. We're in a downturn," answered Michael authoritatively.

"I know, I know..." Danny gave up and moved to the couch. He would take a break then try again to find the bug. "Still, check what you can do locally again."

"I can get you great pay..." Michael started to pull out his tactical weapons. "No one wants to go up there. We can get a nice contract."

"Well, check it out...and then we'll see." Danny was not the type that ran after money. He was divorced and did not have a luxurious lifestyle. As long as he had a modest apartment, a car and a computer, he was happy. He was motivated more by social reasons. He hated to be alone.

"Okay," responded Michael in a skeptical tone. "Besides, you never know. You may meet your destiny there...your dream wife."

Danny was on his way to the kitchen to pour himself a drink when he stopped for a second. Something in Michael's voice or words was going through his mind until they coalesced into a premonition. Ahhh, it's nothing, he thought and sat again in front of the computer screen. This is going to be a long night.

It was almost midnight when Danny again felt there was something different in Michael's words. A strange feeling said he had to go to Washington. He shook his head for a second. It's all nonsense, he thought, common sense tells me there is nothing waiting there for me. It can be in any other place on earth as it can be there. Still, he looked at the bright half moon through the apartment's balcony; something told him that his future wife was indeed waiting for him in Washington State. That night he had difficulties falling asleep. His thoughts wandered over his past few years. He was recently divorced and had a daughter from the marriage. He considered his few past relationships as failures and determined not to get involved with a new one soon. Although surrounded with people almost all day long, he felt constantly alone. His work ended late at night, after which he was alone. It did not matter that he socialized every day, eventually the others went to their homes but he remained by himself. It will pass, he convinced himself, I'll find someone someday. I'll find my life mate. He never gave up on his dream, to find his true love. Day passed after day and many months passed, and Danny remained alone. Somehow he had a feeling that his soulmate awaited him somewhere.

∞

Two weeks later they drove from the San Francisco area, up the Pacific coast, to a small town named Lacey in Washington, about seventy-five miles southwest of Seattle. Michael negotiated them an attractive hourly rate with a prominent semiconductor company there. The plan was to be in Lacey for a few months only, completing the task then returning to California. They rented a small place in a local apartment complex. Michael drove his family van but brought only the bare necessities. Danny was constantly on the move with contract work and didn't own anything that suggested permanent residence. They both planned to buy mattresses (no beds) then trash them or give them away upon leaving. Everything was prepared for a quick arrival, doing the job and heading back south. But destiny intervened, at least for Danny.

∞

They arrived in Lacey on Sunday morning, after two days of driving through beautiful landscapes featuring pine forests and snowcapped mountains. They found their apartment complex and parked.

"See, I told you it could be done in no time..." said Michael as they walked towards the rental office.

"Yeah, piece of cake," added Danny and patted Michael's back. He was anxious to settle into their apartment and take a shower.

It was noon Sunday and the complex manager arrived to welcome them and give them the keys.

"Hello, I am Julie. Nice to meet you guys," said the manager giving them a beautiful smile.

"Hello," said Michael, returning the smile. Danny did not say a word.

∞

Danny was speechless, dumbfounded. He stared at Julie and she at him. Their souls seemed to recognize each other, though there minds told them they were strangers. Daniel recognized Julia, Andy saw Orenda, Janis joined with Darren, Verna greeted Dror, and Anta smiled to Ven. It all happened instantly. Life's powers took over and held them in an emotional surprise. Danny and Julie were not consciously aware they had been lovers across thousands of years. They did not have any way to know that their love was an ongoing story with a new chapter about to begin. They did not have any way to know that from the moment they saw each other, their spirits would control everything from there on. They looked at each other and closed their eyes momentarily. They had to – the feeling was so intense.

Danny wanted to hold this woman, whom he had never seen before, close to his heart – forever. Julie felt that the world had stopped and all that existed was the two of them. The atmosphere was magical, one best left to silence.

"Uh, here is my driver's license," said Michael, breaking the awkward moment. "Thank you," answered Julie as she returned to the mundane. Danny also returned to reality, though still puzzled by the experience. They completed the registration process and Julie took them to their apartment.

Michael went to his van to bring in his belongings. Danny stood and watched as Julie left for her apartment. She would be their neighbor. He was disoriented by the intensity of his feelings. She was not a stranger to him. It's just that she's so pretty, he tried to explain to himself with the logic he earned a living with. It can happen with any pretty girl. But something told him different. As much as he tried to override it using excuses and dismissals, he could not deny it. It was not that he fell in love with her at first sight; he was already in love with her before he even met her.

∞

"You won't believe what just happened!" Julie spoke on the phone with her friend and coworker. "There's this new tenant...and he's simply...cool!" She knew that she desperately wanted to be with this man. It looked and felt awkward. After all, she had just met him. Julie was recently divorced and had a bitter taste about men in general. She was not looking for a new relationship. On the contrary, she thought that being alone was great. Throughout her life men had always disappointed her, and she was done with them – she thought. That is why she was so surprised by the emotions that flooded her when she met Danny, and by how welcome those emotions were. Common sense told her it was a passing fancy, but her spirit told her it was something else entirely.

After the emotional storm she returned to her routine. This is absurd, she told herself. He probably has a complicated life of his own. As much as she could not comprehend the feelings, she kept telling herself that nothing can evolve that quickly. Then her inner thoughts interrupted with the question, really?

∞

Danny just started the project and had difficulties concentrating. All he could think about was Julie. She's too beautiful even to look at a geek like me, he thought. I better focus on my task here. He forced himself to think about his project. He immersed himself in work from early morning until late at night. It was a way to avoid the constant feeling of missing someone.

On Friday night, Danny and Michael searched for a local bar, a place to relax and forget work for a while. They entered one joint, bought some drinks and found a table. The air was blue from so much cigarette smoke. It was the weekend and many people gathered there to start the weekend. They talked about work, life and everything else that came to mind as they unwound. As they were talking, Danny noticed Julie come in. She wore a brown buckskin jacket – something from the Wild West. She was with some other people who, judging from the apparent familiarity, were friends. They talked loudly, laughed and headed straight towards the bar. Michael continued talking, but Danny couldn't hear him anymore. All he could pay attention to was her. The way she handled herself, her flowing hair, her sparkling eyes so full of life, and her lovely smile, all fascinated him. Absolutely beautiful. He was now sure it wasn't just initial physical attraction. Some hidden connection had been activated. He wanted to come up to her and tell her that he had to be with her. He wanted to hold her to his heart. He wanted to kiss her passionately. But she was socializing with her friends. Too much so, thought Danny. They drank together, laughed and hugged occasionally. She was the center of attention, and he did not like that.

Michael noticed that Danny was not really listening to him. "Oh, her..." He noticed Danny's look and suspected what was racing through his mind. "Don't even think about it. You've done enough stupid things regarding relationships in your life."

"Yes, you are right..." Danny responded quietly, though still glued to her. "Still, she is absolutely beautiful..."

"Yes, I know, but she also does not fit with you. She's different... Can't you see that? Look at who she's hanging out with." Michael nodded towards the group.

She and her group were getting louder and louder. They were all drinking beer and having a blast. Obviously, they had all imbibed quite a bit and probably did so frequently.

"Do you see yourself with people like that?" Michael asked pointedly.

"Not really..." responded Danny sullenly.

Danny was a computer guy, intrigued by circuits and apps. This was not his crowd. Michael knew that and hoped to get Danny to realize that he and she were a mismatch. It had worked before. Danny was very insecure over his past relationships and accepted Michael's advice. But what neither could know was that stronger powers in the universe were at play. One of the most powerful ones is Love.

Danny watched Julie and her friends as they noisily left the bar. He saw her hugging one or two of the guys and he felt physical pain. Although it was just sociable hugging, Danny found it excruciating. He felt heartache and anger. How could she do that to me? He looked in other directions, breathing deeply. Then he downed the rest of his beer.

"Who wants more?" he asked Michael with a fake smile.

"Sure, I'll have one." Michael was smiling. "But no more than one. I don't want to get drunk."

"Aahh, who cares..." Danny went to the bar. Michael's right. She's just not my type. She belongs to a different world and I shouldn't even think about her anymore. Encouraged by his reasoning, he brought the drinks back to their table. After a few sips, he found himself looking at the entrance. Is she coming back?

∞

It was Saturday morning and Danny went out to enjoy the sun. The Northwest is known for being overcast and rainy but that morning was sunny. Danny loved the sun and tried to catch it at any opportunity. As he looked for a bench, he saw Julie coming out of her apartment. There were two children with her, one boy about six years old and a little girl about four. She has kids, he thought to himself in mild astonishment. She looked so young that he never imagined her with kids. The realization that she was already a mother hit him. He mumbled good morning to her and added a few compliments about kids just to be sociable.

The thought that she was already heavily involved from a past relationship struck him hard, despite his conclusion from the previous night about their incompatibility. He also had a daughter from a previous marriage and knew what a commitment it is. He felt deep sadness. Not regarding the kids, but from the knowledge that there was a man in her life. She was supposed to be his alone, not shared with another man. He returned to his place and watched her with the kids through the blinds. He nodded in realization many times and took a deep breath. What was I thinking? Not everything revolves around me. Of course she has a life; she must be in her early twenties. She does not even acknowledge me. Still the feeling that she was supposed to belong to him was everywhere deep inside him. Something happened in the evolution of time. Something changed something else and now she and I had kids with someone else... The thought was very disturbing to him. He felt restless.

"So, are you coming to work? It's overtime on the weekend..." Michael was on his way to work. His family was down in California and he had nothing better to do.

"Good Idea. I'm coming too." It would be an escape from an uncomfortable moment. He'd immerse himself in work. After all, that is why he came with Michael – so they can work and socialize together. Forget about her. The drive to work was enjoyable. The skies were clear blue and the sun was beautiful. Yet Danny's ache refused to go away.

He saw her many times after that weekend. Every time, he felt his heart pounding. Michael noticed his moods and reminded him of his bad luck with women. "Don't get involved with her; she already has kids and a life of her own. Besides she belongs to a different world." Danny was torn by his heart urging him on and by experience constantly telling him not to make any more foolish moves. All he knew was that he wanted to take her far away so they could be happy together. But that looked more and more unreal. The next week, they received word that the project would be done in about a month – their contract there would be completed. There's the solution. Destiny will take me away from the unfeasible...the rash. He found himself thinking less about her. Now that he was working long hours and rarely at home, he did not see her anymore. It looked like in no time he'd be away from Lacey...and away from Julie.

∞

It was another Friday night and they decided to hit the same local bar for happy hour. It was as usual very crowded and full of cigarette smoke. They sat down far away from the crowd in attempt to avoid the dense smoke.

"See what type of life you'd have in a small town like this?" Michael was nursing his beer. "You're born here, pop a few kids here, live all of your life here and eventually die here."

"Good chance you never even know about the rest of the world..." finished Danny.

"Most likely."

"You're right," Danny continued after thinking awhile, "I could never see myself living in a town like this. It's just too small for me."

"Let's wrap up this project and get back to the Bay Area. We'll find you someone. Don't worry, someone more your style."

Danny nodded without saying anything and looked at the crowd on the dance floor.

"And a better chance not to get divorced again!" cheered Michael. "You cannot afford another failure."

"This, I know."

Although logic and work seemed to be shaping his prospects, Danny didn't quite feel right about things. There was a vague feeling that he was letting go of something that was part of him. Danny did not have any way to know the transcendent bond he shared with Julie. He had no way to know that their souls had been together for generations and that they would eventually find each other again, one way or another.

"Want another beer?" Danny asked as he headed for the bar.

"Not for me. I'm done for tonight, thanks." Michael pointed towards his head.

Danny stepped towards the bar. "Another Heineken, please."

The bartender nodded with a smile and put a bottle on the counter. In a professional way he popped the top and handed it to Danny. As he handed the bartender a five, he noticed Julie just down from him at the bar. She was talking with someone. All of his logical reasons and explanations vanished. In a moment of panic he tried to regain control of himself but failed badly. He found himself lost in her dazzling eyes.

"Hi," Danny heard himself saying to her, without even knowing where it came from.

"Hi," she answered with a winning smile.

He melted.

To his surprise – to his pleasant surprise – she held his hand and walked away from the bar with him. All of a sudden, she gave him a kiss on his cheek. It happened so fast and spontaneously that Danny had no time to respond. They continued to talk, as though nothing out of the ordinary had happened. Did she kiss me or am I dreaming? They chatted away as though nothing had happened. Danny only slowly became convinced it had happened.

He wanted to kiss and hold her close, but stopped himself. You have to watch your manners, he kept telling himself. The sound of her voice, the sparkle in her eyes, the way her dimples showed as she smiled – all familiar to him. Many times Danny simply closed his eyes momentarily and enjoyed her company. He looked at her intently as she spoke. He sensed her life was not an easy one. The way she approached people and handled conversations told him that, for her, life was something she merely endured. He felt the urge to shelter her. He could not understand where the feeling came from. But his mind still demanded circumspection. For crying out loud, I was just introduced to her not that long ago. What is all this nonsense? He pushed the thoughts from his mind.

"I have an idea," Danny heard himself saying. "Come to New York with me."

"What???" she responded incredulously. "New York?"

"Yes, why not? Let's spend a weekend there."

"Sure..." she continued almost immediately with a smile but he was not sure if she fully understood. After all, they had had a few beers by then.

"Do you really want to go?" he asked, uncertain what was happening. It was beyond his wildest dreams.

"Yes."

"It's a deal then. I'll call you tomorrow...I gotta go now." Danny felt he had to leave. It was too much for one night. He had to regather his thoughts. At the same time, he did not want to leave her there...with all of those men. He shook her hand gently and signaled to Michael that it was time to hit the road. On the way home he realized he did not even know her phone number.

∞

She couldn't believe it. He's coming my way. I'm so glad I've had a few beers – it can help things! Her spirit responded naturally to his. As they chatted she couldn't believe what she did. She leaned towards him, gently held his head and kissed him on his cheek. He reacted nonchalantly, continuing with casual talk, probably trying to hide his surprise. She also pretended that nothing had happened. Another surprise hit. He invited her to weekend with him in New York City. It was more than just a vacation. It was more than just a fancy. It was more time with him. After a short while he apologized and left.

It took time to realize that she hadn't been as happy in all the last few years as she was during the last thirty minutes with him – with Danny. She looked at her beer and wondered if it was the alcohol, but her soul told her it was something more potent.

∞

Danny waited all day long to come home, then it was over to Julie's apartment to spend time with her. Every evening they cuddled on her small couch, watching TV and talking about life. Obeying generations of union, their spirits sought reunion, and in time found it. But just then they fell asleep together – that's all. Mornings, Danny woke up and quietly left for his apartment. He never left without kissing her as she slept. Without knowing why, he used to watch her sleep, often for quite a while. Absolutely beautiful.

It was not an ordinary passion. It was not only the physical attraction that couples treasure. There was something deeper. Neither Julie nor Danny could identify it. All they knew was that they had to be with each other. They had an almost obsessive urge not to miss a moment together. The hours crept by grudgingly until work was done and they could be together for the evening and night. Their lives would never be the same. They did not know it; they did not care. They did not know the road ahead would be difficult. Their graceful unity would encounter great turbulence. What was trivial to their spirits was not to the rest of the world. The issue of children was never confronted. Not his daughter, who was far away. Not her children, who were either with their father or with her.

∞

"She is definitely not for you," proclaimed Michael, looking at Danny in disbelief. "I can't believe you are even considering a serious relationship with this woman." He was almost scolding him.

"But I truly love her." Danny's words came from the bottom of his heart. He could not understand why people refused to accept this.

"She comes from a different world than you. You've already made many bad mistakes in past relationships," Michael shook his head, "and you are going to repeat many of them."

"It was different before..." Danny's defense started to crack. He was divorced twice – well, officially three times. I did fail terribly in the past, he thought as his heart called out for truth.

"You thought it was different then, just as you think it's different now." Michael aggressively pursued his line of reasoning. "You are looking short term only, again."

Danny remained silent. They had this conversation every day since he and Julie took up – at work, on breaks, and during any free time they found. They went back and forth over the same points. Michael had many weapons in his argumentative arsenal: Danny's experiences, past mistakes, her background, the current situation and many others. But Danny still had the inexplicable feeling of having known her across time.

Others were critical of the relationship, too. Almost everyone whose counsel Danny sought just shook his head. The overwhelming consensus was to break off the relationship before it got any further. "There are too many problems ahead," they said. Both had baggage from previous marriages; both had different backgrounds and outlooks. There were other, smaller reasons. The world already rejected their relationship, yet they were happy with it – in what it was and in what they hoped to make it.

Julie did not know about all the criticism and objection that Danny endured on a daily basis. Insecure about relationships, Danny put off any mention. Many times he wished to have no one else around him, beside Julie. Many years later he wondered if he had been granted his wish, would things have turned out differently.

∞

They went to dinner and then to a dance club, and the evening was going well. "Let's get a hotel room for the night," Danny heard himself suggesting. What did I just say? Julie hesitated and Danny was in a state of suspension. But to his delight, she agreed. Although he somehow felt they were not yet ready for intimacy, he also felt their love needed to be fulfilled. They had enjoyed so much time together for the last several weeks, yet to his bewilderment they had not made love. Night after night they shared life thoughts, wishes and desires. They met almost every lunch and spent entire nights together. Maybe the spiritual union was so intense that it made physical union an afterthought.

Late at night they checked into a modest hotel. Something isn't right, he thought as they entered their room. It was clean and basic but something seemed wrong. Julie sensed it too but did not want to say anything that might spoil the magic. Awkward in such moments, he assumed he was expected to initiate things. In later years they'd wonder if things would have been different had they taken the time to talk a while first.

They lay on the chilly but increasingly cozy bed, cuddling under the blankets, feeling each other's warmth. They kissed passionately as their bodies, already familiar, became even more so. Instinct took it from there. Maybe it was nature's way of breaking the nervous tension or maybe it was just their poor timing, but they were so worried about losing each other that their communication with each other suffered. They experienced their first physical intimacy that night and although they expected grand fireworks and amazing sensations, the fulfillment was less than spectacular.

∞

Their next weekend was spent in San Francisco. They walked carefree all day and night. They breathed in the city's spirit. They held hands and the spark was in their eyes for all to see. The highlight was their nights. Their first intimate night had been an aberration. For the rest of their lives, their love life set new heights of ecstasy. It was in San Francisco that their lovemaking became comfortable and then amazing. The passion that slowly accumulated during the day exploded in millions of flames at night. The knowing smiles, the hugs, the frequent kisses, the touches and everything else they shared during the day seared their bodies with passion. As they reached their hotel room at night they could hardly wait to be in each other's arms. For hours they played with each other's senses, bringing their bodies and souls to peaks they never felt before. After their physical hunger was satisfied, they lay together, holding each other and wondering what had happened. They had sensed something wrong that first night of intimacy, but how wrong they were. Their spirits reunited after generations of separation and the ultimate love was recreated.

Julie lay near Danny, deliriously happy. Nothing else was important anymore. They were together and things looked just glorious. They had just spent an out-of-this-world weekend in San Francisco together. She felt that they had something extraordinary, without understanding that they were obeying an ancient calling. Nothings can break us apart. She fell asleep with a smile.

What she did not know was that they were still living in this time and place. She knew almost nothing about the daily criticism Danny had to endure. After establishing such a close connection with someone, she could never have imagined what was about to happen to them.

∞

The first cracks in Danny's defense started to show about a month later.

"The contract ends soon and I'm going back to California," said Michael one night. "What are your plans?"

"I'm...staying here..." Danny sounded unsure, even to himself.

"By yourself," retorted Michael in a skeptical tone. "In this little town? You have no friends or family here. Are you sure you comprehend what you are doing?"

Danny did not answer.

"In California, everyone knows you. You have a social life, friends and a good job." Michael stated this in a calm, determined tone. "You cannot even work in this little town. There is nothing for you to do here."

He's right, thought Danny. But he felt physical pain as he pondered separation from Julie. He could not stand the idea.

"What you are going to do on the weekend?" continued Michael as he slowly ate his dinner. "Spending time with kids that are not yours, not your culture and have no feelings towards you anyway. They already have parents and lives... It's a waste of your time. You'll reach the same conclusion as I have – eventually. I'm just telling you that ahead of time, to give you a heads up."

Danny stared at his plate for a long while without eating. "You're probably right..."

"I know I'm right," snapped Michael. He started to load the dishwasher then turned towards Danny and looked straight at him. "Do not make this mistake. You are not that young anymore. You simply do not have years to waste."

Michael sat in front of the TV and prepared to watch a movie. It was not as it used to be when they first arrived in Lacey. He and Danny used to do everything together. But for the past month he was left by himself as Danny was with Julie every night. Michael and Danny had known each other for many years and worked together for the past two years in California. They were close friends. The friendship had changed a bit. Michael was ready to go back to California, with or without Danny.

"I take it you're going to Julie's tonight..." Michael said without looking at Danny.

"Yes..."

Danny went to take a shower. All he could think about was what he was doing with his life. He felt he was betraying a good friend who was always there for him. On the other hand, his heart could not let Julie go. Doubts had developed over the past month – no doubt about that. Can it be that the rest of the world is right and I am wrong? A profound sadness was filling his heart. After all, the world advised me to back off many times before, but to my sorrow I did not. Eventually it was clear that they were right and I was wrong. I have a bad track record... What to do?

Obeying his soul, Danny dressed and went out to meet Julie. When he saw her, his worried spirit felt relief and he forgot everything else. He gave her a hug and a kiss. Her eyes sparkled. His eyes responded to hers and flamed with love. They had planned to go out for dinner. He had still not apprised her of the turmoil swirling about him, as he still didn't want to hurt her or endanger their relationship. If only he had opened to her then. One day he reached the conclusion that the entire world was right and he was wrong. He and Julie had no future together. They had to separate.

∞

Their trip to Paris was like a movie fantasy. They had an entire week to themselves; no one was around them to interrupt. Seconds, minutes, days and nights were magical. They roamed the streets of the French city by day and let their passions run wild by night. There were no limits. After their week passed, they had to get back to reality. If only daily life were like a vacation in Paris...

∞

Michael left for California and Danny remained in the apartment, though he was in Julie's apartment quite a bit. For a while everything looked okay. Michael got busy with a contract in California and Danny worked in the extended contract in Washington.

"So how are you doing there?" Michael asked in a skeptical tone during a phone conversation over the weekend.

"I am doing well, thanks." Danny sounded unsure. He knew where the conversation was heading.

"Are you coming back to California at some point?"

"I...don't know yet..."

"Okay, I am not going to bother you about this anymore. You're a big boy." Michael sounded more like a father than a friend. "Let me know if I can help with anything." It left a bad feeling with Danny.

Michael did not keep his promise. Every time they talked, the subject came up and it led to pointed arguments.

One month later Danny reached a decision. He and Julie did not have a future. He knew by heart all the reasons why. Yet it was his heart that refused to believe those same reasons.

∞

It was a sunny Monday morning when Danny woke up early and lay in bed. Julie slept calmly near him. Danny looked at her and his heart filled with agony, a sadness he had never felt. It was as though he was going to separate from half of his soul. As every day for the past few months, he was going to leave to work. The difference was, he would not come back home.

He had planned everything for the last two weeks. He arranged for a small apartment in California and everything was ready. He slowly loaded things into his car, disconnected everything in his name and gave his notice at work. Everyone was informed about his departure – everyone besides Julie. He just did not have the will to tell her face-to-face that he was leaving. Many times he hinted that their story might not work out. He used all the logical explanations he could muster to lead her to the same conclusion, but without success. She always found logical reasons for their love to overcome everything. Love would conquer all. His heart agreed with her every time.

How can I do this? he tearfully asked himself while looking at her that morning. How will I be able to go day-by-day without her? His heart ached terribly. Then he heard his friend's words, "It's better to do it now and get it over with than to drag it out for years..." Danny thought his friend must be right. After all, we come from different worlds... It will be okay...We'll both get over it soon enough. He cried quietly.

He lay there for an hour until she woke up.

"Good morning, love..." He could hardly talk but he managed to hide his anguish. "Time to go to work..."

∞

It was about noon when he completed his commitments at work and headed down Interstate 5 for California. He could still hear her words when he left her this morning. "But why you are taking your computer with you?" And her expression when she looked at him. Her eyes squinted and her eyebrows flared. It was painful to see that, but he had to be strong. He made up a weak answer regarding the computer, which didn't even convince him. She looked at him with anger and pain and he wanted to cry. He was convinced he was doing the right thing. He just could not tell her.

All the advice and pressure had accumulated and provided the appearance of decision. She knew he was going to work and would not come back, but she did not argue much or dwell on the matter.

Maybe she did not want to believe that it was really happening, he thought as he was approaching the exit he took for the past few months. For a moment he wanted to turn the wheel and go home. He wanted to go home to his lost love from generations. He wanted to go home and hold her tight, close to his heart. He wanted to go home and kiss her all over. He wanted to go home and cuddle with her and forget about the world.

"You have to be strong now, otherwise you'll be sorry for many years." His friend's words rang in his ears. "If you're weak, as in your previous relationships, you will not be able to recover from this one. You do not have much more time..."

His eyes stuck to the exit sign – one more mile. He forced himself to look at the road ahead. I can't listen to my heart...I don't know what I'm doing...I must leave her...This is the best thing for both of us, for the long term. He saw the exit in the distance and his heart raced. The illusion will fade and you'll have to face reality. But his spirit refused to listen. I need you, my love. Where are you? He asked quietly. Why are you not here with me, to encourage me and tell me that everything will be okay? I need you now...

His eyes teared as he passed the exit. Within minutes he cried like a child. His body shook and he had difficulty driving straight. After a while he calmed down and remembered that this morning he had written his name in Hebrew for her. She wanted to have it tattooed on her back. He had debated writing out his name – after all, he was leaving her. Maybe he should leave "I Love You" behind. Maybe he already missed her so much and he wrote his name so that their only permanence would be the tattoo on her back.

As he drove down the highway he saw places they used to visit. Every moment they spent together came back to him. He began to daydream. The driving became a technical procedure only. They were together in all these places, enjoying their time, holding hands and looking into each other's eyes. There was a magic.

So why did you leave her?

He had no answer.

∞

The world collapsed on her. I am so stupid! I saw it coming and still... Tears came shortly thereafter. And I just tattooed his name on my back... But it was more than the end of a relationship. Her soul cried out that a timeless destiny had been disrupted.

She'd occasionally calm herself. I can manage without him. He's just another man...and there will be others. Things like that happening every day around the world – you're not the only one. But then her soul would demand to know, What went wrong?

He called and told her a perfunctory story about leaving. She did not really care what happened. All she knew was that he was not with her anymore. She sat in her apartment, smoked heavily and tried to understand. It did not really matter why; what's important is the end result. And that was he is not coming home tonight. That was a blow by itself. He will never know how much he hurt her soul. The pain of thousands of years of separation culminated in this one time. She was not consciously aware of this – she lived by the moment. And this moment directed anger towards him, an anger that would take years to forget.

∞

He arrived to California the next afternoon. He was familiar with the process of moving in. He had done it many times over the years – divorces, temporary jobs and relocations. This time was different. He carried his few things from the car into the small apartment. The apartment looked dark and depressing. He usually made sure the apartments he rented were generously lit by sunshine. This one he had not chosen; it had been found for him. The darkness contributed to his depression as he robotically completed moving in and went to sleep on the twin mattress on the floor. He lay there for hours without falling asleep. His soul was anguished.

His spirit, recalling forced, tragic separations in previous lives, sank into despair. He was supposed to be with her, to protect her and provide for her. His soul reproached him for bringing a new separation – an unnecessary one – on his own, from his own free will. The anguish was excruciating. He tossed and turned all night and fell asleep only just before dawn.

∞

Danny started a new job the next day – another integrated circuit design. As much as he tried to focus, his productivity was not good. He functioned, but a bad feeling stayed with him. He thought that if he applied himself, the bad feeling would fade away. But that never happened. He socialized with coworkers and after hours with Michael. But that didn't help either.

Evenings were the toughest. In the few hours he had to himself, memories of evenings with her immediately appeared, in vivid colors. He remembered their trip to San Francisco and how gleeful and carefree they were. He remembered the happy and sad experiences they shared. He remembered how he got angry on hearing sad events from her childhood. He, who hardly gets angry. He remembered the burning anger he felt when she told him how she was treated as a child. He never showed his anger; he did not want to aggravate her injury. But he could have killed the people who had harmed her – without any feeling, like stepping on a grotesque insect.

Now she was far away. He could hardly eat or sleep. He lost interest in almost everything around him and slowly isolated himself from company. On the third day away from her, he felt like a walking corpse.

Danny sat down at lunch with a group of guys he worked with. He joined them simply not to eat alone and didn't even listen to their conversation. Danny looked at his turkey sandwich with disinterest. "I know this woman, Michelle, and she is a psychic," said one. "She is amazing. I called her a few times and she told me things that I had never mentioned about my history and family. I don't know how she knew these things..."

Danny's attention picked up. Though he had never seen a psychic or even believed in their claims, he continued listening. No one can see the future or the past. Astrology books are just statistics. Still something compelled him to learn more about this woman. Maybe it was his lingering sadness. Maybe his soul was whispering about his past life. Or maybe it was just a spur of the moment thing. But by the end of the day Danny had Michelle's phone number.

∞

Danny looked at the number he had scrawled on his notepad many times. He already knew what she would say but he needed to hear her say the words. Maybe his spirit whispered of past lives or maybe it was common knowledge among psychics. He did not know.

His hands trembling a bit, he dialed Michelle's number. Her voice sounded calm and relaxing. His tension disappeared immediately as their conversation flowed. She asked him about general things and he was careful about telling her too much. After a few minutes of friendly conversation, though, Michelle stopped.

"You've separated from a loved one..." she said softly.

"Yes..." answered Danny slowly. How could she know that? He had not told her anything. He had not even told her that he just started a new job in a new town. Well, she could have guessed. After all it's common for people to separate from a loved one.

"You are in great pain..."

He did not respond.

"Yes, you met her not so long ago. It was love at first sight... Well, you two are quite special...your love was one in a million. You are star-crossed lovers, ultimate lovers separated across time."

Danny expected those words, and when she said them he knew it to be the case. This is their story. He did not know what it all meant. All he knew was what he felt, and he felt his soul already knew Julie's from many years ago. He felt relief. Her had found the confirmation he wanted.

"Please explain," he asked.

"You and your loved one are what in astrology we call "star-crossed lovers" – two souls' paths crossing through many lifetimes. Your souls knew each other many years ago. You were together for many years and became separated – tragically." Michelle now talked continuously, without a break, trying to describe what she sensed, as Danny wrote down her words as fast as he could.

"You were separated in the past...many times. I can see that," she continued. "You were both doing sorcery, at some point, the good type. You had to go to war...and you died."

Danny was struck by her words, then returned to writing.

"You left her, of course unintentionally, but it was final. She never got over your death. She could hardly go on. This relationship is a big challenge."

"What do you mean?" he asked, demanding more information. "What challenge?"

"Well, it will not be easy. In fact, cases like yours are incredibly rare. But I must tell you another thing, cases like yours rarely find happy endings. Most of the time they never make it. Unless the relationship is brought down-to-earth, the couple never survives and at some point separates again."

Danny remained intently quiet.

"I can see that she will be very possessive. Because you abandoned her in previous lives, she will want to be with you all of the time. Her jealousy will be enormous and unbearable – as will yours. You feel obliged to provide her everything you can. This is to compensate for your leaving her. Your soul will do anything to provide for her and take care of her, forever. Your love is very deep but neither of you is fully aware of it. Your love comes from many years ago and because of separation you are both in pain. The only way to bring this story to a happy ending is to tame it, to bring it down-to-earth." She paused.

"What about all the obstacles? She and I have kids from previous marriages."

"If you make it and stay together, the children will feel stability and will love to be with you both."

Danny sank into thoughts...of Julie.

"I know how much you miss her..." said Michelle. Danny was startled at her timing. "Your love is very rare but also very hard. Your love is like fireworks and when you argue and fight, the sparks and flames are everywhere. Everything is extreme..."

"Will we make it?" asked Danny somberly.

"It is hard to tell," she answered. "My husband and I are a similar case. We are also star-crossed lovers and I must tell you that it was not easy to reach stability. Now that we have reached it, life is beautiful. But we had many years of uncertainty – and unhappiness. As I said, if you both communicate better, then you'll make it. I must tell you, though, most couples like you do not make it and separate after a few years. They are simply unable to tame their relationship."

"What would you recommend for us?" Danny asked with trepidation.

"This is not the time to leave. You have to try to make it – otherwise you'll never know. Remember that it is better to take the chance than to refuse it."

Michelle became quiet, gathering in more perceptions and reflections before continuing. "You both have to work hard to work out your love story, but the reward may be extraordinary." Danny could hear a smile in her voice. "A love like yours is only rarely found. If you succeed, you'll be the happiest couple in the world...for the rest...of your lives. But if you do not make it in this lifetime, you will have a chance to do it in the next one. Who knows – maybe you met many times in the past and never entered a relationship. Maybe this lifetime is not the right one and you'll make it sometime in the future."

Danny felt calm and relaxed. He knew that Michelle was right in every word she said. He knew what he needed to do.

"Thank you very much, Michelle," he said, concluding the conversation.

"You are most welcome...and good luck to you two... You will need much fortune."

Danny sat for an hour, just looking out at the dark skies. A fresh breeze entered through the window and Danny enjoyed breathing it in. He started to write a letter to Julie. He would put all his thoughts on paper and send it to her. After two hours, he was satisfied that he had said all that needed to be said. He would FedEx the letter on his way to work, and Julie would receive it the next day.

∞

She read the letter briefly but words did not matter so much anymore. The world had already broken down. It did not matter what he had to say. Later that evening, she read it again. This time she noticed that he mentioned an email address.

∞

In the evening he checked his email and found an angry message from Julie. It did not matter to him that it conveyed anger, sadness and love. All that mattered was that it came from her. This was what he was waiting for. Somehow he wanted some communication from her – anything, really – to try to rebuild things with her. Although he thought he knew what to expect, he was filled with nervous excitement as he keyed in her number.

∞

Within a day Danny flew to see Julie. The same day, they flew to Reno, Nevada and on the next day got married. Danny's return to Lacey took some arrangement and he was able to pick up a new contract there. They rented a small house in town and moved there in no time. Their souls reunited, a new season of their love bloomed. But for Julie, another layer of bitterness had been laid that would return later in life.

"I have some news for you..." said Danny one day while they had lunch together at a favorite place near Danny's work. "I'm thinking about starting my own company." He did not understand much about running a business. He did know, however, that many companies with talent no better than his own were making mega-money, very quickly. The hi-tech sector was booming.

"Well, how does it work?" asked Julie, wondering of the consequences.

"It's easy," continued Danny, exhibiting greater knowledge than he really had. "Remember my friend Michael? We've done integrated circuit design for many years now. It's time to take advantage of this experience and go into business for ourselves. Michael and I have talked about it for the past few months and we think we can offer new ideas to the industry. All we need to do is patent our ideas, make the product and market it," he explained in between bites. He drank his soda and looked at her, awaiting a response.

"It sounds good..."

"Well, it won't be easy. We'll need to open a new company in California. Silicon Valley is the best place for our company..." Danny knew such a move had implications. For him, a move was simple. But for her, it meant leaving behind or at least being away from everything she knew – most important of all, her kids.

"Look..." he started with hesitation, "I can move and you can stay here, with the kids. I can visit every weekend; it's only an hour flight." He almost knew she would not go for that. Now that their souls were reunited, any separation would be painful. "But it would be better if you came with me...so that we're together"

"Yes... How long would we be in California?" she asked, still not really understanding what it all entailed.

"Well, we hope to make the products fast and make quite a bit of money fast too.

Hi-tech and the internet are booming. Any corporation with a hi-tech halo can become phenomenally successful."

"We can do that... One year is not too bad. We'll be back in no time."

"My concern is with your leaving your kids..." answered Danny. "Maybe you should stay here...with them." But she would not hear of it; she had to be with him. He did not have any way to know how right he was, but not only because of the children.

∞

Their problems in California started almost immediately. Although they had lots of fun in the Bay Area, past friends and workmates intruded on them almost daily. The same scenario in Washington repeated itself, but more intensely. Julie was more irked by the new environs than was Danny, and she reacted angrily towards him. He tried with all of his powers to calm Julie but found himself constantly under attack. And it was hard on him. Julie's separation from her kids and her new circumstances made their relationship a powder keg.

Julie wanted another child. Danny, preoccupied with his company and distraught from their bickering, was unsure of their relationship and did not want to have more children. Besides, children had been the source of considerable conflict in past relationships. Julie's spirit was breaking. Their bickering had reached new heights. Something had to change. Yet their spirits found occasional times of perfection. Nonetheless, after about six months Danny concluded they should separate.

He tried to communicate it gently to her but never found the strength to tell her directly – his soul loved her too much. He put it off for months until one day, out of misery, he decided to try to break the relationship, irreversibly.

∞

A month or so later and he was completely unhappy, though still with Julie. Without realizing the meaning of what he was doing, he registered on dating websites and tried to find a match. In this way, I will be able to understand my love for Julie.

A handful of women contacted him and he tried to connect with them. He exchanged emails with them but his soul felt numb. It was just a bitter game. He exchanged personal information and even arranged meetings, but he never showed up. He realized he probably hurt them. Communicating behind a computer screen has great potential, but not necessarily for the good. Somehow he felt these women were far away and therefore it was all a game. Unhappy people tend to care only about themselves.

What is the point of all this? If I'm unhappy, then I should tell Julie and we should do something about it. But memories of continuous arguments drained his desire and power to do anything. After a while he simply stopped responding to the contacts, except for one woman from his home country. He could not develop any feelings towards her, but he enjoyed discussing his homeland.

Week after week passed and Danny and Julie's problems only grew. Neither could see a solution. Yet their spirits refused to give-up.

I must get out of this relationship, Julie thought many times. She was driving up to Washington to see her kids. She was not aware of the layers of anger built earlier in their relationship, but she could not direct her anger towards Danny. Many times she tried to relax for a moment and figure out what was going on, but something always pushed them to a corporate event, a trip to San Francisco or another such thing. When things were good, it was heaven. But when they were bad, it was hell. Many times, out of the blue, she became angry towards Danny. Maybe it was because he had left her in Washington. Maybe because she was without her kids and feeling alone. After all, she had left everything she knew to go with him to California. And he did not want children. She wanted to become pregnant and he avoided her for this reason.

Now he was busy at work all day and she was at home alone. Then again, she thought, he has to work hard and long to make his business succeed. She couldn't understand how they had reached this situation. She loved him with all of her heart and it was painful for her to go through this. As much as she tried to analyze their condition, she could not figure out why they were still together. As her emotions stormed she did not notice she was driving well over the speed limit. As she passed Yreka, she noticed movement behind her. The siren confirmed her fear – the highway patrol. She swore quietly and pulled over.

∞

He did not even imagine what an eruption his actions would cause. One day, during one of their arguments, Julie discovered his internet adventures. Strangely, he was almost happy, as this would test their relationship. He knew the internet chats were nothing but a game. Her reaction was not one. She reacted as though the sky had fallen. Fine, he was thinking to himself, this is the end. It was inevitable, it was predicted and it should have happened a long time ago. The way from here can be only up.

∞

Her anger burned her. She felt that she could kill him at this moment. She just discovered that he had some kind of a relationship with a woman overseas. They emailed each other and talked over the phone. She called the woman and talked with her. She told her everything about him and her.

The woman was disgusted when she learned that Danny was married. She despised him. It didn't matter anymore to Julie. For a moment she wondered why she was so upset. After all, their relationship should have ended long ago. But her spirit got involved. Her spirit had waited generations for this meeting and it took over, bringing her anger to new heights. She could never forgive this one. She tried to go along with his whims. She agreed to leave everything she knew for him. She even put aside her desire for children. This crisis was too much for her. Past relationships floated back, showing their ugly sides. All the past times that she was lied to and cheated on hit her with full strength. And to think she once thought of him as her knight in shiny armor. He proved to be like all men, even worse. She lay down and stared at the ceiling. He was at work and probably would come home in the next few hours. What to do?

∞

No! The thought took over his mind. No, I do not want to lose her. He sat at work all day long and had difficulty functioning. No one knew about their marital crisis. Things had become unbearable. They hardly spoke and when they did she accused him of cheating. He hoped it would lead to the end of their relationship, but amazingly it did not happen.

He felt his soul was rebelling against him. He did not want to be without her. He tried to explain to himself that their relationship was no good but then his spirit made its presence felt and refused to let her go. When she eventually talked about a separation, he found himself crying like a child, begging her not to leave. He could not understand himself. All he knew was that it did not matter how badly their relationship was going, he did not want to be without her.

∞

Their spirits won.

Despite personal feelings calling for separation, they remained together but their relationship was damaged. Even amid good moments, there was a cloud over them. The subject of separation reappeared in almost every discussion and argument. Julie's soul was hurt and she could not bring herself to forgive him. The agony of past generations and of her life experience left her empty. She could not forget his actions. How could he have done this to her? What had been a game for him, had hurt her badly, seemingly irreversibly. He tried as much as he could to make up for his thoughtlessness and wished he could turn back time and regain her trust. Her pain was his pain.

Weeks dragged on. They were together, in a sense, but without real connection. Their timeless souls urged persistence, but their temporal selves saw no hope. Julie left for Washington and their paths separated again. This time it looked permanent.

∞

The first week or so was a relief for Julie. She rented a small apartment and prepared to get on with her life. She arranged a schedule for the kids with her ex-husband, and everything seemed to be going well. Yes, she had difficulties finding a job but she knew one would come with a little more time. She talked, briefly, with Danny every week and they both felt they had done the right thing. She refound some happiness, yet something was not right. She just could not point it out.

Danny continued his routine. Every morning he went to work and returned late at night. He felt relief also. There were no arguments, accusations or anger. Life seemed on the right track. Yet one night he found himself calling Michelle, the psychic. She remembered him at once.

"You let her go..." she said almost immediately. "It's sad... You are star-crossed lovers. Yes, as I told you then, you constitute a very difficult case, and it's hard to tell what the future will bring you two."

He did not speak.

"If you let her go now, you both will have lost your chance for this lifetime. You may find each other in the next life...or not. There is no way to know. You may spend many lifetimes searching for each other."

He remained silent. His eyes filled with tears and he wiped them slowly.

"I can sense your pain..." Michelle whispered over the phone. "She too is in pain. Your souls want to be together again. After so many separations in past lives, you both found yourselves but now you've...messed it up. I know it was not traumatic on your side, but she took it much harder. You did not consider the agony that she had to go through during her past...and now it's hit her hard."

He knew in his heart that she was right in every word.

"You both have a unique love for each other. Although I usually feel what is going on and what to do next, I cannot recommend anything for you. You both are sure it's the end, yet I do not think it is. I don't. I can feel your souls' strength. They will not give up easily, even if you both are determined to break the tie. My belief is that you will find your way to each other again. Your love somehow will win."

Danny was astonished but remained silent. The first time he talked with Michelle he felt exhilarated, but this time he felt exhausted. He was too emotionally tired to approach Julie.

"Yes, you will overcome this one. It will take a bit more time but you will be back together – and the outcome may even make you stronger..." Michelle continued as though in a trance. Without waiting for Danny's response she monotonically described events to come. "You both will be surprised to see where you are in the next few years..." she concluded, and then she seemed to come out of it. "I may be wrong... In cases like yours...it is almost impossible to tell."

Danny could not fall asleep that night. Michelle's words haunted him. His soul was in torment and he knew why. Life is one big mystery, he thought. He felt that Michelle was right. He and Julie had been separated for a few months now, and the pain was still there. He listened to his feelings and asked himself a simple question, What is it I want most of all?

The answer came to him instantly.

He called Julie.

∞

"Push, push..." urged the doctor and the nurse. Julie's face became red from the efforts. "Congratulations, it's a girl. Time of birth, 11:25PM..." announced the doctor with a smile. Danny looked at Julie with a tired but happy face. Julie relaxed her grip on his hand.

Life is a big mystery, thought Danny. They had just had a baby girl. They already knew the name they would give her – Rebecca.

All will go well from here, he thought. We will make it.

∞

It was not an easy road for either of them. In fact the difficulties that showed in the early months took the better part of ten years to overcome. Julie found closure and Danny made up for mistakes. They had two more children, two boys – Aviv and Itai. Danny found himself occasionally wondering about Michelle's prediction and how they eventually made it. She had been right in every word she uttered. Julie and Danny were inseparable. They traveled together all around the world and were rarely without each other. To others, it looked strange, out of step with modern relationships. How can they be together all the time? At work, after work and on every trip. But for them it was obvious. After many generations, at last they were together, in a peaceful time that presented no extraordinary force that could separate what had been meant to be.

∞

"But you guys are crazy. At your age you want to fly to America?" Rebecca spoke to her mother with a smile as she shook her head in disbelief.

"It's no big deal. We've flown there many times," Julie answered. "Here, hold Tal's pajamas. I need to change his diaper."

Julie changed her grandson as Rebecca watched.

"Mom, you guys are crazy – but with a great spirit..."

Julie smiled and handed Tal to her.

"He's all yours, which is a benefit of being a grandma. I can quit whenever I want and go home. You have to put this little guy to sleep... Your dad probably wonders where I am – you know how he is."

Rebecca smiled. Danny worried when they were not together, even for a few hours.

"Anyway, when are you planning to go?"

"Next month, sweetie – sometime near the end of June. We want to celebrate our anniversary in San Francisco. It's going to be fun!" she added with a mischievous smile.

Rebecca nodded again in disbelief. Even in old age, her parents had a youthful spirit. It was always funny to see them both, fully grayed but still playful as youngsters.

Julie and Danny had talked about this trip for the past few years. Every year they looked at each other and decided to postpone it another year. They did not talk about the trip in detail, yet they knew its purpose. They would have to leave their children and grandchildren far away. When the time came, that would be the way to leave. They prepared the technical aspects a few years ago and now all that remained was the trip itself. Year after year passed until one night they sat together in their living room and had their evening tea.

Danny looked at Julie and smiled.

"You know, you are the same gorgeous girl I met many years ago..."

"Ohhh, stop it. What do you want?" Julie teased him.

"Nothing..."

"Nothing this time?" Julie arched an eyebrow. "You always asked for something naughty..." She smiled but with a meaningful look.

"I wish I could, love." Danny held her to his heart.

They sat there, without saying a word.

"Do you want to watch a movie?" Danny asked quietly.

"Yeah, let's watch a movie of the kids."

They had created many videos of their children along the years, and now had all the fun in the world looking back on various times in their kids' lives.

Danny selected one and they watched their children play and run about, but after a while they got tired and just watched silently. It was almost midnight when the video was over.

"I think I'm ready for the trip to San Francisco," said Julie quietly.

Danny closed his eyes as he felt them fill with tears. He knew it was coming for the past few years but always wanted to postpone it. He took a deep breath and looked at Julie lovingly.

"Alright, my love... I am ready also..."

They kissed tenderly. Danny caressed Julie's white hair as she ran her hand across his unshaven face. It is part of life, he thought, trying to avoid the deep sadness slowly penetrating him.

"Now don't you be downcast," said Julie. "We talked about this before; it's the way we want it to happen."

"I know, I know. But I always want more time with you, my love..." Danny looked away, trying to hide his tears.

Julie gently turned his face towards her and wiped his tears. "Honey, we are together...forever, remember?"

He nodded his head. The video was over long ago and they lay on the couch holding each other. Without saying a word, they went to their bedroom for the night's sleep.

∞

Tanya, a young lobby trainee at the Embassy Suites Hotel in San Francisco, noticed the elderly couple stepping in. Behind them walked a taxi driver carrying their baggage. She was preparing routine paperwork as the couple attracted her sight for some reason. They entered together, holding hands like honeymooners. They looked tired but it did not detract from the radiance they presented. Almost everyone in the lobby stopped to watch the lovely couple. The woman was probably in her late eighties, the man slightly older. Tanya thought they must have been an attractive couple in their day, a couple that caught the eye of all fortunate enough to see them.

"Good evening, how can I help you today?" Tanya found her words eventually, as she smiled to the old couple in a manner more genuine that the professional one she normally displayed.

"Good evening," the old man replied. "We have a reservation for the next few days."

"Wonderful, I'll be glad to take your information."

Then the old man turned to the cabbie with their luggage. "Could we please hire your cab for tonight?"

The cabbie was surprised. "Sure, but it'll cost you..."

"That won't be an issue," answered the old woman with a large smile.

"We reserved the room with the airport view..."

"Yes, I see the note." Tanya was happy to help them. "It has a spectacular view."

The couple looked very happy. "Yes, we know...thank you," they said in unison.

"I want to have fun with you tonight," Danny whispered as he touched her waist. "I want to go to the mall."

"Of course dear..." Julie rolled her eyes.

How sweet, thought Tanya, this old couple...why they're like honeymooners. They obviously have a very special bond, something out of the ordinary. I hope one day to find such love.

The old lady turned to her with a smile. "Don't worry. One day you too will find your loved one. Just be persistent...and do not compromise."

∞

It was early evening and they requested their driver to take them to the Hillsdale Mall. It was their favorite in the area and they had nostalgic memories of it.

"Here I bought her the engagement ring..." explained Danny to the driver.

"Ha! I picked it out myself" teased him Julie as she nudged him. She was tired but the excitement of the trip gave her strength, too much of which had been leaving her in recent months.

"Incredible," observed the cabbie. He liked them and was fascinated by their stories. "How long have you two been married?"

"Fifty-five years..." said Danny, beaming.

"Wow! That doesn't happen much these days."

"But we knew each other years before we met," Julie added as though revealing a secret. "At least that's what we feel."

Danny nodded.

"We came here to close the circle," Julie added quietly. The cabbie didn't hear.

The Hillsdale Mall was almost the as they remembered it. Some stores were replaced, but many were still there and the ambience remained the same. They walked quietly down the center court.

"Oh look," exclaimed Danny, "the jewelry store." It was the store where he had purchased Julie's engagement ring many years ago. They had to go inside.

"May I help you?" inquired the lady behind the counter. She was in her late forties and wore a bright red suit. She looked at them carefully as they looked about the store.

"The same material... Of course, your ring isn't on display anymore," mumbled Danny.

The sales lady looked at them in a puzzled manner.

Sensing her confusion, Julie explained, "He purchased my engagement ring here fifty-five years ago."

"Ahh, I see." The lady was surprised but did not lose her professional demeanor. "So would you like to buy her another fine gift?"

Julie smiled to her. "No thanks, we didn't come to purchase anything, just...to say goodbye."

The lady nodded and went back to her desk. No sale to them.

They looked at the ring on Julie's left hand.

"It still shimmers like the day I bought it for you."

"Almost!" laughed Julie as she tossed her head back.

Absolutely beautiful, thought Danny. Tears threatened to come.

"May I invite you to dinner, as in the good old days, my beauty?" he asked bowing gallantly.

They ate their usual meal at the La Boudine restaurant at the end of the mall. It was their favorite place, renown in the Bay Area for its French sandwiches and soup.

"Let's get back to our hotel now," Julie suggested. It was clear that Danny was tired.

∞

The moon was full and soft, the skies clear, and the night air slightly warm. Danny and Julie stood outside their hotel, in front of the glistening water, and watched the jets making their way to and from San Francisco airport.

"We knew good and bad times here." Julie was holding Danny's hand.

Danny did not answer. Instead he slowly went down on his knees and looked up into her eyes.

"My love, can I commit to you for eternity?"

Julie wiped tears from her eyes. "I am already yours for eternity," she whispered.

They kissed and held each other. They both felt a tiredness – not a tiredness overcome by a night's rest. They had felt this other tiredness for the past few months. It did not matter how much they tried to ignore it, they knew that it would continue its course all the way to the end, with or without their cooperation. They looked at each other's face, taking in every detail. A few clouds slowly approached the moon.

"May I invite you upstairs, my love?" Danny smiled to her.

"As always, some things never change..." Julie took his hand.

They went to their room. The bed was soft and cozy, and they lay together, holding each other. Through the spacious glass door, they could see majestic planes coming and going in graceful motions, ascending and descending.

"Well, we are here." Danny looked at Julie's eyes as he caressed her white tresses. "How are you, my love?"

"Well..." she answered. "It was always our place." Her voice slowly faded.

"Yes, it was." His voice encouraged her and she felt a bit better. "It still is..."

She turned to him. "How do you feel?" she asked him quietly. "Are you tired...as I am?"

"Yes," he nodded.

The time had come.

"Then let's go to sleep, dear." She lay in his arms.

"Did you set everything?"

"Yes," he answered without details. Reading her mind, he added, "...including the letter for the children."

"I hope they understand."

"Of course, they will. Everyone will."

She took a deep breath and held his hand firmly. He pulled her close to him – just as they went to sleep every night for the past fifty-five years.

He turned to her in alarm. He was trembling. It was her turn to comfort him. "I'll miss you..."

"Honey, I am here..." she pressed his head to her heart and he became calm.

"We made it."

"After so many years and lifetimes, we made it. It is beautiful," she told him with a smile.

He looked at her for a while then smiled also. "We did, didn't we?"

"Yes... Now we can go home together." Her eyes sparkled with tears. "We are going to be together...forever"

Her tiredness became even more pronounced; the excitement had taken a toll. Danny felt the same a moment later. He had to let go. There was no need to worry. Their path together was ordained.

"I love to watch the planes arriving and departing," he told her as he positioned himself for sleep.

"I know," she answered, averting her eyes from his.

They lay together silently.

"I'll be here if you need me, my love," he told her, as he did every night before they fell asleep.

"I always need you..."

"I'll always be here..."

A faint smile spread across Julie's face as she calmly closed her eyes, holding him tight. Danny gently massaged her back, as he always did. Danny was always the second to fall asleep and he could feel sleep taking over now. He kissed her and looked at her as she breathed calmly. We are lucky, he thought. We made it; we fulfilled our destiny after many life times... Then he lay back next to her and watched more planes come and go. This would be the last time he'd fall asleep holding her. The skies were aglow with moonlight. Absolutely beautiful.

A 747 began its descent. It came from Europe, bringing people from all countries to the United States of America. For some, it would be a new life, for others a return. The clear, full moon became dark for a few minutes as clouds rolled across it unexpectedly. It seemed the entire night became darker, as though something bad had happened somewhere and the night had become sad. It did not interrupt the landing though. The jet was visible to many of the hotel guests. Danny hugged Julie for the last time and then closed his eyes.

Danny and Julie missed the giant plane's landing. Many other planes landed in San Francisco that evening. They could not see them anymore.

∞

Julia sat on the floor of the gas chamber. The women around her screamed in panic. Julia sat there, eyes closed. She was in her own world with Daniel and little Isaac. She opened her eyes and slowly smiled. All was well now. She felt no stress. In fact, she looked happy. She sat placidly as the gas spread through the shower room. She closed her eyes forever, but her smile remained.

∞

Andy held Orenda to his heart as his eyes closed. The giant wave slowly arced above them. He felt desperate fear but then something happened. Andy opened his eyes, looked out on the huge wave, and miraculously, was not afraid anymore. Everything became clear to him. He smiled joyfully, though he did not know why. He was still smiling as the giant wave came down on the ship like an enormous hammer and broke it into a thousand pieces.

∞

Janis lay on the floorboards of her cabin and tried to make sense of the vivid hallucinations. She saw a bright light getting stronger. She knew the end was near and for a second her heart felt deep pain – the pain of leaving life, the pain of leaving life with Darren. If I could be with Darren one last time, she thought as her powers slowly faded. Then a feeling of joy flooded her. She could not understand where it came from; she only knew she did not feel regret anymore. They were together now – she and Darren. They were together now – she could feel it. She breathed heavily as light filled the cabin. She welcomed it, without any fear. "I am coming home, Darren..." she whispered. She already felt at home.

∞

Dror lay on the flat rock and looked up at the moon. Near him lay his adopted daughter, little Verna, whom he gazed upon lovingly. I was fortunate to have little Verna, he thought. She gave me reason to continue with life. He felt profound tiredness slowly taking over and knew its meaning. He was not afraid to die; he just missed Verna. I wish she could be with me now. He felt something extraordinary – Verna was with him! He was not sad anymore. Verna is with me. Her being surrounding him, ensuring and loving him. Maybe we closed a circle, he murmured to himself. Maybe we ended together. He felt joy.

He lay back, relaxed and smiled at the moon. "Hey old man, we made it..." His eyes closed. We are together.

∞

Ven was about to die, surrounded by her family according to her tribe's tradition. She had all the reasons to die happily. She had five children, all married with their own children. Somehow, Ven always felt lonely. Since that event in her childhood when she briefly saw Anta as she was being attacked, she never forgot him and always thought of their special connection. She lay on her bedding and waited. Her fatigue told her the end was not far away.

I wish I could hold the boy's hand now, she thought, I wish I could hold his hand now... Then she felt his presence. She felt his essence with her. She was strangely happy. She smiled, laughed and even giggled. Her family told themselves that the thoughts of the dying were puzzling and unknowable. There was no puzzle for Ven. She comprehended all. She smiled ecstatically and reached for his hand. She could see him reaching for hers, just as he had reached towards her many years ago. She took his hand and the room filled with light. Tears came to her eyes. She was not alone anymore. Her soulmate was there with her. He took her hand and together they walked towards the light.

∞

The housekeeping woman found them and the concierge on duty arrived immediately. She remembered the old couple that had checked in last night. They looked like they had come for a purpose and she had wondered why. They mentioned that the hotel had been a beginning place for them. Seeing the couple there together, holding each other, brought tears. They came to die together. She tried to control her emotions but less than successfully. A sudden thought came – she wanted to take their last picture. She used her cell phone to take their last picture together, sleeping calmly, for eternity. She determined to deliver the picture to their children. They must see this. It is as though they are just sleeping calmly and will wake up soon. She wiped her tears.

The feeling was not all sadness. Yes, the world is poorer without this couple, but they died happily, together – and that is the way they should be remembered. Would that we all could have such an end. She took another picture. The siren of an ambulance sounded, though it was no longer needed. Julie and Danny remained in their bed, together to the end.

∞

"I got a letter today from the Embassy Suites Hotel in San Francisco," said Itai as his forehead furrowed in puzzlement. "Along with these pictures taken by the manager."

"What does it say?" Rebecca asked straightforwardly. As Rebecca looked at the pictures, she covered her face and cried silently.

Aviv remained silent.

"Just routine matters." Itai was a prominent attorney and had lived in Chicago for decades. For him everything was business. "Their assets will be shared among all the children."

"I can't believe we did not see this coming. I should've figured it out. They were both tired for many years now." She held her head in disbelief. "I just did not want it to happen..." Rebecca was a renown surgeon in Israel and took the news harder than did Aviv and Itai.

"No one could see this exactly. They were very good at hiding it from us," Aviv, the most sensitive one, spoke at last. "I do not want much," he added, "perhaps a personal item...maybe one of her necklaces or rings..." His voice cracked and he became silent again. Although a large man, a professional athlete on one of the better soccer teams in the world, he was always quite emotional. For the past few years he had lived with his family in Liverpool, England.

"Of course." Itai sounded dry, as though he was closing a deal. Everyone knew this was his way to deal with things. "We'll find you something..."

"Well, what do we do now?" Rebecca returned them to present matters. They all traveled to Israel, to Rebecca's home, after they received the news.

"I'll take care of the arrangements." Itai sounded distant. "They expressed their desire to be buried here in Israel, where they lived for many years."

Everyone looked at him.

"We'll all meet here at least once a year for the memorial service, on their death date." He laughed at the irony that struck him. "I don't know how the heck they did it, but they managed to die together on July 4th, the date that mom said yes." He looked at them. "I know we all have very busy lives, but we should all be here on this date, every year."

Everyone nodded silently.

"Oh, one more thing..." Itai added after a pause.

Everyone looked to him.

"They had an odd request concerning their graves. Do not ask me for an explanation; they never gave me one."

Rebecca and Aviv looked at him in anticipation.

"Their graves will be unique. I'll let you read the letter they left." Itai took a deep breath. "I am going out; I need some fresh air."

He gave the pictures to Aviv, who looked at them silently.

Itai went outside. The night air on Mount Carmel was cold and fresh. From Rebecca's house he could see the entire shoreline of Haifa. It's beautiful, he thought. Dad was born here and spent most of his life here. Mom joined him and they lived near Haifa for the rest of their long lives. He walked slowly down the street in the secluded, affluent neighborhood. The landscape was beautiful.

Itai felt great sadness. In the past few years he hadn't had much time to visit them. At least, I called a few times a month... He stopped at the end of the street and looked out on the shoreline. Far in the distance he could see the lights of Atlit, the small town his parents lived in. The lights gently twinkled in the dark. He took a deep breath and for a second thought he could feel their spirit. They are there, together. He'll visit their grave at least twice a year. All of a sudden his sadness was gone. He was almost sure they were there with him...comforting, loving, assuring. They will be with us always. He wiped a tear he hid from no one and started his way back to Rebecca's house. There was a lot of work to do and he'd do it to the best of his ability, which was considerable. Goodbye, mom and dad...you are always with us.

∞

It was New Year's Eve, 2200, and Times Square was packed with people as always. The area was full of police hovercrafts for security. From time to time, a laser pierced up into the skies, preparing for the big moment. The crowd in the Square sang, danced or simply waited for 2201.

Thousands of miles away, in a small town in Israel, a tour guide lectured his morning group about the town's historical site. "Here is our graveyard...and there is one grave here which has become an attraction for people around the world," he intoned austerely. "Please come with me." He led them to a secluded grave. On a small hill, between beautiful flower beds, were two graves, side by side. It looked as though they had been buried in a very special spot from which they could look out on the calm, blue Mediterranean Sea. A light breeze met the group as they gathered around the graves.

"Wow..." exclaimed one of them. "What is this?"

"No one really knows. There is only speculation," answered the tour guide as he too looked upon the graves. "Maybe their names were insignificant, or that's how they wanted to be remembered. But apparently the couple wanted their headstones to be marked this way." After a pause, he added, "Their actual names were never mentioned anywhere."

The tour guide had to pause once more.

"I think that their names were not important to them, only their love was. This is a true love story – one in a million. This couple wanted to memorialize their eternal love. Nothing else mattered, not even their names. All they wanted the world to know was that they were...and are...together, forever."

The group looked at the site in fascination. The two graves had simple headstones without names or dates. Unlike the other graves, these two were clean and bright, as though they had just been tidied and polished. There were vividly hued flowers of many kinds all about, which didn't seem to have been planted. It looked as though they grew wild, by nature.

This tour group, like all the others before it and all those that came after, was struck into silence by the simple words engraved on the headstones, words that conveyed to each of them a sense of timelessness –

Husband and Wife.

∞